I0788602

CRY OF THE SOUL

RUBY JEAN JENSEN

Gayle J. Foster

Published by: Gayle J. Foster, Carrollton, Texas

Library of Congress Control Number: 2022906474

❀ Created with Vellum

Prologue

J^{ob: 33}

"For God speaketh ...
  in a dream,
  in a vision of the night,
  when deep sleep falleth ... "

"Where does the road go?" the little girl always asked, and the answer kept being the same as long as she could remember. It doesn't go anywhere, it's just there. Her mommy and daddy thought it was funny, and they'd look at each other and laugh.

With summer loud and warm around her, the rocks easy beneath her bare feet, she went around the hill, following the road. She had never been so far from home alone in her life. Sounds grew louder. Birds in the trees screeched at her, and flew, making noises like Grandma flapping a sheet. A deep and booming voice warned her to come no closer, but it stayed in the still edges of the creek below. A bull frog.

The road kept going. Beneath the trees. Cut from the hillside and shadowed by the bluffs that hung above. She followed. Where does the road go? Nowhere. But it didn't end at the corner. Nothing but the road, going out of sight. She looked back around the hill. Ahead it was the same, leading her on.

She stopped. But there, farther on, a pretty little rock with traces like fern upon it. A fossil rock.

And in the hillside above, a little hole like a cave beneath the bluff. Where something lived. A chipmunk maybe, or a snake.

Behind her then, suddenly, a different sound. The chip of one rock against another. A footstep.

Her heart exploded into wild, thundering terror. She whirled.

He was huge, like God, with a long white beard. He stood beneath the layered bluffs where the wildflowers grew, above the bank where the ground fell. She looked up and he was there, and the sight of him took her breath. A stranger. She should run. She wanted to run, but fear held her still.

She had never seen a beard so white nor so long. She had never seen such overhanging eyebrows, nearly hiding his eyes. Like streaks of white clouds over a dark sunset.

"What's your name?" he demanded.

Her chin quivered, her throat jerked. The obedient pronouncement of her name was only a whisper, but he heard.

"Emily," he repeated, then said, "Emmy. You're called Emmy."

She nodded, swallowing. He knew her?

"How old are you?" he asked.

She held up four fingers.

For a time he said nothing. He glared into her eyes, holding her still. She was afraid to move.

Then he said, voice gentling, "You have a mountain to climb, Emmy. A very tall mountain. We all have our mountains to climb, but yours is especially fraught with difficulty. The path is narrow and steep, and the side sheer and long. Be careful that you don't fall."

As if his warning released her, she ran, her legs pumping hard, her bare feet scarcely touching the rocks in the narrow road. At the corner she threw a glance back over her shoulder.

But his hand wasn't right behind her, reaching to grab. The road was empty, as if he had never been there at all. She walked on toward the house, backwards, watching.

What, she began to wonder, is a mountain?

Chapter One

Willowbrook Care Center.

A one-story buff brick building, it stretched like spread wings into its green setting. Large trees spotted the grounds, with benches scattered about for patients and their visitors.

The driveway curved in beneath a portico. Through the open doors of the hospital ambulance, Maggie saw a small group of nurses, one of them holding a wheelchair ready for her.

In the brick above the entry, the name Willowbrook Care Center was formed in script gold. It was meant to be inviting and comforting. But it leaped at Maggie, shot by a ray of sun that turned it the color of blood. She felt the threat of panic.

I can't go in there. It's a living grave.

No, she dared not give in to panic. It was only a transition, a place to heal this broken hip. She'd be home in days, with Minnie cuddled warm and comforting and safe on her lap. Minnie needs you—take a deep breath —don't panic. It had become her mantra, repeated over and over. The sun withdrew, beyond the trees and left a shadow like a premonition.

"Mrs. Maggie Winters?"

The woman with the wheelchair was smiling at her. Chubby, full rosy cheeks, plain brown hair drawn back, her lack of a cap identified her as an aide. "Blanche" was on her nametag. She turned the wheelchair into position near the open doors of the hospital ambulance.

Behind Blanche, with the dignity of authority, came a nurse in white uniform wearing a cap with blue stripes. She paused in the shadows of the portico, double doors behind her open and waiting like the hungry mouth of a monster.

Blanche peered at Maggie as the ambulance attendants sat her like a child into the wheelchair.

"Mrs. Winters?" she asked again.

"Yes. Just ... Maggie, please." It was a name difficult for her to attach to herself. Few people had ever called her Mrs. Winters, and none Maggie. But it was part of her present and all of her future. She must remember to answer to "Maggie".

Sunlight bled through a space between the trees and touched warmly on the white stockings of the registered nurse and the metal curves of the wheelchair arms. Maggie remained in shadow, chilled, drained of energy from her week of hospitalization. She shivered though she wore a long-sleeved robe on this summer day.

A sharp pain pulsed through her hip as she tried to adjust to sitting in the wheelchair. She took a deep breath and clutched the arms of the chair, easing down. Her walker and a small suitcase of her belongings were handed down behind her, and accepted by another nurse's aide who stood to the side.

She dared not flinch with the pain, nor show how much it hurt to be moved. The more pain she admitted to, the longer it would take to persuade the doctor to release her. She had begged her way out of the hospital by telling him she simply couldn't afford to stay there. He had released her on the condition that she spend a month in the care center. She'd had no intentions then or now of staying a month.

"I might be able to use the walker," she told the nurse in authority, and saw the look on her face.

THE LOOK, she was beginning to think of it. That 'you poor thing' look, not true sympathy, but pity instead, because true sympathy required a deeper understanding, a having-walked-that-same-road experience. They didn't know, yet, the desperation of helplessness. Maggie hadn't until a week ago.

The nurse smiled her pleasant professional smile and said, "Oh I think we'd better just ride. It's quite a ways to your room. Sometimes too much exercise does more harm than good."

Blanche said, "You don't look as if you'll be here very long, Maggie," and immediately endeared herself to Maggie even though she sounded as if she were talking to a child.

"Only until I can maneuver that walker."

"Do you have someone at home to help you?"

"No," Maggie said, "no one. My little dog and I are alone."

Minnie, her Chihuahua, her constant companion for the past four years, was trapped in a small cage at the Animal Hospital boarding kennel. Waiting to be rescued. Minnie had never been separated from her before, had never been in a cage. She was still a puppy at heart, totally dependent on Maggie, unable to understand what had happened to disrupt her life. Big dogs and strange people frightened her. Maggie loved her as if she were a helpless child. For the past four years the dog was all that kept Maggie from feeling as if she were in a world alone. When she thought of giving up, Minnie reminded her that she was needed.

Blanche pushed the wheelchair through the wide doors into an entry hall. The tile was so freshly polished it mirrored the brisk movements of the nurse as she walked ahead of them.

A young aide with 'Julie' on her nametag carried Maggie's suitcase and the walker as they went deeper into the long hall. Potted ferns and slender trees were spaced at equal distances with an occasional bench between. On one bench three women sat watching. They smiled and murmured greetings. An aide pushed a wheelchair holding a young man, a cerebral palsy victim.

They entered a large entry furnished in plastic-covered chairs and couches, with a nurse's station against the inner wall. The nurse pinned a prepared nametag to Maggie's robe.

"We all wear nametags, Maggie, with just our first names. I hope you don't mind. We're very informal. Blanche and Julie will help you to your room. If you need anything, feel free to call us. There are activities for all patients who are able to enjoy them. There are no televisions in any except the private rooms, but our solarium has a large screen TV. There are tables to play cards, and we have a bingo game once a week, sometimes more."

The three nurses who accompanied Maggie and the two behind the station all smiled and said slightly out of unison, "Welcome to Willowbrook Care Center, Maggie Winters." It was as if one voice echoed the next, on and on into infinity.

Panic spilled over the narrow edge to which Maggie mentally clung. Heat spread rapidly like a wildfire out of control in her chest and up over her face. Her breath caught, her shoulders pulled forward in some inner, involuntary self-defense. She looked at these new surroundings and recognized nothing familiar. The people who came toward her were aliens, unreal, moving jerkily about and uttering language she didn't understand.

No, no. Close your eyes. Take a deep breath. It's only in your mind.

Reality had been altered for Maggie during this past week of helplessness, as she experienced wave after wave of panic attacks. They came upon her with little warning, bringing a terror different from the fear for life itself. This fear was for her sanity.

The doctor had told her, when she begged for an explanation of this madness. "Panic attack, Maggie. Horrible, but harmless. Just close your eyes and take a deep breath. Take a dozen deep breaths. Make yourself calm down. If that doesn't work call for a tranquillizer."

A deep breath. A dozen deep breaths. How strange that in all of her sixty-five years she had never known what a panic attack was. She had thought it had something to do with heart palpitations. Now she learned the racing of the heart was only a very minor part of it. It was what it did to her mind that she couldn't bear.

A deep breath ...

The voices became more natural, no longer the strange mutterings of some alien beings. She relaxed into the forward thrust of the wheelchair, feeling weak and drained.

They went beyond the nurse's station, turned into the left wing, and continued on through the edge of a large room with windows on two sides. Chairs and sofas, covered in varying bright colors, were arranged about the room. In one wall a large screen TV, tuned to a soap opera, was being viewed by a scattering of people. One man slept in his chair, mouth open and muttering unintelligibly with each outward breath.

The tires of the wheelchair whispered over the tile. A few people glanced at them as Blanche pushed the wheelchair toward a doorway leading to the back. The room became L shaped, the television left behind. Around the corner were game tables where one foursome played cards. Near the windows others sat, talking, or quietly reading. There was more animation than Maggie had expected. But she felt entirely apart.

Maggie's hands tightened on the wheelchair arms. The skin over her hip seemed too tight to hold the replacement. Thin, shooting pains were like threads of fire. Every invisible seam in the tile floors felt like speed bumps.

She drew into her mind a picture of home. Her small living room, whose mauve walls she had painted herself, the burgundy and green furniture chosen for softness and comfort, the draperies she had sewn by hand while Minnie lay on her lap beneath the folds of material. A picture window gave her a view of the front lawn and the walk that reached from the entry porch. Down by the street stood a white mailbox in which nothing was ever placed but an occasional bit of junk mail. Through the window she could see the rounded end of the street, the cul-de-sac. Two other houses were nearly invisible behind trees and shrubbery.

Her home, where finally she had begun to feel safe.

Blanche pointed the wheelchair toward a long hallway from which doors opened on both sides. "As Marilyn said, here we are." The resolutely cheerful Blanche added one of her own. "Home, away from home."

They came to a sliding glass door that opened onto the side lawn. Maggie stared at the man beyond the door. He was a stranger to her, yet drew her attention and stopped her breath.

He leaned casually against the trunk of a large tree, but his narrowed gaze moved in darting swiftness as if he searched for someone. Middle-aged, obviously not a patient, he was dressed in a light grey suit, possibly silk, the coat hanging open. His right hand adjusted something beneath the coat.

His eyes met Maggie's and stopped, a sharp, direct contact, cold and piercing. His coat fell back, hand moving away from his belt, and in that instant she glimpsed the black butt of a small revolver. She heard the warning again, low, hurried. There's a contract on your life, her lover had warned. You have to leave … lose yourself … lose yourself.

A life without the one who filled her life, from that day forward.

Four years and three thousand miles away they had found her. Then the wheelchair was pushed forward past the door, and he was gone.

Chapter Two

It wasn't possible they had found her. The trail was too old and too far. He was only part of the nightmare of these past four years.

Of the increased nightmare of the past week. He might not have been there at all.

The terrifying panic that moved so quickly through her, altering her perception, had taken an ordinary visitor and created the illusion of danger. The flash of black was a belt, or only her fear. Not a gun.

Or perhaps he was a security guard.

"The man on the lawn—is he a security guard?"

"Security guard!" Blanche laughed in her happy voice.

"What on earth for? Nothing ever happens around here."

She guided the wheelchair to the right to get out of the way of one being pushed in the opposite direction.

"We have lots of visitors. They're always welcome."

Maggie pushed back her fears as always to become part of a million other fragmented thoughts and worries.

Blanche guided the wheelchair down the hall, deeper into the Center. Vague, unpleasant odors began to waft into the air layered with the scent of air fresheners. Some of the doors were closed, others stood partway open, showing the ends of narrow beds. If there were decorations on the pale walls Maggie didn't see them.

A groan suddenly erupted somewhere ahead and grew louder as they proceeded along the hall.

Blanche herself groaned. "There goes Thomas."

"That poor man needs help," Maggie said, dismayed that no one seemed very concerned. "I can wait while you help him."

"He hears us coming, that's all. He just wants attention." The groan ceased and a voice demanded, "Nurse!"

Blanche yelled back, "Yeah, just a minute, Thomas."

The moaning picked up again, like an engine revved in the distance.

"There's not a thing in the world wrong with Thomas that constant attention doesn't help. Ignore him, if you can."

Julie paused at a door almost directly across from Thomas's continuing moans and pushed it open. As in the hospital the doors were wide, to allow room for wheelchairs and stretchers.

"Here we are." Blanche gave the wheelchair an artful whirl to the right.

They entered a room barely large enough for the four narrow beds and their accompanying small chests or nightstands, and sturdy plastic recliner chairs. Against the wall to the left was a wash basin with a mirror. In the right wall, between two of the beds, a door opened into a white-tiled bathroom.

Two elderly women were already in the room. A tall, bony woman, shoulders permanently hunched, brushed at a wisp of her straggly grey hair. She had tucked it into the pink plastic band that held it out of her face. She wore a faded housedress belted loosely at the waist, white anklets and house slippers. With a handkerchief she dusted the small, framed photographs on top of the night-chest by her bed. The chest was covered with the pictures crowded like trees in a forest.

The other woman sat relaxed in the recliner-rocker by her bed, broad hips filling the chair. She was dressed in stretch slacks and jersey blouse, her swollen feet up on the footrest. Her hair had been dyed a deep red, white roots as startling as ghosts in the closet. Her eyes were dark and lively, and watched with the acuity and interest of a crow as Maggie entered the room.

Both women looked to be in their mid-to-upper eighties. Although they were nothing like Maggie's mother, still they reminded her of Mom. They occupied the most desirable locations in the room, the corners by the wide windows, and seemed settled, as if they had lived in this room of no privacy for a long time.

Maggie wondered if her mother, who was now eighty-five, was in a nursing home, or if she still lived in the little white house just three houses from Peggy. Did Mom still have grand-children coming to spend the evening or the afternoon with her? Visiting, they had called it, never babysitting, even when the children were small. But Mom's grandchildren would be grown now. She'd be keeping her great-grandchildren instead.

Maggie wished she could call to see how they all were, to let them know she was still alive. But for their protection and hers, she had not dared. They wouldn't know Maggie Winters.

"Hello Hazel and Florence," Blanche greeted. "How're you today?"

Maggie looked about the room, at the pictures which covered the walls over the tall woman's bed, at the blank walls above the other.

White canvas hung on rods between each bed, but were pushed back and held against the wall, leaving no privacy.

"You girls have a new roommate," Blanche announced. "Maggie, meet Florence. Florence, this is Maggie."

The redhead smiled and nodded.

Blanche said, "Hazel, stop working a moment and say hello to Maggie."

The tall woman looked toward Maggie and nodded but continued to flap the hanky at the tops of the picture frames. They were filled mostly with snapshots of children.

Julie bent to peer into Maggie's face. "Would you like to get into bed, dear?"

"No. Thank you." It was only mid-afternoon.

"Then we'll just help you into the chair?"

"I think I can make it."

"Are you sure?"

The redhead, Florence, answered, "Yes. What'd you do, break a hip?"

"Take it easy now," Blanche urged, watching Maggie.

"Did you have a replacement?"

"Yes."

"They're wonderful. You'll be running in six months if you're careful now."

Maggie clamped her teeth and stood up, her weight supported by her good leg and hip, her hands and arms. Careful, she warned herself, as she moved from the wheelchair to the recliner.

Florence commented, "She's doing pretty good."

Maggie eased herself into the recliner and gave Florence a grateful smile. "Thanks for the encouragement."

"Listen girl, I been there, I know. Never had exactly what you got, but I been there. You're doing great."

"Are you a Christian?" the gray-haired lady asked abruptly, "Have you been saved?"

"Good Lord, Hazel," Florence said, "Let the girl get settled before you start preaching."

"The good Lord looks after his own. If He wants her to walk again, she will."

Blanche said in her overly bright, overly loud voice as if they were all slightly deaf, "There you are, Maggie. Now, we'll put away your personal things. Here's your spacey closet."

She opened a door on a cubbyhole about twenty inches wide and began to unload the suitcase someone had filled for Maggie at home the day she fell. They had chosen a couple of robes and grabbed a handful of nightgowns and underwear, none of them her favorites, as well as two pairs of slacks and two blouses. A dress had been wadded in also. The only shoes that had managed to follow her were the sandals she'd been wearing when she fell, and a pair of horribly ugly heel-less house slippers suitable for man or woman that she'd had to buy from the hospital.

Julie said, "No pictures?"

"No pictures." No pictures, not any more. Not even at home. "I don't intend to be here very long."

Hazel huffed. "That's what I thought, too. And here I am. Been here going on two years. Or is it three?"

"But then, Hazel," Florence said. "If the Lord wanted you to move, he'd move you." She grinned slyly, eyeing Hazel.

Hazel huffed again. "The Lord helps those who help themselves. My grandson is finding an apartment for me. He's coming soon. I help him when I can, with a little money now and then. He's coming soon now."

"Ummhuh." Florence began to rock. As with most rocking chairs, this one had a distinctive sound of movement, soft and rustling, plastic rubbing against plastic. "I've been hearing that for two years. We've been here longer than most of the nurses, me and Hazel."

Julie laughed. "That's true."

Something eternally sad flitted across Hazel's face. She turned and eased her long, bony frame down into her chair and sighed. "It doesn't take much to tire me anymore. When I think about the work I used to do … that big old house, nine children, a husband. I never got that man, the good Lord rest his soul … never got that man to pick up after himself. The minute he walked in the back door he throwed that coat at the coat rack. From October to April. And missed it every time. Of course the boys followed in his footsteps."

Florence winked at Maggie. "Preachers, most of them. You surely don't expect them to pick up their own coats!"

Hazel smiled, nodding her head up, down, up, down. Sunlight through the window touched her cheek. In the brighter light she looked ancient and crinkled. Her skin had shrunk into a mass of wrinkles in the cavities of her face, but there was a fine beauty in the shape of her jaw and the bones that held her sinking eyes. She sat, nodding, nodding.

Blanche and Julie arranged the few items Maggie needed.

Tissue, toothbrush, toothpaste, face cream, hand lotion. Julie filled the pitcher with ice water.

"My children turned out to be fine people." Hazel motioned toward the pictures on the table. "These are my grandchildren."

"Very nice," Maggie responded.

Blanche put her hand on Maggie's shoulder and leaned closer. "I'll let you just sit and rest awhile," she said over the drone of Hazel's voice, and the more distant moan of Thomas's, "then I'll show you around. The bathroom is right over there. You can go out into the front and watch television anytime you want. But let one of us know if you want to go anywhere, even to the bathroom. You'll need help for awhile."

Maggie looked for a telephone in the room and saw none.

"Could I make a telephone call, please?"

"Oh sure. I forgot to tell you. The phone's in the hall. I'll just help you back into the chair."

"I'll walk. I have to learn to use the walker."

"Are you sure you want to do it now? You've just arrived, you must be tired."

"I'd like to make the call, please. I don't like being so much trouble, but I really need to call someone."

"It's no trouble, Maggie. I'll just walk with you."

"Thank you. I have to hear that Minnie is all right."

She didn't try to explain. How could she expect any of them to understand? She had visualized herself with the walker, managing alone, becoming more independent. To the doctor, to nurses, to anyone else, a few weeks only meant healing. They would not understand Maggie's need to be home with Minnie.

She stood and eased her weight onto her right leg, balancing insecurely, feeling suddenly dizzy. Oh God, no. She closed her eyes briefly and took a deep breath.

A longing to give in, to collapse and sleep, seized her. She yearned for the vivid and beautiful dreams that had come too rarely in her life, of strange landscapes she had never seen in reality, roads she had never walked, people she had never known. Cities in which she felt no fear. Dreams in which her soul sang with happiness. Unforgettable dreams as different from ordinary dreams as heavenly, soaring light is different from fear and darkness. Experiences mysterious and illusive.

In her last special dream she stood beneath a large tree looking up. Its heavy limbs were crowded with peacocks of unearthly, wondrous colors. They were resting, wings folded. As she watched, the large birds lifted their wings and flew, filling the sky with the beauty of their colors.

The dream had come a month ago, the first in many years.

The memory of it exerted a magnetic pull over her. If only she could enter that world forever, blend with the light, soar with the freedom, the endlessness of the beauty.

In harsh reality came the image of Minnie's fear-filled eyes, the little dog's desperate reach toward her from strange hands. She had to heal, and be there for Minnie.

Maggie saw that both Florence and Hazel were watching her as if they held their breath. She was still standing, she realized, though shakily. Her hands gripped the bars of the walker, quivering with tension.

"She'll make it," Florence said. "See? She's standing."

"God willing." Hazel joined Maggie in a deep breath. Florence began to rock again in the short little jerks the chair allowed.

"But don't try it alone yet, Maggie," Blanche warned.

Slowly Maggie moved into the hall. Balance on good leg and hip, she told herself severely as if she had never walked before, set the walker forward a few inches, put it down, hold on and pray you don't fall! Take a step forward. A painful step. Her hip felt as if it were still broken.

"Want to stop and rest a minute?" Blanche asked.

Maggie let herself droop, relaxing her grip on the walker. In the hall an old man, walking slowly, was helped along by a nurse's aide. He glanced at Maggie and Blanche and nodded in silence. They passed on by, incredibly slowly.

Watching him, seeing within his helplessness her own, gave Maggie the determination to try harder. She followed the walker. One step more. Don't groan, she told herself, wanting to join poor Thomas in his moaning and groaning as one infant will cry with the other. She decided to try a bit of conversation—so lacking in her life these days.

"What is there about a groan that makes us feel a little better?" She had almost forgotten how to make small talk.

"Probably because it makes everybody else feel worse. Sort of equalizes us, you might say."

Maggie headed for the telephone determinedly. It was a black box on the wall, just a few feet from her bedroom door.

Another step.

Two women came along the hall, both elderly but one much older than the other. The younger woman paced her steps carefully. They spoke to Blanche and she replied, "Hello girls. On your way to watch a soap?" They went on.

"That was Maude and Helen. They share a room. You could set your clock by them. At five till three they come out and go to watch television."

Maggie reached the telephone. Her arms trembled and felt as if they had the consistency of cooked spaghetti. Her entire leg pulsed with pain. She felt like throwing herself over the walker like a wet towel to rest for awhile, if only Blanche would look the other way. If she were home, would she be able to manage? There were so many things that she now saw she should have done. She should have installed both an automatic dog feeder and a waterer. She should have had a doggie door cut into the wall that led into the fenced backyard. So many things she could have done to prepare for this.

Holding to the walker with one hand she reached for the receiver. She held it between her cheek and shoulder and began dialing the number of the Animal Hospital where Minnie was kenneled.

"Anne, this is Maggie."

"Hello Maggie. How're you doing?"

"Much better, thanks. I'm at the Willowbrook nursing home for awhile. How's my puppy?"

"Minnie's fine, Maggie. Don't worry about her."

Maggie held to the phone although there was really nothing more to say, reluctant to break her only connection to the little companion who couldn't possibly understand what was happening to her. "Give her a hug for me, will you? Tell her we'll be home soon."

Chapter Three

Dinner was served at five, and Maggie accepted a ride in the wheelchair. The dining room was filled. The tables each held from four to eight people, and Maggie sat with Hazel, Florence, and five other women.

"Let us pray," Hazel said, and began a long prayer. Two of the women at the table ignored her, but others at nearby tables murmured with her.

Maggie sat waiting for the prayer to end, looking around, amazed at how many of the people seemed too young, too alert to be here. There was one who was probably no more than thirty.

But Maggie saw she had the innocent eyes of someone brain damaged at an early age. Several others sat in wheelchairs. One middle-aged man with a wasting muscle disease, and another younger, barely able to hold their heads up, were both being fed by aides. Where had they come from, all these people? What kind of lives had they left behind them? Did they have homes waiting? Would they ever return to them?

I don't belong here.

Breathe deeply, don't panic.

Florence asked, "Is something wrong?" Hazel ended the prayer and looked up.

Maggie murmured, "No," and moistened her dried lips. Both Hazel and Florence looked at her as solicitously as mothers. The others began sporadic conversations or stared out the windows where vapor lights were beginning to replace the light of day. Maggie looked for the man who had leaned against a tree, but he wasn't in the supper crowd.

She drew a deep breath. It was the panic she feared more than the pain. That nightmarish sense of having one's reality tossed to the devils.

After dinner they stayed for television. Maggie sat in the wheelchair at the end of the couch where Hazel and Florence sat side by side. It was as though they had already become a family, eating together, sitting together.

Hazel glared at the screen, her mouth drawn down at the corners, creating an odd arrangement of wrinkles on her chin. Florence watched the sitcom with her eyes shining, laughing occasionally. Hazel muttered under her breath as one sexual innuendo after another bounced from the mouths of the actors.

"Scandalous. Sinful. My Lord have mercy, don't they think of anything else?"

Florence threw her a mischievous glance. "I daresay you thought of it a few times in your life, considering that you had ten kids."

"Nine, not ten. I'm going back to my room."

Florence leaned over from the couch and poked Maggie with her elbow. "What do you suppose caused all them ten babies?"

"Nine! Not ten. The Lord blessed me with nine beautiful children."

Florence grabbed the back of Hazel's dress and said, "Oh sit down here, it's only a show."

Hazel grunted in disapproval, but she sat down again.

"I was blessed," she murmured. "The good Lord blesses as he chooses."

An old hurt opened in Maggie's heart. She was twenty-four years old again and listening to those words that changed the meaning of her life. I'm sorry, the doctor said, as he removed the stitches from the surgical wound on her abdomen. This was her seventh day in the hospital after the exploratory surgery that was supposed to determine why she'd had the miscarriage.

This was the day she was going home to be well, to have another baby. But he said, "I'm sorry."

His words, so final, isolated her and left her completely, coldly alone, as if he had severed her from the human race. As if even God had tossed her into space with no orbit of her own.

So long ago—yet the pain was there, unforgotten, so easily brought to the surface by a chance remark.

She didn't want Minnie to feel alone like that. As she was now. She could imagine the terror of the tiny dog, caged in a hell unimaginable, alone, deserted, trapped by her own panic.

Minnie had been so happy at home, always right there to help Maggie work in the flower garden. Minnie dug if she dug, not always in the right place. Minnie sat down when Maggie sat down, on her lap or by her side. Five pounds of silky smooth warmth.

Minnie was there to help Maggie forget how alone she had become, greenish-brown eyes filled with trust and adoration.

Maggie called herself "Mama" to the little dog, and she always had, since the day Minnie was given to her so tiny she lay in the palm of her hand, rising up friendly and eager with little brown tail wagging. "Her name is Minnie," he had said, "Every time you look at her remember that I love you." During her week in the hospital Minnie's image sustained her. Breaking the hip had happened so suddenly. One moment she was strong and healthy, and the next she was helpless.

She'd been going off the kitchen porch, down the steps she'd run up and down for the past three and half years, when suddenly her ankle turned and she was falling helplessly.

She had struck the cement walk on her left hip, and felt the jarring pain at the same time Minnie screamed. Her first thought, her deepest horror, was that she'd fallen on Minnie. Then she felt tiny feet running up her shoulders, and Minnie began to lick her face. She learned then how helpless a person could be without the use of both legs. With Minnie whining, licking her face, she struggled to turn, to crawl back up the three steps to the porch and the utility room door, dragging her left side. The door was only nine feet away, but in her pain and terror it looked an impossible distance. How would she ever reach it? And once there, she would have to cross the kitchen and go into the dining room where the only telephone in the house hung four feet high on the wall.

She heard in the silences of her thoughts Minnie's whine as the little dog licked her face when she lay on the cement walk at the bottom of the three steps, pain rushing through her like wild rivers with every rapid heartbeat. She saw the concern in Minnie's eyes, the questions she couldn't ask. When Maggie wept it was Minnie who licked the tears.

Maggie tried to cry out, "Help. Help me!"

But the backyard, along the chain link fence, had been planted with shrubbery years before she bought the house. She had wanted privacy, and she had it. Over the fence at the back was a hollow where trees grew, and paths meandered. Her own back gate led down into that hollow, and she and Minnie took walks there, occasionally meeting other walkers. But none walked there today. Across the hollow, hidden by trees, were other homes. But they were too private.

She didn't call for help again. Minnie licked her face and whined, and for one of the few times in the dog's life, she took on a humped appearance, tail tucked under, body trembling.

Maggie tried to comfort her. "It's okay, Minnie ... it's okay." She had to get them out of this terrible predicament.

She turned so that she could grasp the railing, and began to inch her way up the steps. It was like dragging an anchor caught in the bottom of the sea to hold her in place, bobbing on the waves of pain.

At one point, after she reached the porch, she felt faint and had to put her head down. Perhaps she fainted for a moment because her next awareness was of Minnie walking restlessly on her shoulders and nosing into the hair on the back of her neck, whining that sad and wondering cry.

Maggie lifted her head and Minnie ran expectantly to the closed door of the utility room. Maggie wondered, why hadn't she carried in her pocket a cordless phone? Because, that inner voice immediately answered, you don't have anyone to call anymore.

It was true. Over the last couple of years, Minnie had become her family, her only companion.

The next inches were measured in minutes. She made it to the door of the utility room, and forced herself to rise, dragging the useless leg. By holding onto the cabinets and door frames, she crossed the utility room, then the kitchen, into the dining room and the wall phone where she pushed the button for 911.

"The back door is open," she told the woman who answered.

Then she eased down off her exhausted leg. Never before had she thought thirty feet could be so far.

She held Minnie, but still the little dog shivered, curled in her arms. The light brown eyes looked up, begging answers. Maggie tried to make her understand.

"I'll be in a hospital. You'll be in a kennel. It will be all right. We'll be home soon. I'm not deserting you."

Minnie understood a few words, but how could she be expected to understand words she'd never heard before?

When the man and woman from the ambulance entered the house Minnie growled and pushed harder against Maggie.

The world was fading in and out for Maggie, the pain unceasing, growing worse, making her heart irregular, her throat and tongue dry. Her glasses were lying back on the sidewalk, or somewhere, perhaps out in the yard. She hadn't missed them.

"What happened here?" the man asked, bending, a stethoscope being prepared.

"I think I broke my hip. I fell—outside the back door. Will you please call the Animal Hospital and ask them to come get my little dog? I don't want her left alone."

Other people, volunteers she learned later, were entering. She felt so grateful to them, so relieved that there were people who cared, who wanted to help. Her eyes filled with tears, and like Minnie her body uncontrollably began to shake.

One of the volunteers told her, "Don't worry. I'll take your puppy wherever you want her to go."

Maggie blinked her tears away, and clearly saw the look in Minnie's eyes as the strange hands reached for her. Minnie growled, snapped back once, missed the hand, and then stretched her front legs forward like a child reaching for its mother.

Her eyes filled with terror.

It was the last time Maggie saw her.

Her name is Minnie ... every time you look at her remember that I love you ... her name is Minnie ... Minnie ...

His voice blended in her memory with the image of the puppy.

Chapter Four

I promise you, Minnie … I'm coming to get you …

"I'm not going to watch that one for certain!" Hazel got to her feet, using a hand to push herself up from the couch beside Florence.

Maggie's vision focused on the television. It was a news show on child abuse and forgotten or repressed memories.

"Well, why on earth not?" Florence's face had a series of vertical frowns between her heavy, greying brows. But she too got up, ready to leave. All the while she glared at Hazel who walked spritely on ahead, stooped, her body thin and bony except at the belly where the skin and muscles had obviously been stretched too many times to regain its former tightness.

Without asking Maggie if she wanted to watch the show or not, Florence grabbed the handles of the wheelchair and started pushing her back toward their room.

A nurse's aide hurried over and took control of the wheelchair. "Are you ready to go to bed?" she asked Maggie.

"I'm not watching that show!" Hazel said again, her face screwed prune-like with irritation. "I don't believe that anybody forgets anything that happened to them when they were little. Why do they blame their parents? The Lord God says we should honor our mother and father. It's in the Book."

"So," Florence said, "You never whipped one of your kids? Nobody ever beat on you? You were never made to do something you didn't like?"

They tromped on ahead of Maggie.

The aide bent again. "Do you want to watch the show —uh—Mrs. Maggie."

Maggie motioned forward at Florence with the dark red hair, white showing underneath like an old-fashioned underskirt, and the taller Hazel with the undyed grey hair. "Whatever they want to do. Evidently, we're going to bed."

"I'll help you."

Maggie didn't argue. She was weary and longed for her own bed at home where she sat at night and read and watched TV, with Minnie sleeping beside her. She longed for the silence and the feeling of coziness, draperies drawn against the world.

They went down the hall, the sound of the television fading behind. As they approached Thomas's door Maggie noticed that it was quiet. Ahead of them Florence and Hazel still argued.

"I don't think you forget!" Hazel was adamant. "The good Lord don't suddenly let you remember something bad after you're thirty years old. Don't tell me! If it happens, you don't forget."

Florence seemed speechless for a change and didn't answer until they were in their room.

"Well," she said, as if that finished it.

The aide helped Maggie to the bathroom, where she slipped into a nightgown. Then back to the sink where she balanced against the cabinet and brushed her teeth. The aide stood by, young and thin with restless eyes, humming under her breath. Her nametag said Josie. As with other aides who worked part-time, Maggie might not see her again.

Josie helped Maggie into bed. There was a strange, sullen silence between Florence and Hazel as they prepared for bed. Maggie cleaned her face with cleansing cream and wiped it off with a tissue. She hated doing this. It made her feel as if she should go to the sink with a bar of soap and give her face a good scrubbing. She had learned while she was in the hospital that it was baths in the morning, not at night. If you couldn't get around on your own, you were stuck with second best. One of the volunteers over at the hospital had purchased the cleansing cream for her.

Hazel came out of the bathroom wearing a long-sleeved flannel nightgown. Florence didn't bother to seek privacy. She undressed, tossing aside blouse, bra, her heavy breasts released and hanging almost to her navel. She peeled down old stretch slacks, underpants and ankle hose, seemingly unembarrassed by her moment of total nudity. It might have been done deliberately, it seemed to Maggie, as if she gained some kind of inner satisfaction in making Hazel uncomfortable.

Although Hazel ignored her, irritation blinked in her eyes and pinched her mouth.

Florence turned and pulled over her head a knee-length cotton nightgown with short sleeves. Then she picked up an old robe and pulled it on. Instead of getting into bed she sat down in her chair.

Josie pushed the tissue box where Maggie could reach it, and checked the pitcher for water. "The nurse will be in later with your medicines. Goodnight. Call if you need anything." She took the wheelchair away, closing the wide door softly. Eager to get away, probably to an after-hours date.

Maggie took pain pills every four hours, but wanted no sleeping pills. Only twice in the hospital had she taken the sleeping pills and both times they had knocked her out as effectively as if someone had hit her with a mallet. The next day her head had continued to feel as if it had been battered. For the rest of her stay in the hospital, she had watched television until she grew sleepy, or read if she could persuade someone to bring her a book or magazine.

"The thing is, Hazel," Florence said, "You just don't know."

"I know enough to know a lie when I hear it!"

"So your childhood was a good one, that doesn't mean everybody's was."

"In a Christian world that kind of thing don't happen."

"Hazel, this is not a Christian world."

"Oh, Lord have mercy on your heathen soul, Florence."

"Bull shit."

Hazel groaned and lifted her eyes to the ceiling.

"Well, I can tell you for sure," Florence said fiercely, leaning forward, "This God of yours was not around when I was a child. My own mother— my own mother—had me doing things with men for money by the time I was barely out of diapers."

"And you didn't forget it, either, did you?" Hazel shot back, as if she'd heard the story many times.

"You goddamned right I didn't forget it."

"Oh, Lord have mercy on your soul, Florence."

"Yeah, sure."

Florence rocked, the chair jumping back and forth in its narrow allotment, the sturdy wooden base flat on the floor. It was a furious rock.

"But then," Hazel said with a different tone of voice, "You went right on doing the same thing, and you can't blame your mother for that."

There was silence except for the rock-rock-rock of Florence's chair, and a soft rustling of bed clothes as Hazel got into her bed and then sat with her arms crossed. She pushed the button that eased the bed back a few inches, adjusted her pillow and leaned back, sighing.

"My childhood was good," she said. "Papa was a preacher. We traveled around a good deal. In them days with a horse and wagon. If I got a whipping I didn't forget it, and in them days we didn't call it child abuse. It was the right thing to do. Spare the rod and spoil the child."

Florence looked over at Maggie, amusement on her face again. "Bet you've never been in a wagon in your life, have you?"

"A wagon? Hay rides, maybe."

Hazel said, "You didn't come up with lost memories, I'll bet, either."

"Oh no. Nothing lost ... that I know of!"

Florence laughed. Maggie had intended it as a joke and wanted to laugh too but laughter didn't come. No, I'm not sure … gaps in memories … years gathering ... like ghosts rising in an old cemetery. "But who wants to remember?" she added.

"That's right!" Florence said. "You look like you had a good childhood. You can tell about people."

"Yes, I was one of the lucky ones," Maggie answered, her head turned against her pillow. "I had parents, grandparents, uncles, aunts, two little sisters. Lots of cousins. I was fortunate."

Except ...

The door opened and the night shift RN, another nurse Maggie had not seen before, came in carrying a tray loaded with little plastic cups of pills. She smiled and spoke, her voice soft, and checked the chart she carried.

"Miss Florence," she said. "Two sleeping pills."

Florence took them with a full glass of water.

The nurse stood watching until the pills were down. "Want help into bed?"

"Oh no, I'm not ready for that. Yet."

"She's been helped into bed too many times," Hazel snapped. "And not by nurses."

Florence settled into her bed and pulled up the blanket. The bed buzzed as she lowered it to lie flat. "You pray for my wicked soul, Hazel." She laughed and turned to face the wall.

Hazel grunted. "Thank the good Lord for sleeping pills. Maybe we'll have some peace and quiet for a while. Shut Florence up till morning. Poor lost soul."

Florence said over her shoulder, "But I won't be lost long because Hazel is praying for me." She chuckled like an old engine running down.

The nurse smiled and said, "That's nice."

"Somebody has to." Hazel looked into the plastic cup. "What do I have here that I have to swallow?"

"The same as usual."

Hazel struggled to swallow several pills, each one seeming to be almost impossible to get down. She choked and coughed and gulped. The nurse stood by quietly, waiting, and Maggie assumed this was the nightly pattern.

She was next. Two pain pills and one sleeping pill.

"I don't want the sleeping pill," she said.

"Are you sure?"

The room had grown quiet, except for a soft snore from Florence. She had gone almost instantly to sleep. There hadn't been time for the medication to work.

Hazel said, yawning, "If you want to sleep, Maggie, you'd better take that pill. Florence snores."

Minnie snored too, softly, rhythmically. A comforting sound. "I don't mind snores."

"If you change your mind and want the medication," the nurse said, "Just push your buzzer. Here, I'll hang it over the railing within your reach."

She pulled up the railing, which, Maggie noticed, she hadn't done on the other two beds. The buzzer hung in the shadows, a black plastic device with a lighted red button in the center.

As the nurse left the room, turning the lights all out except for a soft glow over the sink, Hazel yawned again, a verbal "Ho-hummm," followed by a long sigh.

Somewhere in the distance, like a storm hovering just below the horizon, a groan rose. Thomas had awakened.

"Good Lord," Hazel prayed, "Let the man sleep. Let us all sleep in peace."

In SILENCE MAGGIE PLEADED, "Bring back my dreams, please, God." From that other existence, trapped in a reality that too often turned dark and terrifying. Would the dreams ever come again?

But she felt closed off from that other existence, trapped too often—in a world turned dark and terrifying. Would the dreams ever come again?

Those strange, marvelous dreams, filled with their pure, eternal ecstasy, had become farther and farther apart as she grew older. Or, perhaps it was that on looking back time had narrowed, like a road disappearing into the distance, with the dreams, those special dreams, spotted along it like highway markers crowding into a disturbing and painful past.

She thought of the old man and the mountain, and felt she understood a portion of what he had meant. He, who perhaps had not even been real, but a warning. Warning her of mountains to climb, a mountain of paths, chosen at her own will.

It seemed that all events of her life were with her in the present, as though nullifying time. What she was, what had happened to her then, created her present. And she had come now to the steepest part of the mountain. She could not bear to look up. She could only look down.

She closed her eyes tightly against both future and past, but they were there, waiting. Waiting.

Chapter Five

Anurse's footsteps came down the hall and went into a nearby room. Thomas cried out.

Hazel mumbled, "Got his shot. Thank the Lord. He'll sleep now."

Thomas's groans softened, faded. An uneasy stillness settled around Maggie. In the corner opposite Maggie's bed Florence's snores acquired a kind of rhythm. Snonk, clunk snonk ... clunk ... in, out, in, out. She listened, then turned one ear against the pillow and pulled the blanket to cover the other.

She wanted to sleep, to dream, to escape. But the memories came, invading her space like aliens from a long forgotten planet.

HER NAME WAS EMILY THEN, shortened to Emmy.

She didn't remember the sex play, but she had no doubt it happened. Her memory opened with the question from her grandmother, her daddy's mother, with the long black hair turning to silver on the top.

Grandma had taken her hair down from the bun and let it spread like a shawl. She washed it in the tub in the backyard. It hung to her hips, dripping water onto the stones beneath the tub. Then she toweled it dry and went into the main room of the two-room house and curled it with a curling iron that had been heating in the globe of the kerosene lamp.

Emmy followed after her, watching, always fascinated with Grandma's long, long hair. Sometimes when it was down Grandma let her brush and comb it, and Emmy would let it fall between her fingers, coarse and heavy like a horse's mane. She wished for hair like Grandma's instead of the straight, white, fine fluff on her own head. She loved seeing the tiny waves the iron made in Grandma's hair. She leaned against the table, her arm resting on the oilcloth, watching. On the floor near the hearth and the fire that burned in the fireplace, her two little sisters, Peggy and Rebba, played with some little stones they had picked up in the bed of the branch down in the meadow.

Grandma began wrapping the bun up again on the back of her head, using thick, brown and tan-streaked celluloid hairpins to hold it in place. There was a touch of silver overlaid on the black hair, like sunshine on a cloud. Then the question …

"You took your bloomers off, didn't you, when you were with Jimmy and Sheila, and you did naughty things. Why did you do it? Why would you do such a naughty, terrible thing like that?"

As if she were acting alone. As if she were older instead of younger than her cousins. Emmy drew back, stung by the accusatory tone in Grandma's voice.

"But Daddy did." If Daddy did it, wasn't it all right if she did?

The black eyes turned toward her, filled with a kind of awful fire.

"What! What did you say?"

Emmy backed away from the table where Grandma had been looking into the small mirror propped there against the kerosene lamp. The lamp was never lighted during the day except when Grandma heated the curling iron. The chair in which Grandma sat turned, scraping on the floor. Several hairpins on the table fell to the floor. The end of Grandma's hair hung out of the half-done coil like the end of a tail.

"What?"

"Daddy did," Emmy said again. "Daddy and Aunt Ketti." Grandma stood up, grabbed Emmy's arm and dragged her out into the backyard. Emmy tried to stay on her feet and run beside her, but kept stumbling, falling to her knees and scraping them on the rocks. Grandma jerked her up and pulled her on, toward the dark hollow with all the trees. Emmy began to cry. She felt Grandma's sudden and awful hatred more than she felt the pain in her knees, the skin peeling back, beads of blood oozing through, She had never been treated like this before. She didn't fight to get away because she didn't understand what was happening. Why all of a sudden did Grandma hate her and want to hurt her?

The little girls came out the back door and stood watching in silence with their mouths falling open.

Aunt Ketti lived around two long corners, almost a mile, up the road with Uncle Willie, Emmy's cousins Jimmy and Sheila, and baby Denton. Emmy walked to school with Jimmy and Sheila.

On warm days when there was no school Grandma walked up to Aunt Ketti's, and Emmy was allowed to go along and play. Their walks along the road were great adventures. Grandma let Emmy run ahead, or run to the side, if she didn't get too far away. She answered all of Emmy's questions, about the flowers that grew on the hillside above the road, or about the little caves beneath the bluffs. Until she got tired. Then she would say, "My goodness, where do you get all those questions?" Once, Emmy remembered in flashes and bits and pieces as she was being dragged out into the yard, she had let Emmy run down off the road while she waited, to the lone apple tree in the field, and pick up apples from the ground to carry up to her cousins. Usually she didn't like to wait, but this once, she had—Grandma had always let her go along to Aunt Ketti's. Why was she so mad at her now?

Grandma stopped at a bush with many branches and with one hand ripped off a limb. It was long and thin and willowy.

It made a rushing sound in the air like a snake hissing and it struck her bare legs with the sting of a snake bite. It began to tear her skin away as it came down and kept coming down against her, on and on, until the limb grew shredded and stubby. "You're lying! You're lying!"

"No!" Emmy screamed, no longer hearing the sound of the switch, only feeling it cut into her legs, her back, her head. "No!"

THEY HAD GONE into Aunt Ketti's house that morning last week, she and Daddy. It was a cold, frosty morning just a few days ago, and she was late for school. Daddy had walked with her up the road so that she could walk the next mile to school with Jimmy and Sheila.

Sheila had already gone. Jimmy was home because his nose was running, and his forehead was hot.

The baby sat in a cardboard box on the floor, and Emmy sat down beside him, holding his hand, watching his smile, listening to his baby talk. She cooed and gooed at him, and wished she could hold him. But she was too little to hold a baby yet.

The heating stove put out waves of warmth in the front room of the house. Daddy stood on one side of the stove, with Aunt Ketti on the other. They talked. Emmy didn't listen. Jimmy sat in a rocking chair, leaning on his hand, sniffing.

Then Daddy went around the stove to Aunt Ketti and pushed up against her. She stood looking over his shoulder, her arms akimbo, fists on her hips. She acted as if he weren't there, pushing against her belly.

Emmy stopped playing with Denton and sat watching. Jimmy began watching too.

Daddy took hold of Aunt Ketti's bottom with his hands and pushed harder against her as if he were driving in a nail with his body.

Then suddenly they laughed and looked at Emmy and Jimmy. "They're watching," Aunt Ketti said.

They went into the kitchen, and closed the door behind them. Emmy heard a chair being propped beneath the knob.

Jimmy looked at Emmy, then got out of the rocking chair and went to the wall. There was a knothole in the board wall, the size of baby Denton's fist. Jimmy had to stoop to look through the hole. Emmy went to stand beside him.

He looked for a while, then glanced over his shoulder at her and stood back. The hole was about the right height for Emmy. She didn't have to bend.

The view through the knothole revealed the kitchen table with its oilcloth cover, worn through at the corners and at the edges, faded by many scrubbings. Aunt Ketti lay on the table, her skirt around her waist, her underwear gone, her leg above the roll of her stocking bare and white. The leg hung off the table, her foot dangling toward the floor.

Daddy lay on top of her, his trousers down around his feet, his bottom white and bare like Aunt Ketti's leg. He humped against her, pushing, pushing.

"What are they doing?" Emmy asked, but Jimmy didn't answer. Perhaps Aunt Ketti heard her, for suddenly her eyes turned toward the knothole. Emmy saw her laugh again. Daddy stopped humping on her, looked at the knothole and laughed too. He got up, and his big pee-pee was sticking up like a bleached pig's mouth. It was so big his hands didn't cover it. He moved baby Denton's highchair to cover the knothole.

She hadn't gone to school that day, though she had wanted to. Daddy and Aunt Ketti finally came back into the front room, and Daddy put some wood into the stove for Aunt Ketti. Jimmy went to the corner behind the stove where it was warm and private, and curled up on the floor, sniffing.

Emmy liked school more than anything. She had wanted to start when she was three, the year Sheila started, and again when Jimmy started the next year. She cried when they wouldn't let her go. She had to wait until she was five.

THE SWITCH KEPT HITTING Emmy's back, even after it became a stub, hurting more than Emmy knew anything could hurt.

Grandma screamed, "You take it back! You're lying! You bad, bad girl, you liar!"

Emmy escaped, somehow. Suddenly she was running, around the house, across the yard, across the narrow dirt road and to the barn where Mommie and Daddy were milking cows. They came hurrying to meet her. No one had ever whipped her before.

She went to them for comfort, for protection. She felt their arms around her.

ANOTHER GAP IN HER MEMORY. It was the next day or perhaps the next, and she was walking home from school. Jimmy and Sheila stopped at their house, and Emmy continued on down the road the next mile.

But no one was home except Daddy, and he seemed angry at something. He didn't look at Emmy.

"Where's Mommy?" Emmy asked. "Where's Peggy and Rebba and Grandma?"

At first it seemed he might not talk to her, but then he told her.

"Grandma's up at Ketti's. Your mother took the little girls and went home to her mommy and poppy."

"Why did she leave me?" Emmy pleaded. "Why did Mommy leave me?" He didn't answer. It was lonesome and quiet without them. She even missed Grandma, even though she still stung where Grandma had whipped her. But there was something nice too about being just with Daddy.

He made a fire in the cookstove, and she watched him. The heat in the house came from the fireplace, and he had filled it with wood. But he looked so funny building a cooking fire. Grandma always made the cookfire, and kept it going from the wood in the box behind the stove.

It was even funnier watching him fry ham, eggs and pancakes. Grease spattered. She stood on the edge of the woodbox and peeked over the top of the stove at the skillet and tried to tell him how Grandma did it.

"She pushes the skillet back when it gets too hot," she said. Daddy shoved it back, but he put it too far and the food stopped cooking. He opened the little metal door of the stove's firebox and shoved in more wood. Sparks flew like fireworks. He grumbled. "I don't know why your mother had to pull something like this. I don't know why she didn't at least bake some biscuits before she left. She's not taking very good care of things around here."

He flipped a pancake. It fell on the stove top instead of into the skillet. Emmy laughed.

Daddy cussed. "Goddamned cocksucker," he said as he tried to get the doughy side of the pancake off the top of the hot stove. Emmy said, under her breath, "Goddamned cocksucker."

The dough stuck and cooked brown before he could scrape it off.

Finally they ate. The pancakes weren't smoothly brown, they were black and white. The ham was still pink except where it was burned crisp. The eggs were soft and runny. She hated the yolks of eggs from that meal forward, all her life, even when they were cooked into a sunny little ball that she could dig out of the surrounding white. If there were a dog handy, she tossed him the yellow ball.

Daddy wasn't friendly. He didn't look at her one time. He didn't hold her on his lap in front of the fire the way he usually did on winter evenings. Maybe it was because Peggy and Rebba weren't there, because usually all three of them sat together on Daddy's lap in the big rocking chair.

The next morning he didn't dress her for school. She wore the same dress she'd had on yesterday, the same dress she'd slept in. But he told her to hurry up, and they went out to the truck and she got in. The ground was white with frost. The black fenders of the truck were coated with white, and frost made fancy patterns on the windshield like cut-out valentines. Daddy showed her the throttle on the steering wheel, a little metal stick with a knob on the end. He had never let her touch it before.

"Now when it starts, you pull this down."

He took the crank to the front, put it into the hole beneath the radiator and began whirling it around and around, his face growing redder, his curly dark hair falling down on his forehead. A deep frown lay over his eyes just as it had last night while he was cooking, while they ate, even while they washed and dried the dishes. He looked very angry, as

Grandma had, his eyes dark and snapping. All the grownups were mad lately, but she didn't know why.

The engine started. Whomp …whomp …whomp. Daddy frowned at her over the hood, and his mouth worked some words, but she couldn't hear what he said. She remembered to jerk down on the throttle. Whomp … whomp … whomp. The cab rattled and shook.

Daddy came running around, threw the crank in on the floor, jumped in and shoved her over. They were on their way somewhere. He hadn't told Emmy where they were going. The truck bounced and rattled up the frozen, narrow road. But the sun was shining over the hills into the long, narrow valley, and as its light crept over the ground the frost disappeared as if running in fear from the sun's fingers of golden light.

They drove past Aunt Ketti's and Uncle Willie's house, past Uncle Elmer's, past the big spring that made a branch down through Uncle Elmer's field. That same branch was the one that passed her own house, where she, Peggy and Rebba gathered the pretty stones for play. They went up the hill. School was toward the left. Her other grandmother lived toward the right.

Now she knew.

They were going to see Mommy.

She leaned forward, eager and excited. She had never been away from Mommy before, and she could hardly wait for the truck to pull up beside the picket fence.

He parked beneath a big tree instead, a ways off from the house, and got out. When she started to get out and run to the house, he stopped her by closing the door against her.

"Stay there." The order was barked short and quick, the way he told the dogs to stay.

She sat still, stretching to peer over the hood and watch him walk halfway to the house and then stop.

Here on the hill there was no frost. Sunshine spread everywhere, throwing funny shadows with lots of arms where trees stood. Even as she watched it ate away the frost on the windshield. Hungry sun.

Mommie came out of the house and toward Daddy where he stood waiting. She was alone. Emmy could see Rebba's little face pressed against the window. Peggy stood behind her, a dark shape in a room crossed by sunlight and shadows.

Why had Mommy come up to Gram's without her?

Emmy was so glad to see Mommy that she wanted to run and hug her and never let go. She was beautiful, her hair wavy, the sunlight filling the waves with pure gold. She came slowly toward the truck, not smiling. Like Daddy, she too didn't look at Emmy. She stopped near the front fender and stood looking down, saying nothing.

Emmy didn't see Daddy get the stick. It was large and heavy, much heavier than the switch that Grandma had whipped her with. When he opened the door she saw it in his hand.

His eyes looked at her, finally. They were like Grandma's, and filled with the same look. She shrank from it. She had never seen Daddy's eyes like that. Cold and furious, and hating.

He got her by the arm and pulled her from the truck cab. She stood on the ground, his hand hurting her arm.

"Tell her you lied," he commanded.

Mommy stood looking at the ground, saying nothing.

"No," Emmy said. "I didn't lie."

Hadn't Mommie told her it was bad to lie? Someone must have. She knew in her heart it was very bad. God wouldn't love you if you lied.

He jerked her forward and brought the heavy stick down on her back.

"Tell her you lied!"

The stick came down, harder, harder. She heard the sounds of cracking and thought it might be her bones. She screamed, screamed, the one word coming.

"NO! NO!"

"You lied! You're a little liar! Liar! Tell her you lied!"

"Nonono ..."

She fell, no longer able to stand up. Her screams settled to sobs. She couldn't get her breath.

Her mother spoke suddenly. "Leave her alone."

The beating stopped.

She lay on the rocks at the edge of the road, gasping for breath. She heard sobbing. Terrible, heartrending sobs. She lifted her head and looked up to see who was crying. Daddy sat on the running board of the truck, his head in his hands. His shoulders shook, hunched by his head.

Slowly, Emmy got to her knees. She had never heard her daddy cry before, and it tore something within her and made it bleed, as if a great hand were squeezing the life from her heart. Her heart hurt. It hurt far more than the beating.

She rose to her feet, went to him, put her arms around his neck and laid her head on his shoulders. She felt his body shaking as the sobs came. "Daddy," she said. "It's all right. It's all right, Daddy."

She looked up and saw Mommy standing by the front fender. Mommy was staring at Daddy, tears in her eyes and rolling slowly like little clear beads down her cheeks. Her lower lip and chin trembled.

Emmy hurt. In her heart, in her eyes. There was something she had to say so her mommy and daddy wouldn't cry.

"I lied."

Mommy's eyes rose from Daddy's bowed head to stare at Emmy. Again, louder, firmer, Emmy said, "I lied."

God might hate her now, but for a reason she didn't understand she knew that Mommy very much wanted to hear that she had lied.

Emmy felt her daddy move against her, pushing her away. He got to his feet, his chest and throat jerking.

They went home. All of them.

She was seven on her next birthday, soon after, while the white frost still coated the hollow with winter.

Chapter Six

Once again it was Grandma who kept the fire in the cookstove. It was Grandma who baked her a birthday cake. She baked a big cake for everyone, and she baked a surprise cake, small and round, especially for Emmy. Mommy worked outside with Daddy, cutting wood, hauling it away to the sawmills for money to buy flour and salt and sugar.

Daddy never whipped her again.

Instead, it was Mommy who started whipping her.

The weather was still too cold for them to play outside without shoes, and Peggy, sitting on the cracked stones of the hearth near the fire, was taking too much time getting her shoes on. Emmy was ready for school. Mommy told her to wait so Peggy and Rebba could walk to the corner with her. Peggy kept trying to tie her shoes all by herself. Her awkwardness made Emmy edgy. "Here," Emmy said, pushing Peggy's hands away from the shoestrings. "Let me show you."

Mommy had been working at the table clearing breakfast dishes, but in three steps she was at the hearth. She jerked Emmy to her feet and marched her outside, just as Grandma had done not long ago. She went to the willow bush as Grandma had and broke off a long, mean switch. Peggy and Rebba stood in the open back door while Emmy was whipped.

The two dogs came around the corner of the house. Rosie, the spotted hound, slunk to the ground whining. Sport, the German shepherd, growled and came forward, the hair stiff along his spine, his eyes sharp with warning. Mommy turned the stick toward him, but he came forward with stiffened legs, growling. She struck at him and he flinched and backed down.

"Go on to school," she told Emmy, shaking the stick in front of her. "You'll be late."

Choking on her tears, sobbing in her chest, Emmy started her walk up the road to school. The dogs wanted to walk with her, but at the corner she hugged each one around the neck and told them to stay. She wished they could go. For the first time she was afraid to walk alone. What if a mad dog came along and bit her?

At Aunt Ketti's house her cousins were waiting and came across the ditch to walk with her. She had dried her tears. She didn't want anyone to know that she had cried. "Like a baby," Grandma had said, every time she cried now. "Emmy's getting worse than Peggy and Rebba to be bawling all the time. And you can't depend on a word she says."

Jimmy had gotten over his bad cold and lagged a bit behind. Emmy and Sheila walked ahead, throwing rocks into the field. Emmy didn't feel much like talking.

They reached the spring, where cold water bubbled out and became a brook that wound its way down the hollow.

"Wash your face," Sheila said suddenly, "It's dirty. Have you been crying?"

For the first time it came to Emmy's mind that Mommy had stopped washing her face in the mornings, or combing her hair to get her ready for school.

She bent to the cold spring and scooped up water and smeared it over her face. Jimmy glared at Emmy as if he didn't like her anymore.

"Why didn't you wash your face?" Sheila asked. "Why didn't you comb your hair? Why don't you change your dress? It looks like you slept in it."

"My mommy didn't ..." She said no more. To finish her thought would be like accusing her mother of something bad.

"You have to do it yourself," Sheila said, running her fingers through Emmy's hair to take out the tangles. "I have to. I've always had to."

Emmy wiped her face on her sleeve, and followed them on up the road toward school.

"Once," she said, remembering another walk up the road, "Mommy and Peggy and Rebba and me walked up to Gram's, and we saw a fox right over there in the trees. It wasn't afraid of us. It walked along the hillside with us."

"Really?" Sheila said.

"Naw," Jimmy said, "Don't believe her. Emmy's a liar."

Sheila walked on, her shoes sometimes kicking the rocks and making little glints of fire.

"I'm not!" Emmy denied heatedly, glaring at him.

He didn't look at her. "Yes you are. Everybody says so. You told a dirty lie on my mommy and I don't like you anymore."

She stared at the back of his head where the hair curled against his neck. He knew. He had seen too, and he knew Emmy hadn't lied. Yet he walked on as if he didn't know, hadn't seen, and didn't remember.

"Liar, liar, liar," he chanted. "A black liar. Emmy lies about everything. She tells dirty old mean lies."

They walked to school, they walked home, day after day. She loved school, especially ancient history with the stories about gods and goddesses. She loved geography, and drawing maps of the world. It was a one-room school, and there were only four other kids in her third grade class. No one else liked geography.

School ended and she was passed to fourth grade.

Almost every day Mommy whipped her for something. She had made a stick for whipping Emmy, and it stood in the corner by the fireplace.

If Emmy talked or laughed at the table Mommy slapped her. Most of the time Emmy didn't know what she had said that was bad. Mommy slapped her so often she began to dodge when Mommy's hand moved, and Mommy laughed and asked, "Why are you dodging?"

One evening in this new winter, the two little girls were sitting on the hearth taking up all the room when Emmy finished drying the dishes for Grandma. Daddy and Mommy were already sitting in rocking chairs on each side of the fireplace.

Emmy went to the hearth and reached down to push Rebba over, without thinking. She used to push Rebba over all the time, a long time ago it now seemed, other winters ago. Immediately she knew that she had done a bad thing.

Mommy got up and got the stick. She pulled Emmy back away from the fire and whipped her for a long time, until Emmy couldn't get her breath. She let Emmy go then and told her to go to bed.

Emmy slept in the bed in the corner of the big front room, with Peggy and Rebba. Mommy and Daddy's bed was the only one in the bedroom. Grandma's bed was in another corner of the front room.

Emmy took off her shoes and dress and went to bed, her breath still catching in her throat. She kept her sobs soundless. If Mommy heard her crying she'd get whipped again.

They sat near the hearth talking, Mommy, Daddy, and Grandma. Rebba and Peggy sat on the hearth playing that the stones were houses and people. All their heads were outlined against the fire as it died down. Emmy wished she could be there too, toasting her feet, playing with the stones.

Finally, they all went to bed. Rebba and Peggy intertwined like two piglets, but they left a space between them and Emmy. They didn't like her much anymore. She was always getting in trouble, and it scared them. When Emmy was around their play was disturbed and sometimes even they had to be quiet.

Emmy was cold and alone, and she couldn't sleep. Her breath kept catching and her stomach hurt.

Now that the lamp was out the only light in the big room came from the dying fire. Red coals glowed on the hearth. They were like one red eye looking at her in this very dark world. Cold air came through the crack in the wall by the bed and Emmy shivered under the quilt.

The room was still, the coals turning black. Everyone but Emmy slept. Her arms were like icicles, and her legs felt brittle with cold. She sat up, and crawled down over the foot of the bed and slipped quietly outside.

In a big cardboard box on the porch the two dogs slept on a smelly old braided rug.

When she climbed into the box with them she heard their tails tapping the side of the cardboard, and felt their warm tongues on her face. They rearranged themselves to make room for her, and she snuggled between them. She heard their long, contented sighs as they took her in and overlapped her, their heads on her body, their necks stretching over her as if they knew she needed to be warmed.

THERE CAME NOW, as she was snuggled by the dogs, the first of those strange, marvelous, vivid dreams.

She is in a country store with Mommy, Daddy, the little girls, Aunt Ketti, Jimmy and Sheila. There are others too, in the store, all strangers, yet in some way familiar.

At the back of the store is a window, with small panes. It is dirty, so black with grime that she can't see through it.

She puts her hand up and wipes away the dirt on one small pane.

Through the glass she sees a view more beautiful than she's ever imagined. It's a narrow valley, with long, silky green grass and perfect, round trees spotted here and there. The grass moves in waves with the silent wind. The valley is surrounded by treeless mountains, rising small peak after peak up, up, high toward the sky. The mountains are solid rock, and the peaks are like steps upward, so high she can't see the top. She just knows it's there.

Emmy turns and motions Sheila to come and look at this marvelous sight.

Sheila comes and looks through the window where Emmy cleaned a small pane, but sees nothing. Emmy knows by the expression on her face that for her, nothing is there, though she nods her head before she turns her back on it. She hasn't seen the lovely valley, or the stone mountains with their rising steps.

Suddenly Emmy is in the valley, standing with her bare feet in the green grass. It's softer than anything she has ever felt before, and brushes her legs like feather wands as it moves. The grass is softer than the fur of a kitten, and she has never felt the happiness she now feels.

She begins to walk, farther and farther into this other world, this valley. She looks up at the mountains made of stone, and feels a glorious beckoning. She begins to run.

Then suddenly overhead, in the sky, she sees a round, white moon. Clouds white and floating like lambs in a meadow gather and cover the moon. They move, pushed by the straight, fresh wind in this other world. They uncover the moon bit by bit. It has grown with the passing of the clouds and is now huge, filled with light, and something else … something … a message, printed in shining letters on the face of the moon.

She woke, curled with the dogs, bathed in the beauty and excitement of that heavenly light. There was a message on the moon, but she didn't understand it. She stared hard back into her mind trying to recall that important message, struggling to see again those printed words. They slipped away like the image of the moon, melting, her mind unable to hold on. The dogs stirred, stretching. The night was ending. A pale dawn filtered into the dark of the hollow. A dim light came through the window. Sounds of a fire being made, the clank of wood, of metal door. Grandma was up.

Emmy opened the door an inch, another inch, until she could slip through and into the house. Grandma was building the cook fire, bending over, getting kindling from the box of wood. She didn't see or hear Emmy as she slipped back into bed.

She tried to go back to sleep, back into that world she didn't want to leave, into the magic of her dream. But it was gone. It left the memory, the burning image of the beauty, and the so-happy feeling. The happy feeling that puzzled her, the understanding that was beyond her, on the other side of the curtain in her mind.

She was eight years old. Dreams became as much a part of her consciousness as the reality. In her dreams her spirits soared. There was no danger in the dark woods she walked past, or from the people who walked the city streets with her. There was a happiness, a glory, a feeling of perfection. She tried to catch the dreams and hold them, but they left her, like a heavenly bird dropping her to the hard ground of a different world. She learned to lie still, eyes closed, savoring that other world.

Wondering about it.

She began to feel she lived in two different worlds. One filled with danger and fear, and an aching heart, the other without hurt or danger, exciting and marvelous and mysterious even in the dark places.

COMFORTING SLEEP ELUDED MAGGIE. Florence had settled into a snore that at times seemed as if she would choke. Even Hazel's deep breathing was audible. Her bed was just beyond the curtain that was pushed back against the wall, and Maggie saw the humps of her shoulder and hip in the pale light that created ghosts in the room. On the wall beyond and above Hazel's bed hung a framed picture of Jesus on the cross, his head hanging in martyred misery, giving off a luminous glow. It reminded Maggie of pictures given as prizes at carnivals. Elvis Presley on velvet. Bull fighters, with lanced-pierced bulls, their painted faces angry as if they were insensitive to pain. Blood and pain on velvet. The insensitive cruelty of men on velvet. Jesus, illuminated, so that you couldn't miss seeing it even in the dark. Jesus, more than a man.

She didn't want to think of the past. It had been a long time since she had let the past into her life. But no, she hadn't forgotten. Memories returned, bits and pieces here and there, part of her always, having made her the conscious human being that she was.

What was Minnie doing? Was she whining and trying to find comfort in a cage that probably had straw for a bed? Minnie had slept with Maggie since she came to live with her at the age of two months. A tiny, warm, breathing touch of silk, she seemed, her fur soft and smooth. Her tiny nose pressed to Maggie's cheek as she curled against her. When Maggie moved, Minnie crept close again, a continuing source of comfort. If Maggie turned over, she took Minnie with her, always keeping her safe and warm. For four years Minnie had slept with her, wherever they had slept.

"Please God, keep her safe. Hold her in your hands."

Her whispered prayer drifted away. Too many prayers, unanswered. Yet still, perhaps instinctively, she prayed.

Her leg and hip ached, screaming for another position. She turned in bed, feeling in the darkness for the button to call the nurse. Movement made the pain worse. Pain slit her hip, separating bone, muscle, nerves. How long before it would quit hurting? She had lived pain free for so many years. Had she been properly thankful for that?

She was reminded of part of a poem, the writer's name lost to her memory:

"CALL TO THOUGHT, *if now you grieve a little,*
   the days when we had rest, oh Soul,
   for they were long."

SHE FOUND THE CALL BUTTON, a red eye against the bed, and pressed it. As if it disturbed Florence with its silent ring, she turned, grunting, onto her back. The walls above and beyond her bed were bare.

Other moans reached Maggie. Softer than during the day, dampened by drugs, perhaps. Thomas.

Her chest tightened, with the full force of panic. Swift and unexpected, arriving with no warning.

I have to get out of here. I have to get out of here.

Please God, help me, help me, help Minnie. Let us be together again. She's all I have. I'm all she has. Help us. The door opened. Maggie hadn't heard the nurse's approach. She drew a deep breath of relief. She would not refuse a sleeping pill again.

The night shift nurse came to the bed and turned off the tiny light that had been activated by the call button.

She bent and whispered, "What do you need?"

"I guess I need something to help me sleep. Something mild."

"Haven't you been to sleep yet? Well, we can't have that. Back in a minute." The nurse slipped away as quietly as she had come. She was back within a short time with two tiny purple pills in a plastic cup.

"Can you help Thomas?" Maggie asked.

The nurse whispered, "No one can help Thomas." Then she was gone.

It had been almost a ghostly visit, leaving Maggie feeling helpless and sad. No one can help Thomas.

Chapter Seven

Sounds of movement disturbed a deep rest that seemed to have only started. A bright light had been turned on overhead. She blinked against its intrusion.

"Wake up, girls, it's time to take showers and get ready for breakfast."

She had taken the pill too late. A drowsy heaviness was worse than the sleeplessness.

"Remind me not to take any more sleeping pills," she said, scarcely realizing she had spoken aloud until the answers came.

"I won't be here to remind you," the nurse said in a loud and cheerful voice, and Maggie saw it was Blanche.

Was she always so happy and energetic? Or did she go home and flop and feel like crying because she didn't have to put on that front for a few hours?

Florence said, "You'll wake up after awhile. Being groggy is better than lying awake all night."

"The Lord has given us another day, praise God. Is there a letter from my grandson?"

"Mail hasn't come yet, Hazel. Who wants to go shower first?"

Florence said, "Maggie needs help, take her."

Hazel had already started toward the bathroom, seemingly more bent than yesterday.

Exercise, Maggie reminded herself. Move on your own. You must. As soon as she could manage the walker without falling she could go home. Would there be enough money to cover her expenses? She had to get home to pay the utilities and the kennel bill. She had to get home.

She managed to get out of bed and stand, holding to the bedside table. Blanche rushed toward her.

"Here you go trying to do it on your own again, Maggie."

The walker stood at the foot of her bed.

"But you see, I have to. I'll be all right. I have to do this."

Still, Blanche held to her, helping her to the walker, then into the shower when Hazel was finished. She helped Maggie dress, in a pair of slacks and a tunic, then helped her to stand in front of the mirror over the sink where she began brushing her teeth.

"Okay?" Blanche said. "Now you stay here and I'll see who all down the hall needs help. Here's your walker. Don't let go of it."

"I promise," Maggie said, glad to be left on her own. Her image stared at her from the mirror, no makeup, hair undone for over a week now.

She was always a bit startled by the wrinkles. Her hair color had not changed much. It was still soft and light, streaked naturally, silvered on top, bleached by the sun. But the wrinkles lay like a baby's palm print on her cheeks. Though she had tried to change her mental image to fit reality, she still saw herself as she was once, with an unlined face, firm skin with no strange brown spots like wayward freckles tossed here and there.

She looked, she thought, every bit of her sixty-five years. It didn't matter. Who cared? Minnie didn't care.

But she began to try to fix herself up as she always had at home, before the fall. She clutched the walker and awkwardly brushed her hair. She no longer felt whole. She was divided into good parts and bad parts.

"Here." Florence's face appeared suddenly in the mirror beside hers. With a small clunk her hand dropped makeup items on the narrow counter. Lipstick. Eyebrow pencil. Even mascara. All new and unused. Florence turned away. "I don't use makeup anymore."

Warmly touched by the offer, Maggie watched in the mirror as her roommate moved away. Florence went back to her own narrow portion of the room and plopped into her chair with a grunt.

"That's sweet of you, Florence. Whoever packed my bag the day I fell managed to get my hair brush, but little else."

"Some makeup'll make you feel better while you're here." Florence leaned her head back against the chair and stared at the ceiling.

"Why is it you're here, Florence? You seem healthy and able to live alone."

"Oh sure. But I don't even have a house anymore. The girls sold it so that I could live here. They decided I couldn't live alone anymore just because I left a burner on once and burned up some stuff. Blackened the ceiling, that's all. A little paint fixed it. Then they took away my driver's license and my car just because my brakes failed and I hit the back of the garage. All it needed was someone to put that wall back in. A little carpentry work. But then nobody wanted to bother with taking me to the grocery store. You know how kids can be. Do you have kids, Maggie?"

"Nieces and nephews."

She didn't add they were strangers to her, rarely seen since they were small children, communication cut away.

"Not the same. You don't expect so much from them. And maybe that's the whole problem, we expect too much from our kids."

Florence had risen this morning as if she were sore and tired. She went into the bathroom. The shower ran, a noise that reminded Maggie of the water over the dam where she had last lived with her family. They had been good years, those last few when they were all together.

Maggie's thoughts returned, kept returning, to that distant childhood that seemed so close lately, so much a living part of her. She didn't understand this reliving of episodes of her life, as if she were slowly drowning. The faces of her parents, and her sisters when they were children, kept returning, obscuring the moment and the walls of this confining room.

They had begun the moves that would occupy their lives during the late 1930's, the dwindling years of the great depression. They became followers of the fruit harvests, like so many other families.

The beatings stopped as abruptly as the moves began, as if that other part of life was no longer important to her mother.

Maggie didn't know what had happened to the dogs that had given her a safe haven one winter night in her childhood. The night of her first beautiful dream.

No, she hadn't forgotten. She had tried to forget the bad parts, but as if the bad more than the good had created the person she became, she hadn't been able to forget. Conversely, she had not forgotten the beautiful dreams, either. They remained as vivid and close within her memory as if they had happened last night. They intrigued her, gave her flashes of great ecstasy, and very deeply puzzled her. She could not pull new dream experiences forth at will, had never been able to. Unlike ordinary dreams, the beautiful dreams came like brilliant visions, from afar.

FLORENCE CAME BACK, drops of water still clinging, and began to dress. Hazel sat in her chair, the Bible open on her lap, her eyes closed. She mumbled quietly her morning prayer.

Florence took up the conversation where she had left off. "Yes, you expect too much maybe. I wasn't a very good daughter myself, to my mother, when she got old. That's the way of life, I guess."

Maggie used the makeup though her heart wasn't in it. She applied lipstick, even mascara, more for Florence than for herself.

"One of the signs of depression," Florence said, as if she knew what Maggie was feeling, "Is when people stop doing their hair, putting on makeup. If you've ever been in a psychiatric hospital, you learn to fake it, so you can get out."

Maggie's grogginess was lifting. Her brain no longer felt saturated with fog. Also, she was getting stronger, she was sure, muscles not so weak.

"Did that happen to you?"

"Once, for a couple of weeks. I had this husband, see. My fourth—or maybe my third. You get to losing track of them after having five and looking back over all those years. Anyway, this crazy man thought it was me who was crazy instead of him. So without me even knowing what he was doing, here came the police to my door that night about dawn when I got home from work, and dragged me off yelling and screaming—I didn't know where the hell I was going. Turned out though they soon found out they had the wrong person. You could have heard me yell from Kansas City to Chicago. I expect them shrinks thought they'd caught a she-bear. I was out the next night in time to go to work."

"Home from work at dawn?" A yearning for her own years of night work was like a thirst. "What did you do, Florence?"

Hazel opened her eyes and looked up. "Now tell the truth, Florence. Don't add lying to your passel of other sins."

A fleeting smile, a wicked twinkle passed like a thought over Florence's face.

"I was a call girl, back then."

Maggie held to the walker with one hand and twisted to take a harder look at Florence. She expected to see devilment on her face, but Florence had settled to a kind of dreamy staring at the pictures on the wall above Hazel's bed.

"Seriously?"

"Oh yeah," Florence answered. "Why would I say I was when I wasn't? High-priced, too. I was a good-looking broad in my heyday."

"Yes, I can see that." Maggie was at a loss for appropriate words. It wasn't as if she'd never known a prostitute, but she'd never lived with one, even an ex-prostitute. "Interesting."

Hazel muttered something unintelligible. Florence grinned. Maggie gathered up the makeup and started with the walker across the room toward Florence. The older woman motioned her back.

"No, keep it. I don't want it. My youngest daughter brought it to me as if it would make up for what they did. My youngest, Ellen. She always was my favorite. I got her from husband number three, I think it was."

Maggie had maneuvered the walker to the foot of her own bed, and stopped when Florence waved her back. She put the makeup into the pocket of her tunic and turned the walker toward the hallway.

"I'm going out to make a call."

Florence started to rise. "Want help?"

"Thanks no, I'm okay." She paused, pain running down her leg. She waited until it eased.

The door stood half open. Footsteps passed along the hall, some very slow, some quick. The distant odor of food signaled breakfast was beginning.

Maggie moved the walker ahead one pace, and then followed it. One step, two. She forced herself to try to use the unwilling leg, clench her teeth against the pain and the sense of helplessness. Her arms ached and trembled by the time she had reached the telephone.

She leaned against the wall and dialed the animal hospital. One of the girls answered and Maggie said, "How is Minnie this morning?"

"Oh hello, Maggie. Minnie's great. She's had her little walk."

"She's really okay?" The weakness that had been in Maggie's arms and legs entered her stomach.

"She's fine. Don't you worry about her. We're taking good care of her. How are you?"

"Much better, thanks."

She hung up the phone and stood resting against the wall, eyes closed, seeing Minnie, tiny, brown, silky Minnie, her eyes so happy as Maggie put the little halter on her. The halter always meant a special walk, or a ride to the store. Wherever Maggie went, Minnie went, sometimes carried hidden beneath her coat into forbidden territory such as grocery stores. Once carried beneath her coat as they ran into the night, and kept running, thousands of backroad miles. Until they found their haven at last.

A groan edged into Maggie's awareness. It trailed away like a sob. Maggie lifted her head.

Thomas.

Bedfast, he would probably be eating in his room. She wondered if he could feed himself.

His door was only across the hall.

She went toward it, moving the walker, taking a step forward, moving the walker. If she were home, she thought, she might be able to manage. Certainly if she could budget her money more closely, enough to hire someone to come in and help out a couple of hours a day, she and Minnie could otherwise manage.

She reached the door that was closed against the groans of an old man, and pushed it open far enough to enter.

The room held only one bed. There was a television on the wall, but it was dark. The head of the bed was lifted to form a back rest. The face that turned toward her when she entered was skeletal and almost as pale as the sheet that was folded back on his chest. His hair was thick and white. His moans ended and he stared at her, eyes watery pale and buried in overlapping skin. His stare grew steady and penetrating, eyes widening with disbelief, a recognition that opened a door somewhere in his mind.

She went toward him, a step forward, pause, a step forward. She had never seen him before, but saw that he viewed her almost as a ghost, the recognition real in its delusion. Perhaps she shouldn't have come into the room, but she couldn't turn back now. Her legs had begun to tremble, threatening to collapse beneath her. She had to reach the chair before she fell again. It was too soon after surgery to put such a burden on her hip, she now realized. Blanche, Florence, Hazel were right.

He suddenly whispered loudly, "Eleanor?"

"Hello. I'm Maggie from across the hall. May I sit down? Before I fall down!"

"Eleanor?"

His hand reached toward her. He tried to sit up and leaned to his right, falling against the side rail.

She took several hurried steps toward him, stumbling and then catching her balance against the walker. She felt their helplessness, his and hers.

She caught his hand and helped him sit back before she let herself down into the chair. The smile on his face was eager, delighted, reaching to his eyes and opening a glimpse into his heart. Whoever Eleanor was, she was very dear to him. His cold hands clung to hers.

"I'm—I'm sorry. Maggie is my name," she said. "I'm just another inmate."

"Eleanor," he cried, clinging to her fingers. "I knew you would come. I knew you would. Thank the Lord, you found me."

Maggie sat with her fingertips caught in his. He caressed them, running long fingers over the backs gently as she would have caressed Minnie's ears. His eyes savored her face, looking from feature to feature as if she an angel from heaven. His hands were icy cold.

She didn't know what to do. Nor did she know what to say. What had been in her mind when she followed the sounds of his groans? She had wanted somehow to help him. But she had only deluded him instead.

"I'm really not Eleanor …"

"Eleanor, where have you been?" His eyes blinked. "They told me you were dead."

At that moment a nurse with a tray of food entered the room. Maggie tried to pull away but Thomas's hold tightened on her hand.

"I'm sorry," Maggie said to the nurse. "He thinks I'm someone else. I guess I shouldn't have come in. Would you please call for a wheelchair for me? I need one to get out of here."

The nurse nodded and pressed the call button at the side of Thomas's bed. "Sure."

Thomas said clearly, "I knew you weren't dead. I knew you'd be here. I knew you'd find me."

Maggie exchanged a perplexed look with the nurse. The young woman began to smile.

"That's the first time Thomas has spoken a full sentence in months." She put the tray down on Thomas's bedside table.

"He thinks I'm someone named Eleanor."

The nurse arranged the food on the tray, broke the soft-boiled egg, took the lid off the toast. "How are you feeling this morning, Thomas?"

"Much better, now that Eleanor is here."

"Well, why don't you turn her loose and get ready for breakfast? Now that she's here, she won't be going very far away."

He released Maggie's hand.

"First, your medicine. Help with that fidgety feeling, Thomas."

The nurse spoke loudly, as if he were deaf, which Maggie didn't think he was. He swallowed pills obediently.

"Who's Eleanor, Thomas?" the nurse asked.

"Why don't you ask her?" he retorted. "She's right there."

Blanche looked in the door. "Ah, Maggie, there you are. I'm here to give you a ride. Florence told me you'd taken off, pushing your walker. She didn't think you'd get this far."

"I'm ready to ride." Her muscles felt as if they'd wasted away during too many days in bed doing nothing. The strength she thought she'd gained, was gone. She wondered how her flower bed was doing without her and Minnie out pulling weeds, transplanting flowers.

"I'll be back, Thomas," Maggie said as Blanche helped her into the wheelchair.

"Where are you going, Eleanor?"

He looked desperate, lost. The nurse at his bedside said, "She's going to eat breakfast, Thomas, if you'll promise to eat yours."

"But why can't she eat with me?"

"She can, when you get out of this bed and walk to the dining room."

"But, I'm sick."

"No, you're not sick, you're just lazy. The doctor says there isn't a thing wrong with you."

Florence and Hazel stood waiting in the hall. Hazel had dressed in a printed duster, and Florence wore slacks and a big, loose blouse that made her look larger than she actually was. Others came along the hallway, the tap of canes among them, the whisper of another wheelchair.

Mixed smells reached Maggie. She didn't drink coffee, but the smell always reminded her of home, where she had awakened every morning to the sound and smell of coffee perking. Grandma would be in the kitchen, keeping the fire hot with cook wood and kindling, cooking the big breakfasts that started the day. The smell of coffee would always remind her of Grandma.

The procession moved along the hall toward the nursing home dining room. Maggie had not eaten breakfast since those days when they started the day at dawn. She would have preferred going back to her room, but Blanche pushed the wheelchair on without asking her.

They passed a door that this morning stood open. Against the far wall was a polished and shining old upright piano.

"Wait!" Maggie cried. "Stop, please."

Her voice stopped everyone. All eyes turned toward her. Blanche stopped the wheelchair. Hazel stopped, and Florence, and others whose names Maggie didn't know. But all Maggie really saw was the piano.

A piano. She had never seen a piano she didn't love. "Take me there, please, Blanche."

"To the music room?"

"Yes, to the piano. I promise I'll play softly."

Florence asked, "You play piano?"

"But," Blanche protested, "It's time for breakfast."

"I don't want breakfast. I've never eaten breakfast." Except when she lived at home and Mommy made her eat, at least a few bites. And, "Drink your milk, Emmy." Always, as long as she'd lived at home, it was, "Emmy, drink your milk." She hated milk, unless it was sweetened with sugar and muddied with chocolate.

Maggie now said, "No milk, no food, not until noon, please. Just leave me with the piano and close the door."

"Well …"

Florence said, "For goodness sake, let the girl play. She knows whether she eats breakfast or not, I reckon."

The wheelchair moved into the room. It was windowless and much smaller than the dining room. There was an organ against the back wall, and boxed instruments leaning near the organ. A bass violin, she judged from the size of the containers, a couple of guitars, a small violin. In the center of the room was a group of folding chairs. And against the far wall the piano.

Maggie held her breath, the feel and smell of the piano reaching her in silent calls. Blanche helped her from the wheelchair to the piano bench. "Thank you, Blanche. Just close the door, okay? I don't want to interfere with anyone's breakfast."

"Play us something," Florence said, "Play us something."

She was back in the nightclubs where she'd played for years, listening to the pulse of the crowd, but playing to her own soul.

Chapter Eight

When Emmy was ten years old they moved into a house that had a big, warped, player piano. She was drawn to it as if it were the missing part of her.

She picked out remembered tunes, found old sheet music in the bench and began the slow process of teaching herself to play. The music class she took that fall helped, and gradually her fingers felt less and less awkward.

Some of the ivory on the keys had curled, and there was a slightly off-key ring to many notes. The player part lay exposed like the innards of some old being, the cover forever gone. It was a big, ugly old piano, and Emmy loved it. She hoped they wouldn't have to move anymore because she knew she couldn't take it with her. Each time they moved they took nothing but their old truck loaded with bedding, pots and pans, dishes, and what few clothes they owned.

That was the way of the families that followed the harvests from south to north in California in the thirties and early forties. The war had started, and during the first years it didn't affect their family. Daddy had found a permanent job far in the north where, Emmy hoped, they could stay in the house with the piano, on the quiet old road across from the creek and the dam where water flowed over. Where salmon came up in the fall, long and sleek, to lay their eggs and die.

They took the big fish after their eggs were laid and their brilliant color began to flake away. When they grew too weak to swim. When they flopped into the edge of the stream to die. They lived on salmon steaks. Mommy canned salmon. All year long they ate salmon, in cakes, casseroles, and fresh steaks in season. But food wasn't important to Emmy. Only the music.

No one stopped her from playing the piano. No one called it noise or racket or told her to go outside and play with the little girls, though at times she heard Grandma grumbling about all the time wasted at the old piano.

Every blues song Emmy had ever heard came to life at her fingertips. When she ran out of old tunes she began to make up new ones. She kept them in her head, in her heart, where something hurt, just a little, all the time.

From then on she never saw a piano she didn't love.

The nursing home piano was old but it was in tune, polished, and the tone was deep and mellow. She broke into a medley of blues and jazz, playing softly, waiting for the door to close.

The nurse held the door open until Florence and Hazel were out, and then closed it. Maggie tipped her head back and closed her eyes, her fingers moving from one tune to another, blues and jazz she had played during her years in nightclubs from Chicago to New Orleans to San Francisco, back to Chicago and Kansas City ... points east, south, north, and west.

Her memory skipped like a small flat stone thrown across a still pond, and came to rest at the beginning, when she had begun the separation from her family.

SHE WAS ONLY FIFTEEN, but she looked eighteen or nineteen if she pulled her long slightly curly hair up and pinned it on top her head, as was the style in the forties. She had reached her adult height and weight by age thirteen, five-four and one hundred five. The war was everywhere, on the movie screens, on the streets where service men strolled. Even in the local dancehall where Emmy learned to dance.

With her girlfriend, Emmy went to Shadowland, a large dancehall within walking distance of home. Neither she nor Betsy were allowed to have boys come to the house to pick them up for these weekly Saturday night dances where girls got in free, men paid a dollar. But they were allowed to be brought home by a date.

Betsy lived across the field from Emmy, the best friend she'd ever had in all her life. They had spent the past five years together, walking to the school bus stop, sometimes walking all the way to school three miles away. They swam in the creek together in the summertime, and went together to whatever was going on in the small town they called home.

Emmy never had to take the little girls along. Rebba was now eleven, and Peggy thirteen. Rebba was chubby and round-cheeked, and Peggy awkward and almost as tall as Emmy. Now, at last, Emmy found herself an object of envy. Both little girls wanted to be like her, but obviously Peggy was going to be taller, like Mom. And Rebba was going to be fatter, like Grandma. Peggy, like Emmy, had the thick light brown hair like Mommy's, gold and brown and silver all mixed together, and Rebba had darker hair, curly and pretty and overlaid with gold. But she leaned on the washstand where the mirror hung and watched as Emmy brushed and twisted her long hair into a fancy bun that she rolled under and pinned on top of her head.

"I want to look just like you when I grow up."

The washstand and mirror were in the big kitchen, which held also the table and chairs, and even the washing machine over in the corner. Mommy and Grandma were cooking. On Saturday nights Emmy didn't have to eat supper at home. She was allowed to eat in the snack bar at the dancehall. Her folks had never been there and didn't know beer was sold without question.

Rebba sighed loudly. "I want to grow up to look just like you." As if all that was needed was Mommy and Daddy and Grandma's permission.

"Fat chance of that," Grandma said, in a tone of voice that brought Emmy to pause and look at her. She worked at something over on the kitchen counter and didn't look up. "I think Emily is one of a kind."

Mommy said, "Be thankful that you're as pretty as you are."

Grandma humphed. "Character is more important, Rebba, and Emmy can't hold a candle to you."

Can't hold a candle? Emmy felt as if she'd been insulted, but wasn't sure how or why. It was the same way she felt when one of the guys in the crowd told a dirty joke that was supposed to be funny, she supposed. She'd laugh with the rest, without knowing exactly why she was laughing.

Afterwards she'd ask Betsy, "What did it mean?"

Betsy, who was two years older than she, would patiently explain the joke. In the beginning Emmy usually slapped one hand to her mouth and said, "Oh, my God!" Then silently murmur a prayer to be forgiven for taking God's name in vain, because it was, after all, a kind of swearing.

Later, though she still sometimes asked Betsy such things as, "What did he mean by cunt?" she already knew what fuck meant. She had learned that so long ago she couldn't remember when. It was as if she'd heard it and knew all about it while still in the womb. It curled her lips in disgust. She found it totally indigestible.

Betsy began to look shocked at her. "You mean you don't know what cunt means?" Voice lowered in a whisper on the new word.

"No …"

"Well …" And Betsy would tell her.

Emmy stopped slapping her hand to her mouth, or swearing in shocked surprise. The dirty jokes were part of sitting in the snack bar drinking a beer. They were part of a bunch of kids piling into one car, four in the front seat, sometimes six in the back, sitting on each other, laughing, necking, hugging, intertwining legs. If Daddy and Mommy knew, they probably would never let her go.

It was at Shadowland that she met him. He was a tall soldier, handsome in his uniform. She stood between dances surrounded by boys she knew and danced with, talking, laughing. On the stage the fifteen piece swing band began to play again after intermission, and suddenly he was there, taller than the others, older. He stood looking over their heads at her. Staring. She felt flushed under his attention. Then she returned his stare. She had never seen anyone so handsome, nor so tall and broad-shouldered.

"May I have this dance?" he asked over the heads of the younger guys she'd known for years.

He had hair the color of rich cream and eyes like heaven.

His face was oval, lips full and sharply cut, nose straight as if nature had laid a ruler along the ridge. His eyebrows were straight, too, and lifted over the inner corners of his eyes as if he questioned everything, or looked on others with contempt. He was, without doubt, out-of-this-world handsome, as she and Betsy described the most good-looking of the guys. He was also older than her steady boyfriend, who was nineteen and had his own car. This blond Norse God was dressed in Army uniform, and was the only one in the group she thought of as a man—and he wanted to dance with her. But …

"I have the next four dances scheduled," she said, wishing she could cancel them all. Would a chance like this ever come her way again?

Her boyfriend, Harold, who took her home every Saturday night, did not really become her date until the dance ended. Until then she was free to dance with whomever she chose, and even if Harold didn't like it, that was just too bad. She could just let someone else take her home, and he knew it. She even at times sat with someone else in the bar. Harold brooded, sometimes, looking over at her with puppy-dog eyes. He wasn't much taller than she. His hair was dark red, and very curly.

She liked him, but his kisses didn't thrill her. He had started taking her home from dances right from the first dance she'd gone to, and it was like dating one of her cousins.

She saw something flicker across Harold's face. A warning? Some kind of fear? His hand tightened suddenly on her arm as he pulled her toward the dance floor, beyond the rows of benches where spectators sat, and through the opening in the railing.

She stumbled, looking back at the soldier.

He held up five fingers, then flicked them again, and again. Fifteen? The next fifteen dances? Nothing this exciting had ever happened to her. The dancehall didn't close until three-thirty in the morning, hours away. She had never had her dances monopolized before. The thought of it made her breathless.

Harold muttered close in her ear, "He's too old for you. He's at least twenty-five or thirty. Too old."

She looked back at the handsome soldier and saw him staring at her with an intensity that caused a weakness in her stomach, a charge, almost electrical, through her veins. This, she knew from hearing older girls describe their own thrills, was indeed a thrill.

Breathless with excitement, she went with Harold onto the big dance floor. They jitterbugged into the crowd to "Little Brown Jug". Every time she looked toward the soldier he was watching her. She scarcely noticed the rest of her partners through the next three dances. The soldier had waited, asking no one else. When he touched her it was with a commanding possessiveness that added to the thrill and romance of the evening.

He danced slower than Harold or the other guys. She would not have liked it with anyone else, the drawing close, the face-to-face old-fashioned kind of dancing. She felt his arms, strong and insistent, and saw his eyes looking at her lips.

"You're gorgeous," he said. "Drop dead gorgeous."

She could have said the same about him, but suddenly felt very shy, speechless. He took her left hand, turned it. "No engagement ring."

She shook her head, gazing up at him. He was at least a foot taller than she. She'd never felt so short and young and tongue-tied.

"I thought by the way that one guy was hanging on to you that he had claims on you."

She found her voice. "Oh no. That's just Harold."

He laughed. It was soft, deep, like his voice. "Just?"

"I mean, he takes me home. Things like that."

"Things like that, huh. Does he have to? I mean, do you have to go with him?"

"No."

"Good, because tonight, I'm taking you home."

They danced and danced, never leaving the dance floor. She even found that he could jitterbug, her favorite kind of dancing. She laughed and whirled, her circle skirt pleating around her up to her hips, sometimes her waist. She felt the air high on her thighs and knew her panties showed. He liked looking at her, she saw, when he whirled her.

Then in the slow dances he cuddled her against him and laid his cheek against the top of her head, closing her in, it seemed, where no one else could reach her. He murmured things she didn't hear clearly. Your hair is so sweet—such a beautiful body—pretty legs—you smell so good—I want to kiss you—forever—I'm going to take you home with me.

Was he really saying those things or was she having a romantic daydream?

He lifted his head when the music stopped between dances and said, "I'm leaving in two weeks, and I'm taking you with me."

She heard him, yet didn't really absorb the meaning.

He smiled down at her. Teasing, she thought. She glanced away, smiling. Smiling, just a little. She couldn't get the simper off her face. Betsy would call it a simper.

He held to her through the rest of the dances. When it was almost three-thirty, between a trio of tunes, Betsy grabbed her arm and pulled her toward the restroom.

"What's going on?" Betsy hissed in her ear. "Have you looked at Harold?"

"Ummm … not exactly."

"Come off it, idiot! You look sappy, letting that guy just take over. Tomorrow he'll be gone and you'll never see him again, and by that time Harold's going to be shit holy mad at you."

"No, he's not leaving for two weeks."

"Two weeks! Big deal!"

"He says he's taking me with him."

"You're not!" Betsy's brown eyes rounded, shocked, believing. Until Emmy saw Betsy's belief, she hadn't believed it herself.

She knew then it would happen.

"You have to tell Harold," Betsy warned.

"About what? About taking me away?"

"Don't be an idiot, Em! I mean tell him about tonight! Are you letting this guy take you home tonight? Forget next week!"

"Well, yes. Harold hasn't asked anyway. Why should I tell him anything?"

"He always takes you home. You, me, Clark, Harold. What about me?"

"You can go anyway. Without me."

Betsy made her feel a little guilty, but not enough to go with Harold instead of the soldier. Harold hadn't even asked, she reminded herself, trying to get away from the feeling that she was doing something wrong.

The soldier was waiting when she left the restroom, and took a masterful command of her immediately, putting his big hand on her waist and guiding her. She felt a little scared when she looked back at Betsy.

"I don't even know your name," he said.

"Emily." She brought her eyes away from Betsy. The soldier was guiding her toward the exit.

"Hi, Emily, I'm Sid, short for Sidney Alexander, from Idaho."

While the last dance was playing he led her out into the night. He guided her around the edge of the building into the shadows, where cars were parked beneath the scattered trees. Sounds of water flowing in the deep basin of the creek replaced the music. At the side of a car he pulled her against him and kissed her, his lips parting hers, his tongue caressing the sensitive interior of her mouth.

From then on Betsy, whom Emmy loved like a sister, was scarcely in her life. Sid took up her time. He came to her house, introduced himself to her family, and won their immediate approval. They didn't seem to care that he was older. When he asked if he could take her for a Sunday drive, they said yes.

He arrived early, before nine o'clock. She had dressed in one of her school dresses, a cotton print. In her part of the closet hung four school dresses, now several months old, and one good dress that she wore to dances. She had two pairs of shoes. One pair of brown and white saddle oxfords, and a dressier pair with straps, which she called her dancing shoes.

She hurriedly slipped the dancing shoes on for this Sunday drive. Like most kids she knew, she worked in the summertime and bought her own school clothes. Parents were poor even though the really hard times of the thirties were gone, and war had brought a kind of prosperity. Factories had opened, jobs were available. But still, hardly any girl she knew had more than four or five dresses. She also had one slacks suit, yellow with brown buttons. But she had decided not to wear it, and later she was glad.

He drove straight and fast, as if he had a destination. He didn't talk to her, or even notice that he wasn't alone. This was one of those times when she felt like a baby, too young and too naive for this mature man. Why did he want her to ride with him on this Sunday drive? She was afraid to break his silence, but finally stammered a question.

"Where are we going?"

"It's a surprise." He smiled at her, for an instant intimate and close, then left her again.

They drove into the mountains eastward to the big trees she loved, past beautiful blue Lake Tahoe, and down into Reno. He drove into town and then parked in front of the courthouse.

He turned and looked at her. In all of the two hundred mile trip he hadn't touched her, even to reach over and squeeze her hand. She looked around. Why had they stopped here?

"How about it?"

She stared up at the walls, the windows, the front door of the court-house. She looked at the wide steps leading up.

"The courthouse?"

She didn't understand what he meant, but she didn't want to appear stupid. She felt a little uneasy about being so far away from home, uneasy, yet excited. She often daydreamed of being free, leaving behind shackles of rules and boundaries, of going on to freely roam the world. Seeing everything that was out there to see. They had passed casinos on their way down from the mountains, through town to the courthouse. She would have liked to stop at one, see for herself all that was inside. But Sidney had seemed to know exactly where he was going. He didn't stop until he reached this place. The courthouse.

"I want to marry you," he said, taking her left hand, turning it and slipping on a ring with a small, solitary diamond. "I didn't ask before now because I was afraid you'd say no. And I'm being shipped out in a few weeks. I want to spend those weeks with you."

"Really?" In her mind suddenly was a lifetime of music and dancing. Not just Saturday nights, but every night. The whole, exciting world was out there for her to see.

From the time they climbed the courthouse steps until they went down again time was lost. It might have been five minutes or an hour. Her memory left it behind. It was a gap never filled. Sid handled it all. She couldn't remember signing anything. Had she said, "I do?" Had he? Had someone said, "You may now kiss the bride?" Or, "I now pronounce you man and wife?" Or had they said, "Husband and wife?"

They came back down the courthouse steps, in silence. She remembered that, the descending. Wide, steep steps dropped away from her and she looked down as if she were a little child on unsteady legs afraid of falling. She gripped his arm for security.

He took her straight home. They drove again in silence.

The big trees in the mountains provided a steady shade like a clouded day. She drew up her knees and curled on the seat, her back toward him, and began soundlessly to weep. What had she done? They drove swiftly through the big trees on the mountains and she looked into their shadowy depths and wished she could go there, blend with them forever. An old song came to her, very sad, notes in a minor key, calling to lonely souls. She had played it often on the piano. It touched something distant and yearning within her.

"In the pines, in the pines,
  Where the sun never shines,
  Where you shiver when the cold wind blows".

WHEN THEY REACHED the house he took her hand and led her as if she were his child now. The sun was going down and Mom and Grandma were cooking supper. The girls were setting the table, Rebba looking sour, lower lip turned down, until she saw Sidney. Both girls had crushes on him, Emmy knew, but didn't care.

He spoke to Grandma, Mommy, and then to Daddy when he came from the front room to stand in the doorway.

"I know I owe you an apology for keeping Emily out so late. But I have an explanation. I love Emily. I took her to Reno today and we were married. I wouldn't have done it this way if it weren't for the war, and the future so uncertain. I just want you to know I'll take good care of her."

Daddy turned quickly away, but not before Emmy saw tears fill his eyes. He went outside, and after a hesitation Emmy went looking for him. Neither Sidney nor Mommy missed her or noticed as she stepped out of the kitchen. They were talking about something or other that Emmy missed entirely, with Grandma and the girls standing close and sometimes joining in.

She found Daddy behind the well house, sitting on a barrel that in hot, dry summer was used for water. He looked up at her, eyes red and tear-filled.

"Don't do this, Emmy," he whispered, hoarse, choked. "You don't know him. He's years older than you, Emmy. He'll expect you to go live with his family. He's a Mormon, Emmy. Family is everything. You'll never come home anymore."

She only looked at him, heart aching, and both of them knew. It was too late. She had already done it. She was married. Marriage was forever.

He reached for her and held her as he had when she was little, and together they cried. She hugged his neck, and listened to his sobs for only the second time in her life, and wished with all her heart and soul she could undo this day, this past week, and know to turn away from the forever change she had committed. She had dreamed of music and dancing and freedom, but there would be no dancing. This she knew as if her eyes had been opened upon a truth of life. There would be no dancing.

"I'm so sorry, so sorry, so sorry, Emmy. So sorry."

She knew what he meant. Once again she said, "It's all right, Daddy. It's all right."

Then, "I'm sorry too."

Chapter Nine

Maggie became aware that someone was standing at her shoulder. She glanced sideways. A man in an easy-fitting, expensive grey suit.

Her hands jerked involuntarily away from the keyboard. His hand clasped her shoulder. She felt the heat through her clothing, and the tight fingers.

"Hey, I'm sorry. Didn't mean to scare you."

The stranger she'd seen through the door? She wanted to believe he was here to see a relative or friend, but a spasm of fear closed her throat and her heart surged with choked, rapid pounding.

She felt ill, quivering … could he see her quivering? Her heart dripping fear like blood, turning to dust in the face of her own death. She hadn't realized she feared them so much. If they killed her, she'd told herself so many times, so what? A moment of pain, then she'd know nothing more about it. Had that been only a feeble attempt to still her fear of them?

At home, two years ago when Maggie had finally bought herself a piano, she had been paranoid to the point of playing very softly, and with blinds closed. Whoever they sent after her would know her style and her preferences for blues and jazz. If they walked along the sidewalk in front of her house they could hear the music. For two years she had given it up, but she hadn't been able to continue to deny herself that outlet. It was her soul that needed nourishing.

But logic always won against the fear. They would never walk her street, this dead-end street that was so much like other dead-end streets everywhere. Lost as it was in a corner of a small city in the middle of the country.

Not even her mother or sisters knew where she was.

She was stalked by fear, nothing else.

She twisted on the piano bench and looked up at the stranger's face, as if something there would reveal his truth. Was he a visitor, did he have someone here? Was his face familiar? Only in the vaguest way was the familiarity there. The easy casualness of big city, the confidence of power.

He could have fit into any crowd. Medium complexion, rounded face, receding hair, he was probably in his fifties. He had mild, blue eyes, and an easy smile. Medium height, but with a strength in his shoulders and arms that suggested time in fitness centers. His fingernails were carefully manicured. No work calluses on those hands.

He could have been a banker, a friendly businessman.

He could have been part of the audiences she had played for in the past.

"Please don't stop playing," he said. "I didn't mean to disturb you. Great music. Mellow. You must be a professional."

"Perhaps," she offered cautiously, "I could play something for whoever you're visiting, if she's able to come to the music room?"

"Play anything. You don't mind if I just sit and listen a minute, do you?"

"Of course she doesn't," Florence said.

He sat by Hazel. Hazel who was the mother of nine children. Some of her sons were ministers. The stranger could be a minister, yes. Maggie drew a long breath.

The rows of chairs were almost filled with people sitting dreamily. They had entered while she was immersed in her music, and now dwelled with their separate memories. Florence and Hazel sat side by side. Hazel leaned away from Florence, toward the man, her chin resting in her hand as if she were deep in thought, or prayer. Maggie felt surprised that she would even listen to the kind of music she'd been playing.

Maggie turned back to the keyboard and played a few strains of gospel music. "Swing Low, Sweet Chariot" and "Amazing Grace." She played slowly, then jazzed it up, and saw Hazel smiling and nodding and tapping her foot.

When she stopped and turned to reach for her wheelchair she saw that

Hazel had closed her eyes tightly. A smile of pleasure softened her face. The man who might have been Hazel's son was gone. Maggie's eyes swept the crowd that had gathered, and saw him standing by the door. He smiled. She looked quickly away.

A nurse entered the room with a tray of medicine. "Where on earth is everybody? Half the rooms are empty. Doesn't anyone want their medicine?"

The group stirred, rising, moving toward the hall. Voices began to murmur, telling Maggie how they enjoyed the music.

Time had slipped by for Maggie, the way it always did when she was at a piano. But now she was aware that her leg hurt, her hip felt stiff and unyielding. She was ready for the pain killer that sometimes made her a little drowsy, that might even help her to be less afraid of a man who watched her from the doorway.

"I think I've caused enough disturbance for one day," she said.

The nurse hesitated, watching as Maggie carefully moved from the bench to the wheelchair. The man was suddenly beside her, putting out a steadying hand. His palm was moist on her elbow.

"Broken bone?" he asked.

"Nothing that can't mend," she said quickly.

"She's doing very well," the nurse observed.

The stranger smiled. A pale blue handkerchief, folded, showed three peaks from his coat pocket. It was the color of his shirt. He wore no tie, as if making an effort to look casual. Both the shirt and handkerchief were the color of his eyes.

Contact lenses perhaps changed the color, gave them that sky-blue softness.

A low murmur of general conversation came from the crowd as the people filed through the door. Hazel and Florence paused, waiting for Maggie to catch up, making room for her and the wheelchair. Blanche pushed it slowly along. The man's presence made Maggie more aware of her new disability, her new vulnerability.

The man moved at her side. He peered around at the nametag pinned on her blouse. "Maggie. Maggie? You don't look like a Maggie," he said in a soft voice that could be inferred as merely curious and teasing, or tormenting, as if he suspected she wondered about him.

She looked quickly into his face, searching his eyes. They held no betrayal, it seemed to her, yet she knew the eyes did not always show a betrayal. She had met killers whose eyes appeared mild and kind. But they could harden, and show in their depths the cruelty that most people never saw more than once.

He evidently wasn't going away, so she decided to meet him on his own level. She returned his almost flirtatious smile.

"What do I look like?"

An Emmy? An Emmy who dressed in sleek and good-looking clothes, who wore her hair in blond-bright softness around a face that was at home in another world? A world of perpetual night—of people escaping reality in their own ways. A world sometimes of danger …

"Oh." he rubbed his chin. His eyes were narrow, hiding behind heavy lids as if they were shades. He smiled, willing to play this game.

Florence said, "An Eleanor. The old man across the hall thinks she's his Eleanor."

He said, "I expect a lot of men wish she was their Eleanor."

Add corny, Maggie thought, to the description of him. She began to relax. This man had never known Emmy, or known anyone close to her who could have told him what she was like, or he would have known she'd never fall for something so obvious.

She caught a glance from Florence and saw Florence's eyebrows waggle at her. She almost laughed. Florence gave her a more direct look.

"Do you know that's the first time I've seen you smile as if you meant it, Maggie?"

They thought her smile had something to do with Eleanor and began to speculate on who Eleanor was.

The nurse listened for a while, then said, as if she weren't sure she should be saying it, "Eleanor is not Thomas's wife."

"How do you know?" Florence asked quickly. As a large woman with heavy hips walking as if her swollen legs pained her, she moved slowly ahead of Maggie,

Near her Hazel walked, her legs thin and slightly bowed, her stockings bagging on the wasted calves and wrinkling around her ankles. Maggie itched to pull them up tight.

"I helped take care of his wife, Mrs. Sherman, last year when she was in here, before she died. Mr. Sherman—Thomas—came every day to see her. Her name was Dellie."

"Oh," someone murmured, "That's sad. So now he's here."

"Daughter, then."

"No, I don't think so. I don't think they had children."

"And who," Maggie asked the stranger, "Have you come to see?"

"A friend," he said, "I thought he was here, but I guess got the wrong place."

"You have the advantage," Maggie said, "You aren't wearing a nametag."

"No." He put his hand down, picked up her hand and shook it. "The name is Mart Stanley, Maggie."

Mart Stanley? As easily a pseudonym as Maggie Winters. They moved for awhile in silence along the hall, footsteps heavy, soft-soled amid the sounds of wheelchairs and the tap of canes.

Blanche said, "No one ever comes to see Thomas." She paused. "He's been here seven months, and no one has come to see him yet."

People began drifting away, the group thinning, disappearing into rooms, taking other hallways. The sound of Maggie's wheelchair set the tone for the small group that proceeded down the hall. Mart Stanley continued walking beside Maggie.

"He's ninety-three," the nurse said. "And really in good health for his age."

"Why does he carry on all the time?" Hazel asked, "if he's in such good health?"

The nurse shrugged. "Who knows?"

Florence said, "Probably Eleanor's fault."

They reached Thomas's room. There was no sound coming from behind the half-open door.

Maggie felt Mart's hand on her shoulder again as the nurse maneuvered the turn into the room. Florence went to her chair and plopped down with a loud sigh. Hazel first bent to brush whatever dust might have gathered on her bedside table and touch tenderly the tops of some of the small frames, then turned and sat down.

The nurse dispensing medicine followed them with her tray of little white containers. She poured glasses of water.

The man that called himself Mart stopped just inside the door. "I'll be back?"

It was a question, as if he were asking her permission to see her again. Or perhaps it was a threat, a warning: Here I am ... It has taken me four years to find you—but you should have known you could never get away.

He pulled the door closed softly. Maggie stared through its thickness, seeing him on the other side, waiting, his smile gone. Listening.

No, she told herself. Paranoia was something she had fought against. She was not going to give in now.

Florence said, "Looks like you got yourself a boyfriend, Maggie."

"You didn't know him?" She carefully weighed her words.

Blanche said, "So many visitors come and go—bed or chair, Maggie?"

Maggie felt a sudden exhaustion, with pain traveling along her side from shoulder to feet. "I think I'll lie down."

Blanche helped her onto the bed and backed away, taking the wheelchair out of the crowded room.

Hazel said, "I never saw him before."

"Me neither," Florence said. "Not bad looking, was he? Reminds me of some of the johns that used to pay me good money."

Hazel shook her head, lips pursed. "May the Lord have mercy."

When the nurse approached with the pain medication Maggie accepted two.

Hazel muttered, "I would have scrubbed floors first, had I been you."

"No, you wouldn't. Why scrub somebody's dirty floor for a dollar an hour, when you could make a hundred just laying on a soft bed?"

The nurse winked at Maggie, her lips working to suppress a smile. She turned.

"Ready for your medicine, ladies?"

Hazel said, "Give Florence a mickey."

Florence snorted loudly. "A mickey? What the hell do you know about mickeys, Hazel, a nice girl like you?"

"Learned it from you."

"Oh, well maybe."

The nurse held a glass of water for Hazel. "I expect you've learned a lot of things from Florence, haven't you Hazel?"

"More than I wanted to know. If Florence had as many pricks sticking out of her as she's had sticking in, she'd look like a porcupine."

The nurse laughed and Florence cried out, "Hazel! Go wash your mouth!"

Hazel wore a tight little grin. "Just repeating what you say, Florence."

"Excuse me." Maggie said to the nurse with the tray of medicine. "The man who came down the hall with us. Do you know him?"

The nurse paused at the foot of Maggie's bed, and she saw her name was Jamie. Her eyes wandered in thought.

"He looked familiar. Why?" The nurse's eyes were so bright blue they were almost turquoise. They pinpointed Maggie. Curiosity, maybe even suspicion from this RN, who was accustomed to watching patients for the unusual behavior. Maybe Maggie showed too much concern.

She shrugged. "I just wondered if he has someone in here he comes to see."

Florence added, "If he didn't, he does now."

Maggie felt the burning sensation of panic building. I have to get out of here. Take Minnie home, lock the doors. Oh God, help me.

Take a deep breath, she told herself in silence, relax. She closed her eyes, opened her lips and breathed deeply. The panic hovered, threatening. The door closed softly behind the nurse.

"What you need to do, Maggie," Florence said, "is smile at the guy. Encourage him."

"Not everyone, Florence," Hazel snapped, "wants a man."

The panic eased away. Maggie opened her eyes.

Florence rocked in her chair, a smirk, almost a smile, on her lips. "Did you know, Hazel," she asked with that glitter in her eyes that Maggie now recognized as pure orneriness, "That most men would rather be sucked than fucked?" Her question ended with a wicked little chuckle of anticipation.

Hazel rocked forward, back and forward again. "Oh my Lord a'mercy. That is an abomination against the Lord. Language like that!"

Florence widened her eyes in innocent pretense, "Well how else should I say it? How would you say it, Hazel?"

Hazel leaned her chin into her hand. "My heavens!" Then, lifting her head and jutting her chin, she burst out, "I wouldn't be saying it! I wouldn't be thinking it! Don't you know the scriptures say the whores shall be cast into hell with the dogs?"

A deep frown settled on Florence's face. "Dogs! Whatever did the dogs do? I mean a dog is a dog, he can't help being a dog, can he?"

Hazel flicked her dust cloth handkerchief at her face. "Dear Lord have mercy on this poor lost soul. Never read a verse from the Lord's Book in her life."

Florence rocked, the stationary foundation beneath the chair stingy with its space. Hazel sat shaking her head. Maggie saw her chin quivering, and felt a surge of sympathy.

Florence said, her moment of anger gone and replaced now by her former impishness, "And a whore can't very well help being a whore, either, can she? I mean, God made us all, didn't he? Or she, or it or—"

Hazel began the long process of rising from her chair. "An abomination unto the Lord, that's what it is."

"As far as that goes," Florence said, another frown flashing through the amusement like cracks in a wall, "the whore doesn't make herself a whore, does she? If I remember right, it takes men. A lot of men. What about them? And what makes them act the way they do, hey? The Lord God made us all, you say. So what about all that, Hazel?"

"Abomination, that's what it is. Never read a word."

Hazel had gained her feet. She walked surprisingly quickly across the room to the bathroom door. But before she could get it closed behind her, Florence twisted to one side, looked after her, and let fly another question.

"And them men that like most to be sucked, Hazel. Do you know what they are? Husbands!"

Hazel shut the bathroom door with a strong thud. The closest it would come to a slam. Maggie watched, her head resting against an unyielding pillow. She saw Florence lean back in her chair, rock a little and laugh. The last word. Then suddenly Florence sobered and looked over at Maggie.

"I might tease her a little now and then, but Hazel's a good old girl. We've lived together in this little room for two years now, and never a day passes but that Hazel thinks her grandson is going to come and get her. She just waits and prays. And nothing happens."

Maggie too waited.

Florence said, "At least she has hopes of getting out of here." She rocked back, put the footrest up and crossed her ankles. She was wearing soft house slippers, her ankles bare.

They had swollen, the blue veins close to exploding.

"How old is Hazel?"

"You mean she ain't told you?" Florence grinned. "She usually tells everyone. She tells me every day. She's eighty-eight."

"She seems very healthy, actually, for her age, don't you think?"

"Sure. But, you know, she's forgetful. Had trouble doing her bills, things like that."

"If she has so many kids, why couldn't one of them do the bills for her?"

"Haw! You know kids." Florence paused. "But maybe you don't."

No, maybe not. Maggie had to admit to herself she might have a romanticized idea of how it would be to have an adult daughter. Closeness. Being able to depend on someone when you needed them.

The way Mom could depend on Peggy and Rebba. They were the good daughters, not Emmy. They were close to Mom, always, as she never had been.

"Is your mother still living?" Florence asked.

Maggie opened her mouth and closed it. She didn't actually know. Florence directed a steady gaze at her.

"Yes. She's eighty-five and very healthy," Maggie said firmly.

"Does she live around here?" Florence watched her, eyes bright and penetrating.

"No."

Florence's gaze seemed too penetrating, too questioning. "You said you have sisters?"

"Yes."

She closed her eyes tightly against the image that crashed into her mind, as it had daily, almost hourly, for four years. Shut her eyes and tried to shut her heart. The box at the door, the face in the box ... the head ... severed. Images of blood.

The unwritten message was clear: Do you have a family, Emily?

Change the subject— anything—but this.

"The weather looks good today. Don't you ever go out for walks, Florence?"

"Oh yeah, sometimes. But Hazel's back hurts if she walks too much."

She heard Hazel stirring about in the bathroom, blowing her nose, clearing her throat, flushing the toilet. Florence smiled and winked at Maggie. "Now she'll come out with a string of Scripture, you listen. That's the way she gets even with me."

Hazel came back into the room, crossed the short distance to her chair and sat down, easing against the too-straight back.

"Florence," she said sternly, "You need to read your Bible. The wicked shall burn in hell, their feet tied in fire forevermore—"

"What on earth for?" Florence asked, her eyes rounded, teasing, urging Hazel on. "What good will that do our everloving Lord?"

Hazel shook her head, back and forth, back and forth. "Florence, what am I going to do with you? I know how the Lord must feel, I truly know, bless Him."

Chapter Ten

Maggie only half listened to the scripture Hazel was reading aloud from the Bible. To her surprise Florence was quiet, her head resting against her chair, her eyes closed. There began to be a laxness in her jowls and mouth that suggested maybe Florence had begun to doze.

The door opened slowly inward. Hazel closed the Bible, looked at the door and waited. A nurse's aide entered. Voices became audible. A woman's voice asked, "Are you all right, Mother?"

Blanche said loudly and clearly, "Here we are, Clara. You'll have plenty of company here. Three roommates."

The group entered. A woman no more than fifty-five or sixty whose eyes were oddly blank and distant rode in the ubiquitous wheelchair. Behind her came a younger woman with shining blond hair that was carefully and freshly arranged.

The daughter carried a small plastic bag of personal items that she immediately arranged on the bedside table. The usual lotions, box of tissue.

Two nurses helped Clara out of the wheelchair. She stood, looked around, confused, uncertain. Her hair also had the look of having just been done. Maggie could imagine the daughter taking the mother with her to a beauty parlor before this final move. Clara wore a neat blue dress with matching jacket. A woman who looked as if she should be going to church or shopping, not into a nursing home.

"See, Mother," the daughter said, "You'll be so cozy here."

Florence opened her eyes and watched. The activity was just beyond the curtain that separated her part of the room from the one that was now occupied by so many people it made the four-bed room seem as small as a closet and as stifling.

The daughter didn't glance at Maggie, Hazel or Florence as one of the nurses attempted to introduce them to the woman named Clara. Coming through the door was a man of forty or so dressed in a casual summer shirt and trousers. He carried a suitcase. A teenaged girl came behind him but paused in the doorway. She looked at Hazel, Florence, the picture of Jesus on the wall, and at Maggie on the bed, her face reflecting horror. She took a step backward as if she couldn't wait to get out of this place.

The granddaughter, Maggie surmised. The family bringing Grandma to the nursing home.

Clara sat down in the chair. A nurse spoke carefully and loudly, as they so often did to the patients.

"We'll be bringing you a nametag, Clara. Everyone wears a nametag, so we'll know one another's names. There are too many of us here to remember everyone all at once—"

The daughter said, "Mother can't even remember her own name."

The man said nothing, nor did the girl. Clara too was silent, but something flickered in her eyes. She looked about the room desperately, reminding Maggie of animals she had seen in cages. She wanted to speak up, say, "It's all right, Clara. We're here." But she didn't. Even if she did it would make no difference. Maggie knew the terror that must be clutching her heart at this moment.

She looked at the daughter, and felt a rush of sympathy. A touch of the horror from her teenage daughter's face flashed momentarily across hers, as if she saw herself here in another thirty years or less. She was anxious to leave, to try to forget what she'd just had to do to her mother. Was the daughter thinking that her time was coming? Right now, she just wanted to get on with her own life. And that was understandable. She had a teenage daughter who needed her care, and perhaps other children, as well as a husband. Life wasn't easy at this moment in time.

"You'll be fine, Mother," the daughter said, leaning down to her mother, kissing her cheeks. "We'll be in to check on you as often as we can. We'll call every day."

A nurse took the suitcase and hung in the closet a robe and three night-gowns, a couple of dresses. On the floor she put a pair of shoes, house slippers, a couple of other items. In the drawer went toothbrush, toothpaste, hairbrush, comb.

The man and girl disappeared silently into the hall without saying goodbye to Clara. But Clara hadn't noticed. She seemed not even to notice the daughter who still hovered in front of her.

"I'll bring a picture or something, Mother," she said, looking about the room, seeing the pictures on Hazel's table. "Which one would you like?"

Clara looked up at her daughter. "I want to go home."

"How about the picture of the boys? The one you always liked so well? The one on the mantel?"

"Take me home, Geraldine, take me home."

"I'm not Geraldine, Mother, I'm Deana."

"Deana?"

A shadow of irritation crossed Deana's carefully made-up face. "Your oldest daughter, remember?"

She turned, and gave Maggie an exhausted and embarrassed smile. "Only three of us kids. Geraldine died last year, but Mother just can't accept it or remember it. She has Alzheimer's."

"I'm sorry," Maggie said.

Deana nodded. "We just didn't have any choice." Her lower lip quivered, but she pursed her mouth, steadied her chin.

"There wasn't anything else we could do. My brother lived with her, but she just couldn't take care of the house anymore, and he didn't try to help." A controlled fury had entered her voice. "He's twenty-five, but acts fifteen when it comes to responsibility. Of course he was against Mother living here, but what can we do?" Her voice trailed away, growing fainter.

"We'll look after her," Blanche said. "Won't we girls?"

"Oh, sure," Florence answered. "We take care of one another around here."

Hazel said, "I'll ask the Good Lord to help her."

Deana blinked rapidly, fighting tears. She turned back to her mother, kissed her forehead and was gone. Her footsteps were swallowed by the walls, the ceilings, by room attached to room and separated by long halls and pathways.

The nurses remained for a few minutes, but Clara did not respond to them. She stared around her at the floor or at the walls as if searching for something familiar.

For a moment after the nurses left the room was silent, then Hazel began to read from the Bible again. Maggie saw Clara's eyes lift, find Hazel for the first time. She looked at the Bible Hazel held up in front of near-sighted eyes. Then she drew a deep sigh and leaned back in the chair, her hands folded in her lap.

She'll be fine, Maggie thought with a strange sense of relief, not until now realizing how tensely she'd been holding herself. Her hip and leg were beginning to throb with pain. But Clara was going to be fine. Maggie closed her eyes and listened to Hazel's soothing monotone.

AFTER THEIR CONVERSATION, Daddy left Emmy and went toward the barn, his head bowed. Emmy stood watching, wishing she could run after him, take his hand and walk with him. But she had a husband now, and he was waiting.

She went slowly back into the house. Sidney sat at the kitchen table talking to Grandma, and Rebba leaned nearby gazing calf-eyed at him. Emmy saw the bedroom door was closed, and quietly slipped through, closing it behind her.

Mommy was folding her few clothes into a paper sack. "What are you doing?" Emmy cried.

Mommy looked at her. Her face was thin, skin drawn tightly on the cheekbones. She looked as if the long winter of rain had leached away all the golden color the sun had put in last summer.

"I'm packing your clothes."

"Why?"

Mommy turned sharply as if to slap her, but didn't. "You're a married woman now, Emily. You have to go with your husband.'"

"But he lives at camp!"

"Didn't he even tell you? He has a furlough and he's taking you home to his parents. In Idaho."

"I don't want to go." She began to weep. She wanted to run to the piano, close the door against the world and let her heartache flow into music. Muscles in her stomach tightened, curving her forward as if they had shortened. She wrapped her arms across the hurting. "Mommy ... he's in the army. I can stay home until ..."

She felt sick. Oh God what have I done?

"Emily, you've always been bull-headed and headstrong. I've never been able to do a thing with you. You've made your bed, Emily. Now you lie in it!" Her voice shook with fury. Mommy went back to folding her three school dresses carefully and neatly. Her hands weren't trembling.

Her chin seemed forcefully forward and Emmy suddenly had the feeling that her mother was glad. Glad to be rid of her. Then she saw the unnatural brightness of tears in her mother's eyes. For her?

Emmy went to her, put her hand out, but Mommy turned away. Emmy needed Mommy to hug her, hold her, love her. But Mommy had long ago turned her back, shutting her out. Emmy ran out of the bedroom. Sidney, the stranger, was sitting at the table, watching the door for her, and his arms opened.

She went to him, feeling his arm go around her waist. He gave her a hug, this handsome Mormon who was her husband. What had she been thinking of? At the courthouse. When she climbed the steps, those high, wide steps—had she climbed them? She remembered coming down, but not going up. What had she been thinking of? She didn't want Mommy to send her clothes away with her. It seemed so … so forever.

Mommy hugged her, finally, held her briefly for the first time in Emmy's memory, and Emmy wept against her, having needed this for so long. She clung so hard, her arms around her mother, until finally she was gently put away.

Her little sisters came, Peggy almost as tall as she. They cried and hugged her. Even Grandma kissed her. At the last moment, when Emmy had thought Daddy would not come back from the barn, he was there.

He wrapped her in his arms, and she wanted to stay there, with him, with her family. She remembered snatches of the song Mommy used to sing to her when she was little. When she must have held her and rocked her, as she had done Peggy and Rebba. "Hush my baby bunting, Daddy's gone a'hunting. He went to get a rabbit skin to wrap his baby bunting in."

Daddy whispered in her ear, "Come home when you need to, Emmy."

She nodded against him and clung until finally he too put her away from him. She didn't dare look at any of them again. With her head down she went to the car and got in, Sid holding the door for her. In his other hand he carried her small sack of clothes.

She felt the bump of the dirt road that led away from the house, but she couldn't lift her head to look.

They rode as they had ridden home from Reno. In silence, with her turned away from him and staring out the window, they drove north, into the high mountains. Where the dark was like a tunnel into which the car lights searched.

They stopped once for hamburgers, but she could eat only part of hers.

They went on, driving through the dark mountains, over roads that seemed to lead them higher and higher, and deeper into darkness.

At home she used to climb the ladder and lie down on the roof and look at white-capped Mount Lassen to the east, so close she felt she could touch it, and feel in her heart something of the strange happiness and breathless excitement that she felt in her dreams. For hours she would lie and soak into her soul the beauty of that old volcanic mountain, where the hot springs bubbled and the ground shivered beneath your feet. Between her and the mountain the big trees grew, their fragrance of pine as clean and clear as the blue skies.

To the north was Mount Shasta, it too capped with white. Sometimes the wind blew off Mount Shasta, fast and hard and cold enough to penetrate any coat and chill the skin. But tonight she saw only the darkness, and heard on the car roof the rain that fell steadily from the Oregon sky.

Ahead, a light flickered, cut by the trees. Then it became a light at the side of the road, and in bubbling neon: CABINS.

Sidney pulled in and stopped by the office. The line of attached cabins curved away into the darkness. Cars were parked at an angle in front of most of the doors. He touched her gently.

"Feeling better?"

She looked toward him. Light from the changing neon stained his face with red, green, red, green. His nose looked very long, then shorter, then longer. Like Pinocchio.

Then he eased her toward him into his arms and held her gently, his lips against her cheek.

"Do you love me?" he whispered. He had asked her that before, and in her excitement of being pursued by an older man, a mature man, she had answered fervently, "Yes!"

Now she only nodded.

"Say it," he whispered, as he had those other times, but added, "I need you to say it, over and over, every day of your life from now on. Promise me."

She nodded. He didn't look the same. He was a stranger and she was a little afraid of him. "Say it," he commanded.

"I love you."

As if putting it into words made it true, she felt a rush of adoration, of pride in this man who was hers. She sank against him. The kiss was long, but the excitement was dimmed by this strange, sad day and night.

"I'll be back," he whispered, smiling, looking more like the handsome soldier she had known.

She sat alone while he went into the office. Down the sidewalk a couple came laughing and staggering out of a cabin door and got into the car in front of the door. It spun away throwing gravel and disappeared onto the black highway.

He came back, got into the car and drove to a space down in the darkness. The small bulb beside the door was like a firefly leading into the black of the forest of tall mountain evergreens.

She entered a cabin where an unpolished dresser stood at the foot of the one bed, with barely space to walk between. A spider had woven a web around the dresser corner, but she only looked at it to see that it wasn't a black widow, the kind that carries a deadly poison.

There was a door into a bathroom with a stained shower. She stood undecided, by the dresser, near the spider. The small brown spider ran and hid. She watched it, not knowing what else to do.

Sidney brought in two Cokes and a bottle of amber whiskey and set it on the dresser a few inches from the nervous spider. Suddenly it was funny, and Emmy began to laugh at the ridiculousness of this, the spider running, his space invaded.

From the bathroom Sidney brought two glasses, and stood looking at her, puzzled. "What's funny?"

"The spider—hiding."

Sidney frowned, unamused. "Where?"

"Oh, don't kill it," she said quickly. "It's gone."

He shrugged, and set the glasses down. "Not exactly champagne. Someday, I'll toast you with champagne. But tonight, this will help relax you."

He drew her down to sit on the bed beside him, putting her drink in her hands. His arm pulled her close.

"I know it was kind of fast," he said. "But I could be shipped out anytime, and I want you with me as long as possible. I thought you understood that."

She realized then that he thought she'd been acting like a baby. She sipped the heavily spiked Coke, and a welcome warmth entered her stomach. It wasn't the first time she had tasted whiskey. A couple of times she'd been in a crowd of kids, all piled two deep in a car, laughing, drinking, not caring if she ever went home.

But this was different.

"You're not as old as I thought you were," he said. "I thought you were probably seventeen or eighteen. I found out from your mother that you're just fifteen. But of course I entered your age as eighteen on the marriage license."

He curled over her, tall and strong, smiling into her face. His eyes were inches away from hers. He wrapped his fingers around hers on the glass and eased it toward her lips. She drank again and made herself swallow without choking.

"I don't want you drinking with anyone else," he said, and for a moment didn't smile. "And in fact, I'd rather you didn't mention this to my family. My parents are pretty strict in their religion. Also, you know, drinks do things to some girls, and I think you're one of them. I want you to stay pure. You're my wife."

She felt protected again, the way he'd made her feel from the night she'd met him. He must love her, though he hadn't really said so.

He bent her back onto the bed and began kissing her. She had never stopped him from fondling her breasts. That was one of the things that girls she knew allowed the boys to do. Necking, some of the girls called it when it was only kisses. But petting when the guy's hands were allowed to feel the girl's body. She had thought nothing of it. It was just part of dating.

But she had never allowed anyone to pull her panties completely off. His hand on her stomach, her hand over his, guided it back away from the curve of her inner thighs.

She tried to stop him. She grabbed his hand and held it, as she had Harold's, but he didn't give in as Harold had. He was stronger than she, and the panties went down, farther, farther, exposing her.

"No! Don't! What are you doing?"

He sat up from her, grinned, wider, wider, than began laughing. He released her panties and she jerked them up. He stood up. His shirt had been pulled out of his pants and he started to stuff it back in, then stopped.

He leaned down and kissed her gently. "You're such a baby," he said. "I love you."

It was the first time he had said he loved her.

It was the first time anyone had ever said they loved her. The feeling that pulsed through and thrilled her was similar to when she lay on the roof of the house and lost herself in the beauty of the mountains. Similar even, though not in quality and intensity, to the ecstasy of those rare dreams that came so seldom.

He went into the bathroom, and she was alone for a short time, her heart beating fast and hard. When he came back he looked at her with that same smile in his eyes. His eyes moved down over her, to her arms hugging her knees, and her bare feet on the bed.

"You can't sleep in your clothes," he said softly. She looked at the light.

"Oh. Okay. The child-bride has to undress in the dark."

He reached beneath the shade and turned out the light. From the bathroom, through the half-closed door, a thin light trailed, just enough that she saw the outline of his body as he stripped down to white undershorts.

She began to remove her dress. But she left her slip, bra and panties on.

He held the covers aside for her. After a hesitation she slid in beneath them and felt the nakedness of his body against her. He had slipped off his shorts.

In the shadows of the bed something happened. She no longer minded so much that he undressed her, though she felt exposed even while covered with the sheet. He took her hand and squeezed it, then put it flat on his chest. There was no chest hair, he was as smooth as she. But she felt the muscles as he slid her hand down from his chest to his waist to his flat, hard belly and then into the hair below.

The touch of his thing shocked her. As if she'd touched a hot iron she jerked away. He had begun to breathe heavily, the way he had when they kissed in the car after the dances. He rolled her onto her back and came upon her.

A girl she knew who had gotten married while still in High school had told her and a group of others who listened so intently, "It hurts, the first time. You bleed."

Her thighs tightened, but he pushed them apart, and the big, hard thing she'd touched was against her thigh. His fingers touched her, felt into the private part between her legs and made way for himself.

She stared at the walls beyond his shoulders and thought of this strange act.

What was there about it that men liked so much?

With pale dawn came a different feeling. He lay sleeping, at last, his head on her shoulder, her arm around his neck. For the first time she felt a deep affection for him. He was hers, and she was his. All night he had made love to her, loving her body, touching her everywhere, and the light from the bathroom became like a moonbeam, showing him the curves of her breasts and hips. Showing him that most private part of her that he adored so much. She still didn't understand the adoration, but she liked being the adored.

She was his, fully, completely, totally, forever. And he was hers.

Her hand caressed his shoulder, and she looked at his face and saw that he looked younger when he was asleep. Asleep he looked almost as young as the kids back home that she had dated.

His eyelashes were long, tipped with gold. They fluttered open. His eyes were blue as deep water. "Do you love me?" he asked.

"Yes," she said. "I love you."

Rain dripped like acid from the roof.

Chapter Eleven

"M"aggie?"

THE CALL CAME from far beyond the boundaries of her rest. Trying to rise from sleep, she was drawn toward it unwillingly. Sweet sleep, soft as floating on a breeze. Safe sleep, protecting her from the world she had closed her eyes against.

"Maggie?"

Maggie? Who was Maggie? Sidney called her Emmy, just as her family did. Emmy was her name, not Maggie.

Maggie woke, opened her eyes, and came back from the past. She blinked at the face of the doctor above her, smiling, his dark hair a short cap of curls. He was probably close to half a century old, but looked like a boy at times to her. When he looked down, the bald spot on the crown of his head was visible.

"How're you doing?" He sat down on the edge of her bed.

"Okay …" Her voice was unclear, filled with sleep. Okay, she thought. Except now she was reliving her life, it seemed. The slow drown, the third time down, the desperate recall of memories as if they would save her from something. Why was she drowning herself in things she had almost forgotten?

"I'm doing fine," she said, turning onto her side toward him. Pain, like live wire, reminded her she was not as fine as she wanted to believe. Her hip felt stiff, her leg numb.

"Doin' fine, huh?" he asked, watching her closely. "They giving you enough pain killers?"

"Oh yes." She managed a sitting position, hating this awful helplessness. "It's just hard being dependent. I don't like it."

"I don't like it either, that's why we're trying to get you past this stage."

Hazel and Florence both sat quietly watching. In the fourth chair the newcomer was staring at the bald spot on the doctor's head. "Doing any walking?"

"Yes. Played the piano, too," Florence said.

The doctor smiled. "Do you play?"

"Can she ever! You ought to hear her sometime."

He patted Maggie's shoulder as he rose. "Well you just keep on playing. Walk when you feel like it, but don't overdo it. You're doing fine."

He started out. She sat up, and pain ripped through her hip and leg into her chest. Panic rose. I have to get out of here, she thought.

"Doctor, I don't see why I can't manage at home."

He paused, looking seriously at her. "I'd rather you didn't go yet. What if you fell again? The damage might be irreparable. You're going to be needing help for a few weeks. You can't be alone. If we had someone to stay with you ..."

She said nothing. He had suggested she try to hire someone if it were so important to be home. But that was one of those solutions with a lining not of silver but of gold. Nursing help wasn't easily available. Also, her invested income barely covered necessities, it didn't include much more. She had known she was riding on the edge. But she'd been healthy, felt well, so she'd tried not to worry.

There were so many little things at home that made life good. Sitting on the step of the back porch with Minnie on her lap, and the two of them watching the little chippies run and play along the walk, unafraid of people or little dogs. Watching the flowers grow and bloom after a gloomy winter. The birds, the butterflies ... she hadn't anticipated being helpless.

The doctor patted her knee. "Let's give it another week or two to heal, okay? You ask for help when you need it. Don't put too much stress on that hip."

He left, going around the edge of the big door with firm, confident steps. Maggie's roommates were silent. Clara got up and started toward the door, following the doctor.

Florence asked, "Where you going, hon?"

Clara paused, her head turning, a vague frown answering the sound of her name.

"Maybe you'd like to go watch television awhile," Florence suggested. "Just go down the hall toward the dining room."

Clara nodded and she too disappeared beyond the big door that stood like a thick barrier between Maggie and freedom.

Florence patted the arms of her chair then she too rose. "I think I'll go walk around awhile. Anybody want to go along?"

"Might as well," Hazel said. "I wonder if the mail has come? I'm looking for a letter from my grandson. He's going to fix an apartment for me in his house."

Florence stopped at the foot of Maggie's bed. "Want to go along? We'll get the wheelchair for you, hon. The doctor says you shouldn't be walking around too much."

Maggie shook her head. She eased down on her bed, and turned onto her right side, legs drawn up. The pain pills had made her feel weak and dizzy, and at times she felt as if she swung in a hammock of pain.

"Don't want to leave you alone," Hazel said.

"I don't mind," Maggie assured them. The two faces looked at her with concern, then they too were gone beyond the door.

Maggie expelled a long sigh of relief. Florence and Hazel were becoming like mothers with one chick. Maggie felt a deep affection for them, and was grateful for their concern. But she was glad for the silence of solitude.

She had learned to like soft sounds around her. The slow ticking of the antique clock, the crackling whispers of the fire on the hearth. The soft snores of her little silky brown dog. The warmth of the curled body against her legs, in her arms. Her yawn. These were the sounds that rested her. Not the chattering of voices, gathering and moving along the hall for another meal, another hour of television., Not sick people groaning behind closed doors.

She listened. Thomas wasn't groaning. People talked in the hall as they went toward the front of the building, but Thomas was quiet.

The voices drifted on.

She buried her head against the pillow.

"Please God," she whispered, "Please let me sleep—let me dream. Give me back my dreams."

In passing years her grasp of her nightly dreams had grown less, so that they stayed beyond her at times like broken webs, hanging in shimmering shreds. She awoke each morning from other worlds and other lives, other experiences vague and distant, beyond an unreachable space. She could no longer live within her dreams as she once had when she was young and so desperately needed an escape. But if she prayed ... maybe God would listen ...

"God, let me sleep. Please give me the dreams."

But sleep eluded her and the memories began, hurting her all over again. The past kept slipping through her mind. She closed her eyes and her mind against memories that hurt and prayed in silence. Please give me back my dreams. But the past came instead like dancing clowns, one behind the next, on and on ... so that she stood within it like someone damned to forever relive.

SIDNEY HAD TOLD her his folks were beet farmers, but she had visualized the kind of farms she'd seen down in the upper Sacramento valley. Small, with orchards, maybe a little green meadow with a cow or a horse.

Instead the farmstead was nestled among a group of huge old trees and beyond it the land spread unimpeded to the foothills. The mountains rose like a huge, natural fence behind the farm land, not close and snow-capped like the mountains at home but huge and distant, on and on. The range of the Rockies, stretching north and south farther than the eye could see.

Nearby, the ground was white with a new layer of snow, and the air colder than any she'd ever felt.

She clung to Sidney's hand until he slid away from her out of the car. He had driven into a long driveway that had a turn-around near a screened back porch, with a private road going on to barns beyond.

He released himself from her fingers when the back door opened and the people emerged from the house in what seemed an endless stream. He had told her he had one older brother, David, who was in the Navy, and three sisters, two of them married, the third eighteen and still living at home. But there were visitors. Behind the women came a small group of men. The oldest wore overalls.

They gaped at her, shocked, disconcerted. No one spoke to her. She saw they hadn't expected their soldier to bring home a girl, especially this one. He hadn't told them about her. Their puzzled and averting stares asked, what are you doing here, while they continued to ignore her.

They reduced her to a small, tacky intrusion. Their lack of friendliness increased her vague guilt, as if they knew what had happened last night. She felt exposed and naked.

Questions came at Sidney, love and pride in their faces. "Did you have a nice trip?"

"How long is your furlough?"

"Are you going to stay here—or go somewhere else—?" Sliding, indirect looks at Emmy head to toe. They moved in a group out of the cold wind and through the kitchen door.

Sidney pulled her with him into the house, and in the large kitchen he put an arm around her waist and said as if making an announcement to all, "I want you to meet Emmy. My bride."

"Bride?" an older woman repeated, her face unmasked and revealing her disbelief. "You're married?"

"Emily's her name, but she's called Emmy. I found her near where I'm stationed. Cute, huh?"

Two of the younger women, tall and blond and beautiful like Sidney, both his age or older, gave each other direct stares.

These were his two older sisters, Emmy knew. They had been his guardians, he'd told her. These were the two who used to appoint themselves his bosses.

Sidney gave her the names of these family members. Mom, Dad, Aunt Mabel, Aunt Norma, sisters Mona, Veda and the youngest, not much older than she, Janice. There was also Uncle Ralph, and two other men, Jim and Wayne. There was a toddler who belonged to Veda and Jim whom Sidney picked up and hugged and kissed. A couple of other kids ran in and out and in again. The family stood in a semi-circle staring at her, half-smiling, trapped, perplexed looks in their eyes. Like her, they didn't know what to say.

Then one of the younger women, Veda or Mona, blurted, "She's so young!"

Like Sidney she was tall and slender, with Scandinavian features. They were all good-looking, healthy-looking, rich-looking. She felt her difference. They had never lived in a tent in an orchard, picking fruit for groceries. They had never known what it was to get only one pair of new shoes a year. She had known Sidney was older, educated. He had told her he was going to be a lawyer, that he had only a few more credits to get before he could take his bar exam.

She wished she were home.

The husband of one of the sisters laughed and asked, "Whose cradle did you rob, Sid?"

Sidney's dad looked at the ceiling, at the floor, out the windows. He cleared his throat, shuffled his feet as if he didn't know which way to move, and stared longingly at the door.

Then they all began to talk and move about. The women were cooking a big dinner, smells of roast, of pie, of vinegar and sugar and spices heavy in the large, country kitchen. The men went to another room, and Sidney pulled away from her. Yet he stayed, for a moment, telling the smiling, adoring faces of the women about his experiences at camp.

Emmy stepped back from the center of the kitchen and looked toward the wide double windows beyond the kitchen table. She looked at a cold, strange landscape and felt like crying for the green world she had left, for the comfort of her own home, the smaller, cozier kitchen. For the first time in her life she knew the pain and fear of homesickness.

Sidney took her hand and she went with him through a door into the next room. A fire burned in a fireplace. Windows faced onto a front porch that ran across the width of the house.

Through a doorway a hall reached to a front door. A stairway against one wall disappeared into an upper floor.

The men gathered near the big windows to discuss the year's crop, Sidney among them, in the center of them, his importance solid.

Emmy went to the fire, cold, shivering, feeling lost and out of place.

On the mantel stood a variety of framed pictures, crowded together. Four children, one boy and three girls. Sidney and, his sisters. Another of a young couple. His parents? Then, a large photograph. Sidney, in uniform, his face close to the face of a beautiful young woman. A shadow crossed Emmy's heart. She stared at the face of the woman with Sidney.

She had dark blue eyes, a dainty, tapered chin, full lips, hair as black as midnight, skin pale and smooth. The way he was leaning toward her revealed a depth of feelings he had not given to Emmy. She felt their closeness in her throat, hurting. It wasn't an old picture.

A voice said softly at her shoulder, "Handsome couple, right?"

Emmy jumped, startled, a guilty surge of having seen something not meant for her eyes. The youngest sister, Janice, stood looking at the photograph. She too had a pretty, oval face, like Sidney and his older sisters, but her hair was dark brown like their mother's.

Janice looked past her at the picture. "That's Sidney and his fiancé, Gloria."

"Fiancé!"

It was the first word she had spoken since she entered the house. The hurt in her throat increased. She felt sick with it.

Janice shrugged, smiled. "Well … was. When he joined the army it made her mad, I guess. Something happened. Anyway, she married someone else."

The hurt didn't ease.

Dinner was announced, and the family gathered in the dining room. Emmy tried to swallow with a throat that fought against her. It didn't help that Sidney was at her side. Conversation rattled over her head about people she didn't know, a lifestyle she didn't understand. Emmy pulled the cocoon of separateness around her, and thought of home.

"She's certainly quiet," Mona said at one point to Sidney, and they looked at each other and smiled. Sidney put his arm around Emmy's shoulders, hugged her and kissed her cheek. Then she was left alone again.

After dinner she offered to help with the cleanup, but was told no. She wandered about, alone, and went outside to look for the toilet, but there was none. Of course there wouldn't be an outdoor toilet. This big house with its porches and big lawn would have a bathroom.

A big, black pup with shiny, wavy fur came and put his nose in her hand. "Hi, Midnight," she said, with no idea of his name. Sidney hadn't mentioned him. He hadn't mentioned a lot of things, she thought as she stood with the dog. He loped off and brought back a stick for her to throw.

She stayed outside until she was shivering. She had never owned a coat in her life, and found the jacket she wore to school too thin for this cold country. She went back inside and asked the least threatening of the women, Aunt Mabel where the bathroom was. Then, following directions, she climbed the stairs to the second floor and stopped at the first door.

When she left the bathroom she heard voices, male and female. Sidney and a sister? She recognized Veda's voice.

"How old is she, Sid?"

"Fifteen."

"Good God, man, what were you thinking of? What on earth did you see in her?"

They both laughed. "Don't be naive, Veda."

"She's a baby. She needs to be home with her mother."

"She's with me," he said with a firmness in his voice that softened the hurt that still clutched Emmy's throat. "She can stay here with the folks while I'm overseas."

"Why did you do this, Sid? You're twelve years older than she. She's still in school."

"Not now," he said.

"What about Gloria?"

"What about her?" His voice sharpened angrily. "She's the one who broke the engagement, not me. She's the one who ran off with some guy down to Reno, first. What am I supposed to do?"

Silence followed his angry questions.

Emmy slipped out of the bathroom and went quietly down the stairs. She had seen through an open door a piano in a small room beneath the stairs, and she went to it. She closed the door, sat down and began to play the blues, so softly only she could hear.

Chapter Twelve

In the dark room, the cold bed, she lay against him, her head on his arm. Through their kisses, their love-making, she saw the face of the other girl. She recognized her own insecurity, her feeling of not being first choice. Something inside her quivered. She was afraid of mentioning the fiancé, yet she must or she would die.

"I saw the picture, Sidney."

"Ummm?" He was sleepy. He always became very sleepy after he made love to her. Sometimes he turned away from her, his back a formidable barrier.

"You and her. Gloria, your sister told me her name is. Why didn't you tell me you'd been engaged? They have your picture there as if you were still engaged."

His breath stopped. Then he said, "It's none of your business."

He turned over, his back toward her. Cold wind blew around the corners of the house shrieking in discordant pitches. She shivered beneath covers that were too thin for her, she who had always lived in a warmer climate than this.

She moved against his back for warmth, warmth for her body, warmth for her heart.

He put an elbow into her stomach and jabbed her away.

In disbelief at what he had done, with a strange new fear of him, she crept to the edge of the bed. After staring long hours into the dark the tears came and she cried herself to sleep.

SHE IS STANDING in a valley surrounded by tall mountains of stone. The valley floor is layered in rhythms of snow. A bright, beautiful light shines on the snow and it becomes filled with diamonds, rubies, sapphires, emeralds, gleaming, sparkling all around her. Tiny flashes of color like heartbeats in blue, red, green, gold dance all across the valley floor.

She stands alone, bathed in the glory and the beauty. She is aware of ageless, timeless continuity, in a world that goes on forever. She stands alone in the glorious valley of snow that sparkles like rare jewels yet she is not alone. The light baths her and fills her with happiness and warmth.

She begins to walk, following the long, straight road that leads to the sharp-peaked mountains encircling the valley. Her soul sings with glory, with ecstasy, and the foreverness of this mysterious world. It's important that she reach the mountains, but there is no hurry.

"EMMY, WAKE UP."

She shrank into the cold covers, trying to protect her consciousness from the world. Don't wake me! Don't take me from my dream.

"Emmy, breakfast is ready."

She opened her eyes.

Sidney was dressed, shaved, wide awake, smiling at her. He kissed her softly. "Do you love me?" He pulled her up out of bed.

"I'll help you dress," he said, eyes eager.

The clean dress she'd laid out from the paper bag was wrinkled. He smoothed the skirt with his hands.

She asked, "Can we go dancing tonight?"

The change came in his eyes, a flash of anger. "You crazy?"

"It's Saturday night," she said, not understanding this sudden change.

"I only have a week here, I'm not going to waste it in some joint."

He turned away from her, and over his shoulder said, "Hurry up. Come on down as soon as you're dressed. Breakfast is waiting."

It was not yet daylight.

THE BEAUTIFUL GIRL in the photograph came on Sunday afternoon. Visitors had been arriving at various times all day. There had been church in the morning, and for the first time in her life Emmy sat in a polished church pew and listened to the words of a preacher. She felt as out of place in Sidney's church as she did in Sidney's home.

At home after church Emmy stood out of the way in a corner of the kitchen, where the women had gathered. Suddenly it seemed a ripple went through the house, the people. Outside the dog barked at a car as it eased quietly in among the others.

The women moved forward in a group, going toward the living room. Their voices spoke of someone who seemed important to them in ways that were mixed, full of awe, surprise, expectation.

"Here she is."

"I knew she'd come."

"As soon as she heard Sid was home."

"What about … you know."

Emmy knew. Even before she saw the woman dressed in fur get out of the shining black car. Through the window the sight was unavoidable. Emmy stayed behind in the kitchen as if she could shrink unnoticed into the corner. But at the door, following behind the others, Janice turned and looked at her. "You have to come and meet her," she said and her voice held something deeper and kinder than it had at the mantel when Emmy had first seen the picture.

Daddy had always called her bashful. Sometimes he had teased her about it. It seemed no one else in the world ever had that paralysis in the throat, the sickness in the stomach, the need to run away and walk alone.

Only where music played did she feel at ease with people. "Come on," Janice insisted, her eyes understanding. "You have to, you know. Just get it over with. It won't be so bad."

Emmy followed, conscious of her wrinkled school dress.

She entered the living room just as the front door opened. Sidney's mother put out her arms and hugged the beautiful young women dressed in a coat of rich, thick brown fur. Emmy's eyes took in the beauty of the coat, and her heart wondered about the animals to whom it had belonged. She felt a surprise burst of hatred for the girl who looked as if she had always gotten everything she wanted.

Taller than Sidney's mother, she stooped a bit to hug her. Her dark eyes found Sidney and held his. Voices of greeting in the big room were a loud background to their meeting.

He went forward to meet her.

Emmy saw the intensity of the gaze between them. Sidney took her hands in his and she said, laughing, "You're not going to get by just with that," and she stepped closer and kissed his cheek. She was only half a head shorter than Sidney.

His lips grazed the corner of hers, as if reaching for a kiss. The longing was deep and soft in his eyes.

Emmy could stand it no longer. She stepped back into the kitchen, ran quietly to the door into the hall, and into the music room. She shut the door. Fighting tears she slid onto the piano bench and her fingers found the keys while tears filled her eyes and blurred her surroundings. With her foot pressing the soft peddle she let her fingers play with the keys, finding the music that numbed the aching in her heart. Her soul went into this music, everything that she was.

Time became like a dream. She played, her eyes closed, tears drying. Played softly, as she always had. Playing only for herself. Playing quietly so as not to disturb others, or draw their attention. The door at home had always been closed on her, but remarks usually filtered through, mostly from Grandma. "There she is making that racket again." Slam. But the slamming of the door released Emmy into the boundless, endless, timeless world of her music, her dreams.

From the corner of her eyes she saw the music room door open and Sidney enter. Behind him Janice stepped into the doorway and stopped.

"What the hell are you doing?" Sidney asked. "I've been looking all over the house for you."

Emmy dropped her hands into her lap, took her foot off the piano peddle and looked down.

Janice said, "I didn't know she could play a piano, did you, Sid?"

"Come on, Emily, for Christ's sake. I want Gloria to meet you."

As he pulled Emmy past, Janice said in a low voice, "Well you can hardly blame her, Sid!"

He pushed Emmy ahead of him, his hands on her arms. They entered the living room where people sat with coffee and small cakes. The fur coat was hidden away in the closet, and Gloria sat sideways on the arm of a big chair where Sidney's father sat. A silk-clad leg dangled, and a foot dressed in a black high-heeled ankle strap sandal. She wore a soft, jersey pleated skirt with a peplum blouse that fit her waist closely. She not only had a beautiful face, but her figure was superb. Emmy had never felt so ugly and so poor in her life.

"Here she is," Sidney said, putting a hand up to brush Emmy's long hair back from her cheek as if it were too uncontrolled. "My bride, Emily. Emmy, meet Gloria … what the hell's your name now?"

Laughter. Gloria mentioned a name, but Emmy was caught by her eyes, the look in them as they traveled down over her to her feet, her blue anklets, her saddle oxfords, the only winter shoes she owned, and back up to the top of her head. A hard glaze covered whatever she was feeling.

Chapter Thirteen

Sidney took Emmy to bed early. As soon as all the company left, aunts, uncles, neighbors who dropped in for a few minutes. He put his arm around her waist and drew her with him into the silent dark upstairs.

He turned on the bedroom light and began to undress her. The uncovered, mirroring window gave her a vision of herself as her breasts became exposed, then her belly, her hips.

"No, the window's open," she objected, seeking to hide from the reflection of her nude body.

His eyes looked at her body, not her face. They sought her flat belly, her pubic hair, a brown, fuzzy mat. His gaze clung to her thighs as he pushed her back onto the bed and began undoing his pants.

"Sidney—the window."

"Nobody can see up here."

The drive curled below, circled and joined itself again.

Who might wander there, drawn to look up? Even the cattle beyond the pasture fence disturbed her. The dark out there, the light in here, exposed her. The door was unlocked. His mother had walked in twice before without knocking.

"Please, Sidney." She tried to pull the blanket over her, but he pushed it away.

She looked up into his eyes and her heart grew still and cold. There was a cruelty within their depths she had never seen before, in anyone's eyes, not even her grandma's when she was angry, nor her mother's.

His trousers came down, pushed with one hand. His eyes looked beyond her, into a distance she had never traveled. His fingers grasped the back of her head, tangling in her hair, and he pushed her face downward toward the erection that stood pale and immense. It reached upward from its own bed of pubic hair like a naked growth.

Her face touched its warm, fat, velvety bulb. His hands gripped and twisted her head, directing her mouth to it, forced her face down and held it against that obscene heat.

She cried out, gagging, jerking back, twisting away. What was he doing? She pushed against him, her hands touching flesh she suddenly found as repulsive as the thing he was trying to put into her mouth.

What are you doing? You've gone crazy—crazy—

Perhaps she only thought it, or perhaps she cried it out loud. She gagged against this intrusion, this invasion of her body and her sense of self.

He let her go suddenly, shoved her, put his hand or fist against her, then his knee. He shoved her violently off the bed, muttering, "Fucking bitch."

She fell onto the floor on her knees and chest and remained there, crying hard, body shaking.

He muttered something that sounded to her like, "Fucking whore—who do you think you are—stupid ignorant bitch." But she couldn't be sure.

She stayed on the floor until her tears were gone. What had he tried to do to her? She didn't understand that naked look in his eyes, a look she had seen yet didn't understand. What had she done that made him hate her so much? What had the look meant? And the rest—what he had tried to do to her.

Was it lust she had seen? Lust for something she couldn't give. Lust for the other girl, the one he really loved? With hatred for Emmy because she wasn't the one he really wanted?

She would never be able to ask anyone for the answers to her questions, not even her best friend Betsy.

She rose when her naked skin became as chilled as her heart. A frigid cold closed around her.

He had gone to bed, far over on the other side, his back toward her. There was no deep, even breathing of sleep. He was still awake. But he was as distant from her and as unyielding as the Great Rockies beyond the snow-dusted fields.

She pulled on the only pair of pajamas she owned, and crept beneath the covers, but sat, her knees drawn up, the blanket pulled high beneath her chin.

"Sidney." It was a desperate cry against the abandonment. She had seen something in his eyes that scared her. A lack of love, after all. A cruelty she had never seen before in the eyes of anyone.

He didn't answer.

"Sidney, I heard one of your sisters ask you why you'd married me. Now I want to know the answer."

His head moved slightly, freeing his ear from the pillow. "What are you talking about?"

"You don't love me. You love her. Gloria."

He put the ear against the pillow again. "You're crazy."

"Why did you marry me?"

"Shut up and go to sleep."

She sat still, the hurt too deep for tears. It held her stomach in a hard hand of reality. Why was she here at all?

"Sidney, I want to go home." You made your bed, now you lie in it.

"Go on."

She thought of the long straight roads beyond the fields, of the town they had driven through that was five or six miles away. She thought of the long roads through the mountains, and the darkness and cold. How could she go home? Walking, with only her light jacket for warmth against sub-zero weather? He knew she couldn't go.

"I don't have any money."

He took a deep breath.

She looked at the hard surface of the window, and its reflection of bits of the room broken by the many small panes, and wished she had the courage to go. The courage to reach the highway and hitchhike home. But her jacket was thin and the night so dark and cold. She didn't even have three cents for a stamp to write a letter to her family and tell them where she was, ask them for money to come home. Money that was needed for other things having nothing to do with her now that she had made her bed.

She edged down beneath the cover and stared at the corner of the room where the rounded edge of the braided rug ended and the polished maple floor began. All the floors in the house were maple, he had told her. They were shiny and beautiful, with rugs, mostly braided, colorful. Braided by his mother and aunts, he had told her. His eyes had shone with what she felt was love when he looked at her as he was showing her around. He had come to her off and on during the day, as if he hadn't forgotten her.

But tonight had spoiled it all.

She closed her eyes and must have slept. She woke suddenly, jolting awake, to find the light out and Sidney's arms around her. He was sleeping, his breath warm in her hair.

She woke again, trying to reach a fading dream in which the world she had wandered was exciting and filled with adventures, a city through which she had walked in the dark with only vague lights ahead but with no feeling of danger.

"Hey, wake up sleepy head," he was whispering. His lips sought her in a warm, deep kiss. She relented and accepted the kiss, this sign of love, but she couldn't return it. He didn't seem to notice.

He murmured, "Here's what I want you to do. I want you to stay here with my folks while I'm gone."

She said nothing, but images formed, bleak and lonely. Here? Where people talked about her as if she weren't in the room? Where she couldn't possibly be wanted?

"I thought I was going with you."

"You can't go with me, silly baby. I live at camp, and I'm going to be shipped out any time."

"Then why can't I go home?" You've made your bed, now you lie in it. Would Mommy even let her come home?

"I don't want you to."

"I want to go home. I have another year of high school."

"No, I don't want you to go to school."

"Why?" she cried.

"Because I know you—you'll flirt with the boys, and I don't want you in school." He turned her face back toward him. "Shhh, kiss me. I'm going to have to teach you how to make love like a real woman."

When he left three days later, she wept, after all, with loneliness. Handsome in his uniform, a duffel bag in his hand, he boarded the train. She stood with his family and watched as it puffed away, faster and faster and through her tears she watched it disappear around the turn. Crowds thinned, leaving the depot, and she at last turned and followed the people she had met less than a week ago.

Days passed slowly, lonely and long. Janice went to school.

Emmy found a tablet and pencil and wrote a long letter to her family, but didn't have an envelope or a stamp.

Two weeks later letters came from Sidney saying goodbye. He was being shipped overseas to Hawaii. His letters would be censored from now on. The European war had escalated furiously and dominated the news. It all would end before the year was out, but now to Emmy it seemed a forever thing.

She received an official letter. In it was a check for fifty dollars. She had never seen so much money in her life. Even during the summers when she worked in the orchards she had never received more than twenty dollars for the summer's work. Now she was going to get fifty dollars a month?

"What are you going to do with it?" Sidney's father asked, with a faint curl to his lips that she wasn't quite sure was kind or unkind. Was it a smile, or a sneer? He had never spoken directly to her before. He had brought the mail in from the mailbox, three hundred feet away down the snow-banked driveway. He stood watching her, thumbs hooked in overall galluses.

"I'd like to go home," she said.

"Go home!" He wore blue denim overalls every day except Sunday, and over the overalls he wore a heavy denim jacket lined with flannel. He walked on toward the kitchen door, passing the black cook stove where a coal fire burned all day long. "Thought you were home."

But he was surely teasing. He was being sarcastic, as Sidney could so easily, dismaying and confusing her. She had not learned in her weeks in his home how to laugh at his humor. The things she laughed at, Midnight stumbling over his own big feet, a pig rooting his mama, made them look at her askance, no more understanding her sense of humor than she understood theirs.

She said nothing in answer to Sidney's father. Sidney's mother said, "You should buy a coat."

She was busy as always, puttering about the stove, or over at the sink. She reminded Emmy of Grandma, the same high-boned cheeks, the black eyes, hair turned almost white now with only strands of the former black. Her eyes were small and hard and unfriendly, like Grandma's, it seemed to Emmy, whenever she directed them her way. Her name was Nolabelle. Sidney's father called her Nolie. Others called her Nola. But Janice had told Emmy to call them Mom and Pop as she did, as Sidney did. Emmy had not yet been able to address either of them. She thought of them as

Sidney's mother, Sidney's father. She spoke when she was spoken to, and initiated no conversations.

She wanted to go home. Home where it was warmer, where her jacket was enough even on the coldest day. Home where she shared a bed with Grandma, she on her side, and Grandma on hers, but at least where she didn't freeze all night, where she didn't feel so misplaced. For the first time in her life she'd been sleeping alone, in Sidney's bed, Sidney's room, unused to the cold nights. The blankets heaped on the bed seemed heavy and stiff, holding the cold in. It seeped up through the mattress, like icy little fingers searching for her.

This was a Saturday and Janice was home from school. She sat at the kitchen table with a history book in front of her and a tablet beneath her right arm. She twirled a pencil in her fingers. With her elbow on the table beside the book she leaned her chin on the heel of her left hand.

Sidney's father went out onto the back screened porch, hung his coat on a peg and came back into the kitchen. A rush of cold air came with him, but only Emmy shivered.

"That's a good idee," he said. "Buy a coat."

Janice said, "She needs to go back to school."

"Yes, I want to."

There was silence for a few moments. They weren't used to her speaking up.

Sidney's father said, "I reckon she could go to school with Janice."

But the mother answered, "You know Sidney doesn't want her in school."

Janice looked up. "For crying out loud! Why not? Let her go home if that's what she wants. Let her go back to school."

"Sidney wants her to stay with us."

"Why? Why does she have to stay here if she doesn't want to? I don't blame her. If it was me, I'd want to stay in my own home too while my husband was overseas."

"If it was you," Sidney's father said tartly, "You wouldn't be married. At your age."

Janice shrugged.

EMMY WENT UPSTAIRS and gathered the few things she had brought, into the same wrinkled paper sack.

Sidney's father and younger sister Janice took her away from the big farm. Sidney's mother stood in the doorway watching, but she didn't wave. She crossed her arms over her stomach and squinted, her face pinched. Emmy felt as if she were committing a terrible wrong.

Sidney's father helped Emmy cash the check and buy the bus ticket. They waited with her until the bus came. At the steps up into the bus Sidney's father took her hand and shook it gravely.

"I want you to know," he said, his eyes meeting hers, the corners creasing into wrinkles that brought an expression of great sadness to his gaunt face, "I want you to know—and remember—you're welcome to stay with us. You'll always have a home here."

The bus idled, waiting for her. The driver's hand held to the lever that closed the door. She didn't know what to say. The old shyness paralyzed her vocal cords and kept her from expressing her sudden gratitude.

The bus engine roared impatiently. Sidney's father and Janice stepped back. Emmy boarded, and they were lost from view. The bus ride eased away the loneliness of leaving people she had grown more fond of than she'd realized. Dissolved the feeling of doing something wrong, of disobedience. Sidney's father's name was Arthur, but she'd never been able to think of him by name, not even as Pop, as Janice called him.

A sense of freedom came gradually as the bus took her farther and farther away from the cold.

It became the most marvelous experience of all her life as she gazed out the window at mountains and rivers, meadows and small towns passing in the shadows of a cloudy day. She had a feeling of happiness similar to her dreams, in which she wandered freely through a world of marvelous beauty and safety from all bad things. She felt totally free and happy, her soul flying, as if she had crossed the boundaries into a perfect world.

Chapter Fourteen

Emmy walked the two miles home from the bus stop in town, turning her face up to the sprinkles of rain, looking at the foothills in the mists and the rising white peak of Mount Lassen shrouded by a layer of clouds. Home. Here was the mailbox, the spot where the school bus stopped, and the mile-long dirt road up to her house. She had walked it so many times since they had lived here. Today it was muddy. She walked on the dryer ridge in the center between the tire ruts.

It was almost dark when the house came in view. Ole Bow, the shepherd dog with the long red fur, came wagging to meet her. She clutched him against her and kissed the top of his head.

A voice squealed, "It's Emmy! Emmy's home!" Peggy, running to meet her, the screen door slamming. She could almost hear someone saying, 'Don't slam the door!' A command spoken more often than any other in their house.

They were glad to see her. Even Mommy hugged her, holding her longer than Emmy could remember. She laughed and wept at the same time.

"You didn't write."

"I didn't have three cents for a stamp."

She was home, but it was different now. She was no longer allowed to go to the Saturday night dances. Her mother was shocked that she even got ready to go.

"Where are you going, Emily?" she demanded. "You're married now. You don't go chasing off to dances anymore."

"But ... I was just going with Betsy, the way I always did."

"You can't go with Betsy the way you always did. You have a husband in the war."

"He won't care," she said lamely, but she knew he did. In his latest letter he had berated her for not staying with his parents. He didn't want her in school, he had repeated. But she hadn't shown the letter to Mommy, because she had already gone back to school, and this was one thing she did not intend to give up. Why should she? She didn't understand Sidney's attitude.

The way he had looked at Gloria made his love for her seem obvious, yet he wanted to rule Emily. Perhaps because he couldn't rule Gloria.

"I married you," he had told her. "Not Gloria." But wasn't that because Gloria herself had eloped to Reno and married another man? Being married had changed Emmy's life, in ways she had not anticipated. She had dreamed of dancing every night, of romance and love forever.

"You have to think of him," Daddy said. "He's off fighting a war. It's your duty to wait."

The war seemed far away, on another world. She'd seen it only when she'd gone to a movie, when it was on the screen preceding the movie. Planes flying, dropping bombs. Big guns blasting. Such a strange and terrible thing.

"He could be killed," Grandma said. "Then how would you feel?"

But he wasn't fighting, he was stationed in Hawaii. Training other men. His letter had said, "I wish I could bring you over here, but I can't."

Her husband was away at war, and she was in a concentration camp without wires and fences. Then in the summer the war ended, but it was two more years before her life changed.

"ELEANOR! ELEANOR, WHERE ARE YOU?"

Maggie became aware of her present surroundings. She felt a need to move, as if it would relieve the nagging ache. It accompanied the voices like bad background noises in a movie.

Hazel said, "Who's that yelling? Thomas?"

"At least he's stopped groaning," Florence said. "Just about drove me nuts sometimes."

Maggie sat up, put a hand up to her hair. The short cut was meant to have a slightly disheveled look, fortunately, but she couldn't get rid, even now, of the old self-consciousness.

"What are you going to do?" Florence asked her.

"I think it's time I had some more exercise."

"I don't know ..." Hazel mused, "the doctor said ..." Maggie put her right foot on the floor, clutched the bed rail for support and looked for the walker. Someone had put it at the foot of the bed.

Across the hall Thomas shouted, "Eleanor?" Then more plaintively, "Eleanor, where are you?"

He sounded lost, and Maggie's heart turned. She reacted to his cry as she would have a child's. Holding to the bed, she began a slow one-footed walk toward the walker.

Florence got up. "Well here, let me help you, if you're going to insist on going to visit Thomas."

The door was suddenly pushed back. It reached from the wall to the foot of Maggie's bed, and effectively blocked her path.

One of the nurses came leading Clara back into the room. The nurse saw Maggie and pushed the door away from the foot of her bed.

"Do you need some help, dear? Just a minute. I just needed to guide Clara back. She was lost, poor thing."

"This is not where I live," Clara said strongly, looking about. "These are not people I know. What are they doing here in my house?"

"They live here too, Clara. Here, dear, sit down in your chair."

"It's a terrible chair," Clara said, eyeing its red plastic cover.

"But it's very comfortable. See, it rocks when the footstool is down, and reclines when the footstool is up."

Clara sat down, looking about. She appeared to be physically strong, and was physically attractive. But her eyes saw nothing familiar, nothing safe, and reflected the fear of being in a world she no longer knew.

"Eleanor?" Thomas wailed.

The nurse uttered a short laugh. "At least he's stopped groaning. They're saying down front that you've managed a miracle of some kind, Maggie."

"She's going over to see him," Florence offered. "Personally, I'd about as soon hear him groan as to hear him yell for Eleanor all the time."

The nurse looked at Maggie. "You really want to go see Thomas?"

"If she don't," Hazel said. "He'll never shut up. Florence and me, we're about ready to help Maggie over there ourselves." She rocked and laughed along with Florence.

The nurse was another aide that Maggie hadn't seen before but whom Florence and Hazel seemed to know. Her nametag claimed her to be Denise. She was young, dark, pretty, and definitely pregnant.

She pulled a folded wheelchair out from against the wall on the other side of Maggie's bed and extended it. "Okay, here we go."

Maggie turned slowly, her hands gripping the foot railing of the bed. She suddenly felt like screaming against this helplessness. Fear rushed upward into her chest, the start of another panic attack. She closed her eyes. Breathe deeply.

"Are you all right?" Denise asked quickly.

Florence said, "She's been doing too much today. Instead of eating breakfast, she played the piano, must've played an hour or more. She walked all the way over to Thomas's room. Doctor told her to rest that hip and leg."

The sound of Florence's voice seemed to come from a nightmare. Never in her life had she experienced the kind of nightmare during her sleep that other people described, the kind that Sidney had suffered several nights a week. Her nightmares seemed reserved for her conscious states, changing her perception of reality and filling it with strange terrors.

A hand touched her shoulder. Florence asked, "Are you all right?"

The panic eased away. Florence's voice was warm and close, her hand warm, not cold like Maggie's. Maggie nodded.

"I'll hold the chair," Florence said. "You help her sit down."

"Thanks, Florence," Maggie said. She pivoted to drop into the chair and the pain responded, shooting through her leg and hip. She almost burst into tears of frustration. Dear God, what had made her think she could use the walker just anytime she wanted?

"There now," Denise said. The wheelchair squeaked with each revolution of the wheels. They went out into the hall.

Behind them Clara said, "I didn't know I had company. Who did you say you were?"

Denise said, "At least you're only waiting to heal a hip, right? Your health is good otherwise?"

"Yes, thank God."

"There's always someone worse."

They paused in the hallway as three elderly women came slowly along the hall. They smiled, nodded, and continued their conversation.

As they waited, Maggie said, "Your first baby?" She had become so socially defective in these years of talking only with clerks in the stores she frequented, and occasionally with a neighbor, that when she was around someone she felt awkward.

"Yes," Denise said, and put a hand on her stomach. "In four more months, I can hardly wait!"

"Are you going to stay home then?"

"I sure am. My husband, Daryl, and I feel that the first five years are very important."

"How lucky you are to have someone to support you—emotionally and financially."

"I know."

They waited for a group of patients to walk past. Denise told Maggie about the new house she and Daryl were buying, the nursery they planned, and the fenced play area. The image of birds building a nest came to Maggie. All things great and small, same instincts. They seemed to go awry more often with people than with other species on Earth. The thinking animals messing up.

The rusty wheel of the wheelchair squeaked rhythmically as Denise began pushing it across the hall toward Thomas's room. Maggie dreaded the question she knew was coming.

"How many children do you have?"

"None."

"None?" As if she couldn't imagine not having children. There was a time when Maggie herself could not imagine not having children. What other purpose was there?

The heartache was like a wound ripped open, after all these years when it should have been long healed. "No, no children."

There was a time when she had answered, Yes. Oh, yes. With such love. Such deep, unconditional love.

She saw the telephone and said, "Stop please."

"Do you want to make a call?"

But she had already called once today to ask about Minnie. She would like to call again, and again before bedtime, just to hear that cheerful voice say, "Minnie is fine, don't you worry about her. We're taking good care of her."

"Eleanor!" the voice yelled hoarsely.

"Maybe I should go see Thomas instead. I can wait until tomorrow to call about my dog. She's in a kennel waiting for me."

"Oh, that's good." Denise turned the chair toward Thomas's door. "Did you know Thomas? I mean before he came here?"

"Never saw him before in my life."

Denise's voice took on amusement. Maggie could imagine her smile. "And you don't know who Eleanor is?"

"Not a bit."

Denise laughed. "Well, as long as it makes him happy to see you—and as long as it doesn't tire you out, I guess it's all right for him to think you're Eleanor."

"As long as it doesn't cause more problems for him."

"Oh no, he's better lately. You're good for him."

He was sitting up in his bed, knees peaked. His beetle eyes watched the door with irritation.

"Well, finally!" he said. Then, staring, "What are you doing in that wheelchair, Eleanor?"

"Sprained my ankle, Thomas," Maggie said. "I won't be sitting in this chair very long."

"Well I told you to look where you're walking. You always were an adventuresome child. Stepped in a hole, huh? What took you so long to come see me?"

COME SEE ME, the voice on the telephone had said in her dream those nights after Daddy died. Emmy, come see me.

Daddy, where are you?

His voice had faded over the telephone line and she couldn't hear. In her dream she thought of Florida. He had always said he'd like to go to Florida. Was he in Florida now? Yet that couldn't be. Daddy, she said, I thought you were dead.

He replied in a clear voice, No, I'm not dead! She woke, the vivid dream replaying in her mind. It had replayed in her mind many times in the years since, that strange, clear dream that had been repeated for several weeks, in which she answered a ringing telephone to hear her daddy say, "Emmy, come see me."

WHEN MAGGIE RETURNED to her room a few minutes later, Florence and Hazel were waiting to hear what had gone on.

Maggie told them, "It's getting obvious that Eleanor was a child, probably his daughter. Once, I asked him who Eleanor was, and he completely ignored me. He doesn't want me in a role other than who he thinks I am."

Denise said, "She tried to talk about the weather and he didn't act as if he heard her."

"So what did he talk about?" Florence asked.

"He went to sleep," Denise said, laughing. "As soon as he bawled her out for spraining her ankle."

"Spraining her ankle!" Hazel said.

Denise told them Maggie's explanation for being in a wheelchair, then asked Maggie, "Want to go back to bed where you can stretch out a while before supper, or would you rather sit in the chair?"

A nurse in white with blue stripes on her cap entered with a tray of pills.

"Miss Maggie?" she asked, reading the name on the tiny cup.

"Yes."

"Pain pills?"

"Bring us all some pain pills," Florence said.

The nurse smiled. "Florence, you'd be dancing in the hall if you took one of these."

"What are they, cocaine?"

"Codeine."

"I'm willing to give it a try, ain't you, Hazel?"

Hazel rocked, leaning her head back against the chair, but Maggie glimpsed a reluctant grin.

"But," Florence said, "Maggie better not do any dancing, so she'd probably be better off lying down. Better put her into bed."

"I agree," the nurse said, and Maggie didn't refuse. She at times felt defeated by this weakness, this frustration as she began the transfer from wheelchair to bed. Yet she knew what others would say. You're expecting too much too soon.

"What are the side effects of those?" she asked.

"The list can be long," the nurse said after a pause. "But most people just feel relief from pain."

"Sleepiness? Weakness?"

"Possibly. If it bothers you, you need to speak to your doctor." She handed the little plastic cup containing two capsules to Maggie.

Maggie considered not taking them as she looked into the cup. But the pain, after her time up and the strain of movements, was pulsing through her hip and legs like lightning in a vicious storm.

Hazel said, "Better make sure you don't do too much getting about for awhile. I knowed one man who had a hip replaced, and he just wouldn't be still. He tried to do his work too soon and fell, and the whole thing tore right through his flesh. You talk about pain."

Maggie could see him, screaming on the ground, the new hip protruding through torn and bloody flesh.

Florence said, "My God a'mighty, Hazel, don't scare the poor girl to death."

The nurse said gently, "Most people do better with the replacement than they did with the original. At least the aches are gone, after the healing."

Maggie took the medication.

The nurses left, the wheelchair was gone, to be used somewhere else or folded against another wall. The soft, fragile pages of Hazel's Bible whispered like silk being caressed.

"Let me read you some Scripture, Florence."

"Well if you can't think of nothing better to do, Hazel, I guess it'd be all right."

Hazel began to read aloud in a monotone.

Across the room Clara sat watching the movements and tapping her fingers on the chair arms.

The door, closed behind the nurse when she left, began opening, so slowly it looked unreal. It appeared to have a life of its own, and moved so as not to be noticed. Hazel stopped reading. Both Clara and Florence stared at a spot about the height of a man's head. Maggie's muscles tightened.

The man who entered was a different stranger, thin, stooped, meek, mild, unsure of himself. His wild gaze darted about the room, then found Clara. She looked at him without emotion, as if she didn't know him.

He slipped silently to Clara. Looking back over his shoulder at the door he knelt in front of her on one knee. He put one hand on hers on the arm of the chair. She sat still, looking at him.

"Mother?" His soft voice was like a small boy's, pleading.

"Donnie?" A light softened her features, made her beautiful. A curl of her hair, touched with grey only as if it had been highlighted at an expensive salon, had fallen forward. She looked almost as young as her son. She put out a hand and touched his cheek. He clutched the hand and held it against him. Then he rose.

"I'm taking you home, Mother."

"Did Deana say I could go?"

"It doesn't matter. Deana's gone home. You're coming home too, where you belong. I can take care of you, Mother."

Her face underwent a miracle of changes. Emotions previously trapped flooded forth. Tears rolled into the smiling lips. She got up. "Goodbye," she said toward Hazel, Florence, Maggie. "It was nice knowing you."

They went out, his arm at her waist guiding her, their voices lingering.

"I have to get groceries—whatever you want to eat, Mother, but I'll take you home first so you can relax."

"Yes, Donnie, that will be fine."

Hazel and Florence exchanged startled looks.

"He's taking her home?" Florence said. "He didn't take her things."

"Maybe it's just for awhile."

"Didn't sound that way to me." They sat still, looking at each other, looking at Maggie, at the empty chair, at the door. Footsteps moved along the hall as always, coming, going.

Then Hazel said, "He can't take her home, her daughter brought her."

They began to discuss other patients who had come and gone during the months they both had been here, and came to a mutual conclusion.

"The daughter brought her," Hazel said. "Against the son's wishes. So he came to take her out."

Florence snorted. "The way my daughters brought me against my wishes. But I don't have a son to get me out."

There was a pause, then Hazel said, "One of these days my grandson will be here to get me."

"Well, Hazel," Florence said in surprising tenderness, "I hope he does."

The voices continued beyond Maggie's closed eyes. Hazel reading from the Bible. Florence making an occasional comment. Hazel's chair squeaked softly as she rocked.

Florence grew quiet, then began to snore.

Hazel raised her voice and kept reading, loudly.

MAGGIE REMEMBERED the packets of letters Sidney had kept while he was in the service, and when he was finally home had given to her. Letters of hers, plus one extra.

She could almost see the psychological working of his mind, now with this distance. His way of preparing her.

Chapter Fifteen

"I saved some of your letters," Sidney said, handing Emmy a large packet of envelopes tied together with a thin cord, Army olive green.

The war had ended three years ago and Sidney had finished both his school and his service enlistment. Sidney's mother and father were retiring from farming and moving into a new house in town. As prearranged, Emmy recently learned, they had given the farmhouse to their youngest son, Sidney. The land was given to their oldest son, David. David and Sue's house was across the section, a mile away, visible only as a few buildings, the newly planted trees too small yet to camouflage. Otherwise, nothing had changed since Emmy was here four years ago.

They were upstairs in his old bedroom, cleaning, rearranging. Movers, downstairs, clanged about, removing the furniture that Mother Alexander couldn't part with. All the arrangements had been made by letters and phone calls between Sidney and his parents. Emmy hadn't known of it until he came back to their apartment at the stateside camp where he was stationed after the war ended and told her, "I have a surprise for you."

"What?"

"We're going to be living in the old farmhouse. Isn't that great?"

He had waited for her excitement, but it wasn't exactly what she'd had in mind. She couldn't imagine the home where his parents lived as being hers. But he put an arm around her and began laying out their future. "Kids," he said. "We'll fill it with kids."

That was three months ago, and now everything had gone as Sidney planned, and they were home.

She was pleased about the letters he had saved. He had loved her enough to keep her letters while they were separated.

She sat on the bedroom floor and opened a letter she'd written not long after they were separated, four years ago. She read a few lines and cringed in embarrassment.

Had she been so dumb, so childish? Her handwriting childishly awkward, her grammar certainly wanting some editing. Good Lord, what if she had done what Sidney requested and not gone back to school? Why had he wanted to keep her that way?

She had no desire to delve into reasons. It was just Sidney, she told herself, when she was confused by his actions, the contradictory person that he seemed to be, one moment one way and the next moment the opposite. One moment kissing and hugging her, the next pushing her away as if he couldn't stand her.

She put the letter back without reading more and idly went through the packet as she would have a deck of cards.

In the middle of the packet the handwriting on an envelope stood out in brutal contrast to her own childish scrawls. Beautiful … fluid …

She knew before she slowly opened it whose handwriting it was. Even as she took the pages from the envelope she knew she shouldn't—couldn't read it. It was like slowly tearing a mask from her own eyes. Her marriage, her trust in his love—so tenuous at best—struggling to believe that the future would be great. That Sidney loved her …

She put the pages back unread into the envelope and sat staring out the window at the leaves of the tall tree beyond. A constant wind blew, twirling and rustling the leaves. Across the fields tumbleweeds blew, today loping along north, leaping like jack rabbits. In the winter they would go south. She remembered so well how the land had looked in the wintertime with its spots of snow like white scabs. She wasn't sure she liked it here at all, but here was where her future lay. In this very room there would be a nursery someday. Sidney had already planned it.

Four times in the years he'd been gone he had returned to the mainland and they'd had two weeks together. During the first furlough he'd whispered in her ear, "Let's have a baby." She began to visualize herself with an infant. Each time he had written afterwards, "Are you pregnant yet?"

He had built within her a desire that burned yearningly, growing with each month that her periods came as regularly as always. She laid the letters aside, all pleasure gone.

Then impulsively she took the letter on top—this letter he had left among hers intentionally or unintentionally—and pulled the pages out. 'Dearest Sid baby. It was so good to see you, to be in your arms again. I was afraid it would make our meetings more awkward once you'd married her. I want to see you as soon as possible so we can get back to making some kind of arrangement. I can't live without you, your lips, your arms. I don't know why I did that crazy thing with Jim, that made you do your crazy thing with her.'

She didn't read the rest. Footsteps were on the stairs, coming up. She stood up and turned just as Sidney entered the room. She felt sick, nauseated, her entire body consumed by this.

He stopped short at the sight of her face, then his eyes dropped to the letter. He snatched it out of her hands, glanced at it and stuffed it into his hip pocket.

"You've been seeing her!" Emmy accused, as if this were a new thought instead of an old fear from the wife of a young Mormon who didn't believe in the laws against polygamy.

"Don't make a fool of yourself, Emily, it doesn't become you." His eyes were blue ice, his voice a calm understatement.

"You met her somewhere! How long, Sidney, how many times?"

"Lower your voice."

"I saw the letter, Sidney."

"I don't give a damn what you saw. Forget it, okay?"

"I don't understand you." She began to weep in frustration. For three years she had lived obediently at home, writing to Sidney daily. After she finished high school she took a job in a library not far from her daddy's job, so she could have transportation. She hadn't danced once. Her only outlet had been the piano. "It just isn't fair!"

"You don't have to understand me. You're my wife, that's all there is to it. Mom wants to see you downstairs."

Her stomach revolted against the inability to express her anger and disappointment. She felt as if she would vomit. She turned away, her back to him, hiding her face. Suddenly there was no real future for her. She realized how deeply Sidney's dreams had become hers. It was his dreams she had followed since her marriage, Sidney's dreams of home and family that she had made her own.

Her choices were disheartening. She could go home to live with her parents, or she could stay and accept whatever decision Sidney made about their lives.

Sidney's hand gripped her arm and jerked her around. His face was set with anger. Hatred gave his eyes the surface of marble. The old cruelty was there again, changing the color, even the shape of his eyes.

"You're going to go downstairs," he said through his teeth, "And you're going to talk to Mom about that old cabinet she wants to know if you want, and you're going to tell her it's beautiful and you want it. Do you hear? And you're not going to say a goddamn thing about the letter."

Choices hammered through her mind again. She could go home and stay with her folks, or she could stay here. Even if there were a job she could get, she would have no transportation. She wanted a family, babies, a life of the only kind she knew.

She went downstairs, and she told her mother-in-law that the old china cabinet was beautiful and she would take good care of it.

She began the pretense of not knowing, not caring. She began the pretense of trusting her husband when he went to work each day and sometimes was late coming home.

On Sunday at church Gloria was there, beautiful as always. Her intimate smiles passed over Emmy's head to Sidney. Emmy didn't look to see the meeting of their eyes, the messages passing between them.

The hurting in her heart became a constant companion. She watched the tumbleweeds rolling on and on and longed for something she didn't have and could not even identify. The longing was deep and as constant as the pain. During the day when Sidney was away at work, she took long walks across the flat fields and along the roads, Midnight at her side. She worked in the vegetable garden. She cleaned house, keeping it as clean as Sidney's mother had, but the longing persisted.

Maybe all she needed was a baby.

Maggie put her hand to her eyes. After this long, it still hurt as it came to her mind, one incident after the other. It must be the medication, bringing it all back in such vivid detail—every emotion as painful now as then.

"What must be the medication?" Florence asked.

"Did I speak aloud?"

"You did. What about the medicine?"

"Just—my life running through my mind. As if I were drowning."

"I do the same thing," Florence said.

Hazel got up, went into the bathroom and closed the door. Florence leaned her head back and looked at the line between the wall and ceiling over Hazel's bed.

"I was just thinking today about my second husband. He was just about as handsome as a man can get, and I hung in there and hung in there while he flaunted his other women. I stayed married to him longer than any, except of course, my last."

"What is it with men that—"

"Women," Florence interjected.

Maggie laughed, and Florence joined her. Hazel returned, coming tall and stooped from the bathroom, using a couple of sheets of toilet paper to wipe her eyes.

"What's funny?"

Florence said, "We were just talking about men and how they can't let a new woman pass by without getting her into bed."

Hazel sat down with a long sigh. "You've knowed the wrong kind of men, Florence. My Jake was faithful all the sixty years of our marriage. He never looked at another woman."

"Hazel, you're dreaming."

"It is an abomination to the Lord to lust after women, and Jake would never have done such a thing."

"Well you're right, Hazel, I never knew men like that. My first one, I guess, was faithful. And, as far as that goes, probably my last one was. He was the one that helped me raise my girls, and I can tell you for sure I've got mixed feelings about him. He wasn't very work brittle."

Across the hall Thomas called, "Eleanor?"

"Woke up," Hazel muttered, opening her Bible.

"I married him partly because of them," Florence said. "I was tired of being— well—a lady of the night, and decided I wanted to stay home and raise my family. But I had to keep working anyway."

"And how did he like that?"

"How does any man like being supported?"

"But he helped you take care of the girls?"

"He did. And loved them. He was the only daddy they knew. But you know how it is when kids grow up. They forget all that. Not a one was there at the end. He's dead now."

Florence closed her eyes.

Hazel said, "The girls—they'll be back, Florence." Her voice was compassionate, soothing, as if she were talking to a child.

"My oldest is a grandmother several times over already. Got her own problems. She's about Maggie's age."

Maggie rearranged herself on the bed, pressed the button that lifted the top. The call came from across the hall, "Eleanor?"

"Well you can't run over there every time he calls." Hazel's voice was sharper and her words faster with irritation.

A nurse's footsteps in the hall had a sound different from the others. They were young and quick and soft-soled. They went into Thomas's room. Voices murmured along the hall, talking about the weather, other patients, relatives … fading away, replaced by others.

The nursing home was like a beehive, filled with its own kind of activity. Food cooked for supper, the kitchen not far away at the back of the left wing. Occasional smells wafted through like ribbons.

The walker was against the wall where the folded wheelchair had been. The sleepy heaviness was gone from her head, and Maggie stirred restlessly. She sat up and put her legs down off the bed. She had never liked lying down dressed as she was, in slacks and blouse.

"Where're you going?" Florence asked, alerted by her movements.

Maggie looked across at her blotched and sagging jaws, at the lips that still were full and was reminded of one of the most beautiful girls she had ever seen. Janna, half white, half black. Murdered at the age of … seventeen? Sixteen? She never knew Janna's age.

"I have to call about Minnie."

Hazel looked up from her Bible. "Better call a nurse." Florence rose from her chair with a grunt, her movements slow and heavy.

"What are you going to do, try the walker?"

"Yes. It isn't far to the telephone. And," she added uncustomarily, unused to expressing her feelings to anyone but Minnie, "I feel if I don't move I'll get so stiff I can't."

"Well, we don't want that to happen," Florence said with a humorous quirk in the corners of her mouth. "Hazel and me'd have to haul you around like a board. Here, wait a minute, I'll give you a hand."

Maggie stood up, balancing on her good leg. She remembered the story about the man with the replacement falling, and the thing tearing through the flesh. Florence handed the walker to her.

Hazel said, "I still think you'd better call a nurse. Here, I'll do it." She reached for her own line to the front desk and pressed the call button. A small light came on over her bed, and another over the door into the hall.

At that moment the nurse emerged from Thomas's room, her footsteps an audio image of her movements. In the hall she paused, then she came across to the room with the light on. She entered, glanced at Florence and Maggie, and passed by to turn off Hazel's light.

"It's our kid," Florence said. "She's bound and determined to break that hip all over again." Florence moved out of the way, and returned to her chair. She sat watching critically as the nurse moved slowly with Maggie toward the hall.

Then suddenly the nurse stopped, looking about in the room. She went to the bathroom, looked in, came back and stood with perplexity expressed in her eyes.

"Where's the new lady?"

"She went out with her son."

"Went with her son," Hazel repeated.

"Her son!"

"What's wrong?" asked Florence and Hazel.

"I don't think she was supposed to go anywhere with her son."

"He said he was taking her home." The nurse looked about as if somehow Clara would reappear.

Across the hall Thomas called, "Eleanor!"

"Will you be all right a minute?" the nurse asked Maggie, "I'll just run down to the desk and be right back."

"Of course."

Secure in her walker, Maggie stood. The nurse ran, her footsteps soft but fast.

Florence and Hazel exchanged a long look. "What do you suppose that's all about?"

"The daughter brought her in, the son didn't like it, I'd say." Maggie put her weight on her right leg and eased the walker forward. Rage against this whole thing immersed her in frustration. You've got no patience, Emily, Mommy used to say. You want everything right now. You'd get along a lot better in this world if you'd just accept things as they are.

Maybe Mom was right.

Over the years she had remembered every criticism her mother had leveled at her, and had tried to change. She had developed what she thought was a very intelligent philosophy about aging. Relax. Accept. Enjoy. But the philosophy had proved insubstantial and melted into the rage, the helplessness.

Though she struggled to relax, her chest tightened, the nerve endings in her body tingled, her breath shortened and her heart began to race.

Oh God, not a panic attack.

Breathe deeply. Move, if it kills you. No, no, no. Minnie needs you. Behind her Florence and Hazel's voices speculated about Clara and Clara's son and daughter. Across the hall Thomas called for Eleanor.

Maggie's breath came more easily. She took another step forward.

She made it through the door and to the telephone. The contact with Minnie, even with distance and people between them, made her feel more in control. If only Minnie could know.

Minnie in her little cage, being fed dogfood, not chopped, baked turkey and mixed vegetables with a vanilla wafer for dessert, not even comforted by the knowledge that the only person who had ever cared for her was here, calling.

"How's Minnie?"

"Oh Minnie's just fine."

Just fine … just fine. "Tell her I'm coming to get her. As soon as I can go home and get my car out of the garage. As soon as I get out of here."

Chapter Sixteen

"**I**'m pregnant."

The expression of irritation disappeared from Sidney's face, and he rose from his desk and came toward her. It had been years since she had entered his office because she knew he didn't like her to come here. He had an old-fashioned view of a wife's place. He wanted her at home. Kitchen-bound.

Today she'd gone to the doctor, just as she had regularly every month for so many months she had lost count. Sidney had promised to meet her for lunch, but she couldn't wait.

He took her gently into his arms and held her, his cheek resting on the top of her head. He said nothing.

She thought she understood how he felt. Tired. Just so tired. The news was too long in coming.

She murmured, "I just feel like sitting down somewhere and sitting there, I'm so tired of waiting for this day. Waiting to be pregnant."

"Then that's what you should do. Go home, kick back, watch TV."

Television was new in their old farm house. They had been married almost eleven years. The war was far behind them. The years since seemed to have been filled with one goal. Pregnancy. The longer it took the quieter and less sociable she became. Where she once had enjoyed conversations with her sisters-in-law and her own sisters, these past few years had changed that. They talked of pregnancy, of babies, then of children and how to handle the things that to Emily seemed so small. Problems that would have been good to have.

Janice's two year old was still messing his pants now and then. A shy little darling, he'd sneak behind something and squat, and the look on his face revealed what he was doing.

"He just won't listen!" Janice would proclaim as she dragged him toward a bathroom to unload.

But she had even less patience now that babies were nothing new to her. She'd had her third. She liked to say that Jennifer, the one year old, and Troy, the five year old, both were potty trained by the age of ten months.

Conversations with Peggy and Rebba were similar. In these days of everyone having a telephone, Emmy called them each once a week and listened as they told about their babies, now grown into active children. Peggy had three and said she wanted no more. Rebba had her second and was pregnant again.

"You have to have three, you know," she said, "to fully appreciate the difference in personalities. Three. Kids hardly ever take after their parents in personality, have you ever noticed that? A little quirk here, a little quirk there maybe, but no one is very much like their parents."

So you have to have at least three children.

Sidney wanted progeny, as many as possible. He believed in replenishing the earth. From what? Dinosaurs? He read his Bible nightly and liked to read to her the verses about no man casting his seed on the ground. Her opinion of all he read to her grew increasingly incredulous. How could an intelligent man believe that this was written by any but another horny man?

Once, years ago, she had said to Sidney, "Did God take into consideration that all this seed he supposedly made amounts to the billions? You don't expect every one of them to take root, do you, Sidney?" And she had laughed. Tis' better to put your seed inside a whore, than to spill it upon the ground.

He had looked at her with terrible disgust, and said coldly,

"You just don't get it, do you, Emily?"

She never again expressed her opinion. Why bother? She was the infidel in a large family of believers.

At family dinners, almost always in the old house in the country, the gathering was noisy. Kids running everywhere. Mom and Pop Alexander gleaming. And without fail Pop would say, at the big dinner table, "When are you and Emmy going to add to the family tree, Sidney?"

Driving the stake into her heart.

She'd spend hours cooking, then hours cleaning up, and be glad of the chance to be busy. But she'd look forward to them leaving, and afterwards as Sidney usually went back to the office to take care of something or other, or simply put his feet up and watched TV, she'd walk into the fields, the dog at her side.

Midnight, she'd named him when it seemed he had no name worthy of him. He had fur as soft as the fur of a seal, and as shiny black as onyx except for a couple of brilliant white spots on his face. He'd grown to weigh about seventy pounds, and walked solemnly beside her wherever she went, summer, winter, in rain or snow or hot sunshine.

She'd found a place to sit just weeks ago as snow blew around her, and Midnight sat down against her. She put her arm around him as always and they sat together. He who wouldn't preach to her of a God as cruel as man. When she wept he nuzzled her cheek. Sad and empty, emotions calmed, she rose and went home, Midnight walking beside her.

She thought of that day three weeks ago as she drove home. She'd been pregnant then, but hadn't known it.

Pregnant.

She put a hand to her belly, and felt no change. But the changes were there in other ways. Sharp stings that ran through her breasts and escaped at the nipples. Stings so quick and unexpected that she'd grab her breast before she thought what she was doing. No matter who was around.

She had mentioned that to the doctor today and he laughed.

There were worse things she could grab, he said.

She was actually having a baby? Her own baby?

Somehow she couldn't visualize herself with a baby. No matter how she tried, she couldn't place a baby in that nursery at home, Sidney's old room, or anywhere in the house. Not her baby.

"It's true," she spoke aloud to herself, "it's true. I know it's true."

Yet, the image didn't materialize.

At home she parked the car in the garage, got out and patted Midnight's head. He was about twelve years old now, old for his breed of dog, part black Lab. He walked slowly beside her.

A frigid wind swept out of the north, tumbling tumble weeds south. They piled up in ditches and crossed the roads. Where there was a fence they stopped until they'd piled high enough to roll on over.

Midnight went into the house with her and headed straight for the bed she'd made for him behind the old stove that burned coal. She kept a fire in it, even though she used an electric stove for cooking. The fire was for Midnight, and for herself and the memory of old times when in her childhood the cookstove had warmed the houses she'd lived in.

Those houses, that kind of living here and there, even in tents at times, were unknown to Sidney. They had nothing to talk about when they were alone, because he liked to talk about people he'd grown up with, of lifestyles different from hers. He enjoyed conversations with his sisters, brother, parents, friends. They talked of old times, and Emmy sat quietly, no longer listening. Her old times were so different from his.

He didn't like having Midnight in the house.

"Is that dog in here again?" he usually said when he reached home in the evening.

"He's getting old. The weather is cold."

But tonight Sidney didn't even look at the dog. He came to Emmy and held her tenderly again, as he had in the office. She drew a long, tired sigh.

"You need to rest more now. When the house needs cleaning, I'll hire someone."

She knew he would say no more about it, other things filled his mind. But it didn't matter. The housework wasn't a problem to her. She had as much energy as ever.

She didn't have the morning nausea that had plagued Janice and Peggy. Instead she awoke with a ravishing appetite. One morning she baked two cherry pies, and ate one of them.

Then, appalled at what she had done she sat looking at the empty pie plate as if the pie would reappear. She felt horribly fat. Even worse, she was still hungry.

She had hot flashes in the evening. The back of her neck burned.

Her breasts had stinging pains, right out through the nipples. She grabbed them instinctively as if she were a primitive grabbing at the site of a piercing arrow.

She took long walks with the dog, watching as he took half-hearted chases after the tumbleweeds. If a jackrabbit leaped and ran he just stood at her side and watched it go. It had been many years since he'd given them a good chase. His face was turning grey, the white hairs forming circles around his eyes.

She didn't feel pregnant. Her stomach was flat, her hipbones slightly protruding as they had since she'd become an adult, her waist curved inward as always. Only her breasts seemed to have changed, being more forward, larger, the nipples darker and more erect. Sidney enjoyed sucking them, a sensation she didn't enjoy. She felt like pushing his head away angrily and telling him it was the baby to whom those belonged, not a man six-feet four. Sometimes she turned away, murmuring they were tender, she was sleepy, or tired. Sometimes she dreaded going to bed and wished she dared sleep in a guest room.

She plied the doctor with questions at her second, third and fourth monthly visit. "Are you sure I'm pregnant?"

"Of course I'm sure."

"Why is it I don't have symptoms like other women?"

"What other women?"

He was busy at the sink taking off the rubber gloves with which he'd probed her interior. She sat up, getting her skirt down again.

"My sister-in-law, Janice. My sisters."

"Not everyone has morning sickness. Some women are nauseated all day long. For months. Be thankful you're not one of them."

"I wake up hungry. I've never woke up hungry before in my life. I never liked breakfast."

"You're eating for two."

"So you're sure."

"Yes." He laughed. "Now go home and eat. We'll watch your weight and tell you when to slow down on the calories."

She tried to feel pregnant. She had wanted a baby for so long that the yearning seemed part of her, never to be fulfilled.

She walked with Midnight, sat with Midnight, talked to Midnight as he lay at her feet. To control her eating she fed him part of the pie she baked and served herself. Then sat watching him eat. He nosed aside the fruit and ate only the crust. Her favorite part too. Then she had the dream. The vision, as she came to think of it.

SHE IS STANDING STILL, suspended in time. In front of her a hillside slopes upward. On it flowers of a thousand beautiful colors, colors she has never seen before, bloom thickly, a carpet of color and texture and shape. In the midst of the flowers sits a baby girl, leaning forward, smiling down at her. The baby's hair is a cap of golden curls. Her eyes are heavenly clear and innocent and trusting. She smiles a toothless welcome.

Light surrounds her, a halo of rainbows, interchanging, the colors of the flowers reflecting within its endless depth. The feeling is of all purity, all ecstasy, all happiness existing at once, reaching her with the baby's smile—her smile of recognition—as if they've been together in many ways, many times before.

EMMY WOKE, breathless with the beauty of the vivid dream. The baby girl was so real, if she went into the nursery she surely would be there, asleep in the crib.

No, no. She belonged in the field of flowers.

Emmy lay thinking of this strange dream and the few others before that held this same beautiful quality. In many ways they seemed more like marvelous works of art, waiting for her interpretation. The brilliance and clarity astounded her and remained with her not only during the days following each rare dream, but forever. She remembered her earlier vivid dreams, so strange, and was puzzled still by them, as if somewhere in her mind there was an answer. An answer she couldn't reach.

She told no one about the dream, but she lived in it as if it were her only reality, still bathed by the beautiful light within it, the colors her human eyes couldn't see. The soul of that child. The living beauty of the flowers, the colors, the moving light, the forever light, the exquisite happiness. So real, and yet so different from anything she had ever seen.

A spring-like day came in March, and she sat on the back step with Midnight and soaked up the warmth of the sun. She was five months pregnant now. She suddenly felt movement, as if something within her belly turned over.

"Oh my God," she whispered to Midnight, clutching the fur at his neck. "She moved. She's there, Midnight. She's real!"

She hadn't really believed it, she realized. She hadn't thought this could happen to her, this ultimate purpose for being on earth.

She went around in a sunny daze, although she felt nothing more. It would happen—it would happen again. That marvelous feeling of light, of visualizing the turn of the tiny, growing body.

At her next examination there was a look on the doctor's face that stopped something within her. The flicker of a frown, a difference in his touch. He said nothing as he moved to the sink to wash his hands.

"What's wrong?" she finally asked, reluctant even to voice a negative question, to admit to herself that something—something was different.

She heard him sigh, but still he said nothing. He knew how much she and Sidney wanted a baby, several babies, a large family of their own. He had done so many procedures over the years, even to examining Sidney's sperm for viability. He had always come to the same puzzled conclusion. "I don't know why you're not getting pregnant. I can't find a thing wrong with either of you."

"What's wrong?" she pleaded now.

"I don't know. There's been no growth."

"But I felt it move just the other day!"

He shook his head. "There's been no growth. Let's wait a couple of weeks, then see again."

Her symptoms ended. The hunger was gone, the sting in her nipples gone. Before the two weeks ended she knew there was no baby. He said, after his examination, "We have to go in and see what's wrong. I'm afraid we may have to do a D and C, scrape it out. We may have to do exploratory surgery."

She sat there—as she'd been sitting lately at home as she realized the baby was dead. Just sitting. Sitting, staring. Midnight silent beside her.

Then he said, "Don't worry. This may be the answer. We'll find out what the problem is and fix it."

She packed a small suitcase that night and sat alone with Midnight.

When she'd told Sidney that the baby was dead inside her, he turned away. She told him of the surgery, her voice a monotone, emotions raging inside her. Talking to his back, a large, immovable barrier, feeling unheard.

He didn't reply. He stood a moment longer, then shrugged and began to undress for bed. When he got into bed he turned his back to her. She understood that perhaps he was hurting too, the disappointment eating him up, but she needed his arms around her.

It would be a cold night.

So she went downstairs and sat on the floor with Midnight near his bed behind the stove. But she couldn't cry. There was a helplessness, a stillness in her that had grown over the years, something that seemed to separate her from the human race.

She wouldn't be having this baby after all.

The vision of the baby in the flowers on the hillside sustained her, the memory of the dream sharp and clear and filled with a marvelous beauty that caught her breath in her throat.

She stared into her memory of the dream, trying never to let go.

Chapter Seventeen

Emmy regained a kind of dark, lost consciousness on the operating table and heard the doctor's voice say, "Doesn't this girl have anyone at all in this hospital? We can't leave her open all day."

Neither time nor space existed. She floated in darkness. She came to consciousness again, drifting on the borders of darkness, of a deep hole that went like a tunnel into forever. She tried to rise and found her body immovable, as heavy as a log.

She heard her voice, a gagged and muffled sound hardly human, words running together in a long mumbling groan. "I have to get out of here." The darkness wouldn't go away, wouldn't release her.

"You'd fall flat on your face," a female voice answered reprovingly.

She hadn't known she wasn't alone.

The next time she regained consciousness she saw light, windows in a wall above the grey, accordion iron of a steam heater. There was a curtain between her and someone who moaned in pain on and on. Other voices there spoke softly. Then a dark-haired, plump woman a few years older than Emmy looked around the curtain at her.

"Ah, you're awake."

Emmy nodded her head and immediately began to gag, nausea erupting with movement. She slapped a hand to her mouth and tried to rise. Pain ripped through her belly, and she reached down to touch bandages.

The woman came quickly to her side and slid a little half-moon-shaped vessel to her mouth. Vomit drooled. The woman dampened a washcloth and gave it to her. Emmy fell back trembling, the cold cloth to her mouth.

"What did they do to me?" she mumbled through the cloth.

"You've had surgery. Didn't you know you were going to?"

She swallowed. The nausea rose when she tried to talk. No, not for sure. I didn't know for sure. No! She had wanted out of there, so desperately.

"Just lie still," the woman said. "You'll be fine. The sickness is from the anesthetic. It'll wear off."

"Are you a nurse?" Emmy managed to ask.

"No. My name is Wanda. But I've had surgery, I know how it feels."

The moans grew louder beyond the curtain and there was a kind of desperate movement. Wanda cast a hurried glance in that direction. "That's my mother. Do you want me to call a nurse for you?"

Emmy shook her head, and suffered another spasm of nausea. Wanda disappeared beyond the curtain.

Emmy lay as still as she could to avoid being sick again, her eyes closed. Then she heard the familiar voice of her doctor.

"How're you doing?"

She opened her eyes. "Sick."

"Okay, we'll give you something for that. The nurse will be in later with an injection, okay?"

She didn't nod, but tried to smile instead.

"You're fine." He patted her leg and hurried out. Too fast, she thought later, when she knew. Sidney came in the evening and held her hand, kneaded her hand nervously between his own and told her about a terrible day. "I got tied up in court and couldn't get away—"

Hadn't he known her operation, the D and C, or the exploratory, had been scheduled for eight o'clock? He had left her here yesterday, in a different room, kissed her goodbye, and hadn't looked back. He had seemed in a hurry then, and she'd felt the old ache in her heart. Gloria? She'd heard rumors of Gloria over the years. Gloria married again. Then, Gloria divorced again. Sometimes months would go by and she'd not hear Gloria's name, then suddenly it would come up again, mentioned among the family members, never to her, but within her hearing.

She hadn't been afraid last night.

Only today, when she had regained consciousness in the operating room had she felt a desperate fear, a need to escape.

"How's Midnight?" she asked Sidney.

He looked at her as if she had caused him to lose his train of thought. Then he said, "Oh, okay."

During her five days in the hospital she learned that her roommate, whom she never saw, was dying of cancer of the lung. She was in her early fifties and was the mother of seven daughters. Six of them were at her bedside night and day. The youngest didn't bother to come except once, though the mother called for her constantly between moans. Then on the fifth day she was there, standing before the dresser against the wall at the foot of the beds, combing her long, black hair.

She was beautiful. Seventeen years old. She reminded Emmy of Gloria.

Then she was gone as quickly as she had come.

"She's Mama's favorite," Wanda told Emmy. "The baby, you know."

No one came to see Emmy. Until then she hadn't realized how few friends she had. She had lived in Sidney's shadow, using his friends, his family. She tried not to be hurt that none of them chose to visit her. After all, she told herself, she'd had to go to another town to its hospital. The hospital in her own small town wasn't equipped for the kind of surgery the doctor had said she might need.

On the fifth day the doctor entered her part of the room with a nurse who carried a tray.

"Your stitches are coming out," he said as he removed the heavy bandage. "And you can go home."

She breathed a sigh of relief. Home, to Midnight, to her piano. To her walks in the fields, to her music. To Sidney, and her life.

She felt the tickle of each stitch being removed. The doctor bent over her, talking. It occurred to her she had not asked questions.

"We had to do exploratory surgery because we found infection. Your tubes were infected, and the little hairs that push an egg to the uterus were destroyed. If you had become pregnant now, it would have been an ectopic pregnancy, and your life would have been in danger."

She lay still, inside and out, staring up at him. She hadn't asked questions, because she had assumed everything was all right.

"We tried to find someone from your family to give us permission to take out your tubes, but no one was here, so—well—we had to save your life."

He had finished removing the stitches. He replaced the large bandage with a small one. "You'll never be able to have a baby."

She covered her eyes with her hands. She couldn't cry. Nor scream. Nor make a sound. She could only sink beneath this ultimate cruelty, this taking away of her purpose for living.

She wanted to scream, scream, but she could only lie as someone stiffened by death, the scream silent inside her.

You'll never be able to have a baby.

She was alone, more alone than she'd ever been. She heard the doctor and nurse leave. "I'm sorry," he said once, and was gone. She would see him one more time, one more checkup, and then no more. No one could help her now.

She felt a gentle touch on her arm.

"I know how you feel," Wanda said softly. "A similar thing happened to me. I had a hysterectomy when I was only twenty-five. I can't have babies either. Go ahead and cry."

She couldn't cry.

Not until that night when she was home and in bed. Sidney held her in his arms as she cried through the night. As morning came he said to her, "I promise you something, Emmy. I will get you a baby."

She had no hopes. She knew the difficulty of getting a baby. Once, three years ago she had gone to the adoption agency and learned the wait was several years.

The tears dried, and became a hard and permanent ache within her. She walked the fields with Midnight at her side and lifted her face to the sky, calling out, crying out against this final hurt.

"God help me, please. Give me a purpose. Give me a purpose, please, God. Don't do this to me."

She spent hours at the piano, Midnight at her side, her music sobbing into the house where it seemed she lived mostly alone.

… her soul into this music … everything that she was …

The summer passed, autumn came, and the snows began to fall. Tumbleweeds raced south, but Midnight no longer looked at them with interest. He walked stiffly and slowly. She gave him bits of painkiller for his arthritis. Spring came again, bringing birds and warmer days.

She had stopped calling home so often. Rebba and Peggy were busy with their own families now. Mom and Daddy were alone. Grandma, homesick for her childhood home and sisters who lived there, had gone back home to live. Mom complained that Daddy, now approaching sixty, was going to die of lung cancer because all he did was drink coffee and smoke unfiltered Camels, one after the other.

Still, the call from home was unexpected, a shock to Emmy. Peggy's voice was strained. "You'd better come, Emmy. Daddy's in the hospital. He's had a stroke."

"I'll be there tonight," she said, and broke off the connection. She dialed Sidney's office, and was told he wasn't in.

"Do you want to leave a message, Emily?"

"No, I'll just leave a note. My dad's in the hospital, very sick. I'll be gone before Sidney gets home."

She packed a few things hastily, and left Midnight outside. On the note she wrote only, "Take care of Midnight. I don't know when I'll be back."

She drove west and south, stopping only for gas. The night closed her in among the big trees in the mountains in Oregon and Northern California. She dropped down into the valley and exceeded the speed limit when it was safe.

It was one-thirty when she entered the hospital. They were gathered in the hallway outside his room, Rebba and her tall, gangly husband, Peggy and her shorter, rounder husband, and Mom. Mom, who Emmy thought of in her heart always as Mommy, even though as an adult she no longer called her that. She saw Mom's tears as she came to hold Emmy and weep on her shoulder.

Peggy bit her trembling lower lip, her eyes red.

"He's gone," Mom said, voice quivering. "We went down to the cafeteria for a bite to eat, and he seemed all right. He was asleep. While we were there they called us back."

Peggy's husband said, "A nurse went in and found that he had stopped breathing."

"I don't know when he died," Mom wept. "He might have been dead when I left him!"

Emmy stepped toward the closed door. "I want to see him!"

She had to see him. She must see him.

At that moment two nurses came out of the room and closed the door behind them.

"That's my daddy in there. I want to see him!"

"We'd rather you didn't," one of the nurses said, and unaccountably stood between her and the door, keeping her from going in.

She was desperate to reach him, as though a whisper of life hovered near him, enough she could cling to. That's my daddy in there.

It was Mom who stopped her, Mom with her need now for comfort. For Emmy. For all her children.

She didn't see him until the next day at the funeral home when his polished oak and silver coffin was placed in a small flower-filled room. In all his life he'd never had anything so fine.

Emmy slipped away and spent indelible time alone in the room with him, seeing him dressed in a dark suit, his arms folded peacefully. The smell of the flowers surrounded them. She sat with him, while at home relatives gathered. Sometimes she talked softly to him, telling him about her life. Telling him about her dead baby, the baby who had never lived anywhere but in a dream.

Sidney flew down for the funeral, and drove her car home while she leaned against the car door and stared at the scenery. Summer had replaced spring here in the Sacramento valley and the foothills were brown and dry.

Over the mountains north the air grew colder, and the wind strong. Patches of snow had not yet melted under the warming sun of spring.

They drove down the long driveway to the house, and Midnight didn't come to meet them.

When she walked from the garage across to the house, still Midnight didn't come.

"Where's Midnight?" she asked.

Sidney said nothing. He was looking down at the ring of keys in his hand, searching for the house key, as he walked towards her. The wind blew his grey suit jacket open, and whipped the striped tie over his shoulder.

"Where's Midnight?" she demanded, searching for possibilities. Had he gone across the mile-long field to Sidney's brother's house? Alone, lonesome? Searching for human company?

Sidney ran ahead of her up the porch steps, the house key ready. As she climbed the steps she saw that Midnight's blankets from behind the stove had been dumped on the porch.

She stopped, staring at the pile.

"Where's Midnight? What is his bedding doing out here on the porch?"

Sidney said, "He was old, Emily. He was in misery."

"What did you do with Midnight?" she cried out.

"I had him put to sleep." Then, as he opened the door and stood back for her to enter, he said, "I have to run in to the office for awhile."

She screamed after him. "You had no right! He was my dog! He was my dog! I took care of him, Sidney ... you had no right ... no right ..."

But Sidney was gone, backing his car around and leaving her without looking back. Running away from the sound of her voice. She went through the lonely house to the music room. She imagined Midnight's footsteps followed her. He stretched out at the end of the piano bench and sighed, as he always had, and she began to play. Soft music for Midnight. Soft music for herself, to fill the hollow darkness in her heart.

Chapter Eighteen

Maggie sat on the side of her bed, preparing to get down herself without aid.

"Now, don't you fall. You remind me of my middle daughter. A daredevil. She'd jump off of the river bridge if I told her she better not," Florence said.

You're stubborn and bullheaded, Mom had told her more than once. Always have to do things your own way.

The walker was just beyond her bedside table. Why was it always just out of reach? As if when she turned her back the little invisible devil that followed her around moved it deliberately. But if she could stand, she could hobble over to the walker by holding to the bedside table. A step for Minnie.

"At least let me hand you the walker," Florence said, starting to rise. She stopped, easing back into her chair, her eyes going to someone entering at the half open door.

Hazel looked up from her Bible. "Come on in. She's right over there." She motioned toward Maggie.

Maggie grew wary and tense. So many years now she had lived in the silence of her own home, where the only voices were on radio or television, or her own voice talking to Minnie. A stranger entering her door made her feel vulnerable and nervous.

It could only be her doctor. Or …

"You got company, Maggie," Florence said, her voice sparked with a teasing lilt, such as she used on Hazel. The smile widened.

She smelled the flowers before she saw him.

He came softly around the door, his head first, forward, looking for her. He was carrying a large bouquet of mixed flowers.

The man who had walked down the hall with her yesterday. A man who might know she was not Maggie Winters, but Emmy Alexander. Her pulses quivered. She grew weak and eased back, her feet dangling several inches above the floor. He came forward silently, timidly from outward appearance. But she knew the deceptive ways of killers, the ability to charm, the boyishness in eyes that felt nothing for the victim.

This man had the same unreadable eyes, light and steady. Though his hair had thinned, he wasn't wearing a hairpiece. Instead he had carefully brushed it back. He hadn't tried to cover the bald spot with hair from the sides.

Today he was dressed in inexpensive clothes off the rack. The only bright spot was a tie with geometric figures in a variety of colors.

"How are you today?" he asked.

She watched him uneasily. So much about him so deliberately ordinary today. Yesterday the suit he had been wearing had looked expensive. If he had come to find her, he would have known that to wear expensive clothes here would make her suspicious of him.

He said, "I came back because I wanted to see you again." His eyes met Maggie's unwaveringly as if he had nothing to hide. She had always thought a human's soul showed in the eyes—kindness, or cruelty. But she had found she could be fooled. She didn't answer him, nor turn her eyes away from his. She tried to find a glimpse into his soul, the truth of his visits.

She was aware of her roommates, watching. Florence was still grinning, but Hazel watched soberly.

"I picked these from my own garden," he said.

Maggie watched his eyes. They were outwardly friendly, with little creases at the corners. He reminded her of any man she would have met in any crowd—in a Mormon church, or a middle-class San Francisco nightclub.

Florence said, "That was nice of you, wasn't it Maggie? You must have a pretty garden."

Maggie realized she hadn't spoken to him. Florence and Hazel both gave her puzzled and critical looks. Why are you so unfriendly, their stares asked.

"Well," he said, "I work in it a good deal. Somebody's going to bring me a vase."

He came closer to Maggie.

"They're beautiful," she said, hearing her voice low and hesitant. Perhaps—perhaps he was a once-married single man, with a home here in town, with a garden he tended. The flowers were lovely. Blue salvia, lemon yellow snapdragons, red dahlias.

Exactly like the ones in her own flower garden.

She felt him watching her as she stared at the flowers. The iced fingers of fear started on the backs of her arms and encircled her.

"You don't mind if I bring you flowers?" he asked Maggie, smiling easily.

Florence said, "We'll enjoy them, all of us, thank you. What did you say your name is?"

"Mart," he said. "Martin Stanley."

One of the nurse's aides entered at that moment with a large vase and helped the man arrange the flowers. Her footsteps joined others in the hall on her way out. The man who said his name was Martin placed the vase of flowers on Maggie's bedside table.

"You're not allergic to anything like this, are you?" he asked Maggie.

She shook her head. She wanted to ask, what flower garden?

Oh, no," Hazel offered. "We breathe worse than flowers around here. Thank you very much. You've gone to a lot of trouble."

"I just thought you might enjoy them."

Florence asked, "Where do you live?"

"Ah—over in the Spring Valley area."

"Those are fairly new places, aren't they? Have you been here very long?

"A few years now."

"Where'd you come from?"

"Up north."

"Where up north?"

"Ummm—Ohio."

"Ah, where the Amish live?"

"Well ..."

Hazel interrupted, "Good people. Serve the Lord righteously."

Florence continued, her eyes bright and friendly, simply curious, "Are you a widower, or what?"

The man moved, almost shuffling his feet. He was beginning to look decidedly uncomfortable. Maggie began to be amused. Prick a blister, she thought. He had some soft, sore spots, and being cornered by Florence was one.

He began edging toward the door. Beyond him Maggie saw Hazel and Florence rocking. On Hazel's lap the black leather-covered Bible lay open. Florence wore a pleased smile. He evidently had passed some kind of test. Yet at the last, as he looked to escape through the door, he had failed to answer Florence's last question.

He turned and was gone beyond the edge of the door. She listened to his footsteps fading along the hall. He had gone toward the front.

"Well!" Florence snorted. "Did you hear all that? You got to ask some questions, girl. He sounds like a good catch. Lives in an expensive location. Here you've got a boyfriend and you act like you can't give him the time of day!"

Hazel began to rock. She let out a breath like a sniff, but didn't voice her opinion.

Florence said, "There for awhile I didn't think you were even going to thank him for the flowers."

She hadn't.

Maggie stared at the flowers, as if she would be able to recognize blooms from plants she had nurtured. She could visualize the intrusion, the backyard gate opening, the stranger in the grey silk suit entering, walking through the grass, going up the steps down which she had fallen. Then he would have entered a back door that no one had locked. Or, easily picking the lock, opening the door and walking through her house, searching carefully through the drawers in search of whatever it was they thought she had. Searching so that she, or anyone, would never know someone had searched. He would have found most of the draperies drawn, and no photographs in frames on the mantel. He would have found nothing to indicate she was anyone but Maggie Winters. That she had ever had another life.

She could see him going back outside, then with a smile to himself, gathering this bouquet of flowers from her garden.

"You could have at least told him to come back again," Florence persisted.

Maggie said nothing. She had lost interest in trying to reach her walker.

Her hip ached. She turned back onto the bed and carefully curled up on her good side. She began rubbing her left hip and leg slowly. Florence's voice flowed over her.

"If I was your age, with your health and your looks, and a man came calling on me, I'd make a husband out of him. Just think—you're needing someone to live with you for awhile, right? Well, girl, you just let him walk out the door."

Hazel began to read aloud, "And the Lord said."

Maggie's thoughts went back, drawn into the past, as if it were necessary to live again the pain she had tried to forget.

THE DREAM CAME upon Emmy as clearly as if she were awake.

The phone rings, and she picks it up. Daddy speaks to her, his voice close and lucid. "Emmy, come see me."

"Daddy!" She feels startled surprise at hearing his voice, so real, yet carrying a tone of anxiety.

He speaks again hastily, "Come see me, Emmy."

"Daddy—where are you?"

His voice begins fading, growing farther and farther away, becoming unintelligible. She can't understand where he is.

Emmy woke and lay staring at the ceiling. The dark silence in the house seemed to vibrate with the ring of the phone she had heard in her strange, realistic dream. Beside her Sidney slept deeply.

She didn't tell him, the next day, of the dream. She had so little to say to him, to anyone, these days. The dream came again exactly two weeks later.

"Emmy, come see me."

"Daddy! Where are you?"

The same words again, the fading of his voice as he tried to tell her again …

Then again two weeks later. And again, always separated by two weeks, always the same words.

Four times the dream came. But the fourth time there was a change. One thing different. "Come see me, Emmy."

"Daddy, I thought you were dead."

"No, I'm not dead!" Frustration cried in his voice. "Come and see me."

"Where are you, Daddy?"

"I'm in …" His voice went on, unintelligible, drifting farther and farther away.

She woke, his voice repeating and repeating in her mind. Beside her Sidney turned as if disturbed by this recurrence of her dream, then grew still, snoring evenly. She stared at the faint light beyond the window and relived once more the strange, vivid dream. Unlike most of her vivid dreams, this one was disturbing, puzzling.

Unable to go back to sleep Emmy got up and went downstairs to the kitchen. All signs of the bedding that had been behind the stove were gone. She had washed Midnight's blankets and put them away in a closet. With permanent, unshed tears in her heart she went to the music room and closed the door. Sidney's parents had not taken the piano when they moved. Mother Alexander had said, "Let Emmy have it. She's the only one who cares about it."

In the moon-splattered room she played the blues softly. Her love for Sidney had totally died with Midnight, another painful loss, like Daddy, like Midnight. So many deaths in such a short time. They seemed tied to her surgery, almost a year ago now, and the death of a baby she had seen only in her dreams.

Marriage, though, was forever. She didn't know exactly where she had acquired that idea. Two of Sidney's sisters had divorced even though they had children, and one of them had remarried. She didn't know much about their lives. They lived a hundred miles away down in Boise and came home only for special holidays.

The winter was passing, and she was lost. Her life seemed to have come to a halt. There was no place to go from here.

The dream came again, exactly as it had the first time. Then again, a bit different, spaced exactly two weeks apart. Vivid and sharp came the ringing of the phone, and her hand picking it up.

"Emmy, come see me ..."

His voice seemed weaker, farther away.

"Daddy," she pleaded in desperation, "Where are you?"

He tried to tell her but his voice faded and the dream ended.

The next day she made up her mind suddenly. She was going home. She called Sidney at the office and heard his secretary say, "He's out, Emmy, can I take a message?" She didn't bother to ask where he was. Yet her thoughts went instantly to Gloria. She had come home again and was living somewhere around town.

On one of their Saturday nights out at a club on the edge of town, where they'd joined other couples, Gloria and her present guy had squeezed in at the table with their drinks. Sidney had spent most of the night dancing with her, and Emmy had seen him kiss her. She hadn't bothered even to mention it to him.

The memory of that night, months ago, hurt her even yet. It was the last time she had seen Gloria, but she kept hearing rumors. Janice, for a reason Emmy didn't understand, had said to her one day a couple of months later, "Did you know that Sid is seeing Gloria?"

She had answered flippantly, as if she didn't care, "He never stopped, did he?" And saw a surprised lift of Janice's eyebrows.

Over the years of their marriage the other woman's name had come up just often enough to hold the cloud over any chance of happiness Emmy sought with Sidney.

He seemed to know when her unhappiness reached its peak, and the promises began. "I heard of a girl who's giving her baby up for adoption. We might be able to get it."

She was afraid to hope.

Her love had turned to hatred with the death of Midnight, yet his love for another woman still could hurt her. She didn't understand herself.

"No," she told the secretary, "no message."

She wrote a note and left it on the kitchen table.

"I'm leaving, going home for awhile. I don't know when I'll be back."

Or if.

She drove south, through the big trees on the mountains, down into the valley. Springtime had reached Idaho, while in Northern California the Sacramento valley had drifted into summertime. The foothills were brown, the mountain peaks almost bare of snow.

She went first to the cemetery and knelt on her daddy's grave.

"I'm here, Daddy. I've come to see you. I don't know what else to do."

Perhaps she expected something other than this silence, she thought as she knelt. She heard the traffic over on the highway, dulled by the trees between. A big truck rumbled over the bridge. Silence fell again. A bird sang in a tree far down near the entrance of the cemetery. Yet even with the sounds she was filled with silence. I'm here, Daddy. I don't know what else I can do. She began slowly to walk, among tombstones where no relatives of hers were named. She was the only one in this quiet place.

She began to feel a sense of peace. As a child she'd loved ghost stories. Scary stories about old graveyards where mists rose and formed figures. But here, in reality, even the nights would be peaceful.

She stayed until dark fell, wandering the little roads that connected one part of the cemetery to another, going often back to stand by the stone that marked her daddy's grave.

He wasn't here, of course.

Finally she left, driving on backroads to the junction where she had stood so many times waiting for the school bus. She drove up the mile long dirt road that was home.

She parked beside the house, behind a car she recognized as Daddy's old sedan. Mom had been forced to learn to drive, so she wouldn't have to call on Peggy or Rebba to go for groceries. In the front yard was a 'For Sale' sign.

Emmy sat still in the car looking at the sign after she turned off the switch, letting the car lights glisten on the white and black of the letters and background. For Sale. She hadn't known, but of course it would be expected. Mom wouldn't want to live here alone, so far from any of the family, three miles from town and shopping.

The porch light came on, the front door opened, and her mother came tentatively over to the railing. "Emmy? Emily?"

She came hurrying down, happier to see her, Emmy felt, than she'd ever been.

Chapter Nineteen

Emmy felt like a special guest. Mom insisted on calling both Rebba and Peggy and their children and husbands, and they all had supper at the big old kitchen table where Emmy had done homework when she was a schoolgirl. The table was the center of the family. It had been a big purchase in the family when they had managed to buy the house a year after they moved in. Emmy was eleven years old then.

Rebba and Peggy each had three children. Mom's house vibrated with voices and sound. The children were beautiful and healthy, very active. Rebba was pregnant again.

Pride sparkled in the eyes of the mothers and fathers, and the grandmother. They watched their offspring solicitously.

They had fulfilled purpose in their lives.

"This is what it's all about," Peggy told Emmy, and Emmy answered, "Yes, I know." She hadn't told them about her surgery.

Rebba said as she brought her younger child to Emmy, "You're wasting time, Emmy. You need to be having one of your own."

Emmy smiled and hid her hurt. She felt reluctant even to hold the infant Rebba put into her arms. This helpless, plump being smiling up at her reinforced the question. Why?

Why did it happen that most were chosen but a few, like herself, were not?

She was glad to hear the phone ring. A change of subject, a chance to

"

escape. When Mom answered and then spoke to Sidney, Emmy rose and gave the infant back to its mother.

"Emmy, come on home."

His voice was gentle, pleading, as it could be when she opposed him. She said nothing, thinking of the winter snows still patchy on the ground, of the constant wind, the tumble weeds. She found she had not grown attached to any of it.

But there was nothing here for her either. Morn was selling her house to move into a small house near Peggy and Rebba. There she would take care of the children so Peggy could go back to work. She was a clerk in a clothing store. A small job that would scarcely keep her if she lost her husband. Rebba worked as a cook in the school cafeteria.

"Emmy, are you there? Emmy?"

"Yes," she murmured.

"Emmy—I didn't want to tell you this until I knew for sure, but I think I have the baby for you—the one I told you about. I think the mother has decided to give it up."

A flicker of doubt entered her heart. A strange feeling that she was not meant to have that connection to life. She didn't understand. She had prayed for understanding, for a purpose, and received no answer. God was silent.

Sidney said, "You'll need to be here, just in case. Come on home, Emmy."

Come on home to hope. Home where Midnight existed only in memory. Sidney had not told her he was sorry, that he should have let her make the choice about Midnight.

But, there was nothing for her here, nor anywhere else. "All right."

"When?"

"Tomorrow."

She said goodbye that night to Rebba and Peggy and their families. She said goodbye to Mom. Their lives were planned, and were going as planned. They were getting ready even as she drove away to move Mom's furniture into the other house.

She stopped one last time at the cemetery and stood in silence by Daddy's grave. She looked across the rolling foothills and to the ribbon of river that lay glassily beneath the sun, too far away to comfort her with its rush between the banks.

She drove home, staring ahead, staring into space when finally she sat on the back step. The air was chilly and she hugged her arms and sat staring, Midnight's ghost lying at her feet. She went into the music room and began to play the blues.

She didn't mention the baby to Sidney. He had wanted her to come home, and she wondered why. Why did he want her around at all? She saw no love in his eyes, nor in his actions. She lived only on the periphery of his awareness, of his real life. Was Gloria still his passion? She thought so, but felt numbed by it. What did it matter? She had to figure out her own life, find a way, a direction, and follow it.

"Perhaps I should get a job," she told Sidney at dinner.

"You have a job."

She didn't have the energy to argue. It was true she had a job. Cleaning Sidney's house. She could stay busy all day and never finish. But it was better than feeling so lost, so without a road to follow.

Three weeks passed, and the dream in which Daddy called didn't come again. Her nights were blank, dreamless. Another month passed. Then the new dream came like a bright painting suspended in the air above her.

She sees him walking toward her, a figure shrouded in mists. He comes up the slope of a hill until he stands above her.

Daddy.

She reaches up and wipes the mists away as she would have wiped a window clean.

He stands smiling down at her, but he is different. His hair is full, black and curly, his face young, unlined, his brown eyes clear and deep.

"It's a lovely day."

Those few words, and he was gone, and she was shocked awake to stare into the darkness, still bathed by the beauty, the glory of the dream.

Her daddy, yet in all her memory he'd been mostly bald, and in later years the ring of hair left around his head was grey.

But Mommy had told her that when she met him, Daddy had black curly hair. "Pity," she had said, "None of my girls inherited that hair." Emmy remembered saying, "Well, none of us inherited his baldness either." The vision of the dream stayed with her, and her mourning ceased. She had gone to see him, and he had answered her.

It's a lovely day.

That place beyond the mists, wherever it was, was lovely. Perhaps, she thought as she rested on the back step, Midnight had joined him there, and they wandered a country road forever and ever, in that glorious light beyond the mists.

The golden-haired baby she had dreamed of near the end of her pregnancy came to her mind, as she often did. She saw again the sloping field of flowers, and the baby leaning forward, smiling at her.

She stared ahead as the vision faded.

Fields stretched long and flat toward the mountains. Across the section green trees had grown now to the rooflines of the farmstead of Sidney's brother and sister-in-law. Sometimes in her walks she crossed halfway between the two granges, but rarely went on to the other house. Sue, like all the other young women she knew, was busy with children and housework.

The phone rang, and Emmy got up and went to answer it, feeling dragged down, tired, uninterested in a telephone conversation.

"Emmy?" Sidney said when she answered the phone. "What's wrong?"

She hated it when he started a conversation like that. It reminded her of her mother-in-law.

"Nothing." She made an effort to brighten her voice. "What's up?" Better than what's wrong, she'd decided long ago.

"The baby I told you about … you can get it now."

She couldn't answer. She stared at the wall. Not once had she expected anything to come of Sidney's promise. It had just been a way to get her in line, she had supposed. Sidney's wife always had to behave a certain way. She belonged at home, not chasing away to visit family.

"Emily?"

"What?"

"The baby is at this address. Got a pen? Take it down. Seven-forty east fifth. Got that? The woman there has been taking care of it. You're supposed to go over and get it. I told her you'd be there within the hour."

Something erupted within her. Pulses raced, her skin grew hot, then cold. She shivered. This was another of the vivid dreams from which she would wake with her breath caught in her throat.

"Are you serious?"

"Yes. Do you want me to meet you there?"

"I—I—no. No, that's okay." If it were really true … if there was a baby for her … she wanted to be alone with it. It?

He hadn't said her or him. Just it. As if he were talking about a puppy.

No clothes, she thought in a rapid rush of changing images, no clothes, the nursery not ready. The baby … where? Oh yes, the address she'd never forget.

"Now?" she asked. "I'm supposed to get the baby now?"

"Yes, the woman's expecting you. See you at the regular time. For dinner."

She stood. Slowly she put the phone back into its cradle. Then she was running. She snatched her purse out of the corner cabinet by the kitchen door and raced out, the door slamming behind her. She didn't bother to lock it.

She backed the car out of the garage, and spun it back into the turn-around. Then she sat trembling, her arms on the steering wheel, her forehead on her arms. Calm came. Her pulses soothed. She didn't know what was happening. It couldn't be true that finally there was a baby for her. Something would come up to ruin it. Maybe when she got to town she'd find there was no such address. Maybe Sidney was just playing a trick on her. Maybe that hadn't been Sidney at all, but someone miming his voice, playing a terrible joke on her.

She drove down the long driveway, turned right onto the wide, graveled road. The roads in this agriculture area ran straighter than strings, every section, each carefully measured to one square mile. She passed only two more farm homes on the way to town, the four miles of gravel road. Fields, now green, stretched away like a calm sea. In the distance, on bluish horizons, lay clusters of other towns, none of them larger than 10,000 population.

She drove into town, along streets shaded with tall trees, and found the address she would never forget. She hadn't written it on paper. It was indelibly inscribed on her mind.

It was an older home, cottage style with a long porch across the front. White, with tall trees in the ample yard. On the porch was a swing, and a middle-aged woman rose from it and came down the steps.

She came smiling. Her greying hair had been permed, and she wore it like most of the ladies who didn't want to bother with elaborate hairdos.

"Are you Misses Alexander?" she asked, stopping halfway along the walk. Behind her the house was quiet.

"Yes," Emmy said, getting out of the car and going toward her. "Emily Alexander."

"Well, I must say I'm glad to see you." She turned, leading the way back to the porch and up the steps. "The baby is sleeping now, but I have to warn you she cries all night long." She. It was real. There was a baby.

Emmy expected someone to come around the house at any minute and tell her she couldn't take the baby.

The woman opened the screen door and held it for Emmy to enter.

There were so many questions Emmy wanted to ask, yet she was afraid to know. Just take the baby and run. Ask no questions. In the center of the small, neat living room stood a baby basket. Emmy went forward with weak knees and quivering stomach. She looked down into the basket.

The baby was tiny, perhaps two or three weeks old. A perfect face was turned onto the cheek. Black lashes looked incredibly long. Her hair was brown and straight, her head as round as a grapefruit and about the same size. She was beautiful. Small arms curled on the blanket that covered her.

Plump knees lifted the blanket. She breathed so softly that Emmy was afraid she had died.

She put her hand down and onto the baby's chest. She felt warmth, and a slow, even breathing.

"I've got her clothes packed. I'll carry the suitcase out. She doesn't have much, poor tyke. She just cries all the time she's awake, as if she knows."

Emmy lifted the baby and brought her up onto her shoulder. The tiny face touched her neck, and love exploded within Emmy. The weight of the infant against her, the smell of her, the complete helplessness of her surged into Emmy and created a protective maternal wall around her.

"I'll take good care of her," she said.

"I know you will."

"Whose—" She couldn't say, *whose baby is she?* That fierce instinct within her already cried, *she's mine!* Instead she said, "How long have you had her?"

"Oh mercy. Almost two weeks now. She was brought to me from the hospital. I suppose you know all that."

Yes, she should, she supposed. Just leave, the instinct warned. Get your baby and get out of here.

She carried her out, the woman following behind her with the blankets from the basket, and a small suitcase.

"I'd let you have the basket," the woman said, "But it was my son's when he was a baby."

"That's fine. I have a crib at home."

A crib, a dresser, but no clothes. She didn't want to go shopping now, though, she wanted to go home. To take this precious treasure and go home.

Chapter Twenty

The drone of Florence and Hazel's voices became more distinct as they entered the room, cutting into Maggie's half-dream of memories.

Hazel was saying, "And it seems that the son had been a problem all his life. He was years younger than the sisters. Well, all he did was sponge off his mother when he growed up, so the sister said. And he didn't help her. The house was a mess."

Florence, nodding, helped out. "Hadn't been cleaned since the daughter was here last year."

"Garbage, everything. Now, he's come and got her."

Maggie sat up and maneuvered around to step down and go to the bathroom with the help of her walker. Hazel and Florence had gone to their chairs, but Florence started to get up again, as always, her hands on the arms of her chair, her body forward, feet down.

"Need help?"

"When I get home I have to be able to take care of myself."

"Well I suppose that's true, but you're not home yet, and I don't have anything else to do."

Florence eased back into her chair, but didn't put her feet up. She stayed ready, it seemed to Maggie, to catch her if she started to fall.

"Bless you, Florence," she said. "Now you sound like Hazel."

Hazel said, "It could be worse, Florence, she could sound like you."

Florence laughed, her head tipped back, her mouth open, a gold tooth flashing. Maggie felt the humor of the moment, and laughed with Florence. Hazel had a rare grin on her bony face. Her fingers agitated the leaves of the Bible on her lap. She rocked, her chair squeaking faintly as the laughter ended.

Maggie closed the heavy door on the room. Their voices resumed, unintelligible drones.

When Maggie returned to the room two police officers were coming in from the hallway, led by a nurse. The nurse wasn't smiling.

They waited until Maggie reached her chair, the nurse in attendance. Maggie twisted on her good leg and eased down into the chair. Even though the officers weren't exactly guests, she felt reluctant to lie down in their presence.

The nurse said, "They'd like to ask you ladies some questions, okay?"

The officers stepped forward. The one who spoke was on the small side, dark, calm. The older man looked at the fourth area in the room where Clara's few personal items still remained.

"When was the last time you saw Clara?" There was a lengthy pause, as Florence and Hazel looked at each other. Then at Maggie.

Maggie accepted their silent assignment. "Yesterday afternoon. She went out with a man, about thirty years of age."

Hazel and Florence began talking at once. "Her son. She said he was her son."

"Her son, yes. He came and got her. I remember exactly what he said. I'm taking you home, Mama, he said to her. And she got up and left with him. Or did he call her Mother?"

"That's probably the son who lived with her—"

"She only had one son. It had to be him."

"House full of garbage, he didn't do one thing but cash her checks, they say."

"The daughter came from wherever she lives, several hundred miles away, saw the mess, her mother's illness, and moved her here."

The officer interjected hastily, "Yes, but could you describe the man for us?"

Again Florence and Hazel looked at Maggie.

Maggie said, "He was about five-eight, perhaps one-twenty-five or thirty pounds. Thin, stooped, hair light brown and thin."

Florence and Hazel began talking again, "He was her son all right. She seemed to know him."

"What happened to her?" Maggie asked, "Didn't he take her home?"

"I expect he just wanted to make sure he got her checks," Hazel said.

"No, that couldn't be it, Hazel. The checks had probably already been signed over to the nursing home," Florence said, "Like mine. And yours." Together they began speculating.

"Well, it couldn't be because he wanted to take care of his mother. If he'd wanted to take care of her he'd have taken care of her so she'd never have been brought here in the first place. She didn't seem sick enough yet to need full time care."

"—taken care of her before, and cleaned the house, and—" Voices and words overlapped one another. The officer managed not to look overwhelmed. "If there is anything else, Ladies, let us know."

Maggie spoke up, "She called him Donnie."

"Yes, that's right, she did," Florence said.

"That's right," Hazel offered, "She recognized him, that's right. She hadn't even known the daughter, thought she was the one who died."

"Well thank you—you've been a lot of help."

"He said he was taking her home. My grandson he's coming to get me, too, as soon as he can."

The officers nodded, smiled, and slipped away. The nurse followed behind them. Hazel reached over and pushed the call button on the cord hanging by her bed.

The young pregnant nurse, Julie, came into the room on thick, silent soles, bouncing along as if the energy of the world lived within her. But a solemnity had replaced the smile on her face. She turned off Hazel's light. "Yes, dear?"

"What happened to Clara?" Hazel asked. "Those policemen left before I could ask."

"Oh, poor Clara. She was found dead this morning."

"Dead!" Florence exclaimed. "But she was—so healthy. Except ..."

Hazel cried, "The Lord have mercy! Poor soul. Her son just took her home. What happened?"

"We don't have much information."

Florence said, "Why are the police investigating?"

A hard knot of anxiety began forming in Maggie's stomach. She wanted to curl away from the question, and couldn't.

"Well," Julie hedged, "She was missing for awhile—wandered away from the house or something."

"Couldn't he keep track of his own mother?"

Julie smiled. "Is there anything you need? Besides information?"

Across the hall Thomas called, "Eleanor?"

Julie looked at Maggie. "It's getting close to dinnertime, want to take a ride in the wheelchair?

"To see Thomas?

"You're better than any medicine. He even got out of bed this morning and took his own shower."

"Then," Florence said, pushing herself up from her chair, "After she doctors Thomas take her to the music room. Do you feel like playing some music, Maggie?"

Maggie let out a long sigh. "Always," she said. "But first I want to call and see how my little dog is."

Always she had needed her music, the soft and soulful cry that expressed something within her that words could not express. Always, except once. Then, a miracle happened.

THE BABY WOKE in the car and began to cry. Her tiny fists pushed against her cheeks. A miniscule index finger reached and scratched her pale skin. She seemed so incredibly small as Emmy secured her on the front seat, murmuring soothingly.

The woman stood with one hand on the open driver's door and looked past Emmy at the baby. "She'll cry till daylight. The only time she stops is to nurse her bottle, and sometimes then it takes a while to get her to take it. Her formula and bottles are in the suitcase."

"Is she hungry?"

"No, it's another three hours till feeding time. You have to wake her during the day to feed her."

Emmy drove away with the baby crying on the seat. The baby ... She hadn't asked for the baby's name. She had a name ready, a name she'd kept from the days of her pregnancy. Lacey. Lacey Mellissa. Her mother's middle name. And her own favorite for a little girl. Lacey brought to her mind a beautiful picture, a little girl with long curls, and a frilly dress trimmed in lace. Perfection.

On the road home, where no traffic held her attention, she put her right hand on the baby's chest and began a gentle massage. The baby's mouth puckered, she paused in her crying, then sobbed and began again. Emmy kept massaging. She began to sing. Somewhere over the rainbow, blue birds sing …

The baby's crying stopped. She opened her eyes, looked at the ceiling of the car, then to the side toward the dashboard.

"Looking for me?" Emmy asked softly. "I'm right here, Lacey. I'll always be right here, whenever you need me."

The baby's eyes found her and for a moment the smokey-blue depths seemed to take her in. Then they closed and she began to cry again.

When she reached the kitchen door, which she'd left unlocked, with the baby in one arm, and the suitcase in her free hand, she found the telephone ringing, ringing. She put the suitcase down, and with the crying baby against her shoulder, the tiny face between her cheek and neck, she answered the phone.

Janice yelled, "You got her! We've been so excited, waiting. Sid told us there was a baby he thought he might get for you."

"I just came in the door …"

"We'll have a big family gathering and a baby shower. I'll let you know as soon as I can get it arranged. Right now I know you probably don't want to stay on the phone. Good luck! Congratulations!"

"Thank you, Janice. Thank you." Tears of gratitude filled her eyes.

She began to walk with the baby murmuring in her ear. The baby kept crying.

"You're going to exhaust yourself," Sidney said on the third evening as she began the nightly walk with Lacey. "Let her cry. You're just spoiling her."

"I sleep when she does."

So far they hadn't talked much. Those questions she wanted to ask were interrupted with the cries of the baby. She woke each afternoon about five o'clock and cried until five o'clock the next morning. Emmy walked the floor with her, all night, up the stairs, down the stairs, outdoors into the moonlight, back into the house, round and round. And the baby cried. She took Lacey to the doctor on the first day, and he pronounced her healthy. "She's just got her days and nights mixed up."

"Do newborns always cry when they're awake?"

The doctor smiled. "Sometimes."

Emmy walked, and murmured in the baby's ear. The nights were theirs, theirs alone. The telephone didn't ring. Visitors to see the new baby didn't come at night.

On the fourth night the baby stopped crying. Emmy looked down at the small face against her shoulder and saw the blue eyes opened and looking at her. Emmy smiled. "Well, hello there, Lacey. I'm your new mommy. We're going to get along just fine." The baby looked at her.

Emmy went to a rocking chair and sat down. The baby began to cry. Emmy got up and walked, and the baby grew quiet.

Night after night they walked. The baby was silent. If Emmy tried to sit down, the baby cried. Emmy laughed and got up to walk again, and the baby hushed.

She told Sidney, and he wasn't amused.

"I told you that you were spoiling her."

They had a chance to talk now. She had a chance to ask him all those questions about the birth mother and if she had signed the relinquishment papers. But he was a lawyer, he'd know the right way to handle it, and something within her kept her from admitting that this infant hadn't always been hers. She didn't even know the name of the woman who had kept Lacey, and she didn't know the name on the baby's birth certificate. She was Lacey Mellissa Alexander now, and would always be.

That night they walked as always, the baby silent on her shoulder. Emmy talked softly to her, on and on.

Then suddenly the baby answered, her rounded mouth struggling to form a word. The soft expression startled Emmy, and a thrill raced through her. She stopped walking and listened, breath held, as the baby kept expressing, cooing, making different sounds. It was like a miracle. It was a miracle.

It was like walking through her dreams, seeing the marvelous light that drew her on into cities that glowed.

Emmy sat down in the rocking chair, too weak to stand, trembling. The baby cooed against her neck, and her hand brushed Emmy's chin as if in a caress.

Emmy rocked. The baby grew quiet. She slept.

Emmy held her another hour then took her upstairs to the crib she had placed within reach of her side of the bed. No way was she putting this precious child beyond walls in a nursery. Not yet.

"You're spoiling her," Sidney had said when he reluctantly moved the crib into the bedroom. "We'll never have a room to ourselves again."

He could look so grouchy with that frown on his face. Emmy loved it. She laughed and he glowered at her.

"What's funny?"

"You."

"I don't understand your sense of humor."

"I know."

The baby slept in the crib, and Emmy slept two feet away in the bed. She woke to see Sidney gawking in surprise at the baby in the crib.

"She actually went to sleep before daylight?" he asked.

"Sidney ..." Emmy sat up. She wanted to tell him, share with him the marvels of the night, of the baby answering her, talking to her, and then falling asleep before midnight. But words could never express the beauty of that experience.

She only said, "We made it, Sidney. She and I."

From that day on Lacey woke at six and went to sleep promptly at six in the evening. She rarely cried. She learned to smile, and the coos that rolled from her were answered by the coos of the doves in the yard outside the windows. She was a happy baby.

She too should be happy, Emmy thought at night as she lay in the light-streaked dark of the bedroom. But she worried, more now than ever before. Was baby Lacey breathing? She was too quiet. Up again, leaning over the crib, touching her infant chest. Warm and breathing, so quietly. Back in bed she started worrying again. When Lacey cried, at least she had known she was all right.

And there was the other worry, coming insidiously into her mind.

Would someone come and take her away?

The adoption couldn't take place for a year. She had finally questioned Sidney, the same questions, getting no comfort from his answers.

"Why do we have to wait a year?"

"It's the law." He was getting impatient with the questions.

"Did she sign papers of relinquishment?" Emmy finally asked, when Lacey was five months old.

"Of course."

But she had heard a hesitation. She didn't repeat the question, but she worried. Every car on the driveway caused her heart to miss a beat and then race sickeningly. Every ring of the telephone caused her to feel weak with fear.

Lacey cooed happily, and watched her with adoring eyes. She didn't want anyone but Emmy to hold her. When the family gathered, Lacey kept her eyes on Emmy, no matter which of the relatives had her for the moment. More than one voice said, "You're spoiling her."

"Wait until you try to send her to school," Sidney's sister Mona said. "She'll be like Benny, and cry every time you have to leave her there."

Oh God, to be able to keep her that long.

In the privacy of aloneness, Emmy held Lacey. They melted together in their love as if they both knew their time together was brief.

Chapter Twenty-One

"How's Minnie?"

"Oh, hello Mrs. Winters. Minnie's fine."

"Is she eating?"

There came a hesitation, just enough to tighten Maggie's throat. She wasn't even sure why she had asked if Minnie were eating her food. Minnie loved her food. She'd never been finicky, but Maggie had fed her bits of everything she herself ate, and at the kennel they'd be feeding her only from a can, or a bag. She was a little on the plump side for a Chihuahua, smooth as satin, round and sleek.

"I don't want her to lose weight," Maggie said in the pause.

"We'll take the very best care of her. You concentrate on getting well."

Maggie hung up the phone and let the nurse wheel her across to Thomas's room, but her thoughts remained with Minnie. She had never seen the cage Minnie was now living in, but she could imagine it. She had seen cages in veterinarian's offices, and they contained no wasted space. Still, it wasn't the space that mattered with Minnie. I have to get Minnie out of there.

"Here she is, Thomas," the nurse said cheerfully. "Eleanor has come to see you. I told you she's always close."

Thomas was up and dressed, sitting in the plastic recliner-rocker, his long spider-thin hands trembling on the arms of the chair. He looked at Maggie, at the nurse, and back at Maggie.

"Where?" he asked.

"Well ..." the nurse hesitated. "Here. This is Eleanor, remember? She was here yesterday."

Thomas's deep-set, pale blue eyes examined Maggie's face. "I believe," he said slowly, "That Eleanor is dead. I believe she's gone on."

Maggie breathed a sigh of relief and smiled at the old man. She knew his age to be in the nineties.

"You're looking much better today, Thomas."

"Thank you," he said solemnly.

Maggie waited, but he said nothing more. His hands tapped the arms of the chair.

"Was Eleanor your daughter ... your wife?"

"No," he said. "No, Eleanor was my sister. You resemble her, young lady. She had hair like yours, golden brown I called it. But she died, don't you know. I recollect going to her funeral."

Maggie nodded. Young lady? She hadn't been called young lady since her mother scolded her for some violation or another.

Thomas looked past them. "I raised Eleanor, you might say. Our parents died when I was fifteen and she was four. So, in those days, Child Services didn't exist. I was big enough to get a job, so I did. Kept Eleanor. Our relatives had a fit, but I kept her."

"That was difficult, I'm sure."

The nurse moved her chair, turning it toward the door. "We have to go now, Thomas. Are you coming to the dining room for dinner? It's about an hour from now."

"That might be nice. Thank you."

"We have to go now. We'll see you later."

Florence and Hazel were waiting and watching and listening in the doorway. They backed up to make room for the wheelchair. Florence had a big grin on her face. She laid a hand on Maggie's shoulder.

"Well, young lady, I told you you're just a kid. You didn't believe me, did you?"

They laughed. Maggie felt briefly the way she used to feel, having reached maturity, knowing herself mature, but holding her own in those secure years between becoming an adult and becoming an 'aging' woman. It was part of her knowledge of herself, and of the human psyche, she thought now, which was why the helplessness of sickness and aging was so hard. There was nothing about it that fit the image formed within one's mind. The ego.

She put out her hand and stopped the nurse. "I'd like to walk," she said.

They all stopped. They stopped talking and laughing. Florence and Hazel peered down at her with concern. "That's quite a ways," Hazel said.

Florence said, "You'll be up for a couple of hours now."

"I have to manage that walker. I'm going home next week."

Going home if she had to crawl.

"Going home?" Florence repeated.

There was a quality in her voice, almost a wail, that saddened Maggie. Their lives had intertwined. Florence and Hazel, Thomas and the others she saw daily, had become a kind of family.

"But I'm coming back," she said, "Every day. I'll bring Minnie to see you, and I'll play for you. Every afternoon."

The nurse said, "That would be fantastic!"

She couldn't drive yet, and perhaps would have to wait another month, but she could call a cab to take her away from here, take her straight to the kennel to get Minnie. Then, she would bring Minnie here to see everyone. Every day, she and Minnie could come. Florence or Hazel could hold Minnie while she played for them.

They went down the hall toward the room with the piano, Maggie going slowly with the walker, the others pacing their steps to hers.

The music brought it back. As she played, her thoughts picked up the past and the months during which she hadn't touched the piano more than a few times.

LACEY HADN'T WANTED to be left sitting while her mommy played with the pretty keys on the piano. She wanted to play too.

Laughing, Emmy held her and let her thump the keys discordantly until she grew tired and twisted away.

She was learning to walk. Her legs were short and plump and sturdy. Her diaper showed beneath her dress as she toddled away from Emmy, with Emmy hurrying behind her, ready to catch her when she toppled.

Laughing, Emmy picked her up. Lacey too laughed. Together the two of them laughed a lot during the day. Emmy kept her worries for the night when Lacey slept so quietly near her. They collected during the day like silver gnats to swarm around her in the dark of night.

At bedtime one night, while Lacey slept the beginning of the long twelve hours she had adapted when she was tiny, Emmy worried aloud to Sidney, "Isn't there something to prove she's ours now? Surely we don't have to wait a year for that."

He looked at her steadily. "You know, all you think about is the baby. Don't you love me anymore?"

Surprised at this sudden attack she blinked at him. A change in subject, a complete switch in her thoughts. "Of course," she said. Then "Of course I do."

"Then …"

He reached for her, and she thought of the baby. What if the noise of Sidney's lovemaking woke her? She didn't feel sexual toward him anymore. She wondered if she ever had.

She didn't mention her worries to him again. She began to count weeks instead. Lacey was ten months old, then eleven months. Eleven and a half months. They would soon be celebrating her first birthday, then she could start counting days until the one year was up.

She planned a big birthday party. All the family would come. They would eat out under the trees where the children could run and play. Lacey would love it. Now that she was beginning to walk, she was also trying to run. The soft grass would cushion her tumbles, and her cousins would pick her up. Emmy had to remember to let her go, let her play among the children, and stop rushing in to protect her from every little tumble. Lacey never cried. Though sometimes she puckered up, she hadn't seriously cried since the night the two of them had walked the midnight floor almost one year ago.

She was a happy baby. She would grow into a happy child, a happy girl, as beautiful as a sunrise, or a moonrise, with her dark hair and deep blue eyes. With the dimple in her chin, her heart-shaped face.

She looked nothing at all like the baby in Emmy's dream, the golden-haired baby on the hillside of flowers. Yet she was the embodiment of all of Emmy's dreams of a child. Lacey held Emmy's love in her chubby little hands. She was all Emmy needed. In Lacey, Emmy was complete. Then one night another dream came. Emmy is walking down a sidewalk in a city, carrying Lacey. Among the people who walk past her is one woman who pauses, a stranger, kindly, smiling, warm, middle-aged. She reaches out a hand and stops Emmy, her smiling eyes looking at the baby.

"This is the one who is of your soul, but your time has not come." Her voice fades as she speaks and the vision fades, drifting away in mists.

Emmy woke, the unspoken message as clear in her mind as the memory of the dream. This is the baby who died and lived again. This is your baby.

There was the rare beauty, the feeling of timelessness which she tried to hold. But she slipped away into the reality of her life and the spoken message of the dream.

But your time has not come.

The dream didn't still the fear, the dread, the worries that came in the sleepless hours of the night while on one side of her Sidney slept, and on the other, in the crib she refused to take back to the nursery, Lacey slept.

To be sure Lacey breathed, Emmy got up and put her hand on the baby's chest.

She breathed, she lived. Sometimes Emmy took her from the crib, moving her gently so that she wouldn't wake, and held her before she placed her back again.

In the afternoons Emmy held her, rocking slowly as the baby took her nap, her head resting warm on Emmy's arm. As she yawned, as her long dark lashes drooped, Emmy rubbed her eyebrows, gently, rhythmically. Lacey slept.

Almost a year old. Three more weeks. The day of the big garden party. Even colleagues of Sidney's were invited.

Emmy rose and carried Lacey up the stairs, past the old family pictures on the wall, into the quiet upper hall. She carried the sleeping baby into the bedroom and laid her in the crib. For a time she watched her sleep, then she went quietly downstairs.

Lacey was a child of habit. She would sleep exactly one hour. Just as she slept exactly twelve hours at night.

Emmy didn't hear the car, it crept so slowly along the driveway. She glimpsed it through the wide living room window as it slid out of sight beyond the walls.

A strange car. A small sedan. Two-toned blue. Yet she had seen it before, she thought, parked on the street near Sidney's office. On those days when Sidney was unavailable.

A salesman, she tried to tell herself, but her heart raced, and her throat grew raspy dry. She stood still, her hand gripping the newel post. The old clock on the shelf tick-tocked slowly, as if coming to the end of her life, ticking away the seconds.

She waited. No one knocked on the front door, no footsteps crossed the porch. It seemed forever before the knock came on the kitchen door.

Perhaps a salesman would go to the kitchen door. Perhaps. Perhaps a driver lost would go to the kitchen door, even though it was less accessible than the front door.

She looked up the stairway, at the long distance that separated her from Lacey.

The knock on the back door came again, more forcefully. Emmy made herself go, down the length of the living room, past the narrow hall and the door to the music room, into the short hallway that connected dining room and kitchen. She entered the kitchen.

The face beyond the glass in the kitchen door was turned to give her the profile. Although it had been years, Emmy recognized the woman instantly.

Gloria.

Emmy went forward. The face, still as beautiful as ever, turned toward her and watched through the glass as Emmy crossed the room. Gloria didn't smile. Nor did Emmy. What do you want here?

A cold nervousness surrounded Emmy. A sudden knowledge, and understanding. Your time has not come. Why had she never thought of Gloria? Even Janice had seen it, the first time she'd seen the baby. "Do you ever hear anything about Gloria anymore?", she had asked. Asked as she looked at the infant Lacy. It couldn't be true, yet it was. The long, black lashes, the deep almost-purple blue of the eyes. Gloria didn't have the dimple in her chin, nor the heart-shaped face, but there were others in Sidney's family who did, she now realized. She had noticed the resemblance between Lacey and some of her cousins in the shape of the face. She had thought it was one of those marvelous miracles that occur, a baby from nowhere, now theirs, part of the big family. Even becoming to look like them.

The weeping started within her, in her heart, cries against this invader, this taking away of all that mattered to her. She didn't want to open the door, but her hand turned the knob.

She didn't invite Gloria in.

Gloria walked past her. The superior contempt with which Gloria had looked at her long ago was gone. The bright confidence had been replaced by an unsmiling seriousness. A nerve twitched at the corner of her left eye. She put a hand up and touched her eyes. The twitch stopped.

She stood in the middle of the kitchen, and looked around.

Her eyes found the toys in the corner by the rocking chair.

For a long time she didn't speak. Her eyes took in the toys. A smile touched her lips, lifting the corners slightly. She went to the toy-box and picked up a small stuffed animal, Bambi, with a pink ribbon around its neck. One of Lacey's favorite toys.

"Is this hers?"

Her hands caressed it, the smile returned, small, private. Emmy drew a long breath. Pain was a searing knot in her, chest and throat. Only five more weeks until the year was up and the adoption could be final. Five weeks, a lifetime. An emptiness. Gloria looked at Emmy.

"I've come for my baby," she said. There was no assurance on her face. Her voice carried a question within it, and gave Emmy voice to speak.

"No. No! She's not yours! You can't take away—"

Gloria's eye began twitching again and her face flushed. "Yes, I can! I didn't sign her away! I told Sid I wasn't sure I wanted to give her up. I told him!"

"Sidney ..."

"He's her father. You didn't know that, did you? She's ours, Emily. I'm sorry, but she's ours, Sidney and mine, and I want what's mine! You've had her long enough. It's not fair! It isn't fair! Also, she needs to be with her sisters."

Emmy stared at her. Sisters?

Gloria said, "We have two other children, Sid and I. We are married in the eyes of God."

Emmy turned, unable to answer. The enlightenment came in a flash of little things said and done over the years. Of course he would have another wife somewhere, one who could bear his children. The puzzle was, why had he chosen to keep her, even to provide for her this infant she couldn't have herself? "Why? Why?" she asked.

"In the eyes of God—"

"I mean—why the baby? Why?"

Gloria didn't answer. Perhaps she had wondered the same. The kitchen that only yesterday had been bright, though touched with shadows she sensed, turned dark and ugly. The old stove where Midnight had slept had rusted spots now because she hadn't built a fire there since Midnight was taken away. The linoleum floor in front of the stove had worn through, the pattern long gone. The kitchen table was scarred and chipped. The old rocking chair's seat sagging and soon to collapse. Emmy turned, turned again, her hands to her face. There was no way out, no road on which to run.

She started to pray, then stopped, her mind still and bowed in submission, powerless, afraid to speak for fear of more rejection. In fear that no one was listening, that no God existed to listen.

Like a voiceless animal she submitted to the forces of nature, her mind a silent cry of suffering.

Chapter Twenty-Two

"**M**a-ma!"

The call came from upstairs. Where are you, Mama?, the cry asked. Why have you left me here alone? No, there was only silence upstairs yet. Lacey hadn't started vocalizing words, only sounds.

Emmy didn't know which way to turn. She started toward the stairway to go up and get the baby, then she turned toward the telephone. Sidney had to be here.

Gloria said, "He's out of his office at the moment, I stopped to let him know I was coming out here, and Genevieve said she'd let him know as soon as he got back."

Genevieve. Gloria knew his secretary better than Emmy. Emmy called her Mrs. Parker.

Emmy sat down. Gloria walked the floor with nervous agitation and talked.

"I want you to know why we're in this mess. I was twenty years old when Sidney and I had a fight and I took off and married this guy who'd been after me. Of course the marriage wasn't a marriage. I'd done it only to spite Sidney, and I think he married you to show me he could do the same thing."

"Why me?" Why me into this torture? This Godless hell.

"Why not you? He could make you do what he wanted. Do you know what we fought over?"

Emmy shook her head. At one time in her life these things about Gloria would have made her ill with heartaches, but those days were gone. Her world had fallen in. What did their lover's quarrels matter? What did it matter that they had continued to be lovers, between Gloria's two or three husbands, and perhaps even during their tenure. The only thing that mattered was Lacey.

"Because of this old house," Gloria volunteered. "He and his parents already had it planned. Sidney and I would move in here, and they would move to town. We'd raise our family here. Sidney would go into law with their parents' friend in town. Our life was measured, cup by cup. Well, I rebelled. I didn't want to live here."

"But now you do."

Gloria walked, her hands in constant motion, touching each other, touching her hair. Emmy didn't look at her directly, but Gloria was in her vision, no matter in which direction she turned her eyes. Gloria was there, just as she always had been. But it hadn't occurred to Emmy that Gloria was the girl who had given birth to Lacey.

The girl Sidney had led her to believe he didn't know. A young girl who didn't want to be saddled with an infant. Why had Gloria left the baby for three weeks with someone else? Gloria sat down, moved uncomfortably in her chair, then grew still. Leaning forward, she clasped and unclasped her hands between her knees. She was wearing denim shorts frayed at the bottom, and a short shirt tied in front. Red strap sandals, flat heeled, were on her bare feet. Her toenails were painted bright red.

"Why did you leave her for three weeks?"

"Three weeks?"

Emmy looked into Gloria's eyes. "The first three weeks of Lacey's life."

Gloria shook her head. "She was taken from the hospital. I thought you took her."

From upstairs the call came again. "Ma-ma?"

Emmy stood up. Gloria's eyes lifted, following the sound. Lacey had called, she had actually called. The sounds she'd been uttering had become a word, a name. The name Emmy called herself to Lacey. Mama will dress you now. Eat this for Mama, it's good for you. Mama loves you, loves you, loves you.

"I didn't know she wasn't with you. Where was she?"

"A middle-aged lady in town. I don't even know her name." Gloria seemed to stiffen slightly, sitting straight in her chair, her hands sliding to her thighs.

"That was when he was trying to get me to sign some papers. But I couldn't—I just couldn't."

The sound of crying came dimly from upstairs. It was a sound that tore into Emmy. Lacey rarely cried. Not for a long, long time.

Gloria too got up, but she stood still. "That's her voice." Her expression changed. The lines softened, anger and fear erased.

Emmy followed her heart, through the dim downstairs hallway to the stairs.

The stairs swayed as she climbed and became long and wavering, reaching farther and farther away, growing ahead of her, a different reality. The faces in the frames on the wall came alive and taunted her, calling her names, baring teeth that grew to fangs. Within this horror Lacey cried. Emmy's tears mercifully blurred it all.

The sound of Lacey's crying brought her to close her eyes, open them again. She was almost there, to the top of the stairs. Lacey's voice sobbed Ma-Ma-Ma-Ma … on and on. Not as she had thought, not Mama, but mamamamama …

She was standing in the crib, her small hands clutching the sides, tears abruptly ending as Emmy entered the room.

Through the window as Emmy brought Lacey up into her arms, she saw Sidney's car zip past. She stepped forward, looking down. He skidded to a stop near Gloria's car, but then sat, staring across the beet field toward his brother's house. Emmy took Lacey to the rocking chair and tried to hold her as she had when Lacey had cried so many months ago. But Lacey fussed, pushing up.

"Are you hungry?" Emmy asked, knowing of course that she was. Lacey always went downstairs after her nap to a snack. She took her to the bed and changed her, while Lacey twisted and fussed. She dressed her in a pink, frilly sun-suit she had made last week. Most of Lacey's clothes came from her own sewing machine.

Lacey stretched an arm toward the door and grunted, mouth wide open.

"Hungry?"

Lacey made sounds, trying to pronounce the word.

Slowly Emmy carried her toward the stairs. Gloria hadn't followed her. She thanked her for that. Gloria had given them these last few minutes alone.

I'm taking you now to …

Her.

Your ... mother.

She couldn't say it. Her mind winced against it. Lacey was her baby, hers, not Gloria's.

But she could go through this torture forever and it would change nothing. The birth mother hadn't signed away her child. Lacey was too young to understand, thank God, too young to be badly hurt by this, she prayed. Emmy had to bring to herself the truth.

Your mother has come for you. I have no rights to you.

Only a year of memories.

She entered the kitchen and saw Gloria's emotions break as she looked at the baby. Emmy turned her eyes away from Gloria's revealed feelings and stood Lacey where she could reach a chair if she needed the support.

"She stands alone!" Gloria cried. "Yes, she's learning to walk."

Gloria knelt in front of Lacey. The baby pushed her hands against Gloria's chest, and drew back, staring at her solemnly.

Gloria said, "I'm a stranger to her." There was a catch in her voice.

Lacey toddled waveringly to Emmy, where she had sunk onto a chair, too weak and trembling to stand alone. Lacey put her hand on Emmy's knee, turned and stared again at Gloria.

"She'll have to get used to me."

The door opened and Sidney came in. His face was colorless as his eyes passed from Emmy and the baby to Gloria. He too stared at her, as Lacey had. Lacey began her wordless chatter, with sounds of da-da-da-da.

Da-da, Ma-ma. She was learning to talk, Emmy realized, only today. Lacey knew them by those definitions. Mama and Dada.

She should walk away, but she couldn't.

"Sidney," she heard herself saying, "Do I have any rights at all to Lacey?" To her horror she began to cry.

Lacey looked up at her, seeing tears on her face for the first time since she was too young to remember, groped at her and began crying in sympathy.

Emmy picked her up.

Gloria's eyes darted, from Emmy and the baby to Sidney. "She's mine! You can't do this to me, Sid! If you don't straighten out this mess I can promise you you'll never see her again. I'm taking her with me."

"No, you can't do that!" Sidney stepped forward to stand in front of her. "Please, Gloria, just calm down?"

Tears streamed down Gloria's face.

"You've been promising me and promising me, Sid. I want my baby. I've waited for you to make it right, Sid. I've waited."

"You knew when you got pregnant that I wanted to take her. You were a surrogate mother, Gloria."

"Oh, my God! Is that all you think of me, Sid? Is that all our love ever meant to you?"

"Now wait a minute!" Emmy shouted. Gloria and Sidney looked at her.

Emmy held Lacey close for a moment, then took her to her highchair and secured her. She brought three small wafers and a glass of milk, and held the glass as Lacey drank. She set the glass on the table and gave her the cookies.

"Above all," she said, "is Lacey. I'm not abandoning her to a mess you two have made. You have to straighten this out and behave like adults. Lacey deserves a secure home."

She stood a moment longer watching the baby eat. Then she left the room, for the first time leaving Lacey with others, and forced herself to walk through the house and out.

Her deepest fear had happened. The mother is here, the mother is here. She made herself utter the words, that word she had feared and avoided for so many months.

"Mother."

"Your mother is here, Lacey."

Chapter Twenty-Three

The sound of the blues carried Maggie away. She forgot where she was, that she had an audience. She had spent so many years playing to an audience, her mind drifting elsewhere, going back, back always to the days when her arms hadn't been empty, that an audience had become invisible to her.

She hadn't given up readily, though she told herself to just walk away and don't look back. She couldn't.

On the day Gloria came to claim Lacey Emmy had stopped at the front step. She sat down, looking past the tall shade trees in the yard, past the road beyond, past the fields. She put her hand out and felt emptiness. Midnight, too, was gone.

Why had she stayed? All those years she had known Sidney loved Gloria. He couldn't stay away from her.

Why me? Why had he married her?

"Love me," he had said so many, many times. "I need you to love me. You do love me. Say you do."

Rarely had he said, "I love you."

A train, cutting the misty horizon, crossed a field like a segmented worm, its passage silent, sound lost in the distance.

She rose and began to walk around the yard, going around the house to the back. She passed the kitchen, but Lacey wasn't crying. Was she still eating cookies, or had she discovered that Mama wasn't everything in her life?

Emmy entered the garage and looked at her car.

She should leave, drive away, but she couldn't. Not yet. Something within her hoped this was a nightmare that would fade and be forgotten.

She was on the far side of the barn when she heard a car start and drive away. She ran, heart pumping in terror. Gloria had taken Lacey.

She reached the porch and ran into the kitchen.

Lacey sat in the highchair. She put her arms out. "Mamamamama ..."

"Hey," Sidney said with a strained smile. "She's learning to talk."

His eyes followed Emmy's every move, searching her face.

Emmy did as she always did in the evenings. She prepared dinner, a small one tonight. She took Lacey upstairs and bathed her.

Then they sat rocking, Emmy catching Lacey's plump fingers in hers as the baby played with her chin. She held Lacey and rocked her, long after the baby had gone to sleep. Finally, Emmy put her in the crib, reluctant to let her go.

She bathed and dressed in a long sleeveless nightgown. She got into her side of the bed. Nothing was right. Her mothering of Lacey had been temporary. The natural mother had come for her.

The mother. "Mother." She made herself mouth the title, that all-important title. Gloria had the rights, not she. She had to make plans to leave, but she wanted to know that Lacey wouldn't be hurt by it. Yet how could she not be? But she was a baby, and though she would wonder why Mama was gone, at least she would have the loving arms of her mother.

But her mother was a stranger.

Grandma Alexander. Lacey loved Grandma. Maybe she could help with the transition.

Sidney came to bed, but didn't touch her. He reached out once, but stayed his hand in the air and pulled it back. "Emmy?"

"Yes," she answered without looking at him.

"We can work this out. You'd like Gloria if you got to know her. There's nothing wrong with a child having two mothers."

"Oh God no!"

"I'm not going to go against your wishes, Emily. I married you first."

"Don't, Sidney! I don't want to hear this."

"We'll work it out."

"No," she said. "It can't be worked out." Her life ahead was like a tunnel filled with darkness. The tunnel of death. But there was no light at the end.

She turned away from him onto her side and closed her eyes. Please God let me dream.

Dreams left her as barren as life. They eluded her, night after night, too pale and faraway for comfort.

Hours, days passed. Gloria came daily and Lacey began to know her, reach for her. Emmy left them alone, going out to walk the paths she had walked when she had lifted her face to God and prayed for a purpose. Prayer was beyond her now. She walked, closed in with nature, her mind dulled as if drugged. She spent sleepless nights, sitting in various rooms, sometimes outside in the swing beneath the massive limbs of a tree. She hadn't made any kind of definite plan. She stayed for Lacey's sake, until she could adjust, she had told herself. But it was almost as if Sidney was preparing to take two wives into his home. His great-grandfather had three wives, perhaps more, all living under this same roof. Sidney's Mormon background made it acceptable in his eyes, although the church had long ago turned away from polygamy, and neither his father nor his grandfather had practiced it. Gloria didn't like the old farmhouse, so perhaps he would buy her a house in town. Perhaps he already had. There were two other children, in school. The day would come when Gloria would bring them to meet Lacey.

Emmy wanted to move to a bedroom away from Sidney but didn't have the energy. She kept away from the bed until three or four o'clock in the morning when she was sure to be able to sleep.

Finally, one night she took a blanket with her down to the living room sofa.

She sat with the light on, a magazine fallen onto her lap, unread, and stared at the wall. She stared, yet saw nothing. Her mind seemed almost to have closed. No thoughts. It was easier that way. Hour after silent hour she sat. The clock on the mantel ticked.

The front door was visible from where she sat, a stained glass pane shattering moon rays. Silence of night had fallen. Even the wind had stilled.

She suddenly had a feeling that a presence stood outside the door, wanting in. She turned her head and stared at the door, a strange outer-space cold surrounding her, a fear of the unknown drawing her into herself. She understood that it wanted to pass through the door into the dimension in which she cringed, but it would not enter without her permission.

It was not human, but something beyond, an entity beyond her experience. It meant her no harm. This, she understood. She feared it, yet within her mind she gave permission. There was nothing there, she told herself, nothing. Only her fear and mental agitation.

But instantly the presence was in the living room, an invisible and supremely powerful ball of energy hovering near the ceiling above the mantel. It communicated with her mentally, in total silence, a rapid passage of information, an instant transition of thought, sent telepathically into her mind, her brain slow and primitive in reception, words lost, information gone beneath her cold, frozen terror. Others retained, to leave her puzzled and trembling.

You are going to die … be taken back where you came from … if you don't … your purpose on earth is … to … The message came in one breathless thought, meanings received meanings lost.

The words faded as the messenger faded, gone, leaving cold terror and total silence.

She sat frozen in this fear of the unknown, staring at the place where it had been. She had the sense that it was a messenger from somewhere far beyond. A messenger from God, perhaps, trying to tell her something. She drew the blanket around her, but the awful fear remained, the strange fear not of physical nor mental harm but of the very nearness of the presence.

She sat unable to move, the message going through her mind like a ribbon unwinding. You are going to die … be taken back where you came from … if you don't your purpose on earth … is to …

Your purpose on earth … taken back where you came from … She went to the downstairs bathroom and got down on her knees and began to recite the Lord's prayer, over and over, and gradually the cold terror left her. Taken back where you came from …

It was that which continued to frighten her. She felt certain it had to do with something that existed before she was born into this present life. She had been put here for a purpose after all, but it wasn't to mother Lacey. That was Gloria's purpose.

She left the bathroom, and found that dawn now lighted the stained glass of the front door.

"Maggie?" a voice said softly at her left. She looked up to see the smiling face of one of the nurse's aides. There were so many of them, she hadn't yet learned their names. Her nameplate said she was Marian. She was one of the middle-aged aides that, Maggie supposed, did volunteer work, and worked perhaps once or twice a week.

"I hate to disturb you or end that beautiful music, but it's time to eat."

The time had seemed so brief. A flash, and it too was gone. Her thoughts went to Minnie, always in her mind. She yearned to sit again in the recliner by the window with Minnie on her lap. The only being on earth who depended on her, she needed Minnie, and her childlike dependence.

The wheelchair was waiting. Marian had lifted the footrests so that Maggie could step into the seat. She stood up. Florence passed by and patted her on the shoulder. Several who had gathered thanked her. "Reminded me of my young days," one of them said.

If she were home, Maggie thought as she pivoted on her right leg to sit in the chair, she could manage. The only thing she'd absolutely have to get up for would be to get water and feed for Minnie. Something for herself— many people had survived on peanut butter sandwiches. She could leave the back door open a few inches so that Minnie could go out when she needed to. She breathed a new breath of relief. She could call a cab and walk out, right now. Perhaps they'd let her borrow a walker.

No, she'd have to wait until tomorrow to make arrangements for a walker, wait to see her doctor again. But she was going to stand up to him and tell him, "I'm going home." The people here were friendly and kind, but she had lived a long time without people, and she wanted the comfort and familiar surroundings of home. She wanted Minnie beside her. The image of Minnie in a cage haunted her every moment. Minnie wondering, waiting, perhaps trembling in fear. Maggie couldn't stand that. Tomorrow she was going home.

In the dining room she saw Thomas. With the help of an aide he had come to join them for dinner. He ate at another table, but seemed to be enjoying conversations with his table companions.

"Who is that man?" Florence asked.

"Oh, that's Thomas. You haven't seen him before?" Both Hazel and Florence gazed at him unabashedly, taking him in from his white hair to his neat house slippers. He was dressed in brown trousers and a white shirt and had an elegant air.

"He looks different than he did in bed, don't he?"

"Heard him plenty," Hazel said, twisted in her chair, staring over her shoulder. "I put him in my prayers, though. I could tell the man was in misery."

"Doesn't look miserable now."

"The nurses always said he was just carrying on for attention," Hazel offered, still looking him over. "My, doesn't he have a fine head of hair?"

"Hazel," a wicked gleam narrowed Florence's eyes and turned up one corner of her mouth, "You're drooling. Settle down. The next thing we know you'll have your hands in his hair."

"Oh!" Hazel whirled back, flushing. "Florence you'll never change. Got your mind on one thing, all the time. The Lord save your poor wicked soul."

Florence laughed. Others at the table looked up, puzzled, wondering what was funny. They had missed out on the low-voiced conversation.

"He reminds me of one of my customers," Florence said. "Used to call me every time he came to town. He lived in the east and flew west on business. Maybe I ought to go over and ask him if he's the one. Paid me well, he did." She grinned at Hazel, waiting for her explosion.

"Oh my Lord!"

Others at the table looked at Florence with puzzled smiles. "What kind of business were you in?" a man asked.

Hazel put her head in her hand, then lifted it immediately. Florence sat with a wide grin.

"Well," she said.

Hazel interrupted. "Florence, have you tasted that casserole? You ought to taste it." And under her breath, almost in Maggie's ear, "Stuff your mouth with it."

The other end of the table was occupied by three women and two men, all strangers to Maggie. There were few people around the large dining room that Maggie had paid any attention to in her few previous trips to the dining room.

"Wasn't it terrible," one of the women spoke up, "about that woman? The one who was taken out of the home by her son?"

Florence sobered, listening. "Clara? She was our roommate."

"You saw the son?"

"Yes, we did. What about him?"

"Well, you know his mother was murdered?"

"Murdered?"

"Murdered?" Hazel repeated. "But I thought she wandered away—died from—from exposure—"

"They found her body in a ditch, but she'd been shot."

There was a moment of silence. Diners stared at the speaker. Then

Hazel cried, "She wanted to go home. It was important to her to go home. If he was going to kill her, why didn't he take her home to do it instead of leaving her in a ditch?"

The man said, "Maybe because that would have left no doubt he did it. This way he can say he's innocent."

"Innocent?" Florence cried. "Then who did it? Why would anyone else—?

"Why would he?" another voice asked. "Kill his own mother?"

"He claimed he took her home, and went to get some groceries. When he got back she was gone."

Florence said, "Police came to our room. Asking who took her away, or if she just walked out. They just said she died."

"No, they didn't," Hazel corrected. "The nurse said that."

"Oh, yes."

Heads shook, no one ate. The food sat in front of them congealing. Maggie looked at her plate. There was meat on it with a touch of pink, and she knew if it were cut into there would be blood.

Images flashed through her mind—the box delivered to her door—his head, his precious, innocent head, nestled in a bed of its own blood—

Clara—lying in a ditch, her body nearly hidden by tall weeds—face down, shot in the back of the head, blood and brains exploded through her face—

Janna, lovely face mutilated, blood dark and stilled upon it, matting her long, thick hair.

She forced her mind from those images and was assailed by another— Janna's face filled with terror. Don't leave me, Emmy. Help me.

"Did she have life insurance?" someone asked, "Everything's for money. There seems to be no limit to what people will do for money."

Or was Clara simply another easy target, another warning to Maggie?

The vision returned—the box—the severed head—blood still liquid. A warning. "I thought of life insurance too," one of the men said. "And I don't think she had any. But she had a house."

Hazel said, "He didn't take her away because of money. He took her because he couldn't stand seeing her in a strange place away from home. He loved his mother."

Florence said, "You're a dreamer, Hazel."

The man said to Hazel, "Yet he didn't let her die at home. He took her to a ditch and left her there, like a roadkill. Is that love?"

"Money has more power than love," a quiet little woman at the end of the table observed. She lifted her fork up and began to pick at her food. Her hand trembled, the veins on the back popping through the thin skin. It was a palsied tremor. Beside her chair leaned a cane, its handle shiny and worn with use.

Dishes and flatware clinked and rattled, odors of food mingled with odors of disinfectants. Aides walked among the tables, picking up a dropped fork here, wiping up spilled water from a glass over there. Voices at other tables murmured, as mingled and mixed as the odors.

Maggie's eyes sought distance and escape, but found at each table the face of the stranger. She saw in the faces of innocent visitors the features of the man who might be the harmless suitor Florence imagined, or who could be the hitman who had killed Clara because he hadn't yet been able to reach Emily Alexander.

Chapter Twenty-Four

She couldn't let herself be overpowered by fear lest it become paranoia, Maggie told herself. The murder of Clara was a cruel coincidence. It had nothing to do with herself.

Around her the murder of the woman who had been so briefly in their midst was still being discussed. Surrounding tables had joined in with speculations. Then a man who had sat quietly listening began speaking.

"I have a son in the police department. He's not in the habit of giving out a lot of information, but he did say she was shot execution style. In the back of the head."

Maggie felt smothered. In her image of blood and death she had seen Clara, face destroyed from the bullets to the back of her head. But perhaps the image had been caused by her memory of Janna's murder.

"Her son seems to have an alibi. He did go to the convenience store. When he got home and found her gone he searched the neighborhood, asked the neighbors if they'd seen her. Then he called the police."

"Her body was found by a road crew mowing the roadside."

"Shot in the back of the head? Like being shot by a hitman," one of the men said. Maggie stared at her plate and saw instead the face of the stranger, going into the house where Clara had been left alone, and cajoling her away. A hitman. Targeted—her roommate, someone who'd left the protection of the care center, someone left alone and vulnerable.

Nausea, a deep sick feeling, seized Maggie. Her stomach surged at the smell and sight of food. She wanted to ask the aide to take her back to her room, or to the music room, but she would be alone there, and she was afraid. He had been here so recently, and walked down the hall with her. He had brought flowers, from her own garden she was now certain.

The conversation continued around her, without her contribution. She absorbed it, without really listening.

"No, I don't think she had money."

"Not even insurance."

"Makes no sense."

"Murders never do, do they?" A woman's voice.

"The son probably just didn't want her to know what he was doing, didn't want her to see the gun. Her son did it."

"No, I don't think so."

"He swears he left her at home, and when he got back she was gone. There's no record of him ever owning a gun."

Maggie bowed her head. Please God, forgive me for bringing harm to the innocent.

How easily she had walked into problems, all her life. Of all the roads available, she had usually chosen the wrong ones. Surely she could have done something different.

At fifteen she had danced with a handsome soldier, and married him without questioning why he would want to marry someone so unsophisticated, so soon after he met her. A child. Others questioned it, but not she.

Only twice, it seemed on looking back, had she made the right decision, followed the right path from all the branches that spread before her.

The first time was when she lied to protect her mother from the truth of what she had seen Daddy do with Aunt Ketti.

The second time was when she left Lacey.

For five years the pain of losing Lacey was the core of her being. It clouded her vision and stood like a wall between her and happiness.

She had known at the beginning of Gloria's appearance that leaving was the only solution, but she delayed.

The birthday party was scheduled. All of Sidney's family was invited, even cousins, aunts, uncles. The night before Lacey's first birthday Emmy had called her mother.

"Did I wake you?" It was past ten o'clock.

"No. I don't sleep as well as I used to. I don't do enough, I reckon."

"Tomorrow's Lacey's birthday."

"Yes, I know. Didn't you get our cards?"

"No. They'll probably come Monday."

"It's nice it's on a Sunday. I suppose you'll be doing a lot of special things."

"Oh yes, a big party, with all the family. Sidney's family, that is. I wish you could be here. It's going to be a—a—"

"What's wrong, Emmy?"

"Wrong?" She swallowed. "What do you mean?"

Only once had she taken the baby down to see her own family. When Lacey was ten months old she had persuaded Sidney to drive them down, although he had a million excuses of why he should not. Busy, he said. This is a bad time, he said. He'd been saying that since Lacey was two months old.

Emmy had taken pictures by the dozens and sent them instead.

Every stage of her development.

But finally, bored half to death, Sidney drove her down to her mother's, and spent two days. He had nothing in common with Emmy's brothers-in-law, nothing to talk about with them. They worked at whatever jobs they could find. They lived in small, simple houses. Her sisters had grown chubby and comfortable, interested only in their houses and their children, their homes and families. They made their own clothes, not because they wanted to, but because it saved money. They had vegetable gardens in their backyards, and canned vegetables from it all summer. Their cupboards and cellars were stocked with enough food to keep them going through another war.

That was the way they lived.

For entertainment they watched television on small screens in small living rooms, and were delighted to have so much.

Their differences in culture were embarrassingly obvious, and there were times when Emmy wished she hadn't come. Was she too as uncultured and old-shoe as her family? It was true her education had ended with high school. She'd been lucky to get that far. But was the difference in hers and Gloria's demeanor so obvious? Was that the reason she had always been so willing to sweep up the crumbs and be happy with them?

She learned a strange disgust for herself that weekend. A contempt.

Her quietness, her old shyness that her daddy used to tease her about, she saw in an oddly sharp exterior vision of herself, was the reason Sidney's family treated her the way they did. Talked about her as if she weren't in the room at times.

Just as Sidney did.

Her family had never visited her. They had never been invited. She had waited for Sidney to ask them, and she had seen that they wouldn't be comfortable here.

Her mother said on the phone, on this eve of Lacey's first birthday, "Don't you think I can tell when something's wrong? You're my daughter. I can hear it in your voice."

"In my voice!" She tried to smile, but it died away, unborn.

"Also, you haven't called for more than a month. Until now, you've called every week."

"Well." She had never lied to her mother, except once, long ago, and she couldn't start now. She wished she hadn't called. Yet they had to know, sometime.

"What's wrong, Emmy?"

Emmy licked her lips. She tried to speak. Tears erupted.

She hadn't cried much, but now they came, wringing hot from her heart, tearing and stinging.

"Lacey's—mother came. I'm not—I won't—the adoption won't go through."

There was a silence. Then Mommy said, "Then get out of there, Emmy. Find yourself a life somewhere else. Come home, if you want."

She couldn't talk anymore. Leaving Lacey seemed the impossible, yet she knew that for Lacey to be happy, she had to be secure within a family. With a mother, a father, and all the others. Just as she had them now, except for one change.

She went upstairs to the nursery into which Lacey's crib had been moved. A Mickey Mouse lamp with a seven watt bulb gave the room a soft moonlight effect. In the shadows of the crib Lacey slept, dressed in her little cotton sleeper, short sleeved for the warm summer weather. The sheet blanket lay wrinkled at her waist. She slept on her back, her face turned away, her rounded cheek shadowed, long lashes black and curled. Lashes like Gloria's. She would grow up to be beautiful.

Emmy didn't kiss her goodbye. But she put her hand on her chest, the way she used to do, and felt the rise and fall of her even, soundless breathing. She whispered, "You'll be all right. You'll be fine." Then she turned away. From the hallway closet she took the small suitcase she had packed a week ago. Just enough clothing to get by, as if she intended subconsciously to change her image as soon as she could afford new clothes.

She wanted nothing of Sidney's. But she had to take enough cash to get away, and borrow his car, the car he had so magnanimously called "Emmy's car". Just long enough to get away. To get to town and start her journey, wherever it led.

Downstairs she went into Sidney's office, turned on the desk lamp, and for the first time began looking into the desk drawers. She found his address book in the top drawer.

Gloria's phone number was on the first page, under special Listings. Emmy dialed.

It rang, and rang, until Emmy was ready to hang up, wondering if she were doing the right thing. Then came a sleepy answer.

"Hello?"

"Gloria, this is Emily. You should come over. Lacey will need you in the morning."

There was no answer. Emmy could almost see the surprise on Gloria's face, her pretty mouth hanging open, her eyes widened. Gloria had never thought it would be this easy.

It's you she needs. It's her mother she needs. If she … grows up without your love she will search for it, and yearn for it. She will resent me for keeping her from you.

These were things Emmy had not spoken even to herself, and could not now, nor ever, speak aloud. But she felt them in her heart. If the mother lived in the same world, the child would yearn, feeling an emptiness, perhaps, that no one else could understand.

She gently and quietly hung up the phone, then picked up the suitcase and walked out. A full, round moon was shining. The wind that had blown throughout the day now rested, calmed for the night. She stood in the back yard and looked across the long, flat fields. Midnight stood beside her, a black ghost. She put down her hand and felt his broad, flat head.

"Goodbye, Midnight," she said softly. "Goodbye."

He had stood beside her during so many lonely times. He had walked with her and heard her cry after the baby in her body died. He had heard her crying aloud at the God who seemed to have overlooked her. God, please give me a purpose. He had stood there, and walked there, and offered his sympathy, sometimes in low whines, but mostly in silence.

He walked with her now to the garage, and stood back as he always had while she backed the car out and turned it around. The shadows absorbed him as she drove away.

180

Chapter Twenty-Five

At the bus station in town she checked schedules. There was no bus out until six o'clock in the morning. She returned to the car and drove to the train depot. A train east was leaving in thirty minutes. Trains west not until two more hours.

She had no destination. She couldn't go home to her family. Her mother now lived next door to Peggy, a few blocks from Rebba. Their town was small. There would be no work.

There were other reasons she couldn't go home. She had cut those ties long ago. She loved them all, but they weren't part of her now. It would be torture to watch their lives unfold so naturally, her sisters discussing births and babies and school for first graders. Rebba's Becky would be going to school this year for the first time, a chubby little girl who still had baby ways and baby looks, round cheeks, pudgy hands. She wouldn't want to leave her mother, and Rebba would discuss it as Peggy had last year when her Jacob entered first grade. Together they had a firm foundation of understanding, of similar experiences. Neither of them could enter the alien world that belonged to their older sister.

What would they say about Emmy's walking away from the heartache that was hers and Lacey's? Would they understand that to delay would only be worse for both of them? Could they, or anyone, understand the hurt of leaving behind all she had known for most of her adult life? Of leaving her heart behind in the form of a little girl whose life would only be made less secure if she stayed?

She didn't need a lawyer to tell her there was no way she could get custody of the child. The mother had the rights. If she stayed she would be subjected to the status of a Mormon wife whose husband had at least one other wife, legally or not. Lacey would not benefit. It would do her far more harm than good.

Emmy had no choice but leave. If she went home, she would have to talk about it, explain the circumstances. Or she would be sitting silently among them, saying nothing, no longer a part of them.

"Ma'am?"

The voice startled her, caused her to jump. The ticket agent was waiting. She had in her purse slightly more than three hundred dollars she had drawn from the household checking account several days ago. It was all she had between herself and a dark future. If she allowed her fear to control her she would get into Sidney's car and drive back to the big farmhouse, and behave in whatever way might be required of her. In another year Sidney's need of her, his need for the love she could no longer give, would no doubt be gone, and her expulsion from the family would be certain. This way she at least had some control.

"Chicago," she said to the agent. "One way."

She left a note for Sidney to be called and told where he could pick up the car.

An hour later she was riding east, hearing the rumble of the train, feeling it beneath her, looking out the window and seeing the wide land. Across the fields she saw the farm house from where she had so many times watched the long trains pass silently east or west, their rumbling distant, only the sound of the whistles reaching her. The big house, almost buried among the tall cottonwood trees, was now like a doll house. A mile away, beyond the road that passed straight as a ruler from east to west. And in that house, with dawn now touching the rooflines with gold, Lacey would soon be waking.

Would she cry for mama? Would her mother's arms help Lacey to forget that once she had been carried in the arms of another mother, all night, until finally they both rested?

Tears ached, unshed, her heart broke and it was as if her skin held together a shattered soul. She yearned back as the farmstead drifted into the past, left behind.

• • •

No city had ever seemed so large and confusing. She stood in the depot, with countless people rushing past her, leaving the trains, going out to enter other trains. She watched meetings in which sisters or friends grabbed each other in great hugs and laughed and went away talking. She watched partings, two parents saying goodbye to a young woman no more than eighteen or nineteen.

With the one suitcase she carried, Emmy went to get a newspaper. She had to start somewhere.

The ad section was as confusing as this huge space of milling humans. She found an information center and asked where the employment agency was.

The dark-haired man behind the desk pushed his glasses up with one finger and looked at her. He was either sitting down on a stool, or he was very little taller than she. His face was thin and good-looking, with a narrow chin. His expression suggested he was either tired, as she certainly was, or he didn't like his job.

"Which one?"

She returned his stare. Which one? Her home town had only one. But it also had fewer than twenty thousand residents.

"The nearest one", she said. He nodded, gave her address and directions, and a city map. He suddenly became very helpful.

"It's about—um—maybe ten blocks from here. There are hotels in the area, cheap, you know, not expensive."

"How far is that in miles?"

He looked at her, and looked again. His glance down made her aware of the way she was dressed. A full cotton skirt and white blouse. She had made both of them, just as she made all of Lacey's little clothes, but she hadn't put the time nor care into hers. She hadn't brought much along, only what she could easily carry, as if she'd known subconsciously there would be long walks ahead.

Finally he shrugged and smiled. "I don't know. How far is a mile? Anyway, it's a fairly safe area. I guess you could walk. You go down this way, see," he continued, drawing out the route on the map while behind her the line grew. He glanced at the people waiting. He pushed toward her the small collection of map, notepaper with address, other information about the city, and smiled. "You'll do okay."

He hadn't asked, are you new in town? The answer was obvious.

She walked and walked, facing at times a wind that seemed even stronger than the winds that had blown tumbleweeds past her. She went through a couple of blocks where the windows were darkened and beer was advertised in flashing neon. In the corner of one window she saw a sign, 'Help wanted'. Sounds of voices came through the door as it opened and a man emerged. He stopped short at the sight of her, and nodded, a grin on his face. As she walked on she felt his eyes watching her.

The world had rolled over and over again during her flight from home. It was morning again, ten o'clock, her wristwatch read. She paused on the corner and wound it. Time was important, she wasn't sure why.

She had slept in the clothes she was wearing, leaned back in the seat, after a delay in Omaha. For one hour, perhaps, she had slept. She had prayed for a dream, a dream that would lead her away from the pain of her reality. But none came.

She followed the directions he had given her until her feet began to burn. She sat on the curb and rubbed the bottom of a foot, her shoe in her hand. People passing by scarcely gave her a glance. She had expected that, and found her anonymity comforting. With her shoes back on she walked again, and came into an area of taller buildings, narrow, cobbled streets. Doors without canopies led into hotels, various small businesses, or bars.

In the employment office she sat and waited, the suitcase at her feet, feeling as if she'd walked for days. When her number was called she rose, suddenly light-headed, and she thought of food. She hadn't eaten. During all the trip she'd had only a few drinks of water.

The woman behind the desk had the disinterested expression that the man at information had in the beginning of their conversation. Emmy had filled out a form, and beneath experience had left a blank. What could she say? Well, I can sew and cook and clean, but probably not well enough to work professionally at any of them. Qualifications and education were left mostly blank too.

"No experience?" the woman asked, looking at her sheet of paper that was mostly blank. Her voice held a question. What have you been doing all these years? But she said, "Housewife?"

"Yes, I was."

"There are some jobs you can get without experience. Some factories are hiring. And of course there are usually waitress jobs, but they usually require experience. Do you have any experience at all in the serving field?"

"No."

She thought of the bar she had passed that had a help wanted sign in the window.

"You don't have an address."

"No, not yet."

The woman pushed back in her chair. "You need to get an address, then check with us again tomorrow."

Emmy left, carrying her suitcase. She stood on the sidewalk seeing the cars moving slowly and noisily along the narrow streets and for a moment felt smothered in this skimpy space. Then she began to walk again. It didn't matter now which direction she went, but she favored the narrow cobbled streets. She wouldn't be going back to the employment office. She had forgotten where the help wanted sign was, but anyway, she needed a room, a bath, a change of clothes.

She entered a doorway over which a small sign advertised "Rooms". The lobby was scarcely larger than her sewing room at home. The sewing room where Lacey played on the floor with scraps of material as Emmy sewed at the machine, its purr accompanied by Lacey's sounds, those baby attempts to talk. Emmy would answer her, as if a conversation were being carried on between them. Would Gloria sew? She suspected not. Would Lacey miss their times in the sewing room? For awhile, but then other things, other activities would take its place.

The woman who got up from a chair behind the short counter was grossly obese. Her huge hips squeezed in behind the narrow counter and a line of open mailboxes. Her eyes slipped over Emmy with envy. No, Emmy thought, you don't want to trade places with me.

The woman waited, saying nothing. She picked up a pen and opened the register. Emmy looked around. Nothing on the walls but a calendar. On the right a narrow stairway rose against the wall, steeply, it seemed. A man came down, steps creaking. He was dressed in blue work clothes. The woman spoke to him, and he said, "Good morning, Irma." The door closed behind him.

"How long?" Irma asked Emmy, yawning. "No less than one day. Five dollars a day. In advance."

Emmy hesitated, then said, "One week?"

"Sure. Here, write your name and former address."

Emmy wrote her name but left the address blank. She laid the money on the counter. Irma looked at her name, at the lack of address and shrugged. She reached for a key from one of the empty mailboxes.

"Third floor. A shower on each floor."

Emmy started upwards between narrow walls. The landings were only as large as they had to be, with stairways stretching narrowly upward. The building was like a tunnel standing vertically, rising on into forever.

Emmy drew a long sigh of relief that the third floor was as high as she had to go.

She found the room and let herself in, closing and locking the door behind her. She hadn't expected anything roomy, but a sense of claustrophobia made her feel she had to open the window or smother. She dropped the suitcase and struggled with the window just long enough to realize it wouldn't open with the strength she had today. On the other side of it the wall of another building was perhaps four feet away.

She turned away from the window and sat down on the bed.

There was one straight chair, a small, scarred dresser, and a door that stood open to a closet with, of all things, a toilet and a washbowl. She was so glad to see she would at least have those luxuries that she started to cry.

For several long minutes she sat on the bed and cried. Then she went into the closet, hung her clothes, washed herself. She had thought to bring a small travel iron along. So she folded a towel on the top of the dresser and used it for an ironing board.

Cleaned up, her hair brushed and hanging long and bouncy over her shoulders, her lips tinted pale pink, dressed in fresh skirt and blouse, she left to look for work.

She walked and walked. Several bars had signs in windows, help wanted. But she hesitated indecisively. She had never walked alone into a bar in her life. Also, what did she know about mixed drinks? What kind of barmaid would she be, with no experience? She had lost track of alcoholic drinks back with a spiked Coke. Yet her memory of the bar atmosphere drew her. Its shadows would be soothing. The world of a false reality. Her soul ached for music, to release the deep pain that had lived with her through much of her life, that now had come to the surface to separate her from the faces of the strangers who lived in the world with her. She tried not to dwell on thoughts of Lacey. But they came, bittersweet.

What would Lacey be doing at this time of day? It was time for her afternoon snack.

Had she met her sisters yet? Of course she had. Gloria would have brought the girls, whose names Emmy didn't know, to the home where they would all grow up together. Three sisters, as there was in Emmy's own family. Lacey would delight in them, Emmy knew, as she delighted in her cousins. So many little people to play with, and with whom to have fun.

Yes, Lacey would be fine.

Emmy remembered she hadn't eaten since she'd left home, and not much before that for weeks. Her skirt waistband felt loose and baggy. She went into a small restaurant and sat with a cheese sandwich and a Coke, able to take only a few bites. The waitress was lively and friendly, talking to the men down the counter. Emmy watched her, wondering if she'd ever be able to project that kind of openness. All waitresses she'd ever known were like that, friendly, liking people, putting up with being at their beck and call.

She left and walked, the address of her room in her purse, keeping in mind corners turned, streets crossed.

She found herself in front of the bar where she had first noticed a small, hand printed sign in the window. Help wanted, right below Budweiser in curved neon smoothly bubbling colors of yellow, red and green. Noises of the busy street drowned whatever sounds might be contained behind the darkened window.

She started in, and a man pushed open the door and stood smiling at her. She thanked him warily and walked from the bright street where sunlight struggled to reach the pavement to a cave of darkness. She stood, trying to see.

"Buy you a beer?" the man said over her shoulder, having changed his mind about leaving.

"Oh—no thanks. I just—I just was thinking about asking the boss about the sign in the window."

"Oh sure," He shouted, "Roger!"

The room and its contents began to take shape. A long counter spotted with figures, both men and women. Tables, small, square, with their chairs upturned on their tops. Against the wall to her left were booths, empty … At the far end of the room was a small stage, and then she saw it. A piano. She stared at it, her heart yearning toward it.

A man approached her from behind the bar. "Yeah? Yes, ma'am?" he amended as if something about her appearance changed something in his mind.

She found herself saying, "Do you have a piano player?"

"Uh—well—yeah, with the band, when it comes in. Why? You want to play?"

"Could I?"

"Sure, help yourself."

Nearly every head at the bar had turned to look at her. The dim interior seemed a haven of silence now that the door was closed. She felt no fear, only a sudden rise of excitement.

This room, long and nearly dark as if going on into the eternity of night, took her back into some of her dreams, where she walked unafraid into strange, new worlds.

Her heels clicked faintly on the hardwood floor as she walked the length of the room. The heads at the bar turned to watch her.

"Want more light?" Roger asked behind her. She hadn't heard him following.

She shook her head and sat down on the piano bench. "It won't disturb anyone, will it?"

"If it does, they'll let you know, don't worry."

His hand touched her shoulder, a warm clasp. She yearned toward it, a touch, any touch. But that wouldn't do. She was vulnerable at this time in her life, and had to be cautious of her own needs, of a hand that offered pseudo-love.

She began to play, her fingers eager for the keys, her soul crying for the music and its comfort.

Hours passed, no one booed. At times when she paused, applause rose behind her. When Roger approached her again she saw that the club had nearly filled.

"Want a job?" he asked. "They like it."

She looked at him with gratitude, unable to speak. She had thought she would have to learn to serve drinks, and perhaps she would later, but for now, her music was wanted.

"I can't pay much," he said cautiously.

"How much?" She didn't care how much, only enough to pay for her room and some food.

"I don't know—thirty-five? I mean, to start, and you know, they'll give you tips. I'll put a glass here on the piano for you."

"Thank you."

"Okay. Just come in like you did today, and stay till the band comes. Okay?"

"Thank you," she said again.

She would walk into many different bars and clubs in the years to come, play piano in different surroundings, different cities, her wanderings taking her from the east coast to the west, from Chicago to New Orleans.

Roger's bar was the beginning of a different life. She had literally walked from day to night.

Chapter Twenty-Six

For five years the pain of losing Lacey was the center of her being. Her music cried the pain, the loss, giving her comfort. Her grief clouded her vision and stood like a wall between her and happiness. During those years she moved from city to city, playing piano in various clubs and bars and learning a kind of oblivion to the audiences she played for. Aware at times that the audience could be oblivious to her was a comfort too. It released her into her own dream-like world where she didn't have to smile at anyone, be friendly and thankful for the dollar bills that were poked down into the glass on the top of the piano. She lived in a smoky, veiled world of night, fed by memories of a wide land where she had walked with Midnight at her side, and with Lacey in her arms. In her memories the two meshed, the old dog a faithful companion, the baby her own.

Her finances improved with each move, and she finally got her own car. Nothing came to her from the divorce. She wanted nothing of Sidney Alexander's, even though she knew it wasn't a practical resolution. "Cutting off her nose to spite her face," Mom would say to Rebba and Peggy.

She moved south to Saint Louis, then on to New Orleans, carrying with her a recommendation. She got an afterhours job in a large club in the French Quarter, playing jazz and blues from one in the morning, after the band left, to whenever she decided to call it a night. She slept most of the day, spent the evening with acquaintances, lived in a small kitchenette apartment. She cut her hair to shoulder length. Once a year she flew to Northern California to spend a few days with her family.

Her nieces and nephews were growing so tall, acting so mature. She tried to picture Lacey growing up, but the image of the baby she'd been stayed with her.

When she went to sleep in the morning hours she hoped for a dream in which Lacey would be with her, but her dreams were of strangers, people she knew in the dreams but who seemed to have no connection to the people she knew in reality. They were filled with adventures in strange cities, or on country roads, exciting and fearless. She woke wishing she could remain in the dreams forever.

During Lacey's fifth summer she packed all her possessions, mostly clothes, and started driving west. She imagined Midnight, sitting in the seat beside her, his head up, his gaze eager for the flat land where he had lived and died.

Nothing had changed. There was a familiar strangeness about the town, with the wide tree-lined streets. A few new places had cropped up outside of town, fast food places, a new larger restaurant, a small shopping center. But downtown was the same, the old drugstore where she had sipped sodas, the department store where she had looked at baby dresses for ideas. Where she had purchased the material, the laces, the ribbons.

"You keep her dressed so cute," the women in the family had said. She drove slowly by the office building on the main street where the law offices had been, and found they were still there. She parked across the street and walked over to read the names. Sidney Alexander. Yes, just as always.

In the car again she drove north out of town onto the graveled road that led past the farm. Here too it was all the same. The long driveway unchanged, the Lombardy poplars as tall and slim as from the beginning. Then she saw that three had been replaced with younger trees. The old ones had died. Grown tall, as tall as they could be, they began the slow passage. A limb dying here, another there. Then, through two or three years, the death closing out the green, the leaves no longer breathing. She had watched it happen during the years she had lived there. One tree had died, and she'd cried when she saw it happening. Sidney had laughed at her. "It's just a tree." She'd replied, "but the symmetry will be ruined." She could hear their voices as if she were there again, hers, his. "So we'll replace it." Now, more than thirteen years later, that tree had blended well into the row. The house between the trees showed its white front as always. Nothing had been added or taken away. She couldn't see the backyard, to see if there was now a play area, slides, swings. She pulled into the driveway, then stopped, the engine idling.

She became aware that a car had stopped in the road behind her. Her small, used sedan was blocking the way.

She pulled over to the side, to the edge of the irrigation ditch that ran the length of the yard, and the larger car eased slowly up beside her.

Gloria.

At first there was no recognition in Gloria's eyes. Then they widened, bugged, and her chin dropped. Fear? Shock? Emmy remembered the feeling, that time Gloria had driven into the driveway, when she had come to claim Lacey.

Then Emmy saw in the backseat a little girl with long dark curls, large eyes, long lashes. That perfect, beautiful face. She was looking toward Emmy with curiosity. Beyond her was a baby seat, and it in a tow-headed baby about two months old, sound asleep. The windows were rolled down, the wind cool and fierce, as always.

Emmy smiled at Lacey and said, "Hello, Lacey."

The child looked perplexed. A smile wavered on her lips. She glanced hastily at her mother, then back at Emmy.

Gloria said, "Her name is Leslie."

"Oh." Leslie. Lacey was gone. Gone to live forever in Emmy's heart, like the baby of the dream who had sat on a hillside of flowers smiling down at her. "Hello, Leslie," she said. "How are you?"

Leslie cried out, "I'm going to have a birthday party. Are you coming? It's on Sunday though that's not my birthday, really."

Emmy smiled at her, overwhelmed with feelings. She didn't have to answer. The child kept talking.

"We've got a baby brother, my sisters and me. His name is Arman, after my grandpa. Do you want to see him?"

Gloria said, "We have to go." The car eased on.

Emmy sat still, watching the little girl turn her head and look back, puzzled at this lack of friendliness on the part of her mother. The car went on, turning into the drive behind the house, disappearing behind the trees.

Emmy drew a long sigh. It expelled from her heart, her soul. She felt relaxed in a way she hadn't felt in five years, more than five years, perhaps forever.

Lacey was fine. Everything had worked out for her.

That was all that mattered.

She had done the right thing when she left five years ago. Backing the car out onto the road, she drove to the intersection, and took the highway west.

A couple of days at home with her mother, then on to Los Angeles. She had in her purse the name of a club, and its manager.

In New Orleans she'd told Bob, the manager of the club where she'd worked for two years, that she was leaving. "Do I have to give notice?" she asked. It was five o'clock in the afternoon and the evening crowd was beginning to come in. It would be fairly quiet until nine, with people eating, drinking and talking. She sat at the bar with Bob, sipping a Coke. Alcohol was not one of her weaknesses.

SHE HAD BOUGHT a bottle of high proof whiskey in Chicago, during her first week away from Lacey, and had drunk part of it. She discovered she couldn't lift her head, misery weighing her down. She thought of the cows who'd been separated from their calves and felt so sorry for them she began herself bawling like a cow separated from her calf. She had always hurt when it was time to take the calves away from their mothers, to be fattened and sold for slaughter. As if the mothers knew, they bawled incessantly for days before they gave up and started grazing again. She often wondered how her brother and sister-in-law could deal in cattle and hogs. The religious idea that people had souls but animals didn't was to her ridiculous. They hurt too, suffered too. Anyone who lived around them could surely see that. If a brain indicated soul, then what was the animal brain?

She wept for Lacey, who might be crying for her mama, wondering where she had gone. Or perhaps Gloria was filling her needs, and her memory would soon solve its own wonder and draw a veil between her and the first few months after her birth.

She thought of her own mother, who'd lived after all with a man who was once unfaithful to her. Mommy had known. She couldn't have helped but know, though her heart told her Emmy lied.

She began to feel sorry for herself. She had never felt so sorry for anyone in her life. This poor soul that she was. Nothing had gone right for her. Bad marriage, bad luck, bad everything. She wasn't born lucky like other girls. She wasn't even very pretty. The people who told her she was cute or pretty were just feeling sorry for her because she was so ugly. She sobbed and cried until she passed out.

She woke, blinking around at the strange room. Where was she? And what on earth was wrong with her head? The pain was excruciating when she moved.

She saw the bottle on the floor, lying like a dead insect, its yellow blood concealed in the lower half.

My God! She covered her head in shame, appalled at the memory of her thinking processes under the influence of the alcohol. Appalled at her self-pity.

She became convinced that alcohol was a psychological poison, even before the stage of a physical poison. In tiny doses it probably had good medicinal qualities, but souse yourself and you became a different person.

She vowed never to take another alcoholic drink.

"WHERE ARE YOU GOING?" Bob asked, and snapped his fingers in front of her eyes.

"Oh, sorry. I was thinking, I guess."

Bob had a round face, a sturdy body, not tall. Sometimes in his eyes she thought she saw something she didn't want to see. She didn't want to become involved with another man. Besides, Bob had been divorced three times. Not a really good record. "Where are you going?"

"I think I'll go west, get closer to my family for a change."

He said nothing. There was a seriousness on his face that made him look sad, and lonely, as if she meant more to him than she should have. He drew a long breath, took the small black notebook from his pocket and wrote a name.

"This is a club in L.A. Tell him I sent you. And if you ever want to come back …"

PERHAPS, someday. Now, leaving the little girl named Leslie, her heart finally at rest, she drove west across the Snake River and into Oregon. She drove into the mountains of Oregon and northern California.

Big trees shaded the highway. She kept to the less traveled roads, enjoying the trees. At a lookout point she stopped, in the shadowed depths of tall, old trees, and yearned to walk into them and stay forever. A narrow road, iced with pine needles, led away into the coolness. She often dreamed of a road such as this, like two dirt paths side by side.

If it is the place of her dream, just over the rise the road angles down into a valley of breathtaking beauty, where people work in gardens of flowers along the road, where a house now and then sits among the flowers. Friendly folks look up and wave. They know her, she knows them. And just beyond is a city built of glass, glowing with an inner light. It's quiet and clean, with no cars or trucks on its wide streets, only people who stand talking, or walking about in their various activities.

Beyond the town a tangle of vines begin beneath ancient trees and a path leads off the winding road. She follows it.

She comes to a large mansion, nearly buried in vines. It's white, built of cement, of concrete, like the wide steps that lead up to its front door. The door stands open, waiting for her. She climbs the long flight of steps to the uncovered porch. There is a white, low wall surrounding the porch, with steps down into a hidden garden. She walks toward the open door ... she longs toward it, toward the mysteries and beauties beyond ... but she never reaches the door.

THE EVENING ACTIVITIES had started at the nursing home. Television for those who wanted to watch, until ten o'clock, lights out time, medicine time. For others, back to their rooms to talk to roommates, or rest or read. Maggie chose to return to the room, as did Hazel and Florence and several others who walked along, pacing their steps to three wheelchairs being pushed to various rooms. Hazel disliked television intensely, and Maggie was beginning to see that Florence was more bluster than gale. She was willing to give up a show in order to accompany Hazel back to their room.

"It's the ruin of the world," Hazel said this evening, which was a compliment compared to some of the things Maggie had heard her say. "It's the work of the devil. It's leading people astray."

"How about the televangelists?" Of course Florence would ask that.

Hazel thumped along, her heels making as much sharp noise as if she walked with two canes.

On the way down the hall, riding in the wheelchair and feeling more than a little ridiculous, Maggie resisted the urge to stop again at the telephone and call to see how Minnie was. At every corner, every hallway, she looked for the stranger. Blanche had taken over the pushing of her chair, arriving for a nightshift. She pushed slowly, waiting for the shuffling slowness of Florence, so heavy on her feet. At times Florence reached out and put her hand on the wheelchair, and Maggie felt she should get up and let Florence ride instead.

"Aren't you feeling well, Florence?"

"Oh, about like usual."

She sounded out of breath.

"After I eat—" she said, breathing hard, "I guess I eat too much."

"What else is there to do?" Blanche said. "I went to a therapist for awhile and learned I eat for entertainment. It doesn't help much to know that. I sort of knew it all along. Nothing like a good show on TV or video and a bag of popcorn."

Florence puffed.

Hazel offered, "A body's interests should be in the Lord, in the church." Then she asked, "Was there a letter today from my grandson?"

Blanche said, "I didn't see the mail today, Hazel."

"It's come and gone," Florence said. "There wasn't anything for us."

They arrived at their room.

Hazel took her robe and nightgown from her tiny closet and went into the bathroom.

"Where does Hazel's grandson live?" Maggie asked.

Florence said, "Oh, somewhere up north. This one's got her believing he's going to make her an apartment in his house. She thinks she can still do her own cooking. She's got twenty or thirty grandchildren, and more great-grandchildren, even a few great-greats, but most of them are scattered all around the country and she hardly knows them. This one grandson is the one she's counting on. A bunch of baloney, of course. He writes her a letter now and then and tells her this stuff about him getting ready anytime to build her apartment."

Blanche folded the wheelchair and pushed it between Maggie's bedside table and the curtain that had not been used since Maggie had become an occupant. Beyond the curtain was Hazel's bedside table, and in front of it her chair. The pictures cluttered on the table, carefully rearranged several times a day by Hazel, were in the direct line of Maggie's eyes when she leaned back in her bed.

A handsome family, so many children and grandchildren. Even a few great-grandchildren. Yet Hazel was here, among strangers.

But, Maggie thought, she wasn't exactly in a position to criticize anyone's children.

Blanche helped Maggie into a nightgown and hurried out to take another call. The registered nurse on nightshift would bring in their medications, and Maggie was more than ready for hers. Her hip and leg ached, a deep down toothache kind of pain that made it impossible for her to relax. But she had determined to bear it out, and not ask for medicine. It was supposed to quit hurting soon.

She stood up and, holding to the bed, made her way around to the washbasin. Balanced precariously against the counter Maggie tried to brush her teeth, and found herself trembling with weakness. She finished brushing, washed her face with one hand, and crawled exhausted into bed. She felt like crying in disappointment at her helplessness.

Hazel had returned and was in bed, her back turned toward Maggie, her reading light out. Florence too had gone to bed, lying on her back, snoring faintly.

Maggie adjusted her bed for reading. She looked at Florence's bulk, Hazel's length. Over Hazel's bed the picture of Jesus, on her table all the small, framed snapshots and pictures. On Florence's table just a box of tissues and a bottle of Jergen's hand lotion. The wall over her bed was blank, as the wall over Maggie's was blank and would remain so. Clara's bed had been cleaned up, her things taken away. It was as if she'd never been there at all. Only her ghost remained. In the shadows Maggie could see her there, a woman not yet old, a pretty woman, slender, still shapely. She looked back at Maggie in silence, unable to tell Maggie if her killer had been her son, or the stranger. Sending a warning to Maggie that she had been found. That she would be next. That her death was a long time coming. Someone wanted her dead.

Maggie hadn't planned on her life coming to this. With Minnie, in the pretty little house she'd bought, life had begun to take on a kind of peace. There was the small flower garden where Maggie whiled away minutes that sometimes turned to hours, and Minnie hunted bugs, or chased chipmunks, or snoozed in the sunshine.

She had begun to feel that the fear was left behind her. The fear, and the danger.

Sitting in bed, trying to get interested in a magazine an aide had given her, Maggie lifted her eyes and stared at the wall above Clara's empty bed. Her memory picked up the past. It was as if her past life had become her present, to be lived and relived, the answer she sought as elusive as the question unvoiced.

Chapter Twenty-Seven

Emmy's sixtieth birthday startled her. One day she woke up and found she was no longer in her fifties, and she lay staring at the wall, trying to adjust to this change before she got out of bed and prepared for the afternoon and evening.

The years between knowing that Lacey, whose name was now Leslie, had become the happy child that Emmy wished her to be, and her own sixtieth birthday seemed now to be filled with nothing.

The years had drifted by, leaving her much the same as before, gaining her very little.

"Why don't you do something respectable?" her mother had asked her, when she'd learned years ago that Emmy was playing blues and jazz piano in a nightclub. "And those hours! It's just not respectable. You used to want to go to school, now's your chance."

Respectable! "Birds of a feather flock together," Mom said sagely. Emmy was speechless. She thought of her life, playing for people who sometimes cried in their drinks, sometimes laughed.

She thought of the people who came up to compliment her and leave tips in the glass on the piano. Many of them she had gotten to know. She had seen worse things in a parking lot at a supermarket than she'd ever seen in any of the clubs and bars where she'd worked. One in particular stuck in her mind. Two children, a boy and a girl. The boy eleven or twelve, the girl six or seven, had been left alone in the car. The boy stretched up looking toward the store, then pushed his little sister down, and the car rocked. Horrified, sickened, Emmy wondered what she should do. She thought of going over and knocking on the window to get the boy off the girl. She thought of writing a note and putting it beneath a wiper on the windshield. Your son is sexually abusing his little sister.

Once again he looked up, and the little girl sat up too and tried to edge away, but he pushed her down again. It didn't seem to matter to him that other people were in the parking lot. Only whoever had gone into the store mattered. He was down on her again, and the car resumed its rocking. No one else sat in a car nearby, only Emmy.

Finally he looked up again, and a nice-looking young couple was coming out of the store and toward the car. The boy worked at tucking clothes back where they belonged and the little girl stood up and pulled up her panties. The children's faces were blank.

It was a Sunday morning, and the parents were dressed for church. They drove on, the boy on his side of the back seat, the girl on her's, each looking out opposite windows as if there had been no contact at all during the time the parents had been gone.

She had done nothing, after all.

Another time, another parking lot, same town, while Emmy sat and considered moving here, a middle-aged man drove up and parked in the slot directly behind her. Through the rearview mirror she watched him, curious about his furtive looks over his shoulders and around at other cars. Her presence seemed unimportant to him, perhaps because her back was toward him. What was he up to? Robbing a bank or something? Or the convenience store a few yards away? Then to her embarrassment and disgust she saw he was proceeding to masturbate, all the while casting those furtive looks around. She felt like sticking her head out the window and yelling at him, "For Christ's sake, man, don't you have a bathroom with a lock on your door? Go home and use the damned thing!"

What did they put in the water in this town? Whatever, they needed a shot or two of saltpeter.

She drove away instead, and went back to Chicago and played piano at Roger's bar again, as she did off and on as long as he owned the bar.

Perhaps Mom was right, Emmy decided after Mom finished explaining all the reasons Emmy should have a daytime job in a respectable place. Foremost, of course, was her desire to do something Mom would approve of.

For several years then she had played piano at night, in a club in San

Francisco, and gone to school in the daytime. She had driven home every month to tell of her progress, searching for approval from her mother. Mom gave it, nodding, nodding.

In her mid-forties Emmy had finally earned a business degree.

"Now you can quit playing piano in bars," Mom said.

But Emmy found office work dull and boring. She felt like a schoolgirl who wanted only to stare out the window, lost in space with thoughts suspended. She missed piano to the depths of her soul. She lived in a tiny one room apartment that didn't have room for a piano even if she had been allowed to have one. Also she couldn't make as much money as she did playing piano. She had been a person of the night too long.

Nor did the respectable job give her the opportunity to travel around, working one city, then another, searching perhaps, for something. So she went again to see her family.

"I'm quitting my job," she said at the Sunday dinner table. They were all there. Mom, Rebba, Peggy, Tim and Cary, and the nieces and nephews. They all stared at her. Aunt Emmy had finally gotten a respectable job and she was quitting it? Her niece, Lydia, looked at her with eyes as large and round as Mom's.

Peggy said, "I knew it. I told you."

They didn't approve. Not even in Tim's eyes did she see approval. Tim who liked his beer and the bar scene. Of course it was no secret how Rebba had to nag him to stay away from the bars.

Emmy didn't tell them she had already quit her job, and furthermore, all her clothes and the few little keepsakes she had collected were in the trunk of her car and she was on her way back to Chicago. She had called Roger's club where she'd had her first job, and been given a friendly invitation to come on, as if she were an erratic relative who dropped in from time to time. At Roger's bar she was willing to play afterhours and only for tips. From there she planned to go on east, Philadelphia, maybe New York, then down to Miami, back to New Orleans. Her time schedule was wide open. She might find along the way that for which she searched, the place where she wanted to stay.

Mom hugged her and kissed her goodbye, and laughed. "Well, Emmy, maybe you should buy your own place. Maybe I'll come and be your barmaid."

With tears in her heart Emmy laughed too and held on to Mommy a moment longer, grateful that at last she had been accepted as she was.

Her visits home dropped to once or twice a year. In the coming years she covered a lot of ground. She met a lot of people, knew them casually, ate with them, laughed with them, and danced. But mostly she played piano.

After a few years of wandering she moved on back west. For the past five years she had worked in clubs along the coast from San Francisco south. In Los Angeles she bought an apartment house and lived in a small apartment as simply as always with scarcely more than sleeping room. She bought more real estate, sold it, and became more financially secure.

On her sixtieth birthday she knew suddenly that she wanted more stability. She was tired of apartments, of her collections remaining small enough to put into one suitcase. If she stopped to admire a cut glass bowl in a window, she passed it by because she might be moving on next week.

She needed stability. She wanted a house. With trees and shrubs and grass, and a backyard fence.

The club she worked in now was the one Bob had sent her to, even though the manager had changed a couple of times. Once, she'd been asked if she'd like to manage the club, but she'd said no. It would have changed her life, tied her down, given her no time for piano, which was her life. Playing for the audience, playing for herself.

She dressed and left her small apartment and drove to her real estate broker. Before the day ended she had bought a two bedroom house in a suburb a few miles away. Behind her house the mountains rose, brown most of the year, greening when rain fell in the winter. No big trees here, just scrub. But the hills were like a barrier behind her house, protecting her from cold north winds.

She wondered why she had taken so long to do this. The house wasn't new but it was a delight. She spent her days decorating, hanging her own wallpaper, painting, planting. Then one day as she walked through a mall she found herself looking through glass at a black puppy.

The little guy gazed up at her with his big smoky eyes, his snub nose pressed against the glass. There was a white dot of hair over each eye.

Chills passed over her skin, tingling, tightening. She drew closer to the glass of the pet shop.

Midnight. Except for the white eyebrows, he could have been Midnight, reincarnated. As she looked into his eyes she saw recognition. I've been waiting for you. I knew you'd come.

Midnight, as surely as she stood here, blundering her way toward him, at last. She put her hands on the glass on each side of his round little head and saw the happiness fill his lonely eyes. A stubby black tail began to wag. Then the whole body.

His face lighted. The recognition was complete, for her and for him.

She went into the shop, barely able to breathe.

Coincidence? Or blind stumbling on her part to this stage of her life? A house with a fenced backyard. A home for herself and Midnight.

"The black puppy in the window," she said to the clerk as soon as he finished a sale with a couple who bought a beautiful kitten that had long white hair and bright blue eyes. The little thing was trembling in fear, but the young woman tucked it up beneath her chin and began crooning softly. She went out the door, the new pink leash trailing over her arm. Emmy tried not to see the other puppies and kittens in their small cages. Cages with wire floors that it seemed would hurt their feet.

"The Black Labrador?" The clerk was a thin, nervous man of about thirty, dark hair, long neck. He didn't look at her as he busily filed away some information Emmy presumed was about the Persian kitten that had sold for three hundred dollars.

"If that's what he is." She'd never known exactly what Midnight was. He was just there, on the farm, when she went to live there.

"A hundred and twenty-five," the clerk said.

She wrote a check, then went through the process of showing identification. Her hands trembled. She was so happy she could have cried.

"He's had his shots. He's three months old." He gave his lecture about house training, about food, vet visits, gave her literature and a little bag of special treats. Finally he smiled.

"Let's get him out of that cage. He's been waiting there a couple of weeks."

The man handed the puppy to her. The soft fur settled into her hands. She felt his heart beating beneath her fingers. His warmth rushed into her heart as she held him against her. His muzzle, short and round, turned to her face and she smelled the sweetness of puppy breath.

"Well," the clerk said, "He's found his mama ..." She also bought a leash. She chose blue. Then, she bought a small bag of dogfood, some canned food, and even a bottle of liquid vitamins and a selection of toys. All this wasn't necessary, she thought beneath the smile in her mind, but the clerk was good at his job.

She drove home with the puppy on her lap, held against her with her left hand as she guided the car with her right.

For the first time in years she had someone to talk to at home. She could talk out loud without feeling she was losing it all upstairs. Instead of talking under her breath, she could actually talk out loud. It was a luxury she hadn't even thought about before.

"I can't name you Midnight," she said to the puppy, "Even though I believe that's who you are. We have to think up a different name."

No name was suitable for this marvelous bit of animal life. She told him, "Now I have to go to work tonight. You go to sleep here, and you stay here until I get back." She made him a bed in the kitchen. Beside it she put a water dish and a food dish, as well as toys.

She took him out into the backyard and told him, "Now here is where you go to the bathroom." She saw his mental struggle to understand. She walked about with him until he squatted and peed, then she praised him lavishly and took him back into the house.

That night at work she printed on a white sheet of paper the words, "Help me name my black Lab puppy," and propped it against the tip glass.

"Nurse! Nurse!"

Florence woke with a snort. "Now what?" She turned over and leaned on her elbow, blinking toward Maggie's reading light.

Hazel drew a long breath and put her arm up over her eyes. Across the hall Thomas called, "Nurse! Nurse!"

Maggie reached for her call button and pressed it. The small light came on above her bed. There would be a light on above the door in the hall, beckoning, calling for help. On the table beside Maggie's bed was the little plastic cup with the pain and sleeping pills she hadn't yet taken.. "Let me put it off as long as I can," Maggie had pleaded with the determined night nurse. "I don't want to be dependent on medication. I want to be able to go home in a few days." The nurse had looked steadily at her as if she were three years old and trying to get by with hiding candy under her pillow. Then she shrugged.

She came into the room now, a severe face set with its wrinkles, its values etched into every line.

"What's the problem?" she asked, turning off the light.

Her white uniform rustled like taffeta as she stretched to reach the light. It had grown tight on her since its purchase, Maggie assumed. She wouldn't have bought it this tight.

Across the hall Thomas yelled, "Nurse! Nurse!"

Florence got laboriously out of bed, her nightgown above her knees, the heaviness of her legs like two tree trunks rubbing bark from each other. "It's the old man," she said. "Can't you hear him?"

"God rest his soul", Hazel murmured. "God rest his body! And let the rest of us get some sleep." Florence padded toward the bathroom without house slippers, her toes slapping the tile floor.

"His light wasn't on," the nurse said. "Yours was. What do you need?"

Over her shoulder Florence said, "We need you to shut him up."

Maggie began to laugh. She sat in bed and laughed, on the verge of hysteria, unable to stop. The sour face of the nurse, the prayers of Hazel, Florence's padding to the bathroom, and Thomas, all meshed into an irresistible comedy. No one else appeared to see the humor in it, so she smothered her laughter, and tried not to giggle.

"Nurse!"

"I gave him a sleeping pill," the night nurse muttered, "What did he do, spit it out? He does sometimes." She went out the door, Florence returned to bed, and Hazel drew a deep breath and gave thanks to the Lord.

The clock on the wall read twenty past midnight.

The night grew quiet. Florence back in bed began to snore almost immediately. Hazel drew another long breath and turned to face the wall beyond her bed. Maggie turned out her reading light and the room filled with dark shadows. She sat wide awake, leaning onto her right side to protect her aching hip and leg. She had spent too many years wide awake at midnight to be able to sleep now without aid.

At home she sat in bed reading, usually until two or three, with Minnie asleep at her side. At home the past hadn't haunted her as it did now in this strange environment.

Twenty past midnight.

Exactly the time she had met him.

Chapter Twenty-Eight

The small dark club she worked in couldn't afford a band, so she came in at seven or eight or nine and played piano blues and jazz until twelve or one or two, as the mood swayed her.

Sometimes it seemed the noise of the drinking crowd drowned her music out, and at those times she drifted into that distant place within herself and let her fingers ease into the music that soothed her. Blues, not jazz, soft, crying blues, wordless, speaking only to emotions that could not be put into words. Then someone would yell, "Hey, Emmy! Put some life into that piany!"

So she would play louder, turning to jazz, sometimes to boogie-woogie, depending on the demands of the crowd.

Tonight, many calls had come, suggesting names for her new puppy. She heard the voices, sometimes saw the faces. "Name him Roscoe", a man said at her shoulder as he stuffed a twenty dollar bill into the tip glass. "It means 'from the deer forest'. Play 'Summertime', soft and easy."

"Thanks," she said and eased into Summertime. Another man, deep in the array of small dark tables and noisy crowd yelled, "Hey, put some life in it, for Christ's sake, Emmy! Nobody in here's dead yet! We don't need a dirge!" There were times when she wished they'd all just go ahead and get drunk so she could play as she chose. When they were swaying over their drinks they loved everything, or they sat with long, silent faces, buried in a faraway or recent past, a love affair gone sour, usually.

Love affairs hadn't been a major part of Emmy's life. She was too busy with her work, her music. She had reached a cynical conclusion late in her thirties. There was no such thing as true romantic love. There was only lust, more so on the man's part than the woman's. Lust that wore off in a few months. The man went on to look for another round of lust, and the woman wept with a broken heart. Sometimes it became obsession, having more to do with the ego than with any kind of love, so Emmy thought.

Too many times a woman alone came to sit at the table closest to her piano, saying nothing, staring, emotions almost palpable. She'd give a cold shoulder to the men who approached her. She'd sit and watch Emmy's fingers on the keys, she'd drown herself in the music and the drinks, then she'd rise silently and leave. Emmy would seldom see her again.

Emmy turned her wrist and checked the time. Twenty past midnight. She'd play on until twelve-thirty, then she was going home. Home to her puppy. She wished she'd brought him along, put him in a carrier at the side of the piano. But then again she wanted him to adjust to being at home, alone at times.

The hand came in view, pale blue shirt sleeve rolled up a few rounds revealing an expensive wrist watch and curly hair on the sturdy arm. The hair turned reddish gold in the circle of light that spotlighted Emmy. He wore a diamond ring on his index finger and one of onyx on the little finger. Short hairs on the backs of his thick fingers caught the light briefly with a glint of reddish gold.

He propped a note in front of the one she had written asking for help in naming her puppy. Then the hand withdrew.

She turned to catch a glimpse of his face but only saw his back as he walked away.

He was on the short side, perhaps five-seven or eight. His shoulders were broad, strong and straight, his arms muscled. His waist tapered to narrow hardness and a tight, rounded bottom. He had an easy, confident sway to his shoulders as he walked that stopped the breath in Emmy's throat, and brought to her body a strange tingling she'd never felt before. A thrill threaded through her veins and shot downward into her groin.

He maneuvered between the tables, and stopped at one in shadows, against the wall. When he sat down she saw his face. A strong nose, a high forehead, steady, narrowed eyes. The skin fit closely over the bones of his cheeks and jaws. There was no softness, no puffiness. His hair was high-lighted with grey and thinning. The corners of his lips moved, a brief, quick smile. He rested an ankle on the other knee, and clasped the ankle loosely in his hand. The tingling in Emmy burst into strong sexual desire. Her skin felt anointed in some strange, lascivious oil, something unknown to her until this moment, a secret lotion that everyone knew about but her. She stared at his face, his body, the easy way he sat in the chair sideways to the small table. He was alone.

He wasn't handsome as some she'd seen. Like his shoulders his face showed strength. A strong jaw, strong nose. Hair a light color, not really blond nor brown. His eyes could have been any color, but she sensed a lightness, like his hair, not really blue nor green nor grey, but flecked with specks of brown in blue-grey depths. There was an intensity in his stare toward her that made her gasp softly for breath.

She tore her eyes away, her fingers faltering on her music for the first time. She stopped playing for a moment and closed her hands tightly. The note he had propped in front of hers had printed letters:

RAVEN: Do you want to play for me?

YES, her heart answered. Yes, yes, yes!

She looked his way again, smiled at him, nodded and mouthed, "What?" He returned her smile, but didn't rise. He lifted a glass on a long stem, which meant he was probably drinking a Marguerita. He toasted her, sipped. He was waiting for her.

She had never gone to the call of strange men, not since the night in Roger's bar when a young guy had hung around staring at her for several nights, and she had felt flattered by his attention and was beginning to smile at him too much. Roger had been watching, and he warned her, "Stay away from him. He's into some pretty dirty porn. Got connections, you know. Big time crime. Don't mess with him." She had left town soon after, nervous and wary of the attention. She'd never seen him again, but would never forget his face.

She'd sometimes sit and talk with customers during minutes of rest, but she detested the idea that some of them expected her to come to their table whenever they beckoned. At times the bouncers would have to uproot some of the more persistent and toss them out. The regular customers expected nothing of her but music.

She continued to play, wishing he'd just go away. She didn't like this feeling his presence gave her. Twelve-thirty came and passed, the night hummed, closed into the smoky darkness of the club. Voices were getting louder. The manager liked to close at one if he could.

Finally she drew away, taking her tips and the note from the stranger. She hoped he was gone.

Her eyes found the table the moment she turned. He had risen and was standing, waiting. He pulled out a chair for her.

She passed through the tables, spoke to those who spoke to her, answered, "Goodnight, see you tomorrow night," to the question, "You're not quitting are you?"

He didn't try to take her hand, and she was glad. She felt so drawn to him she was ready to believe, as she did with the pup, that they'd been close in a former life. She sat down, glad to have a solid force beneath her before her legs folded. Sixty years old, and falling in love at first sight, something she'd never believed in. She felt young and virginal.

"Hello, Emmy," he said, and his voice fit him perfectly. Deep and easy. He touched her shoulder briefly and lightly, and the electricity of contact melted her.

She wanted to say something witty, or at least half-bright, but she said nothing. A dim-wit, he would think.

"You play a mean piano," he said.

She sucked in a breath. "Is that a compliment or a criticism?"

"Great blues, great everything. Would you like a drink?"

"No thanks. I have to get home to my puppy."

"A black Lab, right?"

"Yes."

"Gentle dogs. I used to have one. You'll love him. How old is he?"

"Three months. I just got him today." She told him about the pet shop and the little pup looking at her with round, pleading eyes. He listened, as if what she was saying was the most important thing he'd ever heard.

She was embarrassed by her suddenly loose tongue. He knew about her dog, about her new home, about her backyard, everything she'd done today even to the brand of dogfood she'd bought. She turned the conversation toward him. "I've never seen you here before."

"Oh, I've been here. I've seen you. I've been listening to your music for quite a while."

"You didn't tell me what you wanted me to play."

He had a way of looking steadily into her eyes that changed her entire self-concept. In front of this name-less man she had become something she had never known she was. A woman in need, a woman naive in the face of new experiences.

He said, "Everything. Whatever you want to play."

She stared into his eyes. He was drawing her into him with his eyes, his presence, and she wondered if he knew the power he had over her.

He looked down at his glass, turning it. Light sparkled on the edges and deep within the slender stem.

"My name is Gavin Richards. I own a club, and I'd like you to come play for me."

Disappointment was bitter in her throat. She leaned back. Of course he wouldn't be interested in a woman her age for any but a professional reason. He was probably five or six years younger than she, for one thing, and most probably he was married. There would be no romance in this alliance.

Yet beneath the disappointment she breathed a sigh of relief. She liked her life as it was, she and her new house, and the puppy. There was no place in her future for a man.

Especially one who was probably married.

"I like the name," she said. "The one you suggested for my puppy."

"Raven? The least I can do." He smiled, that intimate smile that had no doubt made him a successful club proprietor over the years. "Will you come work for me, Emmy?"

He named a price then that caused her chin to drop in astonishment. A flicker of doubt washed through her and was gone, buried beneath the silt of her attraction to him.

Still, she had been around the clubs for a long time. She played in one outside a mid-western town once years ago, and was paid a salary so good she didn't have to depend on tips. It turned out to be a front for illegal prostitution. So she wasn't so dazzled that she was completely naive.

"All right," she found herself saying, "What's the catch?"

"Catch? No catch. I need entertainment. I like your style, your music."

His glance passed over her face, brow to chin, to the tie at the neck of her blouse. It was a red blouse, silky and full, long-sleeved, tucked into close-fitting black slacks that hugged her hips and legs. A gold chain belt drooped loosely at her waist. She always wore high-heeled sandals. She liked the feminine feel of them. These tonight were red to match her blouse. She was aware of herself as she hadn't been in years. Self-conscious. Seeing herself through his eyes, an indeterminate age. She hadn't had any kind of cosmetic surgery because a few wrinkles hadn't bothered her. In the muted lights of clubs almost everyone became ageless.

A faint smile turned up one corner of his lips. "I like the way you hold your wrists."

"I only play piano," she said cautiously.

He shrugged, twisted his glass, looked into it, found it empty and pushed it away.

"That's all I want you to do, play the piano, just as you do here. I need music background for the entertainment. It starts at ten, so I'd like you to start playing sometime between nine and ten, if you're interested."

Piano players were too easy to get. She couldn't help her suspicions that more was here than she was being told. Why her?

"Just exactly what is this entertainment?"

He gave her that smile again. There was a shyness about him that must be deliberate. Shy in this business? No way.

"You're a suspicious lady, Emmy."

"I've been in this business a long time."

He nodded, looking at her, his eyes steady but unrevealing. She decided she'd been wrong about shyness. It was just his way, a slow smile, lazy speech, but his eyes, narrow and direct, probably missed nothing. He'd been in the business a long time too, she suddenly felt.

"Don't worry so much," he said, slipping his gaze down her blouse again. "What have I done, offered you too much money?"

She laughed, her head tipped back. "That's what I've gotten from working in cheap bars where I've seldom been paid a living salary," she said. "Offer me some money, and I start wondering why. I just bought my house last week. A real salary I can certainly use."

"Then, I'll see you as soon as you can get free. We open at five. Could you be there tomorrow?"

He stood up. She sat still, looking up at him.

She licked her lower lip and nodded. "Tomorrow. I'll be there."

He laid a business card with the name of the club and the address in front of her.

Then he walked away, dressed as casually as most of the men who came into this particular place to while away an evening, but wearing expensive jewelry. She watched the sway of his shoulders and felt her breath stop somewhere in the far depths of her heart.

Not until he was gone did she remember her question: exactly what is this entertainment?

He hadn't answered her.

Chapter Twenty-Nine

"Raven."

Emmy bent over the puppy. He wriggled and whined and reached his snub little snout up to lick her. She picked him up, burying her face in the silkiness of his wavy, black fur.

"Raven is your name." She added self-consciously, as if he could see her doubt, "I met your future daddy tonight."

He licked her cheek and whined.

During the next several hours, when she was supposed to be doing such things as sleeping, eating breakfast and lunch, or just playing with Raven, her mind went over and over her obligations to Chancy at the club where'd she played for the last two years. The tips there had been good enough, but her major living expenses were paid from real estate profits. The crowd was friendly and some of them had become as close to friends as she had these days. She'd been in one place longer than since she had left the country years ago. Could she just walk out on Chancy and Beverly? They'd been good to her.

She made a decision to leave Raven in the fenced backyard where he could at least be entertained by the birds, and left early for the bar. She wanted to talk to Chancy and Bev. They closed only for a few hours in the night and early morning, opening again by ten o'clock. She found them both behind the bar, sitting on stools, talking to a man unfamiliar to Emmy. The day crowd was different from the night. A few more customers sat at tables, one couple who looked as if they probably had fake ID's, another talking quietly and drinking beer. That was another difference about a day crowd. They were more likely to drink beer.

"Well, hello Emmy. Been shopping?" Bev asked.

She moved her stool away from the men and parked it at the curve in the long bar. Chancy waved at Emmy and she waved back. The young couple also waved. Very often customers recognized her while she didn't know them. The contrast in lighting put their faces in shadow, while she sat in spotlight.

"No, I haven't. I just want to talk to you and Chancy."

"Uh-oh, Chancy! Come here."

Bev was obese, but seemed comfortable with it. It didn't bother her that the stool she sat on was totally lost somewhere beneath her, leaving her looking as if she perched on a stick. She wore what she wanted to, was always friendly and jovial.

Emmy had never seen her eat anything during the long hours of the evening. There was an apartment over the club where Chancy and Bev lived, but Bev enjoyed the crowd and her voice could be heard any time Emmy stopped playing to rest her fingers.

Chancy came close and leaned against Bev.

"Did you see the man who came in late last night?" Emmy asked. "I went over to sit at a table with him."

They both nodded, waiting. A customer came through the outer door, stopped and blinked. It would take a few moments for his eyes to adjust to the change from sunshine outside to the equivalent of moonlight inside.

"He's been here before, been coming in a lot lately," Chancy said. "His name is Gavin Richards, and he's manager or owner maybe of a club downtown. What'd he do, offer you a job?"

"Yes. Did he tell you?"

"Warned me he was going to try to get my lady piano player." Chancy grinned.

They watched her. Bev bit the inner side of her cheek, dimpling the outer.

"I hate to leave," Emmy said. "But ..."

"A lot of money, huh?" Bev released her cheek and stuck her tongue into it instead. It bulged like a chipmunk's full of food.

Emmy nodded. Bev patted her arm.

"You can come back whenever you want, Emmy. But don't worry about us."

But she would worry, she knew as she left. There was no written contract, not even an agreement. But she took with her a touch of sadness and a small load of guilt. There was more involved than money, of course. She wanted to be where she could at least see Gavin Richards.

Maggie watched for the stranger, dreaded the stranger. As police came again to talk to them, asking with different questions about the son who had taken Clara away, she made up her mind. Waited, and carefully considered what she could say.

She waited for Florence and Hazel to explain all they knew, again.

"He called her Mama." Hazel looked at Florence for confirmation. "You heard him call her Mama." Her gaze turned toward Maggie. It was more difficult for her to look at Maggie. She had to turn her head sharply to the right, and she put up her hand to rub her neck and a grimace crossed her features. "You heard him, didn't you, Maggie?"

"Yes. Called her mother."

"That's right. Mother, it was."

"Yes," said Florence, nodding. "We heard him."

The officers were detectives this time, dressed in plain clothes. The younger man, a tall, handsome Texas Ranger type, wore jeans and a western shirt, plaid, fitting him precisely. Although Maggie couldn't see his feet, she figured he also wore western boots, if not cowboy. They hadn't made much sound coming down the hall, so she guessed they were western, with the softer heels. Just recently, the footsteps had separated from others in the hall and entered the room. The shorter man, roundish face, entered first and Maggie's heart came into her throat. But it wasn't the stranger, she saw on second glance.

The older detective said to Maggie, "He called her mother?"

"Yes," Maggie nodded, offering nothing about the stranger. She hadn't seen him today. Probably Florence had scared the peewadden, as she would say, out of him with all her questions.

"Is there anything you can add?"

"No," Maggie said.

With Florence and Hazel, she watched them leave.

Another day in the nursing home. She had begged out of going to the dining room for breakfast, taking that time for a private bath and toilet hour. She made herself put on makeup, as usual, just a touch of lipstick, and powder to keep her nose from glistening like a Christmas tree light.

She hadn't worn much makeup since she had left the nightclubs behind. She brushed her hair until her scalp tingled.

She smelled the roses before she saw them. At first it seemed she was back in memory again, the fragrance preceding the image.

Then a nurse's aide entered, carrying a large bouquet of roses. Maggie's heart grabbed. She knew it was one dozen, in beautiful full bloom.

She saw the mixture, red and pink.

And stood staring, heart chilling, hairbrush gripped in her hand.

She needed Minnie, needed to feel the little dog's warmth in her arms, to make this awful fear go away.

The aide looked at her, and looked again.

"Something wrong?"

Maggie couldn't answer.

She stood at the wash basin, in front of the small mirror, three steps from her bed, anchored within the walker, her left leg resting, her artificial hip carefully protected. She turned, lurching toward the bed, stumbling.

"Oh, my God!" the aide cried, and tossed the roses into the sink. She grabbed Maggie's arm, keeping her from falling.

With the nurse's help, Maggie crawled onto the bed and leaned back on the pillows, eyes closed, breathing hard. "Are you all right?" the young nurse asked.

"Yes," Maggie managed.

"Is there something wrong with the flowers? Are you allergic to roses or something?"

It was a better answer than she could have thought of at the moment. She nodded.

Silence ensued for a short time. Footsteps interrupted, coming along the hall, a man's steps, and it seemed they paused at the door. But they passed on. Across the hall as if awakened by the steps, Thomas yelled, "Nurse? Nurse?"

A familiar sound now, after these few days. A welcome sound. It helped Maggie to breathe easier, her heart to calm. She opened her eyes. The aide was just standing there, the roses gathered up again, her worried gaze on Maggie.

Maggie managed a smile. "You can have them."

"Don't you even want the card? Who would send you roses if they knew you were allergic to them? Want me to read the card?" Her own curiosity at work, she opened the small white envelope.

She removed the card, frowned, turned the card over. "Nothing," she said. "That's funny. Don't you think that's strange?"

She went away, taking the roses, pausing once more at the door to look back and ask Maggie if she were okay. Maggie nodded.

"I'm okay."

More footsteps in the hall, coming now with voices that were familiar and welcome. Florence and Hazel were coming back from breakfast.

Florence brought a napkin-wrapped object and put it on Maggie's bedside table. "You can't tell me you won't get hungry before lunch time. I brought you a cinnamon roll."

She was so glad to see them. These two old ladies, who chatted most of the time when they were awake, as if they were friends from the beginning of their time, or, perhaps, were family. Even with the preaching that Hazel sometimes forced onto Florence, and the teasing that Florence threw back at her, they were more often just friends. And Maggie was so glad to see them, so glad to hear their voices in the background of her thoughts, calming her fears.

"What's this about a dozen red and pink roses?" Florence. asked. "Judy said you're allergic to 'em."

"Yes." How strange that her voice could sound so natural when her heart pounded so hard and she felt breathless and tense with fear.

"Too bad. One of these days he's going to get discouraged and stop sending you flowers. Are you so allergic you can't keep them in the room?"

Hazel said, "Of course she is, or they'd be here."

They sat down. Florence lifted her feet onto the footrest. "If I ever had a man who sent me a dozen roses, red and pink especially, I would have followed him to the end of the earth."

I too. And wasn't it because of him that she was here? … an image of blood, of a severed head … not Minnie.

Unable to wait Maggie struggled up again. The pain pills she had taken hadn't yet deadened the pain. But she had to find out if Minnie were all right. They had found her, she didn't know how. She was four years and three thousand miles away. But it hardly mattered how. Her suspicions had been confirmed by the roses. Only one man had ever sent her red and pink roses. With the walker firmly in her hands she started out into the hall.

"Where're you going?" Florence demanded.

They were both in their chairs, sometimes rocking just a bit, the squeak of the chairs adding to the sounds of their conversation. But they both grew quiet as they waited for her answer. The longer she was here, in uh nursing home, the more familiar their questions were becoming. Like the aide, they didn't understand her refusal of a dozen beautiful roses.

"I'm just going to the telephone."

"I thought you called earlier."

"Yes . . ."

"I don't think you ought to worry so much about that dog, Maggie. Eat more, worry less," Florence advised.

Hazel said, "Go call. It don't hurt a thing."

"Unless she falls. What then?"

"Then we'd help her, wouldn't we?"

"Hazel, sometimes you make sense."

"Thanks," Maggie said, "But I'm fine. I'll be back in a minute."

She went out of the room, one slow step at a time, around the door, into the hall. The hall was empty for the moment, then a nurse came from the front and went into a room farther up. Maggie picked up the telephone.

"Animal Hospital," the familiar voice said. "Ginger speaking."

"Ginger, this is Maggie. I—I'd like to know if anyone has been there asking about Minnie."

There was a pause on the line. Maggie could almost see Ginger's face. Puzzled? Wondering why she was asking the question? It gave Maggie only a moment of relief before she saw she'd been wrong, and the terror encircled her tighter than it had before, drawing her skin cold around her and chilling her heart.

"There was a strange phone call," Ginger said. "Some man asked if we had a little brown Chihuahua, about four years old named Minnie."

Oh god. "When?"

"Last week. He—uh—A year or so ago too—I thought it was kinda funny—I'd forgotten about that other call, until this one came."

"What did you tell him?"

"Back then? Well—no. Of course we had a record of your dog, you know, vaccinations and all, but she wasn't here or anything, and I didn't think about it until after I'd hung up—uh—"

"Today! Yesterday—what did you tell him?"

Maggie's voice conveyed her anxiety, her fear and desperation. Ginger's answer was a stammer.

"Last week—that was last week—well I—I said yeah—yes, there's—uh —one. Uh—I thought—"

"Is Minnie still there?" Her helplessness screamed within her. She wanted to throw down her walker and run, run to get Minnie, run home, get the car and leave. Instead she stood trembling, shaking, the tremors reaching her voice, causing her heart to pound heavily. "Is Minnie still there? Is she all right?"

Maggie held to the phone with fingers that trembled.

The girl at the Animal Hospital said, "Uh, yeah—uh—do you want to speak to the doctor? He's right here."

"Yes! But first, Ginger, no one, I mean no one is to pick up Minnie but me! Ginger?"

"Maggie, what's wrong?" Doctor Callison asked.

"Doctor, don't let anyone take Minnie out of there. Don't let anyone else even see her. Please. It's important."

He too paused, then he said, "Of course not, Maggie. Don't worry. We'll take very good care of her."

"Was there only the one phone call?"

He hesitated. "Yes, I'm sure that must have been all."

Maggie could almost see the look of wondering that passed between the Doctor and the assistant.

She said again, "Don't even let anyone see her! Don't let anyone pick her up. I'll come after her myself."

"She's safe, Maggie, don't worry."

She hung up and stood drooping, trying to gain strength to move again.

When she felt she could walk without falling, she went back to her bed and collapsed on it with her eyes closed.

Neither Hazel nor Florence missed her exhaustion.

"What on earth's wrong?" Florence asked. "You're white as a sheet. I'm calling the nurse."

"No. It's okay."

"Don't look okay to me," Hazel said. "Go ahead and call the nurse, Florence."

She would have to make other plans. She had changed identity once, she could do it again. This nursing home, this living grave as she had thought of it, was now her sanctuary, if a sanctuary existed in this world. She wished she could take Minnie and walk into the world of dreams, those safe, marvelous places that existed somewhere, that came to her so seldom now. She wished they could go.

At night, each night she prayed in the noises and alleys of her mind, the silences, the edges of the darknesses and lights, God, please give me back my dreams. But if they came they were lost beneath the power of medication, lost somewhere so difficult to reach.

Footsteps came along the hall, the steps of men, the voices of men and the voice of a woman. Detectives entered the room, led by the nurse.

The nurse turned off Florence's light as both Hazel and Florence told her about Maggie, their concerns, talking at once, words overlapping in confusion.

"Maggie over there—"

"White as a sheet ..."

"Says she's okay, but ..."

The nurse asked Maggie, "What's the problem?"

"... needs a tranquilizer, or a pain pill ..."

"...never complains ... ought to complain ... squeaky wheels you know, get the grease ..."

"... complain a little ... came back from telephone white as a sheet ..."

The nurse nodded. "I'll bring you something, Maggie. Girls, these are detectives from the police department, and they want to ask you some questions. This," she said to the men, "Is Florence, Hazel, and Maggie. Do you feel like talking, Maggie?"

They had been standing, the tall Texan and the rotund man with the blondish hair, his hands in his pockets, his tongue poking out his cheek. Waiting. Waiting for Florence and Hazel to stop fretting about Maggie.

Maggie nodded, the presence of the detectives calming her more and more. If only she could keep them close. A reminder that perhaps justice existed in this crazy world.

They introduced themselves, and began the questioning. Maggie lay listening to Florence and Hazel, still talking together, each adding a few words here and there, the whole making sense.

Occasionally the men looked at Maggie. They both carried notebooks and made occasional notes in them. The nurse returned with a small white pill. Maggie had been refusing the tranquilizers, but now she sat up to swallow the pill.

The nurse said, "You can have four a day if you need them. They're great for anxiety attacks."

"Maybe I will." Maybe she should have from the beginning. Maybe they would have increased the healing. She had to get out of here and get Minnie ...

Minnie!

Of course—that was how they had found her. A little brown

Chihuahua named Minnie. She had changed her own identity, but it hadn't occurred to her to change Minnie's. A tiny puppy, a pound or so, a gift. He had called her a doglet because she was so tiny. "Her name is Minnie," he had said, " every time you look at her remember that I love you."

Minnie … She had accepted the name as she accepted the puppy, as a gift of love.

She sat remembering, putting now another meaning to the living gift. Minnie … a name distinctive only because the dog herself was distinctive. A beautiful nut brown, with gold eyebrows. A smaller than average Chihuahua. He knew she would not change the puppy's name.

She saw Minnie in her cage, that foreign place where Minnie was certain to feel trapped, her own small mind crying for answers to questions she couldn't express.

Time would pass even more slowly for Minnie in her small cage than for Maggie here in hers. But for the first time Maggie was glad Minnie was there, safe, protected by walls and people who would see after her.

"Is there anything else you can remember?" the tall detective asked,

"Yes," Maggie said on sudden impulse. "A man has been coming here. I think you should look for him. Question him. I think …" She stopped. I think he killed her. As a warning to me. They haven't forgotten me. She was limited in how much she could tell them. She had to protect the family so far away, and Minnie. She had to protect Minnie.

What did she know that was so deadly to them? It was almost like an act of revenge, this killing of those close to her.

It was a startling idea, new and disturbing. Revenge.

But her mind could make no connection. It kept going back to the same question: what do I possess that is so deadly?

She heard Florence give an abrupt laugh. "You mean your stranger? You're joking, Maggie! My lands! Don't you know when a man's after you?" Even Hazel gave Maggie an incredulous stare.

"Stranger?", the plump detective repeated. "What stranger?"

They hadn't heard of him before. Florence snorted again. "Well, this good-looking older man, dressed snazzy as can be, has been—you might say—courting Maggie. He's been here a couple of times."

The detectives' eyes settled on Maggie, waiting for her to say something. She answered slowly, carefully choosing her words.

"He's about five-ten, fifty to sixty years old, very distinguished looking, light, greying hair, thinning on the forehead. I don't think anyone here has ever seen him before. He doesn't seem to have anyone here to visit."

The two men exchanged a significant look. "Did he have contact with Clara?"

"She was here the first time he came, yes," Maggie said.

Hazel relaxed her neck. "But he didn't even speak to her as I recall, did he, Florence?"

"Naw! It was Maggie he was interested in, not poor Clara. Just Maggie."

Chapter Thirty

Gavin Richards' nightclub was on the periphery of an area of topless bars, porno shops, movie theatres with X rated films. Called simply "Night Spot" it marked the line between cheap bars and more expensive, exclusive clubs as if seeking anonymity. She would have quickly passed it by if she had been in a strange city looking for work. She would have avoided the street at all means, but the man was a sexual and emotional magnet. She hadn't been able to sleep for thinking of him. Even when she slept it was restless, and she woke often, the puppy trailing behind her as she walked from room to room, or resting comfortably in her arms as she snuggled him to her.

She whispered in his listening ear, "The man's younger than I, probably married a half dozen times, with his last wife thirty years younger." She guessed him to be in his fifties, perhaps ten years her junior. She could have cuddled him on her lap at one time. He would see nothing in her, a woman of sixty. Didn't men always like youth and nubility? They wanted to pass on their seed, see it develop into sons and daughters. The urge never ended. Nature had made the male animal to have a fixed purpose.

Besides, she didn't believe in love. True love that wasn't maternal in origin.

But she had to see him again. Working for him would mean she'd see him every night, unless his club was managed by someone else.

As the hours passed during the afternoon, she went shopping. She bought Raven a doghouse to keep him warm, or cool, when she was at work. A little place of his own in which she hoped he would feel secure while he guarded the backyard. She bought two more dog dishes. Now he had food and water dishes in the kitchen, and outside by his house. He looked at her with sad, puzzled eyes when she left to meet Gavin, as if he knew something she did not know, sensed a wrong turn in her life.

She hadn't expected a street like this, as narrow as old Boston streets, buildings rising high on each side of the narrow strip. A street where young people were beginning to gather for the night, standing about, girls in revealing clothes, teenage boys with their shirts open halfway down showing smooth chests.

A street fairly deserted and quiet at five in the afternoon, but where music and voices would later intermingle, where light would be filled with shadows and shifting darknesses.

The club interior was not a surprise. She knew that, like Roger's place in Chicago and others where she had worked, the nondescript front would be deceptive. Length and depth would make up for width, and inside it was at this time of day like a quiet and enveloping cavern stretching away toward the night.

To her left were tables and chairs, all unused at the moment. The closing of the door left the street noise behind her. At the long bar, stretched along the wall on her right, a few people sat drinking. One bartender was at work. All eyes turned her way when she entered, and conversation lapsed. The bartender came toward her, wiping a glass. He was young, muscled from daily workouts, strong enough to be a bouncer, and probably doubled as one if necessary.

"You looking for Gavin?"

"Yes."

"He's expecting you. Down that way."

Emmy walked the length of the room, and saw that beyond the bar the room widened. The center was filled with small tables, four chairs to each table. To her surprise there was no dancefloor, not even a square, dime-sized floor.

But, to the right, curved near the end corner, close to a wall, was a platform about five feet high. Several spotlights on the ceiling would later outline three distinctive areas there. Steps down at the back led to a narrow hall on which two doors marked "Private" were closed.

Dressing rooms, she thought, and beyond, the alley for quick disappearances.

To her left, at the end of the L shaped platform, was the piano. A spotlight angled onto the keys. It would keep the musician in view. She went to the piano, her fingers slipping softly over the keys. Mellow toned, well-tuned, beautiful.

"Like it?"

His voice sent a ripple of excitement up her spine. She felt her face grow hot, and was glad the spotlight missed her face and outlined her hands. She hesitated before she looked at him. This was going to be a business relationship, she reminded herself, and that was all. All.

But, she would get to see him every night, if …

"Are you the manager here, or just the owner?" she asked.

"I hang around," he said, his voice soft and personal and as mellow as the piano tones. She knew he was smiling that half-smile. She had to look at him sometime. But not yet. She didn't want her hands shaking like an amateur on amateur night.

She sat down on the bench, the spotlight falling fully on her. It had a rosy cast. She began to play. Evening Dreams. A few strains, slipping into the blues she loved.

Tension drained away, her hands stopped trembling, her cheeks cooled. She was in love with the man. For the first time in her life, she was in love. She would have to work at not being crazy in love. The thought of leaving and never seeing him again made her future seemed dark and empty, as if even Raven would then be gone. She could handle it, she decided, her mind working with the speed of her fingers as she trilled to a close.

She could handle it.

"How do you like the club?" he asked, a touch of almost boyish pride in his glance around at the mahogany paneling, the muted light, the dark red carpet and tables that seated no more than four.

"Very nice," she said.

He was still dressed casually, though he had added a jacket. She thought he would probably look very casual and at ease even in a formal tux. He was just that kind of man. But she had a sudden feeling as she looked around at the decor of the club, at the arrangements of bars and the platform near the piano, that there was nothing naive and unworldly about Gavin Richards. The man, the presence, obliterated all else. Even his name was a pleasure to her. Gavin. GAVIN. Speaking it silently his name slid across her tongue like whipped cream.

She did have presence of mind to observe those very obvious platforms and note their purpose. "This entertainment of yours ..."

Standing, her fingers went back to the keyboard for confidence, for comfort, to make more casual her question, to ease her own mind about having come to work in a place like this because of a man. She played a few bars of 'Blues In the Night'.

"... stripping, isn't it?"

His smile came, and the slide of his eyes down her to her sandals, the only frivolous part of her outfit today. She had deliberately dressed in a neat, white suit with a blue blouse. But she didn't own anything but high-heeled strap sandals and wasn't about to go buy anything more practical. She had left that behind her too, when she had left her saddle oxfords and the country.

"Not stripping," he said in intimate, teasing correction, his hand pressing her elbow. His fingers spread heat through the thin material of her suit jacket, into her veins, into crevices of vulnerability she hadn't known existed. He stood close to her, pulling her against him, shoulder to shoulder, arm to arm. "Dancing."

She let herself lean against him for just a second, then she eased away. He was a married man, she was sure. She wasn't into becoming a third party.

Besides, Raven hadn't really understood what she'd said about Gavin being his daddy. If he had, perhaps he'd also known that he'd probably never get a daddy at all, most of all not Gavin.

SHE STARTED WORK a few nights later. When the girls came in to dance, one or two at a time, she noticed something she hadn't noticed before. The angle of the piano was such that if she looked toward the dancers she'd have to turn sideways to the keyboard. She faced instead the wall beyond, a dark corner by the office door, and a few smaller tables, one of them marked Reserved.

The crowd here was different too. In all other clubs where she had worked there were as many women as men. Here, the women were scattered, though some came, and some watched. None of the audience came to the piano to request a tune. They were here to drink, and to watch the girls. Emmy was left to play as she chose.

Emmy hadn't been able to see any of the dancers, but knew when they entered because of the change in the crowd. The applause, the shouts, the laughter. When she saw the girl who leaned over the edge of the piano she stopped playing.

Her first reaction was a frown. Though the light almost blinded her when she turned her head toward the girl, although the young face was in shadow, she was shocked by the girl's age. Sixteen, was her first thought. She thought immediately of Lacey. This girl looked exactly as she pictured Lacey in her mind when Lacey was sixteen. Supple in body, a bit lanky and long, her dark hair hanging almost to her waist, and that beautiful face. She had to remind herself that Lacey was long past the teenage years now. She could very well have a teenager of her own.

"Hi," the girl said. "You sure can play awesome."

"Thank you. I'm glad you like it."

"I love it! The rhythm is really—uh—easy to dance to." She gave a small example, hips rotating, shoulders dipping in opposite direction. It had an awkwardness, like a child just learning, with a naive and natural sexiness. A man's voice at a nearby table urged her on. The girl flipped a hand toward him, and leaned back to Emmy.

"I just wondered if you'd play something special for me."

"Of course. That's why I'm here. What would you like?" Does your mother know you're here? Mother was probably knocked out on drugs somewhere.

Stop being so cynical, Emmy told herself.

"Night Train."

"Night Train it'll be." She toyed with it, wanting to keep the girl longer, trying to find in her face a sign that she was older than she'd first thought. But this girl was not in her twenties. Of course it wasn't against the law to dance in a bar at eighteen. Against the law to drink in one but not to dance, not even in a skimpy little bikini costume such as hers.

Emmy asked, "What's your name, sugar?"

"Tara. What's yours?"

"Emily, shortened to Emmy for family and friends."

The crowd began to cheer and Emmy twisted around to see a girl running up the steps to the stage. She too was young, so young she scarcely had any figure at all.

"Here comes Jennie. She's my partner. Play, Miss Emmy!" Tara cried, running away, going behind the platform and up the steps.

They usually danced in pairs, Emmy saw as the night drifted deeper. In all she glimpsed six girls, coming two at a time to dance, taking a break, coming out again.

After midnight the stripping began, and before the club closed three of the girls had run naked from the stage, costumes dangling from smooth fingers as they waved goodbye. Emmy caught glimpses, seeing young breasts not fully developed. Her feelings that these girls were underage increased.

She began to play for herself, as she always had when her feelings were confused, when something deep within her cried to be understood. She would have left and never come back, but then she saw, as closing hour came, that Gavin sat at the reserved table. Listening, sipping a drink, watching her.

A waiter leaned over her shoulder and said, "Gavin wants you to join him for a drink. What can I bring you?"

"A Coke will be fine," she answered, "with lots of ice." She turned, leaving the piano, and joined Gavin at the table-for-two. The crowd was drifting away, club closing.

It was the beginning of a ritual in which conversation would become natural and easy, but she didn't mention her feelings about the girls until the night Tara was suddenly no longer there. She'd been replaced by a little blond, shorter, curvier, but no older.

"Where's Tara tonight?" Emmy asked, keeping her voice nonchalant, though an uneasy feeling rode with her. She sipped her nightly Coke. There was something not quite right about Tara's dancing so eagerly one night, and gone the next.

"Oh, who knows? They don't hang around long. It can be hard work. Not as glamorous as it sounds. How's Raven?"

It was clear he didn't want to talk business with her. Their conversations had so far been more about bits of nothing, though he'd asked a few questions about her past life. She'd told him that she was divorced. She didn't mention her family, but told him only that she was alone here except for her dog.

"Great little guy, Raven," she said. "House trained already, no accidents."

"Do you leave him in the house when you're gone?"

"No—no, he has his own house in the backyard, but he sleeps with me when I sleep."

"I'll have to come see him sometime—move him over."

Gavin's voice was always as soft as a lover's voice, his attention solely on her during their hour together after closing. But she detected now a flirtatiousness she'd sensed was there from the beginning. It might just be his way of talking to women. She couldn't be sure. But it made her very nervous, very self-conscious, like a schoolgirl on her first date.

She laughed at his sexual innuendo, but didn't answer it. Instead she asked the question that stood between her and her nearly unbearable desire for him.

"Do you have a family?"

She didn't look at him as she waited for his answer. How multi-purposed were drinks, she thought, something to inspect while you were waiting for an answer, something to hold onto as if it were an important action that you were intent upon. Different lifelines, in their different ways, these drinks.

Glasses of purpose.

The length of his pause gave her the answer. "Does it matter?" he finally asked.

"Of course it matters!" She glared at him.

"Okay, okay!" He spread his hands and shrugged like a little boy caught. Then he reached for his billfold. "Want to see my kids?" He brought out snapshots of two young adults. A boy, a girl. Good-looking faces, happy smiles.

"They're in college, out of the house for the most part. But I'm proud of them. They're mine." He smiled. "I think."

"Congratulations. Is that all?"

"Isn't that enough?" He put his billfold away, grinning. He didn't show her a picture of his wife.

Jenny, Tara's partner, was replaced a month later by another new girl. This one was dark and beautiful, and perhaps eighteen, judging by the development of her body. Yet some girls developed very early, Emmy reminded herself as she turned on the piano bench for a couple of minutes to watch the girl dance. She herself had been as mature at age thirteen as most of these who danced here. And for that matter, some of the girls here could be as young as a mature thirteen. Or even twelve. Those younger girls, she noted, danced later, and for not as long. They were the ones who stripped before they ran off the stage, sometimes clumsily, bringing an almost rabid reaction from some of the men. The bodyguards began hovering near the stage at that time of night.

She told Gavin, in a way that she hoped would prompt him to answer some of the questions that bothered her, "The new girl is absolutely stunning. But what happened to Jenny?"

"Who knows?"

It was his standard answer. At first it seemed he would say no more. Anytime she tried to get him on the subject of the girls he led her into other avenues. But then he said, "They're restless. They try a little of this, a little of that. They want to be dancers. They hope for a spot in a big show. They want to be actresses. Some of them work just for awhile to get money to take more lessons."

"Who hires them?"

"I do, usually, sometimes my assistant does."

"Your assistant?"

His look at her was long and steady. There was nothing flirtatious about it. His eyes, always and naturally narrowed, were difficult to see into. The meager light was behind him. She faced into it so that he could see her eyes while his were hidden.

"Is something bothering you?" he asked.

"I just think the girls are a little young."

He smiled. "Girls are always a little young."

She laughed. "You're impossible."

She let it go. Maybe he was right. The older she got, the younger the girls looked. Of course they were eighteen, or nineteen. Not even Gavin would be able to charm the cops into thinking otherwise if he were hiring fourteen and fifteen year-old girls.

Yet that was what they were in some cases, Emmy was almost sure. They came in to dance, some of them very well, and disappeared again into the back door. She never went back there. She had no reason to go back there. She reminded herself that at that age she hadn't been at home doing her school work either. For all she knew these girls went to school in the daytime, danced a few hours at night, and earned enough money to go on to college and learn something respectable, as Mom would say. Something to carry them into old age, in other words.

A pattern began to emerge. The girls stayed from a few nights to a few months, and then were gone, replaced by new girls. Emmy stayed, playing whatever she wished, soft blues, rhythmic boogies, wild jazz. The girls rarely requested any number. She threw in Night Train at least once a night just because every dancer-stripper needed a Night Train. The audience didn't care. They weren't there to listen to music, but to drink, and watch the girls dance. At the end the last two girls always zipped off their little bras, and sometimes the panties, running off nude.

Once Emmy attempted again to talk to Gavin in the quiet of the club when the only sounds were the waiters and waitresses cleaning up, wiping tables, clattering chairs as they upended them onto the tables. Tomorrow morning the cleaning crew would come in and vacuum.

"You said this wasn't a strip joint."

His eyebrows lifted. "Hey, it's not."

She gave him a sample of his own silent, direct looks. He grinned. "Can I help it if they are in such a hurry to change they take their clothes off before they leave the room?"

She didn't try to talk to him about the girls again.

Anyway, she told herself, if she didn't like what she saw, she could always leave.

She didn't leave.

At home she thought about quitting, about buying her own piano and playing at home when she needed music and otherwise getting a daytime job. But another year passed, she was now sixty-one, and the older she got the less her chances would be. Also, the pay would be like pigeon feed compared to what she now had.

She bought more property, feeling a real estate boom would be continuing. She had to plan for her own future. There was no one else to look to. Do your job, she told herself, invest your money. The club seemed to run smoothly, girls coming and going, never returning. It was none of her business.

She had known Gavin several months, had gone through the sweet torture of seeing him every night. She had learned he was in his second marriage, was six years younger than herself, and that he frequently traveled. He had business connections elsewhere which he didn't discuss with her. Their conversations might explore some depth or other, but never Gavin, nor business. Then one morning came the knock on the door.

Raven barked, running from the bedroom with his hair ridged. He looked almost comical, this clumsy-footed, year-old pup ready to eat alive whoever was at the door.

Emmy pulled on a robe and went droopy-eyed to see who it was. None of her friends would be calling this time of day. She hadn't ordered anything, so it couldn't be a mailman. If it were a salesman, he hadn't read the sign on the front gate. 'No solicitors.'

She opened the door. Raven got behind her, growling between her knees.

Gavin stood on her porch holding a beautiful bouquet of a dozen roses, pink and red mixed.

"Does it matter that much?" he asked.

She understood the meaning behind the steady blue of his pleading gaze. Does it matter that much if I'm married?

It should. It should.

She took the roses, and stood aside to let him enter.

Chapter Thirty-One

Emmy learned she had never understood passion. She had never understood that a woman can want a man with the intensity a man can want a woman, or perhaps even more. Her desire for Gavin was wild, dangerous, destroying her image of herself.

She made love to him. She lived to taste him, to feel him, her body opening and sucking him in, as if she could absorb him, take him into the womb of life, conceive him, give birth to him over and over again.

He lay naked and exhausted on her bed, arms and legs flung weakly out and looked through narrowed eyes at her.

"You are the horniest, hottest woman I've ever known, Emmy. But why is that no surprise to me?"

Sidney had told her many times in one form or another—"You have no passion in you, Emmy, you're as cold and distant as the northern lights. I've heard of cold women, but you're the worst. There's something missing in you. You're not a whole woman."

All these years she had thought that Sidney was right. Something was not quite right with her. But now she had learned the secret of passion. Love. She had never been in love before. All these years, so many other men who had searched for a spark within her, from whom she had sought something they couldn't give because it had to come from her instead. Suddenly now it was all so simple, so clear. LOVE.

She caressed Gavin's chest, leaning on her elbow closely against him, loving the feel of his skin. "Just a matter of perception," she said.

He lay looking up at her, then he too rose to an elbow to face her.

"I want to tell you a few things," he said without smiling, "about my marital status. Then, I don't want to talk about it anymore. Agreed?"

In other words, no questions, ever. She would prefer to pretend it didn't exist. She didn't want the intrusion of his other life.

"Agreed."

"My first wife died. Cancer. She was the mother of my kids. My second wife ... well, we've been together close to twelve years. We don't share a room anymore—that ended a few weeks ago—but we share a lot of other things—property, mostly. She doesn't want a divorce. Not now, or ever."

With a long sigh he flopped back on the bed, one arm a pillow. His eyes looked up at the ceiling, and Emmy imagined she saw sadness. She leaned down and kissed him.

Every month on the anniversary of their first time together, he sent her a dozen roses, a mixture of red and pink, buds opening among full blooming flowers, luscious and fragrant.

He never mentioned his other life again.

MAGGIE, lying in the nursing home hospital bed, put her hands over her face and cried in a whisper, "Oh, Gavin."

Her tears had dried, but the longing was still there, too easily brought to the surface of her feelings.

"Gavin, why?"

Why hadn't he just let her go?

"I love you," he had said, his voice low and filled with emotion. "I love you. I don't want to see you hurt. I'd rather never see you again. I love you." It was the last time she had heard his voice, coming almost inaudibly over the telephone.

Gavin, Gavin, Gavin.

She heard a gasp. Then a breath, loud and rasping. Tortured. Maggie rose to her elbow. The room was quiet, the nursing home quiet, lights dimmed. She heard the rustle of bedclothes as Hazel moved, a sharply soft noise beneath the continued long rasp of indrawn breath. The sound of a squeak, of a bedspring, or a tube of metal at the side pulled, merged with the other sounds.

In the shadows of the room Florence's bulk rose upward and then seemed to tumble in slow motion from her bed. She fell onto her bedside table, arms flailing, hands grabbing. The table came over on top of her and the chair scraped across the tile as it was pushed. Items from the top of the table scattered across the floor.

Hazel's overhead reading light came on. Then she too was pitching from her bed, doubled, her length a burden now as if her torso sped forward leaving her legs behind. She went reaching and calling for Florence.

Maggie sat up and put her feet on the floor, standing, forgetting that she didn't have two good legs, that she couldn't run to help someone.

"Florence!" Hazel screamed. "Oh my dear Lord, Florence!"

Maggie fell, her left leg giving in when she attempted to step forward. She grabbed at the mattress and clutched the bottom sheet, pulling it with her. She stopped her fall, but felt a piercing pain in her hip.

"The nurse!" Hazel cried. "We need a nurse!"

Maggie twisted around, and grabbed the call button. The small red bulb on the wall above her bed began to glow like one eye of a devil.

On the floor Florence gasped, then laid still, eyes half opened. Hazel lifted her shoulders, cradled her head and cried out. "Help us! Dear Lord, help us!"

Minutes passed it seemed before Florence gasped again. Maggie tried again to reach Florence. She had taken a course, just enough to be able to attempt to revive someone if the need ever came.

"Lay her down!" she cried. "Lay her flat, Hazel."

Still with her arms supporting Florence, Hazel laid her on the floor. Her chin jerked as she tried to talk.

"What—what do I do? What do I do?"

Maggie got down on her hands and right knee and started across the floor to help Hazel, dragging her left leg. Her hipped throbbed as if freshly broken.

"Press on her chest, Hazel, hurry."

"I'm afraid I'll hurt her!"

"Push!"

Hazel put both hands on Florence's chest and pushed. "Harder!" Maggie crept, as slowly it seemed as if time had stalled, leaving her trying desperately to reach Florence and Hazel. The night was a nightmare where the door kept being farther and farther away, a nightmare unknown to her dream world.

A nurse popped in suddenly, then out again and ran down the hall.

Crying, moaning, calling on God for help, Hazel pushed harder on Florence's chest, and Florence gasped again.

The night RN came running in and pushed Hazel away, beginning resuscitation with vigor and youth. A nurse's aide helped Maggie up. She stumbled on her right leg back to the corner of the bed where she grabbed for support.

Another aide, rushing in, checked on Hazel and helped her to her chair. In the light Maggie saw that Hazel's chin was still jerking. Her prayer was continuous, moaning and low.

Florence began gasping more often. The voices of the nurses' were subdued, but Maggie heard.

"Looks bad. Did you call?"

"It's on its way. A doctor will be waiting."

Within minutes the medics arrived with a stretcher. Someone pulled the curtains that closed Maggie off from the rest of the room. She heard the curtain around Hazel's bed closing, scraping along on rusty rings seldom used. The sounds indicated the movements, Florence being taken away on the stretcher, nurses running, medics running. An aide looked in at Maggie.

"You need some help back into bed, don't you?"

Maggie became aware that she was still standing at the corner of her bed, clutching the foot rail, her back against the drawn curtain.

The young nurse came and carefully helped her up into bed again and straightened the cover and bottom sheet. Pain continued to course through Maggie's hip. There was medication on the table that she hadn't taken. She reached for it.

"Want your curtain opened?"

"Yes … is she … do you know?"

Maggie stopped. Of course the nurse's aide didn't know if Florence would make it through the night, or even make it to the hospital. The nurse didn't ask her to continue her question.

She seemed glad to turn out the lights again and leave the room.

Hazel's murmuring prayers became the only sound in this deep night, these hours before dawn. She was asking God to be merciful.

"And help Maggie, Lord, she needs you, perhaps, more than any of us. Be merciful Lord, and remember us here as we need you more than ever before in our lives."

Maggie thought of her own prayers, unanswered, so many of them in her younger years, such deep, heart-felt cries, becoming less frequent now as she had become resigned. Somehow, she felt, she had not managed the contact with God that others seemed to have. Yet she was not willing to admit her silent fear that God existed only as a human creation, in a desperate need to be not alone.

As she lay dazed with pain killers, the past ran dreamlike through her memories.

FOR ALMOST TWO years Emmy put aside her feelings that something wasn't right about the constant change in dancers. One young woman, older than the others, stayed several months. She danced with an eagerness that disappeared the moment she ran down the steps in the back. Her face serious, smiles and winks gone, she'd go through the door and Emmy wouldn't see her until the next night when her dancing began at eleven.

The remainder of the club seemed constant. The waiters didn't change. If needed they doubled as bouncers. They treated Emmy with respect and distance. She knew only Gavin. Although he never talked business with her, she gradually learned he had connections in other cities. Once a month he would tell her, "I'm going to be gone a few days. Behave yourself. Don't flirt with the boys. Keep playing those good blues for the girls."

A teasing smile, then, and a kiss on the cheek at the door of her house. Then one of his tight hugs that seemed to come so effortlessly from this strong-shouldered man she adored. Blindly adored. Blindly lusted for. Just seeing him walk away turned her to liquid, held together by bones and skin. Weakened, she'd hold to the door and watch him go around the walk to the driveway and his Mercedes.

The questions in the back of her mind stayed there. Of course the girls didn't intend to make dancing, with a strip at the end, their career. Of course not. As Gavin had told her more than once, when she allowed those puzzled questions to the surface, of course they don't want a career wiggling their cute little asses in his club. For another thing, they had to be young. And age had a way of moving on. The men wanted young dancers, they didn't care if the dancers were any good or not. So long as they wore those brief costumes and bent over to show their rear once in a while, the men were happy. They weren't allowed to get close to the girls. The waiters-bouncers were right there, polite, helpful, but capable of throwing them out into the alley at the back. Emmy had seen it happen only twice in her nearly two years at the club.

The faces of the customers became familiar, as they had in every bar, club, whatever, Emmy had worked in. Each nightclub, each bar, had its own group of customers who were regulars. Among them would be those groups, usually mixed, that were out clubbing, bar hopping, slumming.

Then one night Emmy glimpsed faces that caused her fingers to falter on the keys. Three men, dressed in dark business suits, filed into the door marked OFFICE.

The door closed behind them. Two of the men, younger, were unfamiliar to her. But the one who had led the small, serious procession was the man she had seen and been warned of years ago at Roger's club. His hair had receded now, and appeared lighter than it had those years ago. He was also clean shaven now, mustache gone. But it was a face she would never forget. I've heard he's into real nasty stuff, Roger had warned. You don't want an offer from him. You may never show up again. Organized crime, he had said. Emmy hadn't asked him any questions.

The man hadn't been alone then, either. Two other men had walked with him into the bar late at night. They sat at a table and watched Emmy. Dressed in suits, they looked out of place in this bar where most men wore jeans. She had seen Roger keep looking their way as he wiped the bar, washed glasses and mixed drinks. When they finished their drinks and left he was obviously relieved.

Later he warned her, "If they offer you a job, turn it down. No matter how good it sounds. That one guy, the big one with the mustache, is pretty high around here in organized crime. He deals in porn and prostitution. So stay clear of him."

The men had come back several times and seemed to be watching Emmy. Uncomfortable, she moved on, telling Roger goodbye and thanks for letting her play. Tonight, in Gavin's place, she made herself continue playing. But she kept her head turned toward the corner where the door opened into Gavin's office. She had never been in his office, only at the small table reserved just outside the door. But she pictured it in her mind as predominately brown leather. Brown desk, brown leather chairs. The red carpet that covered the club floor and the stage would be there also, soft underfoot.

Gavin was still closed into his office with the Chicago men when the club closed. Emmy went home without seeing him.

She hugged Raven to her, unable to go to bed, anxiety keeping her alert. Finally, at daybreak when it seemed the night had been somehow resolved, she went to bed and to sleep.

She went to work early in the evening and saw with relief that Gavin was there as always with his easy smile, his good disposition. Nothing had changed.

He winked at her and disappeared from her view. She played, her vague, unrealized fears drifting away with the music.

One of the girls, the most beautiful girl Emmy felt she had ever seen, came over to talk to her. She leaned on the piano as she had been doing every night since she'd started three weeks ago. Small talk. A few questions from the girl-child. Janna was her name, she'd told Emmy. There was never a last name, never very much of anything personal, as if they were robots, instead of young girls, whose only life was lived in the club.

Emmy had stopped asking the ages of the girls when they came over to talk to her. In every case they were eighteen or nineteen, even twenty. But Janna had the indisputably delighted look of a much younger girl. Her body was perfect, breasts small and pert, waistline thin and round, hips beautifully curved. She had long black hair, just curly enough to hang in tight waves, and eyelashes that might have been false yet which Emmy felt were natural. She looked of mixed race, the deep-gold skin, the very dark eyes and hair. She reminded Emmy of Lacey. Of course she saw Lacey in all the girls.

She asked, "How old are you, Janna?"

"Siii- uh, eighteen."

Sixteen. Emmy smiled at her.

"You started to say sixteen, didn't you, Janna?"

Janna put her hand briefly on Emmy's shoulder, leaning forward. "Hey! Don't say that so loud."

"You mean Gavin doesn't know?"

Janna's eyes surveyed the crowd. They were cheering on the two girls who now danced on stage, to the right and behind Emmy, out of sight unless she twisted on the piano bench. Emmy watched Janna. The girl's eyes were searching the crowd as if she watched for someone special. It couldn't be a date. The girls weren't allowed to mix with customers. Gavin had looked for a moment almost angry when Emmy had asked if it were permitted. "They can do what they want when they're off the premises, but not here. We're not a dating service."

Janna shrugged. At first Emmy thought no, Gavin doesn't know. Or he wouldn't have hired her. But then Janna said, "Yeah sure, he knows. Nobody lies to Gavin and gets by with it."

"Oh, really?" Emmy asked, an uneasy tenseness entering her body. She kept smiling. "What do you mean?"

The girl shrugged. "Nothing."

Emmy gave her attention to the piano to dispel the questions that were crowding together too much since last night.

Then Janna said, leaning forward and speaking in a low voice, "Hey, Emmy, I just wanted to tell you goodbye. You've been great. Really backed me up, I felt, every time I went up to dance. You know, I hadn't danced much before. Just kid stuff. And having you here, the moment I saw you, it was like seeing a mother, having me my own mother, you know what I mean?"

A connection was made in Emmy's mind. With the speed of lightning, she knew. That was why she was here. The mother image. Perhaps even the grandmother image, because she was certainly old enough to be the grandmother of these girls.

Janna's eyes kept covering the crowd in jerky movements. Emmy suddenly decided it was unease, or indecision.

"Where are you going, Janna?"

"Another town. You see, I was offered this really good deal. I'd be a fool to turn it down. So after my next dance, I'll be leaving. I'll really miss you. You've been great."

Janna's eyes came to Emmy's face with a tenderness that touched Emmy deeply.

"If I could have had a mother of my own, I would have wanted her to be just like you."

She started to leave, whirling and running, the fringe on her brief bikini bouncing like the fringe on a baby's fancy rubber pants, the kind she had put on Lacey years ago.

"Janna," she called, her fingers stopping for a moment. The dancing continued, the calls and whistles behind Emmy filling in the pause in the music.

Janna whirled back. "Yeah?"

"Where is this deal?" Emmy asked. This feeling of dread, of anxiety, of a sense of impending doom, had it started last night when she had seen the Chicago men, or had it started when she first wondered why the girls disappeared, never to be seen again? "Who offered it to you? Is it in Chicago?"

"I don't—no, not Chicago—I—it's time for me on stage. Gotta go."

Janna's eyes went sharply beyond Emmy, and she smiled faintly. Then she ran, going quickly out of sight around the corner of the stage.

Emmy felt the familiar touch of Gavin's hand on her shoulder.

"Hey, how's my favorite blues musician?"

Thirty minutes to closing time. Gavin went to the reserved table, and one of the waiters brought him a drink.

Emmy had never been so glad to finish a night. The voices of the customers filed away beyond the entrance, muted with the lingering traffic. Her Coke was waiting for her on the table.

Gavin gave her his intimate smile. "Your place or mine?" he asked in his low, slow way, that lazy, devil-may-care voice that Emmy had never heard lifted in anger or irritation.

But tonight she had questions, and they couldn't be pushed away by her love for him, her need to please him.

"Gavin, what was the real reason you hired me?"

His eyebrows lifted a little with that look. It could mean anything, be interpreted in any way. She had always found it sexy, or little-boyish, or just a plain puzzled look, depending perhaps on her own mood at the time. Tonight it did not change her mind.

"I'm serious, Gavin."

The eyebrows came down, the smile changed to a quirk. The half-light of the club surrounded him like fog.

"All right. First, you're good. You know you're good. Actually, you could have done much better than playing in places like this, you know."

Her eyes fastened quickly on his. They were serious.

"Yeah, you could have. You're talented. I needed someone just like you. So, when I found you, I knew you were what this club needed."

She continued to look into his eyes, and allowed her own quirk to touch her lips. "The mother image? The grandmother image?"

His eyes opened wider than she had known they could. He actually looked surprised.

"Hey, if anyone in this world ever didn't fit the grandmother image, it's you. I'm not even sure you fit the mother image."

Perhaps he saw the pain that flashed through her. About children she had told him only that she had none. It was the truth. She hadn't wanted to talk about it, the love she'd hold all her life for Lacey was like a secret past buried too deep to share. His hand covered hers, and his voice became even more intimate.

"And I was attracted to you, Emmy, you know that. You know I love you."

It was the first time he had told her. When he made love to her the compliments came, soft and easy, but never, I love you. She was the one who sighed those words to him, over and over. She had never realized the power those words carried. She felt her eyes mist and her chin tremble. But she steadied it and waited a moment for the threat of tears to subside.

"Gavin, that man last night—those men—"

He sat back in his chair, withdrawing from her. Closing her out. Throwing the wall up. "Yeah?"

She hesitated against doing anything, saying anything that would keep that wall between them. "What were they doing here?"

A long pause, then, "Hey, what do you mean, what were they doing here?"

She waited.

He said, "Business, baby, business. Don't fret it, okay?"

"Gavin, I'm seen that one before. I know what his connections were— and probably still are."

For the first time she saw Gavin with a blank face. She sensed his eyes might have turned hard, his lips tightening. Then he sat forward, smiled, and squeezed her hand.

"Business, sweetheart. Let's just say it's none of yours, okay?"

He smiled, and the wall was down. But the subject was closed.

He stood up, put his hands on the back of her neck in a warm, sexy touch. They slid to her shoulders and pressed, urging her up.

"Your place," he said. "I have to check and see that you're not mistreating my dog."

Chapter Thirty-Two

The night was long. Every sound magnified as Maggie's fears mounted. Every footstep coming along the quiet hall was at first the footsteps of the stranger, then as they came closer she knew the softness of the soles were nurse's shoes.

Once in the night Thomas called, "Eleanor?" But his voice sounded muffled and far away as during a dream, throat paralyzed by sleep. Hazel stirred often, moaning faintly. She woke and began murmuring softly aloud a prayer. Maggie caught the words, 'dear Lord', and 'Florence'.

Maggie tried to make plans to escape. Could she get her money out of her bank without being followed? Could she go home to gather clothing, drive her car? They knew where she lived.

If only one hitman had come, she could possibly evade him. But if there were more—two or three—there would always be someone watching her, waiting for the moment to strike.

Was she that dangerous? What was it she knew that they would kill her for? Why wasn't it enough that she chose to lose herself in this world? Gavin—Gavin—what kind of game had he been playing with her all these years?

THEY HAD MADE love that night almost four years ago with something special from him, a tenderness that seemed real. Even as she was more withdrawn than usual, remembering that face from Chicago, so burned into her memory, but reluctant to believe Gavin's involvement in organized crime. He must have felt her withdrawal, her lack of total giving, and gave more of himself instead.

He left her at dawn, as always, and this time she was relieved to be alone.

She got up, showered, and fed Raven. In her thin summer robe she sat on the back step and looked into the backyard, staring at shrubs against the privacy fence, staring into shadows created by the trees that grew on her small lot. Stared, but saw faces from the past. There was no way she could have been wrong. The one face, then young, had been indelibly printed on her memory, for some reason. Perhaps because he'd been the first crime figure she'd ever seen.

Her eyes focused on Raven. He was almost two years old, a big, beautiful dog with wavy black fur and two small white spots on his face. He was doing one of his favorite things, sniffing beneath the shrubs.

As she watched him, thankful for the diversion, he raised his head, the hair on the backbone lifted, and woofed. Deep, low in his chest. He padded in a trot toward the back door. At that moment she heard the doorbell ring. When she opened the kitchen door Raven entered and bounded past her down the front hall woofing. But only his size would intimidate anyone. The only danger he posed was in his friendliness. His tail wagged with every woof. He waited at the front door, the hair on his back stiffened. Gavin stood on the stoop, carrying a small basket in his left arm. His right hand reached out and patted Raven, but Raven's fur grew stiffer as he lifted his nose to the basket. His tail wagged widely, slapping Emmy's loose, long robe.

"I came back", Gavin said with the with the little-boy-done-wrong grin.

"I see."

She wanted to cry out, what's wrong. But his demeanor was as calm and reassuring as always. Gavin as she knew him, loved him. He had brought her a gift, for some reason of his own. Not a bouquet of red and pink roses this time.

In the living room, with Raven still sniffing at the basket, Gavin extended it to her.

"Open it."

The top came up under her fingers and a tiny reddish-brown head with pert ears looked up at her. It had a tail, no larger than a toothpick, but it wagged as wildly as Raven's.

"A dog?" Emmy cried. "Is this a dog?"

Gavin shrugged like a boy offering a gift, "Well … a doglet."

Emmy laughed, and put out a finger to the incredibly tiny puppy. She felt the lick of the warm tongue, and a burst of love within her own heart.

"Gavin! A puppy! Good Lord, it's so tiny."

Gavin said, "Sometimes I say the wrong thing, and this is my apology." He picked up the puppy and put her into Emmy's hands. His eyes were serious and, she thought, sad.

"Her name is Minnie," he said. "every time you look at her, remember that I love you."

Raven stuck his nose up to the puppy and she growled and struck quick as a snake. He jerked back. She was not half as large as Raven's muzzle. One bite from Raven and the puppy would have been gone, but he had a wide-eyed respect for her growl and the sharpness of her baby teeth. Emmy and Gavin laughed at Raven's look of surprise.

Emmy caressed the tiny creature, and she turned wiggling to lick Emmy's face. She was beautiful. Smooth as satin, nut brown with little golden tuffs over each eye, triangular eyebrows.

They stuck out like patches of gold pasted on as a last thought by nature, always so generous and with such a sense of humor.

"One pound of doglet, two months old," Gavin said. "Purebred Chihuahua if you want to register her."

"I'm not a breeder. She'll be spayed."

"Shh. Don't let her hear you say that."

Smiling, Emmy glanced at Gavin. "Do you suppose Raven knows he's been neutered?"

Gavin faked horror. "Is she serious?" he asked Raven.

Raven was interested only in the puppy. His suspicion and surprise had changed rapidly to adoration. He got down on his chest and elbows, ready to play.

Gavin went toward the door. "Gotta go," he said. As he went out he turned back. "Don't forget, her name is Minnie." He blew Emmy a kiss and the door closed behind him.

* * *

Minnie. Not once in these past four years had it occurred to Maggie to change that name. Not once.

She went to sleep with alternative plans of escape tossing erratically in her mind. The walker was a necessity. Home no longer a sanctuary. She wept into her pillow for that small home she had felt safe in, a place where Minnie was happy and safe. Minnie, who needed her. She who needed Minnie.

... every time you look at her ... remember that I love you ... Instead, she now wondered, had the puppy had been a way of finding her?

Please God, give me a dream. Let me live for awhile in the beauty of that other world, the other side of our existence. Let me escape, for awhile, this nightmare of reality. Please God, let me go into my dreams.

They had come to her so rarely, spots of beauty and light through a life of shadows. Yet never at will, never when she wanted them most. And they didn't come now.

Morning arrived abruptly with Blanche entering the room, calling out cheerful greetings, turning on lights, adjusting curtains. Maggie sensed the remnants of a vague dream, not the vivid beauty she longed and prayed for. Her thoughts went immediately to Minnie. But security was good at the kennel, she knew. The dogs were kept inside the animal hospital, and the caretakers would keep Minnie safe. But what if someone in charge did not know Minnie was not to be released to anyone but herself? The image of death lived in her mind, surfacing, the severed head, the dulled eyes, blood surrounding it in the box.

She flinched against the memory, pushing away the thought of strange hands reaching out for Minnie too. She felt a rising urgency to call the kennel to make sure Minnie was safe, but at this hour she'd get only the answering service.

Hazel began her preparations for the day. "Is Florence all right? Have you heard anything?" she asked the nurse.

"Oh yes. She's going to make it."

Hazel almost collapsed. A rare smile crinkled her face. She grabbed the foot of Florence's bed as she passed by on her way to the bathroom. She leaned, supporting herself, then straightened her back and went on. "Thank the good Lord."

Blanche followed her into the bathroom. "As soon as you can, Hazel, you need to return a call."

"A telephone call? From Florence?"

"No, from your grandson. I think he's coming to get you."

"My grandson! Oh my."

The large, heavy door closed, and the voices grew muffled. But Maggie heard the eagerness in Hazel's voice. Her grandson, finally. After her two years in the nursing home she would be leaving to live with her grandson. She had daydreamed of it, prayed for it, talking aloud of her plans.

Within an incredibly short time Hazel emerged from the bathroom, showered and dressed. She left the room with Blanche, walking faster and more eagerly than Maggie had seen her walk. Her plans hung in the air. She looked forward to the excitement of having her own room again, of privacy, of an independence she had left behind. Her granddaughter-in-law would take her shopping. She would be allowed to prepare her own meals if she wanted to, because the apartment had its own apartment-sized stove, and a sink. For the first time in years she could wash her own dishes. What a pleasure, washing dishes.

She laughed. "I'm not feeble yet." Her excited voice grew faded as her footsteps with their solid heels clunked on down the hall, merging into the hollow distance.

Maggie was alone. She got out of bed, stood carefully balanced and reached for the walker. She dragged it close, and clenched her teeth against the pain, against the feeling that she was going to fall again. She went to the bathroom, slow step by step. She managed a quick shower, came back to the small basin in the wall by her miniscule closet and brushed her teeth and hair. On the way back to her bed she closed the big door, muting sounds that grew beyond it. Closing off Thomas's call for a nurse and a nurse's answer to him as she went in to help him dress for the day. Maggie wanted to dress, go out to the hall, call about Minnie. But a trembling had begun in her arms as she clutched the walker, and she turned to the bed, needing rest.

She pulled herself onto the bed and lay on her side, heart racing. With her eyes closed she rested as the calm came.

She had to have strength in order to leave, she reminded herself. Breathe deeply. Relax. Another day, two days at the most, and she must leave.

She had to get Minnie and keep her safe.

FOUR YEARS ago Minnie had been one-fifth of her present, adult size. No larger than Gavin's fist. A little live-wire who seemed to know immediately that Emmy was hers. If anyone tried to take her from Emmy's hands,

Minnie set up a vicious growling. Tail wagging all the while. All growl, as if her ferocious growling could keep danger at bay.

Emmy hadn't wanted to leave her when she went to work. What if Raven played too roughly with her? Good Heavens, what if he stepped on her? Minnie seemed to delight in running between his feet while he looked down trying to locate her as he did when he accidentally stepped over a bug. So Emmy put her into the basket and took her along to work. Word passed among the girls and if they weren't dancing they came to pet Minnie.

"Ooooh, isn't she the cutest thing? Where'd you get her?" Girls who had barely seemed to notice Emmy was there, suddenly were kneeling on the floor by the piano, unselfconsciously, legs askew as if they were nine years old.

People from the audience came up, held Minnie, petted her.

"Hey," Gavin said when the club closed for the night and Emmy joined him at the table, Minnie exhausted and sound asleep in her basket. "Your dog is stealing the show."

"You gave her to me. It's all your fault."

Their conversation centered around the pup, from then on. The puppy had a grand time with all the attention, and the girls delighted in putting her on Emmy's lap and then calling up a customer to try to pick up the puppy. They all laughed at her miniature growls. The very ambience of the club changed, in those nights of Minnie coming to work with Emmy.

Those were happy nights, Maggie thought in retrospect. The puppy kept her from worrying about the contacts Gavin had made, or which had been made with him. Pushed to the back of her mind it became a part of all the things she had pushed back.

The happiness lasted less than a month.

She had barely gotten to bed and to sleep when the telephone woke her. She rolled over and turned on the bedside light. On the foot of the bed Raven sat up, stretching his neck, leaving the rest of his body lazing on his part of the king-sized bed.

Against Emmy's pillow Minnie lay curled. The puppy's eyes opened, but she didn't lift her head. Emmy glanced at the digital clock.

4:17 AM

Her thoughts went immediately to the family. Mom, now eighty, might be ill. She visualized her in a hospital, taken in on a stretcher from an ambulance. Peggy and Rebba would be at a telephone in the hall, faces white and drawn with worry. Mama had a heart attack. Mom, always healthy.

"Yes?"

"Emmy—Emmy—"

Puzzled, disturbed yet relieved, Emmy listened. Not Peggy or Rebba. Not one of their daughters, she was sure, not Lynn or Clair, yet they grew so fast, voices changing. "Lynn?"

"Emmy—this is—"

The voice sounded so far away, name muffled. Background noises were like loud track sounds in the back of a movie.

"What? Who is this?"

"Emmy …" She was crying. Emmy could hear that. She was in a place where large trucks revved heavy engines, and pulled away changing gears.

"Who is this?" Emmy said again. Raven, alarmed at the tone of her voice, sat up, watching her.

"Janna—Janna—"

Janna. In desperate trouble, it sounded. "Where on earth are you, Janna?"

"Emmy, can you come and get me? Help me, Emmy, please."

"Of course I'll help you. Where are you?"

"Las Vegas. Out at the edge at a motel. I'm calling from this telephone and I have to talk fast, I'm out of money."

"Just give me the location, the name of the place."

Emmy wrote it down on the pad she kept by the telephone just as the operator interrupted telling Janna to deposit more money.

Emmy broke in and told her to reverse the charges.

"Now, Janna, are you checked into the motel?"

"No," Janna's voice was drifting away it seemed, drowned by the noises of the big trucks and other traffic. "No. I don't have the money. Just come and get me please?" She had begun to sob again. "Don't tell anyone —please—please Emmy—just come and get me."

"I'll be there as soon as I can get there." The phone clicked in her ear.

Raven jumped off the bed, ears lifted. The puppy raised her head. Emmy began hurriedly to dress, pulling on jeans and a shirt. She looked at the dogs. It would take her the rest of the night and tomorrow to get to the motel where Janna was stranded, pick her up, and drive back home. She couldn't leave the dogs alone.

She hurried to the kitchen, bag strap over her shoulder, and grabbed

Raven's leash and tiny Minnie's halter. They followed her, happy to be allowed this adventure in the middle of their night.

"Get dressed, pups," she said as she began trying to thread them into collars and halters while they danced with joy. "We're taking a ride."

She'd be home in time for work tomorrow night at nine, with any luck at all.

Chapter Thirty-Three

The dogs settled down in the car, Raven in the back seat, Minnie curled beneath the steering wheel on Emmy's lap. The night was beginning to break in the east with thin streaks of rose and magenta as she drove onto the freeway and headed east out of the valley. The only traffic at this time of day was an occasional truck.

The sun had grown hot by the time she pulled into the motel parking lot in the southwestern edge of Vegas. Here was blowing sand and brown stretches of landscape, nothing of the flamboyance of downtown Las Vegas. The motel was old, one-story, each cabin separated by a carport. It reminded Emmy of the cabins she had stayed in with her family back when she was a child. A sign out by the road would read, "Cabins, kitchenettes." The kitchenettes were usually one or two hot plates or gas burners. But once in Wyoming, she remembered, the kitchenette actually was a small kitchen in the corner of the large cabin. It was almost like having a real home. Then, in their homeless days, it seemed a luxury. She drove slowly through the blowing sand of the unpaved driveway. There were strings of gas pumps, and a cafe. Several eighteen wheelers had parked haphazardly in the parking lot that extended on out into the desert. A few smaller trucks and pickups parked closer to the cafe. Only two of the carports sheltered a car.

She circled and drove back again, feeling more and more that the phone call had been too strange to be real. Here she was, long hours and miles from home, answering what might have been a hoax call. A lot of people knew her. More people knew her than she knew. The audience had the advantage. Her phone number was available in the book. It had never been necessary to have an unlisted phone number.

She drove back past the cabins, slowly, letting the car creep under its own volition. The cabins needed paint. The curtains beyond the windows needed to be replaced. They had grown colorless, and two were torn. She became more uneasy.

Raven whined. The back windows were up, air conditioner on, but Raven scratched at a window as if that would lower it. She pressed the button that lowered his window, and one slap of sand in his face made him draw back. She rolled the window up.

She had stopped at a roadside park a few miles back to let the dogs out to relieve themselves, so that wasn't Raven's problem. She had given them water there too from a hydrant.

She came to the last cabin.

"We might as well go home," she said aloud.

At that moment a figure separated from the shadows in the corner of the last carport and approached the car rapidly. A boy, was Emmy's immediate impression. He wore dark sunglasses, a cap pulled forward with bill down, a long-sleeved shirt and baggy jeans. When he reached the sunlight Emmy recognized Janna's face, thinner, rich complexion grown pallid.

Emmy unlocked the car doors, and Janna jerked the passenger door open and climbed in. She glanced over her shoulders in both directions, ignoring Raven's muzzle leaning on the headrest behind her head.

She was terrified, Emmy saw, and her own uneasiness increased. She found herself looking around too, for someone following Janna, but there was only the end of the cabins, and the desert beyond.

"Have you eaten?" Emmy asked.

"No. I'm not hungry. Let's just go, okay?"

Glancing at her, dividing her attention between the highway and the girl, Emmy pulled out into the traffic and headed west. Janna suddenly jerked forward.

"Where are we going?" she cried in alarm.

"Home." Emmy slowed, pulling into the right lane. "Where did you want to go?"

Janna didn't answer. She stared down the road west, her lower lip drooped, mouth open, eyes hidden behind the glasses. Then she slumped "I don't know. It's just—I don't want anyone to know where I am, okay?"

Emmy didn't know what to do. The girl was scared half to death of something. She was trying to hide herself, and had done a good job of it. She wanted to continue to hide.

"Do you need to talk to the police, Janna?"

"Oh, God no, Emmy. Please, can't I just stay with you?" Her face turned toward Emmy, her mouth drooped pleadingly. Then she saw the puppy, on the seat beside Emmy, and without another word reached for Minnie and held her cuddled against her neck, beneath her chin. Her breath, pulled in, was like a labored climb of steps.

"Have you—" Emmy thought of how to put her words. "Have you done something, Janna, that you're running from the law?"

Janna threw her a rapid glance. "Oh no! Not that." She stared down the road again, one hand holding Minnie, the other gently caressing her.

Minnie hadn't growled as she usually did when hands tried to take her from Emmy's side. The puppy licked Janna's fingers, as if she understood the girl needed comforting. Janna stared down the road.

"Where're you going?" she cried again. Anxiety and desperation made her voice unnaturally high-pitched. She caressed the puppy nervously, but Minnie tolerated it.

"Home. There's nowhere else to go. I have to be at work tonight at nine or ten. We have to go home."

Janna reached over and clutched Emmy's upper arm. "Look—they can't know I'm there. No one. Please, can't we just go somewhere else? Please?"

"Janna, you're going to have to tell me what's wrong."

Janna scooted down into the seat, her knees up, her cap covering her forehead. She cradled the puppy in the curve of her body and stared, it seemed, through the dark glasses at the dashboard. Glancing frequently at her, Emmy drove, picking up speed.

"Janna, do you have family at all anywhere?"

Janna shook her head. "My mom—she left me in foster care. I don't even hardly remember what she looked like. I had some sisters and brothers, I think, but I'm not sure. I had a grandma once, but she was old and sick. I think she died. I ran away from the last foster home."

Her lips pursed, chin dimpled. Emmy kept glancing at her, trying to read between her words, trying to understand this fear.

Janna said, "That's when I came down to Hollywood, you know. I was just sort of trying to get enough to eat—I wasn't about to do what some of the others were doing. That guy, you know, in the last foster home—I knew from that that I didn't want no more of that." She drew a long breath.

"How old are you, Janna?"

She hesitated. "Sixteen. I ran away when I was thirteen. Then a guy told me I might dance at this place, since I wouldn't—you know—nobody's going to make a whore outa me!" Anger pushed away the fear.

"Gavin hired you knowing you were only sixteen?" She wasn't really surprised at her age. But she searched within herself for an excuse for Gavin. She couldn't bear disappointment in the only man she'd ever truly loved in her life.

"Oh, no," Janna said, and Emmy felt some of the tenseness go out of her arms. Then Janna added, "He didn't ask. He said I looked eighteen, and he said if anyone asked, anyone at all, I was to say I was eighteen. Actually, I was sixteen then."

"You—you're sure you didn't misunderstand him?" Emmy asked. "Maybe he just said ..." No, there was no way Gavin could avoid knowing how old she was.

"No, that's what he said."

"The other girls—were any of them eighteen or older?" She knew the answer before it came, and her consternation increased. She felt it in her stomach, a weakness that spread to her hands on the steering wheel. Love had blinded her. Perhaps it still did.

"No, most that I knew were sixteen, seventeen. One of them, remember Sheila? She was fourteen. She didn't stay very long. I knew another girl, met her on the street, she'd been like selling herself. She came and wanted to dance after I told her about it, about my job, and how much money I made. She was kind of my friend. She was older, nineteen. And she was really pretty and all. He wouldn't hire her."

"They had to be under eighteen?" What was Janna trying to tell her?

"Yeah, that's what I found out. I found out too much. You just don't know, Emmy. They want to kill me."

"Who wants to kill you?"

Instead of slowing, trying to find a place to pull over so she could comfort Janna, Emmy speeded. They had to get home. She had to understand what was happening and try to figure out what to do. Why would anyone want Janna dead?

Janna stared out her window and said nothing for several heartbeats. Then, "I don't think I should tell you. If I told you, then you'd—they'd have to kill you too."

"Janna—whoever this is doesn't even know you're with me. You must tell the police."

Janna turned toward her. "Oh no, oh God no!"

"But the police will stop them."

"Not from me, they won't. Do you know what happens to people who tell? I just have to—have to go where it's safe. Be with someone I can trust. Maybe ..."

Her thought silenced into the sounds of the engine, the tires on pavement. Emmy waited a few minutes, but her own thoughts were a boiling caldron. Not Gavin ...

"You said you'd been offered a great opportunity, Janna. It wasn't Gavin, was it? He didn't send you down there, did he?" He's not involved in something this dangerous, is he? She couldn't put it into words. She would never be able to believe Gavin had sent Janna into something so dangerous.

Janna didn't answer for awhile, then she said, "I can tell you this—most of the girls at the club are sent down there. Like me, they're promised this big shit, you know. They're going to pay a lot of money to work at these clubs in New Orleans, in Houston and places. But they took us to a house down somewhere, Houston or El Paso or somewhere close to the border. You're not allowed any freedom, so it's hard to tell. And they give you stuff, whatever your pleasure, so your head is messed up."

She grew silent again. Emmy could see her hand trembling on Minnie's back. Emmy waited, waited and drove. They were in the hills, rising brown and dry, shrubs as brittle as papier-mache. One spark and the hills would be alight with a raging fire. Emmy pressed on the accelerator, trying to drive away from this, the heat, the dryness, the revelations of suspicions long hidden. Obviously it was worse than she had feared. What had she thought was happening to those young girls, off the street, runaways ...

"All of you—were all of you runaways?" Emmy asked. How many girls had she seen come and go in the almost two years she had worked at the club? Thirty? Some of them stayed as long as two months, others only two weeks or less. She had never seen any of them again after they left, until now.

Janna was nodding. "All that I knew, and all that I found out about down on the coast. When I found out I couldn't get out of there, that I had to give in, I decided to go for the main man, the guy who managed the house. And that's—well—that's how I found out."

"Forced prostitution?" Emmy frowned down the highway. Heat shimmered in waves above it like layers of water. Cool, clear water, drawing one on hopelessly.

"Yeah."

"Why on earth is that necessary" So many girls? Girls ready to sell themselves for drugs, her thoughts added.

"Well, it's this thing with guys who like a thrill. Besides, no diseases, you know. It's all kinky. Some of them, the girls, had to do films, you know. Snuff."

"Janna!"

"It's true. I know it's true. The boss, down there, he liked me. I could tell you these names, Emmy. I'll never forget them. But don't ask because it would put you in danger."

Don't ask. Later, when Janna was more relaxed, Emmy vowed silently to talk to her again.

"Some of the girls are shipped out," Janna said softly, "They threatened me, too. This one guy said if I thought I had it bad there, I could just wait until I got to that other place. Places. It's a whole weird setup, and that's when I figured out that it's really headed by this one person."

One person. Gavin?

Emmy believed her fear, but rejected Janna's story, trying instinctively to keep Gavin out of it. Here was a girl with an overactive imagination, she told herself. Perhaps Janna had been led into prostitution when she hadn't wanted to be, but actual porn snuff? Surely it had to be faked.

Janna sat up higher, her chin lifted. "One thing—when they got me they didn't get no dummy. I might be young, but I can read, and at my last foster home there was a computer. So I know how to work computers, and I got into my boyfriend's information. I got names, Emmy."

She put up a fist and wiped her nose. She thumped her head. "And I got a photographic memory."

Emmy kept looking at her. She saw the pale skin, the attempt to disguise herself. She saw the long dark hair beginning to fall down from beneath the cap. There was no makeup on her face. She carried no clothes with her. The jeans she wore, Emmy saw, were rolled up several inches, and held up with a belt. A man's jeans.

"How did you get back to Vegas, Janna?"

Janna smiled for the first time. "Oh, boy. I got my guy to believe I needed drugs, you know, and I stashed 'em. I kept staying around, getting this information, see. Some of the girls when they'd first come, cried to go home. They'd be put in a room, locked in, and I could hear them crying. They did it to me, too. So I knew. You learn fast. Either you cooperate, or you get in more trouble. You get these kooks who like the rape scene. And you get raped over and over."

Gavin knew what happened to these girls once they were taken away? It didn't fit the Gavin Emmy knew. Not Gavin, poised, affable, easygoing, gentle … He had brought her Minnie, he was gentle with Raven, he had children of his own.

"Those were the girls," Janna said in such low tones that Emmy barely heard her. "They were the ones put in the snuff films."

"You must be mistaken about that. Surely, not here, in our country."

"I saw a couple of the movies, Emmy. They'd didn't fake it."

"Why didn't you go to the police? Why don't you let me take you to the police?"

"No way. It'd be in every newspaper, and I'd be out on the street. At least this way I got a chance, see?"

Emmy drove, facing into the sun. She remembered then, she hadn't stopped for Janna to eat, or the dogs to drink or relieve themselves. But she was closer and closer to home, and it was imperative that she be at work tonight. Especially if what Janna was telling her was true. She only half believed it.

"How did you get away?"

"I dressed like I am, in his clothes. I found five dollars in change in a drawer of his desk. I got out onto the street. Then, this guy saw me, and stared at me, and I knew he recognized me."

She paused, Emmy said nothing. Her skin felt as if it had tightened unbearably all over her, pulling across her cheek bones, around her head. Not Gavin. He didn't know. He wasn't part of this. His expensive clothes, cars and homes weren't bought with this kind of money. No!

"I wanted to run but I walked, didn't want to draw attention. This guy back at the house, a bouncer type, began to talk to someone on his phone, the one he carried. So I knew … I went to the bus station, and I saw a guy there waiting. I knew his face, I know his name. Not important, he just works for them."

"All those names could be important, Janna. If—what you say is true."

"I knew when I saw him that they had the exits closed, you might say. The bus stations, the depot, the airports. Not that I had money for any of that. But I was going to call you from there and ask you to wire me some money. I didn't know who else to turn to, Emmy. So I managed to slip out. Away."

She began to weep, soundlessly.

Emmy reached over and held her hand in a tight grip. "I'm glad you called me. We'll figure this out."

"Don't tell Gavin! Please."

"No. I won't tell anyone. How did you get to Vegas?"

"Truck drivers. Two, long-haul. When I got that close I called. The truck was going north from there, and I didn't want to try anyone else."

"Janna—is it possible Gavin didn't know the girls are underage? How could he get by with it?"

"Fake IDs, Emmy. We had IDs claiming we were eighteen. No big deal."

"Janna isn't your real name?"

"Well yeah, that is. But the last name is different."

"The other—the films—the connections—he wouldn't know about that."

"He was the one who introduced me to this jock and said there was the great opportunity," Janna said. "So what do you think."

Emmy heard the sarcasm in her voice, but it gave Emmy a small bit of hope. Gavin would never send one of his girls into a dangerous situation. There was much more to it than that, other people involved. Gavin had made the wrong connections, that was all.

"You're not going to tell him where I am, Emmy!" Janna cried.

"I'm not going to tell anyone where you are, Janna, I promise. Now relax, okay? I'll take care of you, don't you worry."

Janna sighed, a long, soft breath. She curled into the seat, onto her side, arms around Minnie. The puppy looked at Emmy over Janna's arms, a silent plea on her face.

Chapter Thirty-Four

"Where are you going?" Janna cried.

"I have to go to work."

Janna clutched her sleeve, holding to her, eyes misty and fearful. She had slept most of the way home, then eaten the soup and sandwich Emmy made for her as if she hadn't eaten since she'd started hitchhiking. When Emmy went to her bedroom to get ready to go to work, Janna followed her, keeping both dogs close.

"Don't leave me," Janna pleaded.

She talked low, fast, urgently. She had pulled the blinds before lights were turned on. Even if part of her story were exaggerated, the fear wasn't. It was real. She needed help. During her shower Emmy's mind had tossed possibilities about like marbles, with about as much cohesion. She had thought about taking Janna straight to a hospital for mental problems. She thought about taking her to the police. She thought about taking her and simply leaving. She was a teenager who needed a parental figure, and Emmy was willing to fill that need. There were so many things that had to be done.

"If I don't go to work," she explained carefully, her arm around Janna's trembling body. "Everyone at the club will wonder why. Gavin might come here to see why. If I called in sick, he might come over. The only thing I can do tonight is to go to work. For a few nights. I'll give notice that I'm going to quit."

"Emmy ... I'm scared."

Emmy took Janna's face in her hands and held it steady a few inches from her own, making eye contact. They were about the same height, but Janna was thinner now than she had been three months ago when she had danced to Emmy's music.

"Listen to me. Here's what we'll do. Tomorrow I'll take you up to my mother and sisters. No one here, not even Gavin, knows about them. Their names or where they live. You can stay there until I can liquidate my properties, understand? That might take a while. You stay there. As soon as I get my money, you and I will move somewhere, where you'll be safe."

"Really?" Tears were dewdrops in her eyes, catching the light and sparkling. Hope was in her voice. "You mean, like a real family?"

A warmth entered Emmy. She felt a closeness to this girl at this moment like nothing she had felt since Lacey. Back to the country and the mountains, she thought. Back to nature.

"Absolutely. We'll make plans. But now, you take a shower and find something in my closet to put on. Keep Raven in the house with you. I'll be home as soon as the club closes. You're absolutely safe. No one even knows I left town last night."

Janna glanced around, the fear returning. "No one knows I'm here, right?"

"No. No one. You just relax. Let the dogs out into the backyard to go to the bathroom. It's quiet and private out there. You don't have to be afraid. It's fenced."

"Okay."

She was calming down, eyes less worried and searching. "We'll make plans tomorrow, right? While we drive up to your mom's? Where does she live?"

"In the north, almost in Oregon. I'll take the night off."

"Will that work? Gavin won't get suspicious?"

"No, he won't." But the worry that had surfaced increased. "I don't have to tell him or anyone anything. I'll quit my job and say I'm tired of working and want to retire. It'll be all right, don't worry. I didn't sign a contract."

"It'll really be all right, won't it?"

"Absolutely." Emmy hugged Janna, and felt the pressure of the girl's arms clinging.

"We'll have a nice home in the mountains where the big trees grow. You can be my daughter." She added, "We'll change your name. How about—" No, not Lacey, there would never be another Lacey. "How about Leigh?"

Janna nodded, her smooth cheek against Emmy's.

"I have to go now," Emmy told her. "Relax, Rest." She left Janna curled on her bed with the two dogs.

Not until she reached the club, had parked the car and locked the doors and was on her way in did she remember that she hadn't brought Minnie. For the first time in the two months Minnie had been with her, she had left her at home. She stopped, torn between going back after her and going on in. The street lights were beginning to come on. Shadows lurked between parked cars in the area behind the club. The sounds of the street beyond the club and the tight row of other bars and movie theatres and book stores seemed only like background in a drama. All of it slightly askew from reality. She'd had a growing sense of nightmarish unreality since she had picked up Janna, seeing her fear, which was increasingly real to Emmy.

Emmy suddenly was anxious to get away. To be done with this life. Gavin had never been hers anyway. She had chosen to be the other woman because she had loved him so much. He hadn't promised her so much as separation from his wife, and she hadn't expected him to. She was not a home-wrecker. She preferred not to know Mrs. Richards, so that in her mind Gavin's wife never gained the status of a real person.

Night was coming to the world outside, as night was always in the club. Street lights emphasized shadows in the unlighted corners. Emmy walked quickly through the parking lot and into the club. She walked through the patchy crowd, saying hello to familiar faces, the waiter-bouncers, to Cindy behind the bar, who leaned on an elbow, talking to a couple of customers. Emmy spoke to the bartender, a handsome man who could have worked as a dancer-stripper himself, and might have.

"Hey Emmy," he said, "Where's the pup?"

She knew the questions would come, and had her answer ready.

"She wasn't feeling very good this evening and—"

Cindy cried, "What's wrong with her?"

A customer who came each night to hold Minnie for a few minutes asked, "Did you take her to a vet?"

Emmy paused, seeing the piano at the other end of the long room angled away from the dancers' platform. Her sanctuary, her escape. She hadn't planned this well enough.

"If she isn't better tomorrow, I'll certainly take her."

She went on and slid into place on the bench. Her fingers tested the keys, and the questions stopped. A couple of requests were called out, and she began to play. The spotlights came on, two on the stage, and one on Emmy, the soft, rosy light outlining her, cutting her vision of the growing crowd.

It allowed her to think, make plans. As soon as she got back from taking Janna to Mom, she would arrange for her real estate broker to have her property turned to cash as quickly as possible. She'd take what she could get, rather than wait for better prices. She had purchased at good times, and the present value was a few multiples of the original.

A voice came at her shoulder, asking, "Where's Minnie?"

Emmy said merely, "I left her at home tonight," and smiled at the woman who had asked.

The girls came in still dressed in jeans or shorts and disappointment dragged their faces down. "Where's Minnie?"

"She'll be here tomorrow night, I promise."

She looked at the faces of the girls and wished there was some way to convince them to get out of here, go home, go anywhere. But of course she dared not talk to them. She had to smile, play blues and jazz as she always had.

The night progressed slowly, trying never to end, it seemed. She should have told Janna to call if she needed her. No one here at the club would have recognized her voice. So many girls, staying such a short time. It had been months since the bartender or Gavin, the only people who took the calls, had heard Janna's voice.

Time crept by slowly. Her fingers missed a note. She covered it as quickly as she could.

Jerri, a thin, not very friendly little blonde, came to Emmy and leaned with her elbow on the piano. Her face was just at the edge of the spotlight. She watched Emmy's fingers on the keys. Emmy paused. She usually took short intermissions between the dances, when the girls were off stage. The last girl had run off with an extra wiggle of her rear, the tassels of her bikini swinging. The men loved it.

Jerri, too, was in costume now, but it was covered with a silk kimono, hanging open. She was one of the few people who paid little attention to the puppy. Emmy doubted that was the reason for her visit at the piano, the first she had made. Her face carried an expression that puzzled Emmy. A half-smile, a faked interest in the music.

"You play good," Jerri said.

"Is there anything special you'd like?"

Jerri shook her head. The smile faded. Her eyes covered the crowd in a quick, nervous glance.

"No. I was just wondering something."

Emmy waited. Jerri's glance passed through the crowd again and finally to the office door and lingered. Emmy turned her head. The door was closed.

"Wondering what?" Emmy prompted.

"I was wondering if you ever hear from Janna."

An iced ripple passed through Emmy. The hair on the back of her neck felt as if it visibly lifted.

Jerri hadn't even been here when Janna was here, Emmy thought rapidly, had she? But of course she might have known her from somewhere else.

"Did you know Janna?" Emmy asked carefully.

"Yeah, sure. We were friends."

This was too much of a coincidence.

"No," Emmy said carefully, flexing her fingers, looking down at the keys. "I haven't heard from her. Have you?"

"No."

Jerri seemed to relax. She remained at the piano, watching Emmy play for several minutes, then she wandered off. A few minutes later she ran up on stage for her dance.

Emmy stole a glance at her wristwatch. Another hour to closing time. She turned her head and caught a glimpse of Jerri dancing. Men hooted and yelled when the girls made special moves, but mostly the crowd was fairly quiet, nursing their drinks, staring at the girls, having their fantasies. A surprising number of the regulars paid little attention, carrying on conversations with someone at their table, or at the bar talking to Cindy or the bartender.

The last hour was the longest hour. She found herself often turning her wrist to look at her watch, surprised that only a couple more minutes had passed.

She became aware once of being stared at. She, not the girls dancing. She felt the stare and was drawn to turn toward it as she seldom had been in her life.

She was surprised to see it was a woman. She stood between tables a few tables away, tall and slender and elegant, with dark hair arranged on the back of her head. She wore dark sunglasses.

As Emmy turned, the woman walked away, and soon was lost in the crowd near the bar.

A waiter came near with a tray of drinks. Emmy motioned him close.

"Did you see the woman in the dark glasses?" she asked.

Dirk looked over his shoulder. "You mean Mrs. Richards?"

Emmy's hands froze. There was a lull in the music before she began to play. Mrs. Richards! "Gavin's wife?"

"Yeah."

He moved on to serve the drinks at the table in the corner near the entertainment platform.

Gavin's wife.

Had she only imagined the steadiness of the stare? It had been impossible to see her eyes. Even without the glasses, the smoke and shadows that filled the club would have obscured any special expression.

She continued playing, turning to her favorite blues for inner comfort. No one yelled an objection.

The last hour tonight was the longest hour of her years of music. When it was finished, and the spotlights went off, Emmy closed the piano. When she turned, she saw Gavin at the table waiting for her.

He winked and smiled, his eyes narrowed and steady, holding her. She had a feeling that he had been staring at her during the whole of this past hour. Often he sat listening, watching her play, but never before had she felt such intensity in his gaze with, it seemed, wordless questioning. You're being paranoid, she warned herself. Very much of this and you'll have to check yourself into a mental hospital right along with Janna.

She sought an excuse as she went to the table. She didn't sit down. He stood up and waited. She remained across the table from him. Don't touch my hand. Don't weaken my resolve to leave him, forever. I don't want to look back, I just want to go.

She let her eyes love his face, one last time. Goodbye Gavin. She just had to get away as quickly as possible. "I understand your wife was here tonight."

"She's gone now," he said. "Where's the pup? Cindy said she's sick."

Emmy saw something flicker in his eyes. A concern? A criticism that she hadn't brought Minnie? But why did it matter to him?

She looked away. Get out of here. She dared not look at him again. His eyes had almost as much power over her as his touch.

"She was just off her feed a little. " Emmy caught herself fidgeting nervously with her belt. She kept wanting to look over her shoulder. "I won't be staying for a drink. I'll go home and see how she is."

Gavin said nothing.

She hesitated, hoping he wouldn't choose this night to want to go home with her. "Well … goodnight."

"Goodnight," he answered. "Hope the pup's feeling better."

She nodded, gave him a quick smile and hurried out, relieved, yet feeling the pull to stay, however she could, with this man she loved so much. Too much. Too much to see beyond him, to have allowed her vague suspicions of the purpose of his club to surface.

The streets through the nightclub area were alive and working, but she drove away from the traffic and onto streets quiet and empty. Careful to watch her speed limit she drove home as fast as she dared.

She pulled into the driveway and pressed the button that opened the garage door. A dog began barking in a deep, slow voice. Raven. He barked as he did every night when she returned home. Why had Janna left him out in the backyard?

She noticed then that no lights were on in the house.

She drove into the garage, pressed the button to close the door, and hurried into the house.

Minnie met her in the hall between garage and kitchen, wiggling happily in the shadows where only a nightlight kept the dark away.

Emmy picked her up. In the backyard Raven continued to bark. Something was wrong. Raven never barked after she drove in. He'd be standing at the kitchen door, tail wagging, watching expectantly for the door to open.

Emmy sensed the emptiness of the house. Minnie, here alone, inside. Raven outside. Emmy hurried through the house turning on lights, looking everywhere, even into the closets. But the house held silence and a feeling of terrible emptiness, and Emmy knew that Janna was gone.

Emmy's own voice was silent. She walked through the house, Minnie in her arms, and opened the back door for Raven. He bounded past her without his usual effusive greeting, put his nose close to the floor and made a couple of circles in the kitchen, then went down the hall, into the bedroom hall, through the two bedrooms, back to the front hall and to the door. There he stood and whined, then he came back to Emmy as if he'd been chastised, and pressed his big head to her leg. She reached down and held him against her, wishing he could tell her what had happened.

She went through the house again, this time looking for a note. She found on her desk a notepad that belonged in a drawer. A pen from the box of a dozen pens, lay beside it. But there was no note, not even in the wastebasket. It had been cleaned, dumped somewhere.

She went searching again. All the wastebaskets in the house had been emptied. Emmy had a habit of bringing mail through the house and dumping junk mail into whatever basket she was close to, the one in the entry hall, the one in the living room, in the kitchen, wherever. Every room had its waste basket, and there was junk mail in all of them, ordinarily. But not now.

Why would Janna empty the baskets? Had she simply busied herself, alone, scared?

Emmy looked into the big, plastic trash can at the outside corner of the house, but the junk mail hadn't been emptied into it. Raven followed closely behind her, occasionally whining. Minnie huddled in her arms, subdued, silent.

Emmy went back into the house and checked all doors and windows. They were still locked.

She went to her bedroom and sat down on the bed. Raven leaped up on the foot, and sat, alert, his ears perked as much as nature allowed. He was listening. But the night was quiet, as always.

What had Janna done? Had she grown frightened of being here? Had she lost trust in Emmy?

Had she simply slipped out and melted into the darkness, on her way to another place that might be safer?

Emmy said softly aloud, "What happened, Raven?"

His tail flopped once against the foot of the bed. His head turned, listening.

Chapter Thirty-Five

Janna wasn't coming back, Emmy decided as the business day arrived. She had not come home, as she had hoped she might. As Emmy lay on the bed during her two hour rest, waiting for the night to end, she'd played over in her mind Janna's possible actions. Perhaps she'd only gone down to the convenience store on the corner four blocks away. Maybe she'd be back.

But the sun rose, and the silence in the house remained. There was no way someone could have been following her after all. No way. She had escaped from wherever she had been, come a thousand miles, and she hadn't been followed. So therefore it couldn't have been the people Janna was afraid of.

No, Janna left on her own.

Emmy kept listening for the phone to ring. It didn't.

She showered, dressed in a suit, took care of the dogs, left Minnie in the house and put Raven in the backyard. She drove aimlessly through the neighborhood at first, hoping to catch sight of Janna.

As she drove she became more anxious to finish her life here, to sell out and get away. Where to? There were so many places she had lived and liked, but she felt a need to go back to the country. To the big trees. A little mountain town, in the north. She saw the sign of the real estate broker from whom she had made her purchases, and parked.

"I want everything liquidated," she told Clair, her broker, a middle-aged woman who knew the business and whom Emmy trusted. With Clair's help, she had made money on all her real estate purchases. "I don't want to wait months to get as much as possible. I'll take what I can get now, as soon as possible."

Now. Before she saw Gavin again and lost her power to leave him.

"Today?" Clair's eyes enlarged.

"Yes."

"You're really in a hurry to leave."

"Yes."

"I'll see what I can do. If you're really in a hurry the company can buy from you. I'll let you know as soon as I get everything arranged."

She drove home wondering if she should go on to work tonight as if nothing had changed in her life. Wherever Janna had gone, would it help cover her? Or were her accusations baseless? Surely not all the girls disappeared. Emmy searched her memory for even one who showed up again to say hello, or to dance again. None?

By the time she entered her house, bringing in Raven, holding Minnie in her arms, both dogs delighted to see her, she had decided to go ahead and go to work as usual. Meantime, during the days she would get her things packed.

With the dogs in the car she went to the nearest market and filled her back seat with cardboard boxes. Raven sat up front in the passenger's seat, and seemed more himself. He watched eagerly down the road, and put his nose out the window. Minnie curled on Emmy's lap as she always did.

At home she tried to concentrate on the confusing job of packing. Taking another walk through the house, she stopped at the desk where the notepad and pen were lying on top, as if Janna had planned to write something. But staring at them wouldn't help her understand Janna's thoughts during the moments before she left the house. The notepad and pen merged in her vision and became one, misty and unreal.

She turned away, refocusing her eyes, wandering aimlessly about the house. Raven followed at her heels. Minnie grabbed one of her toys and followed Raven.

Emmy didn't know where to start. The movers could pack it all, but there were some things Emmy wanted to take with her. Clothes, books, sheet music. The rest could be stored until she had bought her next home.

She went to the utility room to get one of the boxes she had stacked in the corner. Might as well start, she told the dogs.

Raven went to the back door and whined. She turned him out.

Returning to the bedroom she snapped on the radio to dispel the sense of emptiness in the house, the feeling of someone important having just left, of part of herself having gone. She realized she had created a dream life in her mind that she didn't want to lose. Janna, and a home. A chance to be a grandmother, if not a mother. Janna, who would be the right age to be a child of Lacey's.

She opened a chest drawer and looked at the folded sheets within. But the movers could pack those. She went to the dresser and looked into a couple of drawers.

The end of a newsflash on the radio caught her attention. A girl's body? Music began. She had absorbed only the last few words. She stood unmoving, trying to recall all that had been said. Unidentified girl … found in park. The radio was turned to a local station. Very few murders ever occurred in this quiet suburb. The only park was three blocks away, a small area of benches, tennis court, and trees. Lots of trees and nooks.

She dialed the local police, dread increasing, conviction growing, hands shaking. Janna, her heart told her. Janna had been followed after all, somehow. Somehow they had found her. Janna hadn't been exaggerating.

The argument nearer to the surface of her consciousness came, trying to overpower the dread. No, it wasn't possible. Janna had simply left.

"The … the girl whose body was found," she said to the woman who'd answered the phone. "Was she in Crescent Park?"

"Who's speaking please?"

Yes, the cautious reply had in a sense said. With a crushing weight growing in her chest, Emmy gave her name and address.

Her call was transferred to a male officer who identified himself as Sergeant Ingram.

"May I—see if I know her?" Emmy asked.

"Why do you feel you might know her?" the man asked. "Is someone you know missing?"

"Yes."

"Would you describe her for me, please?"

"She's about sixteen, small, petite, long black, curly hair, very pretty. Her name is Janna—I don't know her last name."

"You don't know her last name?"

"No. I'm not a relative, only a friend."

"When did she become missing?"

"Last night."

There was a pause.

Emmy said, "I didn't report her missing because she's—she's homeless, and I thought she had just moved on."

"All right," the male voice said. "Give me your name and address and I'll come and get you and take you over there."

Emmy had seen mutilation only in brief clips on television, and never in all her life could she have been prepared.

"There's not much left to ID," the officer said as he touched her back, guiding her into the chill of the morgue. "The body hadn't been there very long. It was discovered at daybreak. The crime scene had to be taken care of, so it was several hours before the body could be moved."

He had asked her questions, in his office, in his car. She understood his need to know the answers, but she held back everything except that Janna was spending the night with her, and she had come home from work at one-thirty AM to find her gone.

No, she hadn't left a note. She thought of the tablet, but didn't mention it.

She saw the dark hair first, lying on the table behind the turned head, matted with dark blood. The sheet, lifted, revealed a face slashed repeatedly until there was nothing left of it but a portion of one eye and the corner of the mouth. The throat had been cut all the way through, and only skin held the head to the body. The face had been mutilated. But there was no mistaking the hair.

Emmy closed her eyes.

"Yes," she whispered, "It's Janna." No, there was no mistaking that lovely hair, nor the little of the features she was able to see. She stifled a scream. Rage ran like molten lava through her, rage at faceless people, at circumstances that would lead to this. Then the rage was gone, leaving her limp and sick.

Suddenly needing support, she turned, looking for something to hold onto. She had thought she could do this without caving in, but it took the support of the police officer to get her out of the room.

For several minutes she sat in an office, her head resting in her hands.

"I need to know where her family is, her friends, anything you can tell me. How is it you happen to know her?" She had to think. Her mind seemed a dark mass of confusion. Janna hadn't been exaggerating her fear.

Someone had followed her, somehow. Yet Emmy felt that wasn't true.

The trail had been picked up again here. At her house. They had known to come to her house. How had they known?

She remembered the girl asking about Janna last night.

Quite early in the night, around ten o'clock, before she started dancing. She had been nervous, as if she knew what was going to happen.

It was too much of a coincidence that another girl in the Club would choose that night to ask about Janna.

"I have to go home," she told the sergeant. "I don't feel well." I have to think.

He nodded, and led her out to the car. At her house he said, "If you remember anything, any little thing, let me know?"

It was evening again as she entered the house. In another hour she would be expected at work. She couldn't go.

She sat down, trying to gather some wits about herself. She could never go back to the club. She couldn't even call Gavin and tell him goodbye. She loved him, even knowing that he might be part of all this—knowing he was part of all this, she still loved him. But she could never see him again.

Minnie!

She hadn't taken Minnie to work with her last night, for the first time. Was that the small change that brought the killer's attention to her? Of course they knew Janna was out there somewhere, and Janna had been in terror of them. Now, it became obvious that someone had entered the house, someone Raven had told her without words was a stranger. More than one, probably. How had they gotten in? Janna would never have opened the door. She got up, Raven and Minnie at her heels, and went through the house checking locks. Would she know a forced lock if she saw one?

She went to her bedroom and looked at the notebook on the desk. Someone had entered the house, and torn away the sheet of paper Janna must have been writing on. What had she written? Information? Names?

The police had to be told Janna was here. It might help find her killers. Emmy started to pick up the phone, and drew her hand back.

She thought of Gavin. Would Janna's trail lead back to him? She could not involve him. She was incapable of it. He couldn't possibly know what had happened to Janna.

No, not Gavin.

She reached for the telephone and dialed the number Sergeant Ingram had given her.

"I think I have information for you, about Janna. But could you come here? I'd like you to look at my locks to see if they might have been forced."

"Why do you think they were forced?"

"Because—I think the killers came into my house. By the way my dog acted when I got home last night—I think someone was in here."

"On my way."

Minnie had been scared and trembling, cowering into her hands. Raven was scared too, the hair on his backbone stiff. He had trailed someone through the house, following a scent only he detected.

The telephone rang. She reached for it, then stopped. Her mind flipped through the possibilities of who it could be other than the strangers, the killers.

Slowly she picked it up.

Clair said crisply, "Just how fast do you want this money, Emmy?"

"As soon as possible."

"Here's what we'll do. The company will buy the real estate, including your house, if you'd like. We'll pay you market price, minus a ten percent fee. We—"

"I'll take it. When can you have it ready?"

"Tomorrow, as soon as the banks open. We'll need you to come down and sign things."

"Yes. I'll be there tomorrow morning."

She walked through the house, Minnie and Raven following at her heels. When she heard the car in her driveway she went to the back door and let Raven out into the yard, then she went to the side door and opened it. Sergeant Ingram had another man with him, younger, with serious dark eyes.

"Officer Thurow," he said. The other man nodded. They climbed the four steps to the hallway.

Emmy paused, then before her throat should close against her, "She danced at the night club where I worked—work—" Worked. She wasn't going back, ever. "You might ask there about her."

"What's the name of this club?"

A scene played like a video through Emmy's mind, police entering the club, questioning the bartenders, the waiters, Cindy, Jeff, Raoel. Gavin. Blank or wary faces with no answers.

She told him the name and address of the club.

"I met her there," Emmy said, in answer to the question. "That's all I know about her."

The younger officer's dark eyes looked at Emmy as if he were suspicious of her. Suspecting there was more than she was telling. She averted her eyes.

"Can we see through your house? Check those locks?"

She led them from room to room, Minnie held tight against her chest, window to window, door to door.

They looked at all the locks. The younger man shook his head.

"No," he said, "None of these were forced. She either let the killer or killers in, or someone had a key."

"Does anyone have a key to your house?" Sergeant Ingram asked.

They looked at her. She felt as if she were being interrogated, as if they increasingly suspected her. They had no one else. She was the only person to give them any information on the dead girl, and she felt as if they were turning on her. "No," she said defensively. "I've lived her two years. Alone."

"You haven't given your key to anyone? A house cleaner?"

"No. No one."

Former owners, the real estate company, none of them likely to keep a key. "How about someone who had a chance to make a copy?"

"No!"

Gavin? Dear God, not Gavin.

She shook her head. "No, no one." She felt cold, tired, yet filled with nervous energy. She wanted them to leave now so she could choose the things she wanted to keep with her until she found another house.

Officer Thurow shrugged. "Well, this kind of lock is simple to pick, as far as that goes."

Emmy wanted suddenly to get away from here. She wished she could just close her eyes and leave it all behind. But wasn't that what she had been doing for two years? And wasn't that what she continued to do? They'd be going over to the club to question everyone about Janna, she knew. But she had involved Gavin only in telling that she worked in his club, and Janna had worked there.

She let them out, and locked the door behind them, even though it sounded now as if the locks were virtually worthless. She had to think, yet she couldn't arrange her thoughts into a cohesive whole. Her emotions filled in the spaces, and her memory kept replaying Janna, from the moment she had picked her up at the motel, until she last saw her.

She went to the back door to call Raven in. It was fully dark now. Her backyard was filled with black areas untouched by the street light on the corner.

"Raven." she called softly. Her fingers flicked the backyard light on. She walked out onto the patio staring into the darkness beyond the rim of light.

"Raven," she called again, concern turning to panic. "Raven!"

The shadows didn't change. Nothing stirred in the shrubbery. For the first time in his life Raven didn't answer her call.

Chapter Thirty-Six

Raven was gone.

She grabbed a flashlight from the kitchen and searched through the shrubbery in the enclosed backyard. The front gate was closed. There was no hole in the wood privacy fence or beneath it. He couldn't have jumped or climbed over. She checked the gate that opened onto the alley. Hidden by shrubbery, it was never used. Only she knew it was there. She ducked beneath low-hanging limbs to reach it, and found it locked as always. Raven hadn't gone out anywhere around the fence. He could only have gone through the front gate into the driveway.

Crying, "Oh God," over and over beneath her breath, she ran down the driveway, her light searching, searching for gentle eyes that would reflect green lights back at her.

"Raven," she called, and slowed to a halt at the end of the short driveway. Her small front yard was filled with slanted light from the street lamp. The grass was a dark quilt of light and shadows.

Puzzled and sick with dread she clutched Minnie and walked slowly back to the gate between the edge of the one-car garage and the secure privacy fence that surrounded the back of the lot. The only way Raven could have gotten out was through that gate. It was closed. But why hadn't she had it locked? Her mind set up its own silent argument.

Maybe a neighborhood kid had let him out.

Raven might wander through the front yards of the nearby houses. He was a dog, after all, with a dog's sensitive and curious nose.

She went through the gate and around the back of the garage to the patio. The yard light reached to the shrubs and left a black jungle within them. Once again she shined the light beneath the shrubs and on the hidden wood gate in the back fence.

She ran into the house, and called the number Sergeant Ingram had given her.

"Ingram," the voice said almost immediately. The sound of traffic came muted through the phone. He was still in the cruiser.

"Officer Ingram, this is Emily Alexander. My dog is missing from my backyard. I'm afraid he's been stolen."

"The Chihuahua?" There was incredulity in his voice.

"Oh, no. She's here with me. I also have a black Lab. He's two years old."

"Oh. Okay. Could it be he's cruising the neighborhood?"

"There's no way he can get out except through the gate, and it's closed. Why would anyone want to let him out?" She had begun to tremble, and she sat down. "Do you think this has any connection to Janna's murder? Why would they want my dog?" Her voice ended on a sob. Raven, dear gentle Raven. Why would they want him?

"We'll come over and take a look around. Just sit tight." She walked the floor, the puppy in her arms, waiting.

When the doorbell rang Emmy hurried to let the two police officers in. Officer Thurow's eyes searched beyond her, even into the corners, as if a missed clue was ready to jump out.

They didn't sit down. With flashlights drawn, they went through the house and into the backyard, Emmy showing them the way. They flashed their lights through the shrubbery and examined the gates, inside and out. Emmy provided the key for the padlock on the hidden back gate. Thurow walked out into the alley. He returned shaking his head. Nothing. No dog at all.

He carefully closed and locked the gate. Sergeant Ingram's light flashed against the weathered fence on the other side of the yard like lightning silent and close.

He asked, "Do you have any idea what time the dog disappeared?"

"I put him out when you came over today. I tried to call him in this evening, and he was gone."

"We usually don't have the department look for missing dogs, but in this case we will. I can see that he wouldn't be able to get out without help, unless you think he could have jumped the gate."

It was about two feet shorter than the wood fence, and Emmy's hopes lifted a moment. The officers' flashlights examined the horizontal boards nailed across the vertical boards. Thurow said, "He could have climbed over if he really wanted to."

"I hope you're right. He's a large dog. I haven't taken him for a walk down to the park in several days. Maybe he decided to go alone." The park, she remembered, was where Janna's body had been found. She added, "But he never has before."

They went back toward the patio. Thurow shined his flashlight into the small door at the back of the garage. Emmy knew what he'd see. One car, a Buick. One lawn mower, which she'd seldom used, a few garden tools with which she took care of her few flowers. A hedge trimmer that she didn't use either.

The shrubs grew wildly in all directions. She liked their tangled, jungle effect. They harbored squirrels and birds.

She followed Officer Ingram up onto the patio.

"We'll see if we can find your dog, Mrs. Alexander." At that moment the doorbell rang.

She thought immediately of Gavin. He would be the only person to be coming to her house this time of the evening.

"Excuse me," she said, aware that they followed behind her. She looked at the kitchen clock as she passed through the room. Nine-thirty.

No, she suddenly knew it wasn't Gavin. Even if he were in the office, he wouldn't necessarily be missing her yet. Though she usually arrived at the club by nine, she sometimes spent a few minutes talking to people before she started playing.

She opened the door. A youth who looked no more than nineteen or twenty stood outside the door. At his feet was a box wrapped in plain brown paper. Her name and address were printed in large black letters on the top of the box. "Emily Alexander?"

"Yes." She wasn't expecting a delivery, hadn't ordered anything in months.

"Nothing to sign," the delivery man said. "I'm just to make sure Emily Alexander gets it."

He hurried away to the delivery van that sat in the driveway with motor idling.

"Thank you," he called back. He hadn't waited for a tip.

The officers came up behind her, and Thurow stepped past her to watch the van back out and drive away. "Expecting something?"

Emmy shook her head, staring at the black print on the box. Her name in such large letters, printed with a wide-point marker.

"I think we'd better open it." He picked up the box, and brought it into the living room.

She asked, "Who's it from? What is it?" Something made her afraid to touch it. Afraid suddenly of everything.

Thurow turned it, handling it gently, looking for a return address, a label, perhaps. Whatever was in it made a hollow thump as it tumbled from one side of the box to the other.

The two men exchanged a look. Thurow placed it on the floor, got down on one knee, and used a pen knife to rip it open. The lid came up.

Black fur, like a crushed hat—streaked with something dark and red—blood—still liquid it was beginning to congeal in the bottom of the box like a bed made of raw liver.

A severed head.

Raven's eyes stared beyond her, as flat and soul-less now as glass. Blood had crossed his face like rips from long fingernails. His swollen tongue protruded.

—blood—everywhere—on   Raven's   face—on   Janna's—Emmy screamed.

She reached ... Midnight ... Raven. The dog too friendly, who would never hurt anyone. Hands pushed hers back.

One of the men put an arm around her and turned her away.

In one part of her mind Emmy was aware that Minnie too screamed, frightened at the sound of Emmy's cry, of the smells from the box. The puppy ran, tail tucked between her legs, toward the bedroom hallway, then made a quick turn and ran back toward Emmy.

"Take it out," Sergeant Ingram ordered. "Put it in the car. Let's start a trace on the delivery truck."

Emmy felt pats on her back. Like Daddy's pats when she was young and had been hurt, they were awkward and a bit rough, more like thumps than pats. But she understood and was grateful for the effort to comfort her.

"He never hurt anyone—never—hurt. He couldn't talk and tell what he saw—he couldn't ..."

The puppy put her front feet on Emmy's legs, and Emmy picked her up, grateful for this small being, this puppy, unhurt—so far—unhurt. The tiny body trembled as Emmy cuddled her.

"There's a connection to the girl's murder, obviously," Officer Ingram said. "We'll make arrangements to give you some protection. I suggest you have a friend come and stay with you."

Carrying the box, Thurow went out the door. The phone rang.

She was afraid to pick it up. At the door, ready to follow the other man, Sergeant Ingram waited. It rang three times and the answering machine picked it up.

"Emmy." Gavin's voice, distant, as if he spoke softly, hoarse, as if filled with emotion. "Are you there Emmy?"

She put out her hand and lifted the receiver.

"Emmy?" Gavin's voice came louder, still strange and tight. "Are you all right, Emmy?"

"Yes." It seemed for a moment that all life went out of her. She sat down weakly, herself trembling as Minnie was. "Wait a minute."

She looked up at Sergeant Ingram. He asked, "Is it all right?"

"Yes, thanks. A friend."

"You'll be getting someone to stay with you tonight? Or go to someone? Family, friend?"

She nodded without answering. She had to be alone, to try to organize her thoughts. She shook harder now than the puppy. She still wanted to scream, scream, against the horror of these deaths.

Gavin asked sharply, "Who's there?"

Officer Ingram said, "We'll leave you now. I'll see to it that there's extra patrol in this area."

"Thank you."

"You've got our number. Call again if you need to." He left, locking the door before he went out.

"Who is that, Emmy?" Gavin demanded.

Her breath expelled in a cry into the telephone, "Gavin! They—killed Janna—now Raven. They sent me—his head. Why? Who's doing this?"

There was a pause, then, "Raven? When?"

"Just now. The box just—was just delivered. Why are they doing this? They killed Janna. Gavin—" It was as if he could change it all, put it back where it was yesterday, or last month. Though she knew in the depths of her mind he might be connected to all this horror, her heart still clung to him, and forever would. She could no more speak against him than she could point a loaded gun at him and pull the trigger.

"Who's there with you?"

She had never heard such sharpness in his voice. She could almost imagine it was someone other than Gavin. The killers, perhaps, impersonating him.

"No one, not now. The police—they just left."

She wanted to cry, but there were no tears. She clutched Minnie to her throat with her left hand. The small body still trembled.

"Listen to me, Emmy. I didn't know about Raven. Believe me, I didn't know. You have to get out of there, do you hear me?"

"Yes—yes—"

"I mean now. Don't take anything. I'm sending a car for you. There will be two of the guys in it, bodyguards, to get you away from there. They're bringing cash, enough to take care of you, and a new ID. Are you listening?"

A coldness enveloped her as all this he was saying entered her consciousness. She didn't tell him she had been planning to leave anyway. But not to use her name?

"Emmy, you have to listen very carefully. There's a contract out on you. Do you hear?"

A contract. As there had been on Janna. A contract to kill her?

"Why?" She cried.

"They think you know too much. They know Janna was in your house, and she probably gave you information that is dangerous. I can't protect you, Emmy."

"Gavin! I don't know anything!" Only the story Janna had told her, and the first names of girls who had danced at the club, names that might have been as fake as the color of their hair.

"Listen," Gavin hissed, "get your coat on and get out of there. Everything's ready for you. Get away from here, Emmy."

"They're wrong!" she cried. "I don't know anything!"

"There' s something—I don' t know what—but something. You're marked for death, Emmy. Get ready to leave. The guys are on their way over to get you."

Her thoughts swirled, stirring in a dark funnel visions of Janna, alive, dead, visions of Raven's head with a body of blood, visions of death, dreams of life and happiness sucked beneath the horror in the vortex of her mind.

"Emmy. Emmy ..." It was a desperate sound, as if he had begun to cry. "Emmy, I love you. I love you more than life. Remember that."

The connection between them was broken.

Emmy sat stiff and hollow, frightened, cold, and stared at the floor. Then she realized she was sitting, just sitting, and time was moving on.

She hurried up finally, went to the bedroom and took a black London Fog coat from the closet. Over her head she tied a black scarf. The puppy huddled, shivering, looking up at her with silent, pleading eyes.

She needed Minnie, as Minnie needed her.

"I'll never leave you," she whispered to the puppy as she picked her up and tucked her beneath the coat.

She started to leave the bedroom, then turned back to the desk and the notebook. She turned the desk light on. Janna had written something on the notebook. But she hadn't thrown it into the wastebasket. It was empty. Emmy held the notebook up to the light. Nothing. Nothing that she could see. But Janna had taken it from the drawer, and had probably used it for a note that was now gone—or perhaps she had started to write names on it.

Emmy hurried to the kitchen. She got her shoulder bag from the drawer and tucked the notebook deep into the bottom beneath billfold, makeup, keys.

She went through the house turning out all lights. In the darkened living room she stood and waited, watching the street.

How could she trust him?

The car he was sending for her, who was driving? Was there really a plan ready for her to disappear into another identity, or was this a trick? Or, if he told the truth, who was watching, outside her house, this change in the making, this going from the house to the car? Who had watched Janna, and who had taken Raven. Who now waited for her?

Whoever watched the house would be distracted by the arrival of the car. It was her chance. Her only chance, to get away unseen. She got the key to the concealed and locked back gate and held it ready between her fingers.

Minnie breathed softly beneath her coat. Emmy's heart pounded.

The car slid almost silently into sight, coming up the short driveway to park at the end of the walk. A door opened, and Jesse, the six-three, two hundred and fifty pound bouncer from the club, got out and came toward the house. Emmy turned and ran, her running shoes quiet on the carpet. She went through the kitchen door, leaving it open. Keeping in the depths of darkness she went into the shrubs at the back of the yard. She unlocked the alley gate and slipped through into the alley.

She hurried away, keeping to alleys and dark places, going deeper into hiding.

Chapter Thirty-Seven

Emmy stayed in the city overnight, hiding with Minnie where other homeless people took refuge. The next morning the money from her real estate was transferred to an out-of-town bank, and Emmy slipped away and began the process of changing identification, holding her breath against being found before it could happen.

She waited in a cheap hotel in San Francisco, while she contacted a man she knew would supply false IDs for cash. She purchased her new identity, Maggie Winters, with a new Social Security number. With Minnie hidden under her coat, she bought a small used car and started driving eastward.

She didn't dare go see her family. Her presence there would be putting them all in danger. She had to keep going, follow the road, wherever it took her, accompanied, God willing, by Minnie whom she kept closely beside her.

She drove a varying route, a wandering course, two thousand, four thousand miles. Each morning she felt a bit surprised that they were still alive, she and Minnie.

In the south central United States amid incredibly green hills and valleys, clear, sparkling creeks, she chose a town in a community of small cities, and bought a secure little house on the curve of a cul-de-sac.

For several months Emmy lived in terror, suspicious of every movement around her, wary of anyone, old or young, who came close to her. Minnie was her comfort, small and warm, hugged tightly against her.

Gradually, she began to relax.

There was a back yard sloping into a hollow where trees grew and paths meandered. Her chain-link fence did not obstruct the view. Her neighbors' yards were shrouded from hers with shrubs and trees. There was a patio tucked between the back of the garage and the side of the house, a private little place where she and Minnie sat on a warm day, a cool evening. She made a flower bed, and planted it with a variety of flowers, claimed by two hummingbirds and one bumble bee. She cautioned Minnie against chasing the bumble bee.

"You don't want to catch that," she said.

The fear gradually left, and a kind of contentment came.

In the first year, she bought newspapers that might give her information on arrests, convictions in the murder of Janna—Janna whose last name she never knew. But there was nothing.

She carried the puzzle with her. What did she possess that was so dangerous to someone? The story Janna had told her? It wouldn't stand up in court. It was only hearsay. She had proof of nothing.

She wanted to forget it all, even Gavin. Forget too her love for him. Her heart pleaded for oblivion to the past. She asked nothing more now than to live in peace with Minnie, who had become her family, her child. Minnie, who was never out of her sight. She even carried her tucked beneath her jacket when she went shopping, and she shopped only as necessity dictated.

Her money was strictly budgeted, to last through her lifetime. Unable to use her legal name of Emily Alexander and her legal Social Security number, she didn't even have that to count on. So she sought contentment. And the beauty and release of dreams, which came less and less as she grew older.

Each night her prayer ended with, "Please God, give me back my dreams."

But her nights were silent and dim, the figures that moved through her dream-mind vague and lost to her when she awoke. She pondered at times the pure ecstasy of the dreams that stood out in her memory, and it seemed in retrospect that they were more than dreams, something beyond dreams as dreams were known to be. Perhaps they were visions, special visits to a different reality, a world available only by some unknown means.

But she lived in this world now, with its dangers. The killer had found her, and she had to plan a way to take Minnie and move on. The thought of leaving her little house, surely the only home Minnie remembered, brought a sick yearning.

She had escaped once, she could do it again. This time both she and Minnie would have to change identities, Minnie's name would never be listed again in a kennel or animal hospital.

She didn't dare drive her car. Now that they knew her name, they knew her license plate number. They knew the address of her home. She had to rise from her hospital bed and somehow get away. Beyond the pulled-back curtain she heard a long sigh from Hazel. She was gathering the pictures from her bedside table and lovingly folding them into garments already laid in the suitcase one of the nurse's aides had placed on her bed. She seemed tired today, somehow dispirited.

"Are you all right, Hazel?" Maggie asked.

Turn your thoughts to Hazel, forget yourself for awhile. Minnie's fine where she is, and now the nursing home has become my own fortress. Think of Hazel, of Florence. Think of Thomas across the hall who calls out periodically for the nurse, his real wish for a companion underlying his demands. Think of Peter, who spends his days slumped in a wheelchair, but who loves people and is always out there, going up and down the halls, pausing to talk, playing cards if he can roust up a foursome. Think of Clara, who became a pawn in a game too deadly.

No. Don't think of Clara.

Hazel said as she turned and sat down in her chair, "Any effort seems too much, somehow. I was just thinking about these past two years here in this room. I've seen maybe ten or twelve roommates come and go. Some of them died, not like Clara, but gone, anyway. Florence was here when I got here. The poor old girl was just sitting here alone most of the time. Her daughters you know—well—they're like my children, all have their own lives, and in most cases live hundreds or thousands of miles away. They can't just drop in."

A long pause issued, and Maggie felt a need to fill it, to bring in a stroke of happiness. "But now you're finally getting to leave, live with your grandson."

"That's right," Hazel said with more animation as she rose from the chair. "And not feet first." She chuckled, and Maggie smiled with her. Then

Hazel sobered, "I never thought I'd live to see Florence carried out of here. She's four years younger than I am."

"But she's getting better, I'm sure. I'm glad it's working out for you, Hazel."

"You'll be out of here soon yourself, Maggie. You're young compared to some of us in here. You're like one of my daughters. You've got years ahead. I've knowed others with hip replacements, and as soon as the healing is done, they're better than they've been in years. The hurting goes away. Artificial joints can't hurt."

"Maybe not, but the skin on the outside sure does."

Hazel laughed. "Don't mean to make light. But you'll be fine. The hurting will stop."

Maggie carefully maneuvered herself out of bed and stood, wondering if she could make it to the walker without calling for help. A brief distance away Hazel went back to work wrapping the framed pictures.

Footsteps moved along the hall in both directions, fading, coming near again, fading. Voices sometimes accompanied the sounds of walking, and sometimes the walker moved in silence. Maggie watched the door each time the sound of steps grew near, dreading the sight of a bouquet of pink and red roses, or the face of the stranger.

She looked with suspicion at medicine given her, yet knew she was being paranoid about that. Pills were dispensed by the nurses. She wanted to say, "Don't let him in. Don't accept roses." But that would mean too many questions that she was afraid to answer.

The collection of voices coming closer along the hall were those of women, and Maggie paid little attention until Hazel straightened, turned and looked at the door.

"Is that Florence?" she asked, wonder in her voice.

Maggie secured her position against the bed, holding to the lowered railing for support. Her left hip that wasn't supposed to hurt shot pains toward her shoulder and her foot. The door came slowly back toward the foot of her bed.

Hazel's face shone and a long smile sent wrinkles streaming like sunbeams toward her hairline.

"Well, I'll swan!" she cried, and hurried forward to embrace Florence.

Florence gave her a hug, smiles radiating over her face.

She patted Hazel's shoulder and back and came to Maggie and laid a hand that had never softened against her cheek.

"Are you doin' okay, kid?"

Maggie felt the warmth she brought into the room. The two nurse's aides following her looked as happy as if they had delivered a special gift. Hazel, still patting Florence's back, asked, "What on earth are you doing back here?"

"You didn't think you could get rid of me that easy, did you?" Florence went toward her part of the room, and patted the bed. "I missed this old hard thing. Those hospital beds are too soft."

The aides laughed. Florence sat down in her chair and leaned back. "Ah, now this feels good. Home."

One of the aides unloaded Florence's suitcase into her now miniscule closet, and the other put out on the bedside table the tissue, water pitcher and glass. All personal items were returned to the table.

"Welcome back," they said, almost in unison as they went out the door and pulled it within six inches of being closed.

Hazel sat down and began to rock gently, as she hadn't done since Florence's heart attack.

Florence noticed the wrapped items on the bed, and sat forward.

"What's going on, Hazel?"

Hazel drew a deep breath and directed her gaze at the line between ceiling and wall over Florence's bed.

"My grandson called. He's going to make a private sitting bedroom for me. He's coming after me."

A shadow crossed Florence's face, but she said, "Well, finally. Finally you get to go."

"Yes."

Hazel stood up, pushing herself with her hands against the chair arms. She crossed the room to the bathroom door, and closed herself within its privacy.

Maggie turned on her right foot and let herself down into her chair. Florence sat with her head leaned back on the headrest of the chair looking, it seemed to Maggie, at the picture of Jesus that hadn't yet been taken down from the wall over Hazel's bed.

"You know, Maggie, I thought I was going to die," Florence said slowly, softly. "And I swear to God I saw angels around my bed. They lifted me."

Tears came to Florence's eyes. Her chin puckered and her teeth clenched. Her eyes batted to hide the tears. Maggie waited in silence.

"I want to confess something," Florence said. "That stuff I told about being a call girl and all—it's not true. I just set out to aggravate Hazel, her being so pious and all. It was the best way to get her goat."

Maggie waited. Florence still looked at the picture on the wall. "I'm not saying I didn't—make the streets my home for awhile. I mean, well, my mother, that's true—and I didn't know any better until I was older—but after that I was just a factory worker. Sometimes when the work got hard, or I lost a job, or the girls wanted something I couldn't buy, I'd think—look what I might be earning. I wasn't a bad looking woman."

"I know. I can see that."

Florence's gaze found her and lingered a moment. "But mostly I was just teasing Hazel. I missed that old soul, and I swear to God her angels visited me."

Maggie thought of the prayers she had heard in the night. "They dismissed you rather quickly, didn't they?"

Florence leaned forward. "You bet your life they did. I told them I wanted out of there, and if I was going to die, I'd die right here where Hazel can pray for my soul!"

Florence laughed, and Maggie laughed with her.

The bathroom door opened and Hazel came back into the bedroom, clearing her eyes. Maggie saw the remnants of tears, reddened eyes, an attempt to close her emotions off. Hazel went to her bed and began unwrapping the pictures.

"What are you doing?" Florence asked.

"I'm unpacking."

Hazel pushed her call button, and the light came on above her bed.

"What's wrong?" Florence's voice hovered on the edge of alarm.

Hazel sighed deeply. "Well, I've been thinking and thinking about the trouble my grandson runs into to come and get me and fix me a place to stay. He's got his job and his family, what does he need with me?"

Florence leaned back. She began to rock slow and easy. "So, you're staying with us?"

"Yes. I'm staying. I have to ask the nurse to help me make a call. I expect my grandson will be glad to get it."

Florence rocked, a small smile playing like dimples at the corners of her mouth.

"Besides," Hazel said, "What would you do without someone to tell your big whoppers to?"

"You eavesdropped!"

Hazel chuckled.

They rocked, the whisper of their chairs the only sound in the room.

Then they began to talk, a back and forth dialog about the weather, about the hospital, the nursing home, about nurses and aides and doctors.

Perhaps the teasing would continue at times, but Maggie felt it was gone, blown away by the wings of the angels.

The stranger didn't appear at her door.

Roses weren't delivered.

Maggie got up and found the walker put in her hand by Florence and Hazel, as both of them came to help. She thanked them and made her way slowly into the hall.

Steady now, she told herself. We have a long way to go.

She reached the telephone and called a cab company. Send a cab to Willowbrook Care Center. Plans formulated as she hung up. She could manage to carry Minnie and use the walker too. She had to manage. They were leaving town.

Perhaps they would end up as part of the homeless in the streets and parks of some southern city, but they would be together.

She dialed the animal hospital. A feminine voice answered.

"This is Maggie Winters," she said. "I'm coming after my little dog, Minnie. I'll be there within an hour."

There was silence on the phone, then the voice of the girl said, "Just a minute."

Maggie clutched the telephone in her left hand, and held to the walker with her right. Her hand grew tighter and tighter, her knuckles whitened. A vast distance of time seemed to pass before the silence ended.

The doctor's voice said, "Maggie?"

"Yes."

"Maggie, how are you doing?"

"I'm coming after Minnie, doctor—"

"Maggie, we didn't want to tell you this. We wanted to give you a chance to get well first—"

"You didn't let him take her!"

"No one took her, Maggie," the doctor's voice remained calm and even in tone, but lowered. The moment she had heard his voice, speaking to her as he was, her soul writhed in anguish.

"What—what's wrong?"

"She's dead, Maggie. We did everything we could, but she simply wouldn't eat. We of course put her on an IV, but that didn't save her. I'm so sorry. I'm sorry. She was depressed. She couldn't understand. We wanted to take her to you, but you were still in the hospital, and we couldn't. She's been dead since her first week, Maggie."

Maggie said nothing. There was nothing left to say.

"I—we—had her body disposed of. That was all we could do."

ACROSS THE HALL THOMAS MOANED, his voice dimmer and more distant than in had been a few days ago. Or perhaps it was she who was more distant.

Chapter Thirty-Eight

Maggie hung up the phone, set her walker forward one step, and followed it. Step by step she went back to her room. The drone of Hazel and Florence's voices surrounded her, drew her in, yet left her on the edge of humanity, slipping toward the bottomlessness of grief. Minnie gone. She was only a baby, a puppy, four years old. How could she be gone?

She walked toward her chair, aware that the two ladies had stopped talking and were watching her. Beyond the window dusk was filling the air beneath the trees like soot, and summer insects were rasping.

"What happened?" Hazel asked. "What's wrong, Maggie?"

Two pairs of eyes, concerned and caring.

Maggie abandoned the walker at the foot of her bed. Holding to the bed she went to the chair and sat down. Pain filled her chest, her arms and legs.

"She's dead. My little dog is dead. They didn't tell me. She's been dead several days, and they didn't tell me."

They were silent, trying to understand. Maggie felt their efforts in their silences. It's only a dog. The world is full of dogs.

Maggie turned her face away and closed her eyes. She'd had no premonition of Minnie's death. How could she love a living being so deeply, yet not know when that being drew its last breath? It was as if her own senses betrayed her, severing the connection in dark silence.

She heard the squeaks of their chairs as they began to rock. Then their voices started again, lower, as if they didn't want to disturb her.

The sounds and smells of dinner increased, reaching Maggie like fingers from another world. She felt nauseated. Meat cooking. She couldn't bear the thought.

Across the hall Thomas called, "Nurse?" Then, plaintively, "Eleanor, was that you?" Then the moaning began again.

"Oh, Lord," Hazel said, "There he goes again. The next time my son comes in I'll have him pray for the poor old man. We must remember him in our prayers."

A nurse came along the hall and stopped in Thomas's room, and for a moment before she closed the door her voice reached Maggie.

"Time to get ready for dinner, Thomas, you want to go eat, don't you? You don't want to start eating in your room again, do you?"

Maggie sat still, head against the headrest of the chair. She sat with her eyes closed, permeated by sounds, movements and odors of dinnertime. A nurse entered the room and turned on lights. Beyond her eyelids Maggie saw the faint glow.

"It's dinnertime," the young voice said. "What's wrong with all you people down this way? I had to come and get Thomas, and now you. Florence, Hazel, you're usually the first ones down there, and here you make me come and get you."

Her smile said she was teasing, at least partly. The plastic of Florence and Hazel's chairs made their rustling sounds as the ladies got up.

"You need the exercise," Florence said. "We're just doing our duty and seeing to it that you get enough."

"Yeah, yeah." The voice came closer. "And you, Miss Maggie. How come we didn't have our dinner music today?"

Florence said quickly, "She's not feeling very good."

"Had some bad news," Hazel said.

"Maggie? I'm sorry. Can I help?"

The young voice was suddenly more serious. Maggie opened her eyes to see the pretty face leaning toward her, a hand out to touch hers. Maggie saw the face of Janna, and the other girls who danced for a few weeks, months, sometimes only a few nights and then were gone.

"Yes," Maggie said. "Would you cancel the cab for me, and bring me some stationery, a notebook or something, and a pen?"

"Of course." She looked puzzled, but she would do these simple things without questions.

Beyond her Florence and Hazel stood at the door ready to go out, looking back, waiting, listening.

"And something for pain," Maggie said. "Pain, and sleep, please."

The young aide nodded. "Do you want it after dinner?"

"No. I'm not coming for dinner." She had to be alone.

"You have to eat. You need to eat to keep up your strength." The nurse's aide nodded. "You should come to dinner."

"No, please. Could you just bring me the pen and paper, and the medication?"

They left, sounds in the hall merging, blending, moving.

Voices, footsteps going toward the dining room. Others going along the hall toward the back, where patients were bedfast.

Maggie watched darkness fall beyond the window as she waited for the nurse. She walked across a field with Midnight at her side, tumbleweeds blowing past them. She opened a box and saw Raven's head. She saw a cage, small, made of wire, Minnie's living grave. She saw a young girl on a table in the cold morgue, her face barely recognizable. She saw Clara leaving the room with her son. Then, leaving her house with someone else.

The nurse's aide returned with the pen and several sheets of paper. She bent over Maggie.

"I'm really sorry about your little dog."

Maggie nodded. "Thank you."

"The nurse will bring the medicine, okay?"

"Yes, that's fine."

Her voice was natural to her own ears, low and smooth, revealing none of the devastation within her.

"Would you please close the door when you go out?"

Alone, she began to write all Janna had told her. Janna's voice was there, in her memory, low but clear, above the steady purr of the engine as they sped across the desert.

She wrote the few names Janna had mentioned, names her memory would not bury. Maybe somewhere there among them was Janna's killer, and Raven's, and Clara's. At the end she paused.

Her name is Minnie. 'Every time you look at her, remember that I love you.' And now she was dead.

Maggie closed her eyes against the pain of losing her, of losing him, of knowing finally that she would never see him again. The hurt of acknowledging what he had done, what he was, combined with the hurt of losing Minnie and became a roiling darkness within her.

"Oh, Gavin."

With a pen that quivered, she added his name.

Gavin Richards. Her lover. Her betrayer. He who had named Minnie, he of the dozens of red and pink roses. He who had known how to locate her, through the records of the veterinarians.

She folded the sheets of paper into the envelope and wrote on the outside: POLICE.

Then she remembered, and reached for her shoulder bag. From the bottom she extracted the notebook on which Janna might have written four years ago. She added it to the envelope marked for police. She prepared for bed, changing to a nightgown, brushing her teeth and hair. Then she waited for her medication. Florence and Hazel returned, visited a while longer, then went to bed. Sounds in the nursing home became muted, as did lights. Thomas moaned softly across the hall, and finally he too was silent.

Maggie closed her eyes.

Would God forgive her for never finding her purpose in life? Her mind slipped back to her earliest memory. An old man, as tattered as she was ragged, who had stood in the middle of the narrow country lane. "You have a mountain to climb ... you must not fall ..."

The memories of her life meshed and slid forward, and she was one with them. She was then, and she was now, and she was forever. Finally she understood. It had taken a lifetime to fully create herself, her own soul. She had learned to love all living things, to care. To have sympathy for their condition. That was the purpose of her life.

SHE IS STANDING in a valley where the floor is made of stone and cluttered with large, black boulders, lost in shadows.

Around her the mountains of stone rise, barren. They rise in small peaks, one layer after the other, up, up almost as far as she can see. She stands alone.

She sees a narrow path to her left, going up the mountain side. She goes toward it and begins to climb. The path is narrow, and the mountain-side sheer, dropping to the dark valley below. Sometimes she pauses on the narrow steps.

There are other people on the path she now sees, but they are looking upward, climbing their own steps, separate from hers.

Understanding is like the removal of a curtain in her mind. She can go forward, or she can go back. Steps of her life, of all life, leads towards the steps upward to that distant, mysterious summit. Steps marked by shadows and sorrows … steps marked by light.

She chooses to go onward.

Mists like clouds filled with a strange glowing light obscure the path, but she keeps climbing, and suddenly above her on the tallest peak she sees light. A great joy enters her and takes her breath away. She climbs eagerly, hurrying, no longer seeing the narrowness of the steps nor the long drop down. She reaches the top, far above the shadowed valley, and sees a land stretching away into forever.

Lights of infinite colors flood this beautiful new land.

Becoming visible ahead of her people move about through the blending colors of the mists, and the colors of grass and trees and flowers blend into a rare beauty. There's a city beyond, and many roads and pathways where people walk, going on.

She takes the last step upward and enters, following a grassy pathway through a forest of delicate beauty. Figures move along the path ahead of her, their warmth drawing her on, the beauty filling her soul.

She pauses, and understands a truth. Life is only one step of the journey. She begins walking forward again.

She sees a child forming in the mists, golden, violet, and recognizes herself. She sees a mature woman, grown wiser with age, and sees within the woman the love of all living things emanating from her as the rainbows emanate from droplets upon which a brilliant light shines. She sees the whole of life, and knows the choice is still hers, that here she will find all that has been important to her, and that which will become important.

In eagerness and total ecstasy she rushes onward.

The path comes to a small footbridge that curves above a glistening stream, and a figure, small and silky brown sits waiting at the apex of the bridge. The tiny tail wags wildly. Minnie rises, her head lifted, her wait ended.

Emmy begins to run forward, onward. Behind Minnie, now coming onto the bridge is a large, black dog; the fusion of Midnight, of Raven … those her heart keeps and makes immortal.

Behind them are others of her life, Daddy … faces from her dreams, her visions. There comes now another figure and is suddenly before the others, her heart bringing him forward. He smiles and holds out his arms.

She stops, her thoughts wrapped in silence. Gavin? Here before her? Waiting for her.

Gavin, emerging before the others, outlined in glorious colors, surrounded by soft music, coming toward her to gather her to the light.

Chapter Thirty-Nine

The doctor drew the sheet up over Maggie's head and a nurse pulled the curtain that closed off her bed. The police had been called in too, for reasons Florence and Hazel weren't certain of. There was an envelope, that was all they knew.

A stretcher came along the hall and paused by the door. Florence and Hazel watched, silent since the nurse had found Maggie dead early this morning.

Beyond the curtain from Maggie's roommates, the body was removed. Police quietly gathered her things from the closet and night-chest drawer.

"She said a strange thing last night," Florence offered. "Didn't she, Hazel?"

The policeman and the nurse stopped to listen.

"Yes she did," Hazel agreed. "It was the last thing she said."

"She said, 'I never found my purpose in life. I wonder if God will forgive me.'" —"Didn't she, Hazel?"

"Yes she did. She wondered if God would forgive her for not finding her purpose in life."

"I don't know what she meant."

"She didn't say what she meant."

"She never talked about herself."

Chapter Forty

Blanche and a new nurse's aide entered the room with fresh sheets and towels.

"Hi, girls," Blanche said. "Over there, sugar. You make Hazel's bed, and I'll make Florence's."

She talked as she worked, pulling off used sheets, stretching on clean sheets.

"Have you ladies seen the newspapers today? Well, you're going to be shocked when you do. There's a big article about Maggie. You remember that envelope she left for the police?"

Florence and Hazel nodded, and stilled their rocking chairs.

"Well, her name wasn't Maggie Winters at all, but Emily Alexander. She used to be a blues and jazz player in nightclubs and she got mixed up in a bunch of stuff. That man that killed Clara?"

They nodded, and waited, and were silent.

"He was a contract hitman, and he was after Maggie, and had been for four years. After Emmy. He traced her through her little dog. The dog was given to Maggie by her lover, a married man who owned the club she worked in. The man, Gavin Richards, was tortured and murdered three weeks after Emily Alexander disappeared four years ago. Maggie probably never even knew he was dead."

She stuffed a pillow into a clean case. "She might have thought Gavin was the one who traced her, but he wasn't. He was dead long ago. Gavin was the one who had previously sent her red and pink roses. I guess the ones that tortured him found out about the details of the little dog and his habit of sending roses. The hitman tried to use the roses to get close to Maggie."

Florence and Hazel sat still, staring at Blanche as she made the bed.

"Maggie had something in her possession that led the police right to the top—and do you know what it was? A sheet of notepaper a girl had written on in Emmy's house. The killers took the girl out of the house and murdered her to keep her from talking. They tore off the top sheet from the notepad, but left the under-sheet with the indentation of writing—and there was also a fingerprint on it. Do you know whose it was?"

Florence and Hazel slowly shook their heads.

"It was his wife's—Emmy's lover's wife."

Blanche looked from face to face, and finished the bed in silence. She straightened.

"Her name is Petra Richards, and she's the leader in a prostitution and pornographic film ring, and some of the films included torture and murder of the girls. She even filmed the torture and death of her husband. She had connections to organized crime, but she did this stuff on her own."

Florence and Hazel stared at her, trying to absorb this foreign information.

"She's been arrested for her husband's murder, the girl who was in Maggie's house, and—gosh—girls who were used in movies and videos in which they were killed—I don't know what all. Even Clara's murder. Petra was responsible for it all. She'd hired the killers."

Florence asked, "Was Maggie's death …?"

"I wondered that too. But no, they said. It was a natural death."

Florence and Hazel began slowly to rock.

A brilliant light suddenly angled through the window. Rainbow colors layered through the room.

Blanche said, "Looks like the sun is going to shine after all."

The glass prism Hazel had hung on her window rotated slowly, scattering the sunbeam into a spray of brilliant colors.

"From the unreal lead us to the Real,
From darkness lead us to Light.

From death lead us to immortality."

THE UPANISHADS

Other novels by Ruby Jean

1974 The House that Samael Built
1974 Seventh All Hallows' Eve
1974 House at River's Bend
1975 The Girl Who Didn't Die
1978 Child of Satan's House
1978 Satan's Sister
1978 Dark Angel
1982 Hear the Children Cry
1982 Such a Good Baby
1983 The Lake
1983 MaMa
1985 Home Sweet Home
1985 Best Friends
1986 Wait and See
1987 Annabelle
1987 Chain Letter
1988 Smoke
1988 House of Illusions
1988 Jump Rope
1989 Pendulum
1989 Death Stone

1990 Vampire Child
1990 Lost and Found
1990 Victoria
1991 Celia
1991 Baby Dolly
1992 The Reckoning
1993 The Living Evil
1994 The Haunting
1995 Night Thunder
2022 Cry of the Soul
Pending Bear Hollow Charlie
Pending Pride of Bella Terra